COYOTE BIRD

COYOTE BIRD

Jim DeFelice

ST. MARTIN'S PRESS
NEW YORK

FIC
D3136co

This novel is a work of fiction. All of the events, characters, names, and places depicted in this novel are entirely fictitious or are used fictitiously. No representation that any statement made in this novel is true or that any incident depicted in this novel actually occurred is intended or should be inferred by the reader.

Editor: Jared Kieling
Production Editor: Mark H. Berkowitz
Copy-edited by Karen P. Thompson
Design by Glen M. Edelstein

Library of Congress Cataloging-in-Publication Data

DeFelice, James.
    Coyote bird / Jim DeFelice.
       p. cm.
    ISBN 0-312-06939-1
    I. Title.
  PS3554.E357C6   1992
813'.54—dc20   91-36498
                                                                                                        CIP

First Edition: April 1992
10 9 8 7 6 5 4 3 2 1

The technology described in this book either exists or is being developed. This being a work of fiction, I have taken advantage of expedients unavailable to those who must operate in the real world. To those in the know, I offer a wink and a smile, as well as sincere admiration.

1

HANDS OF GOD

Europe
Apx. 120,000 feet.
Mach 4 +
04:10
The near future.

Fingers of colors began crawling across the windshield canopy, a bright mix of purple and red that burnt thin, long streaks in the night above his head. The Merc pilots called them the hands of God, or joked that they were sparks from bumping against the earth's ceiling. But without exception, the pilots were awed by the lights, a phenomenon seen only occasionally in the Mercs, sleekly curved spy planes that flew with the angels. There was a complicated scientific explanation for the lights, something to do with the high temperatures and friction caused by going four or five times the speed of sound; the window's glass was blisteringly hot, and if Lt. Col. Thomas Wright reached up and put his hand against it he would be able to keep it there only a second or two, even though he was wearing fire-resistant gloves. Wright, who had flown the Mercs since their first shakedowns, preferred to ignore the science and the explanation: there was more poetry in leaving the lights unquantified. Everything else in the SR-91 was explained and explainable, ad infinitum; you needed at least this one mystery.

"Yo, Millertime," Wright called to the mission specialist sitting in the cockpit behind him. "How's the backseat doin'?"

"Not bad. We still have seven and a half minutes to Alpha," answered Maj. Harvey Miller.

"I thought I heard snorin' back there," said Wright.

"You must be piping in your own intercom," answered Miller. The backseater—officially known as the Reconnaissance Systems Operator, or RSO in air force parlance—ran the Merc's cameras and spy equipment, as well as handling navigation, countermeasures, and some other odds and ends. He had flown with Wright since the plane first went into service at Mildenhall nearly two years ago. The Merc people were matched practically for life. When you were traveling this fast over potentially hostile territory, the theory went, knowing everything down to the other guy's taste in underwear tended to build your confidence in him.

The computer clicked out a milestone marker, and the pilot pressed his screen to acknowledge the electronic nudge—Mother, as the pilots sometimes called it with a tinge of disdain in their voices.

The video screen was the largest of three cathode-ray tubes stuck in the middle of a sea of dials, gauges, and buttons. Officially, it was an Integrated Control Interface—ICI, or Icky, another of the nicknames—and it was Wright's main link to the flight-control computer. He had only to press his index finger to the screen (his right glove was fitted with a special contact) and the computer would bombard him with information. Two jabs in the right corner and he could reset the "mission profile," adjusting the plane's optimum flight parameters. A wipe across the screen cleared the display; a tap in the lower left corner prepared the computer to take the controls or relinquish them on voice command.

Mother was only a small part of the system that helped the pilot fly the plane. The aerodynamics profile selector (APS), a collection of fast processors and several gigabytes of RAM the pilot had no control over, was actually much more important, translating his stick commands into movements of the wings, flaps, and tail. At subsonic speeds, where the Merc was barely stable, the APS was crucial; there were so many different factors to adjust for that even with the computer's help it was hard to keep the plane from stalling. And at high speeds, the electronic brain made it much easier to control the Merc; just throttling the engines properly as the plane turned required a major exertion of higher calculus—not an easy thing to do when you were trying to keep your eyes on the road.

The Mercs, named after the Greek god Mercury or the first American spaceships or the old car, depending on whom you asked, didn't exist, officially. Roughly based on the SR-71 Blackbird, the SR-91 had much more powerful engines, supplemented by hydrogen-fueled boosters. Stronger and faster than the Blackbird, it was a fraction more maneuverable and infinitely uglier. Its mission was essentially the same, though—go real fast, real high, and take a lot of pictures. The new plane just did it all a little better, not to mention more expensively.

The people who had built the plane liked to compare its computer systems to a subordinate officer who has been given a command to follow and left to figure out how best to carry it out. Wright, who knew a thing or two about officer initiative, was less than comforted by the analogy.

The pilot reached forward and swept his hand across the screen, "asking" the computer to give him a run-through of the plane's vital signs. Mother dutifully began filling the main screen with row after row of numbers. They became increasingly arcane as the computer scrolled, and Wright found his mind drifting even as he watched for the telltale red that would indicate one of the specifications was outside allowable parameters. (Why, he wondered, would anyone be interested in knowing the temperature of both the top and bottom of the tail fin?) He flexed his fingers like a pianist preparing to play before pulling the throttle to increase his speed.

Wright and Miller were flying south, just west of Bonn, well above any of the commercial flight zones and beyond the ability of the local civilian radars to detect him. NATO military radars were a different story, although in theory even they would have an extremely difficult time tracking his stealthy plane. That was the theory; Wright knew of at least two flights where Mercs were spotted on German radar and even tracked, briefly, by USAFE TAC, an eight-plane, full-alert squadron, the only U.S. interceptor unit still based in Europe. The Merc's flights were a gray area in the Allied notification rules; supposedly, the SAC recon unit remained in England to verify Soviet compliance with the '93 troop drawdown treaties, but in the last two years the primary mission had been to keep tabs on reunified Germany. NATO or not, history cast a large shadow on the continent.

There was another theory that all American flights were to be precleared with the NATO command, but that had about as much basis in fact as the one about the world being flat. Not even USAFE was on the microscopically short list of those to be briefed on missions. Despite the electronic identification gear that would show the plane was a friend (and incorrectly say it was the mothballed SR-71) if properly queried, the Merc's flight rules directed pilots to avoid all contact, including turning the ID system on. That was because the Soviets—not to mention the Germans— would almost certainly be tracking any fighter patrol that picked up on the Merc, and might inadvertently gather information about the plane.

On the detected flight that got followed, the TAC interceptors (brand-new F-22s, thank you very much) somehow got close enough to tickle the plane. The Merc pilot, however, left the identifier off, laughed (or so he claimed later), pointed the nose up, and let the plane's engines out. The engines gobbled fuel—set up to constantly accelerate, they would clean out the tanks if you just let them go—and the Merc quickly outpaced the fighters. "I didn't even hit the hydrogen," the pilot bragged to Wright much later, referring to the scramjet booster that could have increased the speed, for a few seconds, to close to Mach 7.

Of course, the fighters also carried new Starlet AIM180-ALRAAM missiles, which had at least a 35 percent chance at bringing the bird down, and the pilot's radar detector had been going crazy when he'd hit the gas. If that hadn't worked, his next option was to turn on the electronic countermeasures, designed to confuse the fighters and their missiles, and pray. There wouldn't have been much sense in pouring out the Good Guy signal at that point: they wouldn't have believed an ID that had suddenly popped out of nowhere.

That would be a hell of a thing, shooting down your own spy plane. Dumb fighter jock would probably be proud, even after they busted him to floor sweeper. Wright smiled, nudging the stick ever so lightly to come back one degree to the west, perfectly on course. He had started out as a dumb fighter jock himself, before being granted enlightenment. It was something like a hand reaching down and anointing you, deciding that you ought to be put to a higher use. It took you into the Brotherhood—but not quite. Just because you were good didn't mean you were really a member. You had to prove yourself. And that wasn't necessarily easy when a computer was looking over your shoulder.

Wright swept his eyes across the cockpit screens, back up to the window, down to the stick and throttle, back to the window. That took maybe a quarter of his attention. The other three-quarters floated, his imagination looking for stimulation.

A little more than fifty years ago, army air force B-17s might have taken this same route, looping down to strike Frankfurt and then make the long run back to England, where another flock of British bombers waited to take off for a night mission. No, actually, the route was all wrong; they would have come over the Continent much further west. But Wright saw them anyway as his mind wandered. He saw the lumbering Flying Fortresses stretched out across the early morning sky, their escort, a group of P-51s, darting in and out. Tough little planes, the Mustangs; they were maneuverable as hell and went like all get-out, for their time.

Flying a Mustang would give you good odds at getting into the Brotherhood. Tangle with a couple of Messerschmitts, 109s or the deadly 190s. No relying on missiles and color-coded heads-up displays; all you had were machine guns and your guts.

Or did they have cannons? Wright knew so much about old planes that he sometimes mixed up the details, which armament went with which engine in the Thunderbolts, how far whose drop-tanks would take you. He knew it, but that was the problem: the information occasionally overloaded in his brain.

Ever since he was a little kid he'd studied and dreamed airplanes, absorbing them into his blood. He'd read so many books and seen so many movies and just imagined it so much that when he actually, finally, got into the cockpit himself he prepared himself for a letdown. Nothing, he thought, could compare to his imagination.

He was wrong. The excitement quickly outpaced his dreams. Even on his first flight in a prop he knew he had to blend himself into the airplane, fly with it like it was part of him. The first jet trainer he'd sat in rocked his pants off with the feeling of speed and all he could do the whole way was grin, a lockjaw smile so wide his oxygen mask threatened to split in half. As routine as the mechanics of flying had become since those trips, and in spite of all the computers—and all the time you had now just to daydream, hanging out while the computer did your job—at some point on nearly every flight he still felt a piece of that original thrill.

"Hey, check your six, would you?" Wright said to Miller, asking his RSO to turn around and see if there was a plane behind him. It was a standing joke. "Checking your six" was standard procedure in a fighter, but about the only thing that could sneak up behind a Merc was a meteor. Miller had a small periscope, à la the SR-71, that he could look through. It was virtually impossible for either the RSO or pilot to turn around; they were strapped in tight in cumbersome astronaut-like suits.

"Great view this morning," said Miller. "You ain't expecting company, are you?"

"Hey, you never know."

"Jesus," said Miller in mock horror before putting on his most officious voice. "Backseat to Captain Fantastic. Backseat to Captain Fantastic."

"Roger, Backseat."

"There's a flight of, well, I can't quite make this out. Yes sir, I'll be damned—we got a Fokker Albatross on our tail, comin' in strong at, Jesus, eleven o'clock. We're goners."

"I'm gonna roll so we can check below."

"Oh, I'm sure there's all kind of things under there," said Miller sarcastically. Wright liked Miller. Rolls weren't exactly part of the mission plan, and another backseater might have tried to talk him out of it. Not that he would've had much of a chance.

The pilot leaned his body back into his seat, and then, with a quick flick of his wrist, pulled the plane over. Fast, easy, and smooth, a perfect invert.

The Merc flew just as well upside down, more or less, and with the pressurized suits and snap-ins you almost couldn't tell the difference. But the plane wasn't exactly a fighter. Built to go very fast, it did that perfectly; it was when you asked it to do anything else that you potentially had a problem. Turning over was easy enough—in fact, the plane liked to turn over. It liked it so much that it had a nasty tendency to become a speeding, rifled bullet, spinning over and over in a perhaps unstoppable roll.

Two Mercs had crashed since they were first flown. The first crash was a flubbed landing in the very beginning, during the operational tests. The pilot, a friend of Wright's, had bought it. The other crash happened on one of the last missions out of Kadena on Okinawa (the Japanese had kicked the Americans out about a year ago), fortunately well out to sea. The crash, the air force believed, had resulted from a power dive brought on by a spin that probably hadn't ended until the plane drilled itself into some trench on the Pacific floor. It thrilled no end of people—all the Mercs were grounded for two months and then ordered back to their home base at Beale, California, for modifications. It was never clear what the modifications were, if any. Just like the

Blackbirds, the planes were regularly gutted and reglued every couple of months anyway. Wright suspected that no changes had actually been made. Probably the brass just wanted the pause in case some congressional committee asked why the air force's billion-dollar spy planes were corking themselves into the sea.

Some pilots, though, believed that the Merc's cruise control had been altered to put a "check" on the pilot, a governor to keep him from doing anything stupid. Wright wouldn't put it past them, but he hadn't seen any evidence of this. As far as they could tell, speed hadn't killed the Merc that went down, and it wouldn't have made sense to do anything that would cut back your maneuverability, such as it was.

The flight rules had been revised and reemphasized after the Kadena crash; flying outside of the ridiculously cautious parameters was officially verboten. But as far as Wright was concerned, once you stopped doing things that could or probably could be done because you were worried, you might as well let the goddamn computer fly.

He looked at Mother, saw the big red letters flashing INVERTED at him. No shit, Sherlock. The computer kept a complete record of the flight; the turnover would be there, if anybody wanted to make an issue of it. But then again, it was on just about every flight Wright had ever made.

"How's it look down there, Millertime?" Wright asked. "You see any more Albatrosses?"

"Man, there are all kinds of Fokkers coming at us. There's a flight of those damn triplanes. I think it's the Red Baron himself, Captain Fan. We're goners."

For just a moment Wright pictured the Merc slipping through a time loop and buzzing some poor World War I pilot into a mental breakdown.

"Say, Fantastic, tell you what," said Miller, his serious voice breaking Wright's daydream. "I got us an Alpha. How 'bout you flip us around and hit our mission profile?"

The pilot looked over his head, down at the earth. It was just starting to lighten, but there was cloud cover and more than enough shadow to make it impossible to see all the way to the ground. He knew, though, that from this altitude the mountains they were just starting to cross would look dark green and black, with white splotches thrown across them. They wouldn't look like mountains at all; more like a piece of earth around a tree trunk, with a network of roots poking out of the moss-covered dirt.

But it was time to dance, not admire the scenery. Wright slowly brought the plane back over, using the maneuver to change his course and begin the climb to station at the same time. Upright, he increased the power, the engines gulping fuel as the plane climbed. He was going to 165,000 feet, about as high as the Merc operated. There might be as much as 20,000 feet more up there in its service ceiling (Wright had reached 190,000 feet briefly during testing, and with the supplemental air and the scramjets, no one was really sure how high it could go in a pinch), but there wasn't any need to strain, not today, anyway. Their mission was fairly simple: Wright and Miller were to fly over Yugoslavia, inside the Dinaric Alps. Yet another civil war had broken out in the Kosovo region, an area with a lot of ethnic Hungarians. It wasn't the Yugoslavians they were interested in, however. Somebody back in a Washington cellar was worried about what the real Hungarians were doing about their brothers in Yugoslavia, and what the Czechs were doing about the Hungarians, and what the Germans were doing about the Czechs. So the Merc had been sent to take some pictures—radargrams that would show where everyone's soldiers were. They didn't have to go over Hungary to see in; their flight plan kept them over Yugoslavia, all the further from whatever the Russian air defense had moved into Rumania last year.

The Yugs, even if they decided to get belligerent, didn't have anything that could reach him. In fact, they didn't even have anything that was effective against the U-2 that had flown in from Greece two days ago on roughly the same mission. But the U-2 didn't have quite enough gear or range to see farther than Hungary, so Washington had put the Merc on call.

They'd given Wright an unusual flight plan—two double eights over the euphemistically termed "occupied territory." Generally these things were just straight through, in and out; somebody was either feeling cocky or wanted incredible detail. "Counting license plates again," Miller had said when they'd gotten the orders. It didn't make much difference to Wright. He didn't actually fly the plane during the photographic run, anyway. Procedure called for the pilot to turn it over to the computer's autopilot section so there would be a stable platform for the RSO to do his thing—which basically involved turning on his own set of computers and watching them work. If the fuzz-buster went off, of course, things would be different—Wright would retake the helm and start looking for the quickest way out, no fooling around. But the odds on that weren't exactly too high—the Yugs would most likely go about shaving and getting the coffee ready, oblivious to the American spy plane trotting around over them.

The pilot tapped his control screen and gave the spoken command for the plane to take control. The screen flashed a dull purple at him, and he tapped a confirmation; there was a slight nudge as the controls went completely automatic. "Magazine time," he told Miller, but his RSO was already concentrating on his gear. Wright surveyed the cockpit and watched as the plane flew flawlessly along the coordinates.

They banked to the right, the run beginning as the first rays of the sun hit the corner of his eye. It was so clear and alone up here, so high and so fast that you felt like God.

And then, right in the middle of a turn, angled thirty degrees for maximum exposure and held there not by the flaps or wings but by the engines themselves, there was a bump, something like what you'd feel if, traveling at a million miles an hour over sheer ice, you suddenly fell into a hole.

All three screens and every light in the cockpit flashed in unison. For a dark second—no, shorter than that, a sixtieth of a sixtieth of a second, and yet a span of time that seemed much longer, days longer, an entire year filled with complete and empty darkness—Wright panicked. His mind was cut off from his body, isolated and immobile. It gave out not a single impulse, let alone a plan for action. The sudden rush of g forces as the plane pitched downward caught him completely off guard, demolishing the mechanisms he had built over the years to control fear.

Slowly, slowly, slowly, an entire lifetime in a fraction of a fraction of a second, his mind climbed back, swam up to the surface of the body, and regained control.

"Hold tight," were the first words Wright managed to say. They were strained and high-pitched, a cross between a screech and a plea, ostensibly directed at his backseater but made entirely for his own benefit: they were an action, an assertion of control. Having made it, Wright vanquished self-doubt and fear. He punched the screen with his fingers, poking the computer in the ribs for having screwed up, and grabbed the stick, yanking at the same time on the throttle, something the autopilot had already begun doing.

This was instinct, and it almost killed him. He expected to power out of the dive, gently moving the stick back, but the throttle was useless. The plane's sudden lurch toward the earth had been caused by a complete failure of the engines, and, instead of swooping up gracefully, the plane's plummet deepened. It took a great deal of concentration (and all of the computer's help) to regain control with just the stick; though the controls were electrically operated and physical force was not an issue, Wright's exertion opened every pore in his body and bathed the inside of his suit with a torrent of sweat.

Flaming out was a notorious problem in the U-2s, which were a decidedly older breed, but Wright had never heard of the Mercs doing this, especially under autopilot and at Mach 4; the momentum alone should have been enough to keep the engines going. Nevertheless, the video screen and his controls confirmed they were dead, despite the fact that there was plenty of fuel—and onboard O_2, which the computer could have tapped to prevent a blowout.

"What's going on?" Miller said from the backseat.

"Don't know," said Wright, waiting for the inevitable next question.

"We hitting the ball?"

"Not here," said Wright, dodging the issue temporarily. Ejecting at this altitude was not a good idea; the little oxy whippets they carried would help them breathe, but it was too damn far to fall, pressurized suits or not. Besides, they'd been flying inside the mountains, deep in Yugoslavia. That would not be a very good place to come down, if they had any choice about it.

Had they been hit by a missile? Something that had totally fooled the detection systems and snuck up on them? Wright didn't think so. He'd never actually been in a plane that was hit, but he knew there would have been more of a shake. There would have been a sound, a pop or a loud thud, even with a near miss, and a near miss wouldn't have taken out both engines. In fact, to take out both engines, a missile—two missiles—would have had to wipe out the wings and half the fuselage. Unless he was hallucinating, he was still there and the plane was intact.

Wright punched the engine starters a couple of dozen times. He was more of a computer than the plane was now, hitting this, trying that, going down his checklist as he tried to get the plane out of it.

The controls, powered now by battery backups, were still working, though the plane responded with about as much enthusiasm as a cement truck being pushed uphill. He switched the fuel service back and forth, through all the reserve channels, trying all different combinations with the supplemental air, but no dice. The engines—assuming they were still sitting back there in the wings—had decided to stage a permanent sick-out.

The Merc still had plenty of forward momentum, and while they were losing altitude, Wright had prevented the plane from slipping into a full dive. As long as he kept it relatively stable and his airspeed up, there wasn't any immediate danger.

"Hey, Miller, you back there?"

"Yeah."

"Mega flameout."

"Uh-huh."

"No sweat, man. I've practiced this a couple a dozen times in the simulators. Never crashed."

"You figure we can restart?" asked Miller.

"Tried that. Your navigation shit working?"

"Looks like it."

"Locate us and try and find an airport."

"Where?"

"How's about Greece? No wait—Italy," said Wright. "I never been to Rome."

"Rome?"

"Make it Naples. Big base there, right?"

"NATO COMAIR South. Basically Air Italia now. We also got Bari on the coast."

"Let's go with Naples—I always heard it was a good spot for tourists."

There is an unwritten code among pilots that the more desperate their situation gets, the calmer their voices become. Wright was speaking in his Sunday picnic voice. They were pretty far from Italy, and he knew the momentum they had, which was a tricky thing to manipulate, was not enough to get them there. Not even in a simulator would he trust the plane's aerodynamics to make the significant contribution in the fight against gravity that gliding in required. But it was a noble goal.

The best thing, probably, would be to get the plane out over the Adriatic, where they could break radio silence and bail out. There was going to be hell to pay, losing a Merc like this, but at least they'd have a chance to face the firing squad in one piece.

Except that he couldn't swim too well.

They were still very high—110,000 feet—but their speed was dropping fast. If the plane went subsonic he'd never be able to control it—that was hard enough with the engines on. Still, he had to use his altitude sparingly.

"So you got a fix?" Wright asked Miller.

"We're still a couple of blocks from the coast. You OK?"

"All that and we're still over the damn country?"

"Those figure eights got us in there pretty far," said Miller apologetically.

"Watch us for bogies while I play with the engines some more."

"Scope's clean."

But Miller had no sooner said that than the fuzz-buster started going wild. A radar wave had run up in the thin air near the plane.

"Ground station," said Miller. "Turn on ECM?"

"Let's tough it out. Odds are he's way too primitive to see us."

"Gotcha."

Now they were below 100,000 feet, and theoretically within range of surface-to-air. But putting on the electronic countermeasures was problematic—it would scramble whatever they had, but it might also tell them something was there. That would complicate whatever cover story Wright's bosses would have to dream up to explain his sudden appearance in the middle of the Adriatic. Besides, the U-2s ran the coast all the time at this altitude without getting tagged.

"If it looks like they're locking, we'll have to put it on," Wright said. "But if we can slip away, it'd be better for everybody."

"I make us just over the mountains," said Miller. "Doesn't look like we're being tracked."

"Good."

Wright continued trying to restart the engines, alternately punching and massaging and tickling the controls.

"Airspeed's dropping bad," said Miller.

They were below Mach 2.

"Yup," acknowledged Wright. There wasn't too much time left. "How much longer to the coast?"

"Thirty seconds, I'd say. Hard to project our speed."

He had maybe one more good dive left. Going lower would make them a more vulnerable target, but it was immaterial now.

"We may be punching out, Millertime."

"Okay."

It was an admission of failure. But nothing else was working.

It was immensely quiet here, without the engines in your ears. The sun was just behind them, a warm, bright ball below. If it weren't for the inevitability of their fall, the beauty of the moment might be overwhelming.

Wright and Miller had to go out together. When he reached 400 nautical miles an hour, a bit before the worst of the shakes, he'd put the plane on its side, pull the stick over and hit the green ball—unlike the older planes where the knob had to be pushed before you ejected, the oxygen cutoff was automatic in this plane, but the slang for bailing out was appropriate enough.

If he'd been in a P-51, he'd have had a chance to glide onto the beach below. Or if he'd been in a P-38 Lightning, there'd be a chance that one of the two engines would restart. Of course, that was supposed to be true in the Merc, too.

"We're over water," said Miller.

"I'm going to light us up and break radio silence," said Wright. "Give them a position."

"Okay."

Reaching for the identifier switch, Wright realized that there was one thing he hadn't tried. It was whimsical, a joke, really—he reached over and hit the hydrogen booster button. There was a sudden shock of power and the Merc shot forward so abruptly he almost lost it; the pilot pulled his finger off the switch and yanked at the stick with both hands to hold the ship steady.

"What the hell?" said Miller.

"I just woke up," said Wright.

"Yeah!" yelled Miller, realizing what it meant.

The boosters were an either-or proposition; there wasn't any question of controlling them like he controlled the engines. Still, he could play with the toggle to keep the plane's momentum up. A strategy crystalized in his mind and he gave a triumphant laugh. Not only did he feel for the first time that they might survive and land the plane, but the improvisation was a source of immeasurable pleasure.

He had to do it just right, at just the right times, or he'd run out of fuel or overshoot his mark.

"You got that course laid out?" he asked Miller.

"Sure."

"You think you could program that computer to tell me when to fire the boosters? Get us down there at just the right time?"

"I think it ought to be able to figure it out," said Miller.

"Well kick some butt," said Wright. He wasn't complaining about the computer now. No sir. About time it pulled its own weight.

All of this, from the failure of their engines to his hitting the hydrogen and bursting over the Adriatic, had taken only a few minutes, and these were blurred together so that they seemed a single second. The next few minutes, flying over the open sea and approaching the lower boot of Italy, passed just a little slower. They were moving slower, too, hovering just over Mach 1—fast for a lot of planes, but like molasses for the Merc.

Wright broke radio silence and broadcast a terse message to Naples, telling them he was flying under severe constraints and giving them a code word that was supposed to put the base at his disposal. There was some difficulty with that. He had to repeat the word three times and then tell the Italian controller to go up the line to England, not NATO or USAFE.

According to Miller's calculations, they could swing around Italy's toe and "glide" into Naples, assuming they could keep the plane's speed up. Once they got there, they'd collapse on the runway in a huge ball of fire—the computer unhelpfully showed a series of zeroes at Naples. Wright figured he might get the plane down to a few hundred miles an hour just as they hit the runway without losing control. If he did that, and popped the chute right away, stood on the brakes, and bent the flaps backward, he'd probably stop by the time he got to Mount Vesuvius.

The Naples controller wasn't quite with the program, but he understood Wright well enough to tell him not to worry about stopping; they had a *grosso* barrier at the far end of the runway.

"Company, Captain Fan," said Miller from the backseat as they crossed over land. Two bogies appeared on the screens, fifty miles away and on an intercept course: a pair of Tornadoes, according to the computer, probably Air Italia. The Tornadoes were older planes, but formidable in mid- to close-range combat—certainly capable of shooting them down if they decided to.

Wright had kicked on the friend-or-foe; he just hoped the Italians weren't spooked by the fact that it ID'd a plane that hadn't flown for years. He also wondered what they'd think when they saw the Merc; it didn't wear any military markings outside of a ghosted insignia you'd need a magnifying glass to see.

"You guys speak English?" Wright asked over the air.

They didn't reply.

"Probably can't read us," said Miller. "They got their radars on, but we're still pretty far away for their gear."

Wright didn't like the other possibilities.

Another blip appeared on their screen, much bigger; this plane was moving directly toward them on a diagonal intercept from the Mediterranean.

The computer ID'd it as an American, an F-22M, the navy's

version of the country's top-line fighter. Finally, the navy had a design with the right size engine in it—courtesy of the air force. But of course the navy had thrown in its own two cents, and when it was done with its alterations, the plane, not exactly small to begin with, was a good 20 percent larger and heavier than the air force version. Even with its vaunted "stealthy characteristics," anybody with a little bit of finesse and some long-range missiles to burn would have no trouble shooting them down.

"Navy fighter running up from the south," said Miller.

"Yeah, I got him," said Wright. The scope was on its widest sweep; the plane was a good hundred miles away.

"Think SAC alerted him?"

The air force cooperating with the navy? They'd have called the Russians first, thought Wright. But the navy pilot, using the service-integrated long-range communications system, came on with the proper acknowledgment codes; apparently they had.

"Understand you have operational problems and I have orders to escort you down," said the pilot.

"You figure these Italian guys are going to shoot us or something?" Wright responded.

"They're going to escort, too, once they find you."

Great, thought Wright; I'll get Miller to stand out on the wing and wave a red flag. Then we can all party while I crash this sucker into the volcano.

"I just happened to be in the neighborhood," said the navy flier. "We were flying a long intercept to Naples."

"What a break," said Wright. "Must be my lucky day."

"You must be big-time," said the pilot, who was still too far away to actually see the Merc. "They're getting everything up to chase you down. I never heard so much top-level radio traffic in my life."

"Yeah, well, blame my RSO. He's related to the pope."

"SAC wants to know if you can swing it over to Bari on the coast," asked the navy pilot, who didn't seem to know what to make of Wright's joke. "I have contact with them through my carrier."

"Hell," said Wright. "I was thinking I'd crank this sucker around and fly all the way back to England."

"Repeat?" said the pilot.

"With all due respect, Captain," Wright called back, "I'm surprised we're not in the water already. My machine says I can just about glide on down to Naples if I say three Hail Marys, and we're sticking with that. Unless the engines suddenly decide to start up, in which case we'll land on your carrier."

"You have no engines, over?"

"Every so often me and my partner here get out and push," said Wright, hitting the hydrogen on cue from the computer. "I don't want to blow your security clearance or anything, but I'm a glider."

The pilot was confused, but Wright had too much to do to keep pulling his chain. The fuzz-buster and radars were alive with traffic. The Tornadoes had finally found the Merc and taken up respectful positions a mile behind him. The navy pilot caught up and pulled alongside, practically whooping when he saw the Merc.

"What the hell are you flying?" he asked. Wright gave him a little wave and told him not to get too close and, above all, not to drool.

They were relatively low now; punching out would be easy. Wright considered the option—they'd lose the Merc, but they'd save themselves. If he'd been alone in the plane, the decision would have been easy—you bring the sucker in whenever there's a chance. But he wasn't alone. And he couldn't just tell his backseater to save himself. They had to go out together.

"Say, Harv," said Wright. "You think we ought to hit the ball?"

"Huh?"

"The rest of this is going to be pretty touchy. The computer says we ain't gonna make it."

"What the hell are you talking about?" said Miller. "Since when did you start taking advice from the goddamn computer?"

"Just making sure you don't have second thoughts."

"Screw you, buddy. We got this far, didn't we? I ain't woosin' out."

"Don't get testy," said Wright, thankful for the vote of confidence. "I just thought we'd consider the possibility."

"Jesus, Tom. This crap's so easy from here on I could do it."

It wasn't, but they made it anyway. Remarkably, the plane kept a stable glide until maybe five hundred yards short of the runway, and then, bucking and pitching, its nose threatened to give itself over to gravity and stick itself directly into the earth.

Against the computer's advice, Wright hit the hydrogen a brief second, a burst, and worked the controls with everything he had. The wheels of the plane hit the edge of the runway with a sharp scrape and a pair blew out immediately on his right side, the worst possible moment, but at least it was something he expected. He pulled the nose down and with the chute flailing behind them they swerved and skidded down the runway, managing an almost straight line, the plane a drunken sumo wrestler falling down a stairway and across a floor forever.

For a second it seemed to Wright that the hands of God had returned, that all of this had been a split-second hallucination induced by a failure in the oxygen system. And then he realized that a crowd of people, perhaps all of Italy, was running toward him, yelling.

"Holy fuck," he said, not knowing whether it was aloud or not. "We're alive."

2

THE INTUITION MACHINE

Hunter stared out the limo window, catching glimpses of the battered ghetto they were driving through. It was almost rush hour in the nation's capital, but the streets here were nearly empty; the limousine, which had picked him up at Dulles, hurried past the deserted industrial buildings and the squalid rows of frame houses so quickly it seemed as if the way had been cleared by a police escort. But this limo would never have company like that. The cross-country movements of its lone passenger, leaning back now in the vast rear compartment of the auto, were so secret that anyone who divulged them could be brought up on charges of treason and possibly shot.

There were only two people who knew all the details of these weekly trips. One was Hunter, who was trying to maintain his nonchalance by flipping once more through the newspaper he'd picked up at the airport. The other was National Security Director Henry Morse, the man he was coming to see.

Lieutenant General William "Billy" Hunter—there was supposed to be a "retired" after his name, but no one used it, especially now—had spent a short but important part of his career at the

Pentagon, and coming back to D.C. always reminded him of that terrible experience. Of all the things he'd done in his nearly sixty years, including dropping napalm on peasants he couldn't see, working in the Pentagon had been the most morally repugnant. Not one project he'd been involved with there, including his last, the production of the Mercury spy planes, had escaped the heavy weight of personal and professional jealousies, rival empires, and petty bullshit, to say nothing of the usual vendettas and disputes between the air force, the other services, and especially the CIA, NSA, and all the other damn alphabet phonies who wanted in on the action. Billy Hunter considered himself pretty patriotic, and willing to put up with a certain amount of indignity to accomplish his mission, but several times he had come close to strangling fellow officers, more than occasionally ones who were nominally in a position of authority over him. He had gotten the new SRs flying, but only after threatening to quit several times and finally moving his headquarters out to the field, "going operational" as the Pentagon fags had derisively called it. His tremendous (and still highly classified) success with the plane cut off any possibility of meaningful advancement in the service: he'd bruised too many egos and irritated his way into a permanent place in too many memories to do anything but retire when the airplane flew. But he'd had enough of the air force and military by then anyway.

And here he was, back. Not just in D.C., but up to his ears in an ultrasecret government project: the production of yet another airplane. The Coyote, as it was called, would be more than just a successor to the Mercury. It made the SR-91 look like a World War I biplane. Powered by hydrogen engines, with an airfoil that could twist itself into different shapes depending on the demands of the moment, it was literally a pilot's dream. But that wasn't the half of it. The Coyote was meant to be the key to a new kind of flying, and a new kind of air force. The plane was connected to a vast computer system, which acted as the jet's eyes and ears, accepting inputs from radars, satellites, and drones stationed across the Northern Hemisphere. The computer could coordinate its activities with those of a dozen other aircraft. The full interface wasn't perfected—right now they were still having trouble getting the computer to work well with just the one plane—but you could see the potential. Boy, could you see the potential.

So Hunter, a former pilot himself, could put up with the Washington bs. Admittedly, there was less on this project than anything he'd been involved in. He had real control over what he was doing, acting literally as the deep black project's "czar," answerable to only the NSC director, a man he had known for over thirty years, and through him, the president of the United States. He had an unlimited budget, with access to even more money than he felt he needed. He had the ability to practically kidnap people if he wanted them. And all he had to do—besides make the whole thing work, of course—was hop back here every other week and listen to his old friend tell him why they had to move faster.

Morse always had good reasons, of course. There were the worldwide implications and the need to jump America far ahead of potential rivals, make the universe safe for democracy and all that boilerplate stuff, but mostly the reason he had to hurry was this: sooner or later, Congress was going to ask where they were spending all this money they couldn't afford to spend. At that point, they better have something to show for it, something so impressive that Congress wouldn't mind all the commas and zeroes after the dollar signs in the appropriations bill.

Today the general was going to do more than just frown and say some things couldn't be rushed. For even Hunter had to agree that after the tremendous gains they'd made in the last six months, they were starting to slow down. He was apprehensive, however—not because Morse was likely to oppose his request; on the contrary, Hunter had always been given a free hand. But his plan involved a personnel change involving his main—only—pilot. And Hunter hated doing anything that hurt his people.

Still, they were being held back because the pilot, Maj. Stephen Pelham, just wasn't right for the project. On paper, he was one of the air force's top test pilots. He had worked with Hunter on the Mercury project, where he had done an excellent job. But here he just didn't mesh.

Part of it turned out to be his utter predictability, ordinarily not a drawback in a test pilot. But because the computer that helped fly the plane depended on the pilot to learn, the fact that he followed straightforward patterns every time he climbed into the cockpit meant the computer's learning track looked as if it had been read in from a book. The computer was a major part of the project, more important than the plane itself. It was learning not merely how to fly from the pilot, but how to think. The success of the whole project depended on its moving ahead, and if Pelham couldn't push it fast enough, everything was held back.

Pelham had another problem. He'd managed to alienate everyone at the small base, including and most especially the scientist who acted as his interface with the computer system back at the base during the test flights. Sooner or later, there was going to be a major blowup that would bring the project to a crashing halt. Because of the way the pilot and the scientist had to work together when the plane was flying, one of them would have to go. And since the scientist had invented a lot of the computer system, was still coming up with important changes, and was, far and away, the most likable person at the base, the choice between them was a no-brainer.

Still, having Pelham reassigned would be perceived as a demotion, a washout even; it would kill his career. Even if Pelham was a jerk, Hunter felt he owed him more than that. The guy flew for him, after all.

The limo spun around the back of a nondescript building in northwest D.C. and Hunter got out, glass crinkling under his feet as he walked across the parking lot to the rear door. It looked old and beaten down, ready to collapse if the wind shifted, but like so much else in the nation's capital, you couldn't trust appearances. The one remaining glass pane in the door was actually a receptor for a retina scanning device. If the computer didn't know and approve of you, not even a tank could have gotten in—the flimsy-looking plywood panels covered eight inches of steel. And that was just the outside door.

A pair of marines in civilian dress stood inside. They greeted Hunter with detection wands, and then walked him through a machine that took an ultrasound image of his body, making sure he hadn't had any plastic explosives for breakfast. Having run this gauntlet, he waited beside an elevator shaft at the far end of the hallway. To get the elevator to come up, he had to put his hand on a smooth metal plate—it matched his finger and palm prints with its memory, making sure they jibed with the retina that was checked and recorded at the door. When the elevator arrived, he had to give his code word—Hammerhead—and wait while the machine checked his voice pattern against the other evidence that he was who he was. The door hesitated. "Hammerhead," he said again, this time in a firmer voice; the implied threat registered and the doors swung open immediately.

Hunter thought the security excessive, even by D.C. standards. It seemed a symptom of Washington Disease, and though he didn't like to admit it, it seemed obvious that Morse had contracted a major case of it. Hunter understood the director's desire for face-to-face briefings, even if the nearly thirteen-hour affair of flying out from Coyote Base in northern California, talking for twenty minutes, and then jetting back was a tiresome waste of time, but they could just as well have met in Morse's White House office. Instead, their meetings took place in a never-ending series of clean rooms throughout the city and surrounding area; in three years he didn't think they'd used the same place twice in a row. All of this high-tech spy gear must be awfully expensive. Hunter probably could have built another four or five planes with the money Morse spent keeping secret the one they had.

Real spying was much more likely further down the line, on the operational side, where Hunter had already taken considerable precautions. But the professor had grown increasingly fond of the trappings of his job, and got a thrill out of the gadgets and procedures the retired general found so annoying.

"You're late, Billy," said a disembodied voice as he got off the elevator.

"Sorry," said Hunter, walking toward the door that stood at the end of a long hallway opposite the elevator. "All your electronic shit slowed me down."

"Got to have security, Billy," said the voice, which was piped in from speakers in the ceiling. Hunter's progress down the hall was being monitored by hidden video cameras.

"The Russians wouldn't bother bugging us," said Hunter in a voice he thought low enough not to be picked up. "They know too much of this is bullshit anyway."

"It's not them I'm worried about," said Morse. The door opened, and the national security director put his hand out. "I'm worried about some congressman getting it into his head he ought to figure out what we're doing with all his money."

Hunter snickered as he shook his boss's hand.

The room was austere, its whitewashed walls bare, with only two couches and a table in the corner set up as a small bar—scotch and water, an ice bucket, and a few glasses. There wasn't even a lamp—overhead fluorescents flooded everything with a harsh, bright light.

At the start of their meeting, Morse always played the gracious host, the college professor with unexpected guests. Four years at Columbia did that to you, Hunter supposed. Morse swept him in and moved around like a thin, graying elf, fixing drinks. The jacket of his dark blue suit unbuttoned, his solid red tie pinned neatly to his shirt, Morse looked relaxed and friendly, even five years younger than he was. When he sat down, drink in hand, the national security director reemerged, fully sixty-three now, several pounds heavier, his shoulders hunched.

"You look like you've gained a little weight," said Morse.

"Not enough time to work out," said Hunter. Actually, he'd lost a good twenty pounds since he'd started Coyote. But you didn't argue with Morse if you didn't have to; you saved yourself for the bigger fights.

"Can't neglect your health," said Morse, handing him a scotch. "I schedule my day around my workouts—eight A.M., even when I'm out of the country."

The director's preoccupation with his health was fairly recent, and obviously wasn't of sufficient fervor to dislodge older habits, such as the scotch.

"You look like you've lost weight just in the last week," said Hunter.

Morse smiled, for a second the old friend poking through, but the director quickly returned. "I have something I want you to look at," he said, reaching down to his briefcase and pulling out a folder. He passed it to Hunter, watching him carefully as he sipped his drink. There was a single photo in the folder, a crisp black-and-white glossy reproduction of a 64-shade, computer-dithered spy shot of Coyote Base. The runway was there, the concrete command building, two of the miscellaneous aircraft they had, and, last but not least, the tent hangar where, perhaps only by luck, the star attraction had escaped unphotographed.

Hunter grunted and tossed the photo on the table. They'd known the Russians would eventually catch on.

"I'd have smiled if I knew Ivan was going to take my picture," he told the director. "How'd you come up with it?"

"Look at those characters in the corner. They look like the Cyrillic alphabet to you?"

Hunter picked the photo back up, and with a start realized that he hadn't paid nearly enough attention: there were a series of ideographic characters along the border of the photo he hadn't even noticed.

"This is a great day in the history of mankind," said Morse sarcastically, mimicking a speech the Japanese prime minister had given upon the launching of the shuttle several weeks ago. The reference was lost on Hunter, who was aware of the puzzled look on his face but couldn't do much to change it.

"That came off a satellite that the Japanese Hope Shuttle launched last week," explained the director.

"The Japanese?"

"Private satellite, owned by a corporation called Netsubo. Officially, it was launched to look for mineral deposits, but someone noticed its orbit took it over North America, and the NSA thought it might be worth stealing a few of its transmissions."

"Why are they taking pictures of us?"

"Why, indeed," said Morse, digging back into his briefcase. "I've got the CIA trying to figure out if there's been a security leak," he said as he fished through it.

"There hasn't been," said Hunter stiffly.

"There better not have been," said Morse. He tossed another folder on the table between them and picked up his drink.

The photos in this folder were American, off a Keyhole satellite controlled out of Maryland. These were expensive, low-altitude satellites that didn't go up very often, because of the cost. Hunter examined the pictures carefully, but even so, he couldn't figure out what their significance was. Ironically, the man who had spent much of his career developing spy planes was not very adept at deciphering intelligence photos, and these looked particularly benign.

"Why do you think there is an air base on an atoll in the Kuriles?" said Morse, prompting in his professorial manner.

Hunter went through the pictures slowly. They were all pictures of a small island, a mountain or perhaps an inactive volcano practically in the center, with some scattered rocks offshore. There was a close-up of some seemingly abandoned huts and a broken-down concrete structure on the side of a hill. Another shot focused on the flat plain nearby, but there were no signs that it was a runway.

"It's cleverly disguised," said Morse. "They tell me there's a light covering of sand over a packed lava base, done so well it might almost be natural. This mountain here," added the director, reaching over and pointing at the photo, "houses a base left over from the Russians. They used the complex inside for satellite tracking. Everything was supposed to have been taken out before they gave the islands back to the Japanese three years ago."

"This is a Japanese government base?" Hunter asked.

"That's not altogether clear," said Morse. "The island seems to have been leased by Netsubo two years ago."

"Same company?"

"Apparently. We don't have much information on it yet. With everything else that's going on in Europe with Yugoslavia and with the coup in Syria, this hasn't gotten a lot of attention. But I'm concerned."

"You're not trying to tell me that the Japanese have a plane of their own," Hunter said incredulously.

The more serious Morse was, the more his eyebrows formed a straight line across his forehead. Right now they were a thick, flat smudge over his eyes. "It would explain why they're so interested in ours."

"Do you have any proof?"

"Of course not. I'd share it with you right away."

"Why would they even try to build one?" said Hunter. "Why would the Japanese be interested?"

Morse frowned. He took the folders into his hand, rearranging the photos into their original order. "Why would they take photos of your base? Obviously there's all sorts of scenarios we can construct. Working with even a small air force, a plane like that would give them tremendous capacity. They could make a true break with us—you know the debates that are going on in Japan right now."

"You've said yourself they're nothing to worry about," said Hunter. "That sort of thing happens periodically."

"Yes," said Morse.

He said it the way a man says something when he is reluctant to acknowledge it may be wrong, a little too quickly, with a little too much emphasis.

"Coordination on that level is several years away," said Hunter. "Even for us."

"Whatever is going on in Japan," said Morse, "we've got to move ahead as quickly as possible. This is all the more reason to push forward."

"Some things can't be rushed," said Hunter. This was familiar ground, and now he suspected that Morse was inflating his suspicions to fit in with the constant theme: push forward, faster, faster.

"I called you out of retirement to head this because you could cut through the obstacles," said Morse.

"I am cutting through," said Hunter.

"You're behind your own time schedule."

"Only by a few weeks," said Hunter, "and only on the updated timeline. Nobody has ever flown anything like this. We have a lot of things to work out."

"Yes?" The director said this with an intonation that meant get to the point.

Hunter frowned. He'd come here ready to can Pelham, but when it came time to actually say the words, he felt as if he were betraying his pilot. Hunter repeated the arguments to himself for the hundredth time.

"For one thing," stalled the general, "there are problems with the computer."

"Fix them."

He's right, thought Hunter. My responsibility is to the project, the plane. I'll keep Pelham on and fix it so it doesn't hurt his career. Just his ego.

"I have another problem," said the general. "I need another pilot."

"What?"

"The computer scientists think that another pilot would add variety to the computer's learning routines. We've always talked about having a backup pilot, anyway."

"You told me a backup wasn't necessary," said Morse. Hunter could see by his face that Morse thought this was going to delay them further.

"We're not going to lose any time. I can slip him right into the schedule. We'll be back where we started with the plane inside a week, and the computer will end up ahead."

"The designers contend that we don't even need a pilot—"

"They're flat-out wrong," said Hunter heatedly. "It's crucial during the testing. Once the computer has learned, maybe, but now—"

"Relax," said Morse. "You convinced me of that two years ago. But you also convinced me that we didn't need a backup."

"Well, I was wrong." Hunter took a sip of his scotch. It stung slightly—he only drank scotch with the director. "I have someone in mind. He helped develop the Mercs and is flying them out of England. He's done a lot of flying for me, and he's a quick study. Extremely quick."

"Get him," said Morse with a preemptive wave of his hand. "Get as many pilots as you need. Just get the damn thing moving."

"I am."

"We must be in position for all contingencies," said Morse. His passion reminded Hunter of a tinhorn dictator—or of a fat-assed three-star general.

"Listen, Henry," said Hunter, his voice taking on the tone that had won him so many enemies when he was in the air force. "We're moving as fast as we can."

"Move faster," said Morse, standing to signal the end of the discussion.

Hunter knew it was at least partly a performance, but he didn't like it, not at all. "I'm supposed to screw up my project because of some sand and a Japanese photo expedition?"

"If they're really working on a plane, Billy," said Morse, his voice low and serious, full of the intimacy of a friendship that had started over watered-down beer in a Thailand bar during the Vietnam War decades before, "we're going to have a lot more problems than finding another pilot."

Fisher lit another cigarette and flicked the extinguished match to the floor. It landed at the Italian major's feet. The major, still waiting for his connection to come through on the phone, looked up and glared at him. Fisher glared back. He'd been standing in the small room at the Naples Air Base, waiting to be cleared through to the gate, for over an hour. The FBI agent had decided he might just as well be as obnoxious as possible, hoping the Italians would get tired of him and let him go.

It wasn't like he was acting all that much. FBI Special Agent Brian Fisher was used to waiting and used to taking crap, but he wasn't in the mood for either tonight. He hadn't been able to sleep on the plane from America, which meant he'd been up for more than thirty-six hours now. Worse, far worse, he was down to his last American cigarette. From here on out it was the Italian cardboard he'd bummed from the taxi driver. He'd had to resort to foreign cigarettes several times in his life, dark days all.

It was his own fault; he should have hunted down a shop that sold American cigarettes at the airport. But he'd been in a hurry to get here, and for one of the few times in his life hadn't remembered to check the contingencies.

There was an excuse: he wanted to see the plane before it was moved. Fisher wasn't merely interested in the aircraft because he was on the sabotage watch; the mysterious failure of the engines fit perfectly into the profile of a case he was working on. While he didn't want the air force or the Defense Intelligence Agency (DIA) to know specifically what he was doing—he'd learned from past experience that the more they knew, the more they got in the way—it was important to establish his claim in person. There would be a question of jurisdiction in any event; without being there, the military types would limit his standing to observer status, at best. More importantly, he wanted to talk to the mechanics himself, before their opinions got interpreted. Last but not least, there was the pilot—it would be something of a novelty, Fisher thought darkly, to talk to one who'd survived.

So the FBI agent had hopped the first available commercial flight, landing in Rome at the height of rush hour. Air traffic to the south had been suspended due to the "continuing emergency"— once they got excited about something, Italians tended to stay excited for a while—so he'd ended up giving a cabbie enough money to retire on to drive through half the country to get down here. The ride wouldn't have been bad had either of the taxi's headlights worked with any consistency.

They'd made good time nonetheless, and Fisher had actually trotted from the cab to the Italian HQ building, huffing as he ran up the steps, bursting into the well-appointed office with a rush of enthusiasm and adrenaline. Both faded quickly. The FBI agent had watched three television crews cleared through with a wave while the Italians played chain-of-command with him: a sergeant called a lieutenant, who called a captain, who called the major, who was now waiting for a colonel to give clearance. They might not run out of officers until they reached the pope. The newspeople would never get past the American guards, who were actually controlling access to the hangar. Still, the idea that reporters could be passed through without so much as a name check while his top-level credentials were questioned galled him. And it didn't help that the Italians hadn't offered him a chair, let alone coffee.

The lieutenant said something to the sergeant, who disappeared into the next room, reappearing with an ashtray.

"Grace us," said Fisher, exhausting his Italian with a rough approximation of what he thought was the word for thank you. "You got any real cigarettes?"

The sergeant shrugged that he didn't understand.

"Smokes. You know," said Fisher, pointing to the cigarette.

The sergeant shrugged again.

"You don't understand cigarette?" said Fisher. "Cigarette, smoke." He puffed on the cigarette, drawing it down almost to the filter. "You aren't deaf, are you?"

"He doesn't speak English, sir," said the major, hanging up the phone.

"Well, obviously you do," said Fisher. "You got any cigarettes?"

"I do not smoke," said the major.

"Tell you what—let me through, and I'll bum one from the Americans."

"My colonel is checking with your people right now."

"Your colonel," snarled Fisher. "Why don't we just go right up the line to el presidente?"

"You don't have to be discourteous, sir," replied the major, standing stiffly, almost at attention. "We have regulations."

"What about the TV people?" said Fisher. "You pushed them right through."

The Italian smiled. "We can't interfere with the press."

The smile was a bad sign. He hadn't gotten under the guy's skin at all. "What, the CIA paying you to keep me here?"

"The CIA? Non capisco."

I've found the only person in the world who's never heard of the CIA, thought Fisher. "So nobody's got a cigarette?" he said, real exasperation creeping into his voice.

The major looked at the captain, who gestured to the lieutenant, who prodded the sergeant. "Ecco," he said, taking a package of Italian cigarettes from his pocket and flipping it to Fisher, who caught it and in the same motion flipped it back.

"No grace us," said Fisher. "I got my own camel shit. Thanks anyway."

So much for annoying them into submission. Fisher returned to the window, looking out into the dark for a trace of the colonel or his car. He'd give them ten minutes. If they didn't let him through by then, he'd call Washington and have them find somebody who could do an impression of His Holiness.

In the meantime, more pressing problems. He dropped his cigarette butt to the floor, squished it a little to make sure the fellow who had brought the ashtray noticed, and then took out the Italian cigarettes. He almost gagged at the first puff.

The sergeant and lieutenant suddenly snapped to attention, and Fisher turned to see the latest participant in the authorization round robin. But the colonel was different; Fisher could tell by the way he walked in. Tall, thin, self-possessed, he walked swiftly to the middle of the room and smartly returned his countrymen's salutes. Turning to the FBI agent, he wished him a good evening in Italian, and having thus determined that Fisher spoke only English, asked him in a slightly British accent what he required.

"I'm here to investigate the airplane," Fisher said, reaching for his identification.

The colonel waved it away. "My men have checked that."

Fisher nodded, his suspicions about the colonel's competence confirmed.

"You are with the FBI?" continued the Italian officer. "I didn't know that the FBI came to Italy for anything but the Mafia."

"These are special circumstances," said Fisher.

"Yes," said the colonel. "I see. You expect sabotage?"

"I expect nothing," said Fisher. "But possibilities have to be checked."

"Yes," replied the colonel. "I believe we have more American investigators here than are in Washington, D.C."

"Did they all get such a hard time?" Fisher asked pointedly, pushing the smoke from his mouth for emphasis.

"A hard time?" The colonel looked innocently at his men—they shrugged in ignorance—and then back at Fisher. "We have to take normal security precautions."

"Yeah," said the American agent, stubbing the half-smoked cigarette out in the ashtray. They not only tasted bad, they were stale.

"You know, Mr. Fisher, my own men are not permitted in the hangar. This is very embarrassing," said the colonel.

"Embarrassing?" Fisher asked, as if he didn't understand.

"This is Italian soil, after all," said the colonel, seeming almost apologetic. "We are allies."

Fisher shrugged. "I'm not responsible for these military jerks."

"You know, the pilot took out a pistol and fired a shot when some of our men approached the plane. Imagine! He is lucky that our soldiers kept their heads."

Just like the air force, Fisher thought to himself. "I woulda shot him, if it was me," said Fisher. "Teach the son of a bitch a lesson. Who could've blamed you?"

"Yes," said the colonel with the hint of a smile. "But then I suppose we would have had other problems."

"Be worth it, don't ya think?" said Fisher. The Italian smiled. "I'll slap him around a bit when I see him, if you think it'll do any good."

"That won't be necessary," said the officer, amused.

"What do you say, Colonel? Time for me to get to work."

"You may proceed," he said, extending his hand. "If we can do anything else—"

"How about a lift to the hangar?" Fisher asked.

The colonel said something to the lieutenant, who nodded at the sergeant.

"Sergeant Scacciaferro will take you there," said the colonel.

"Say, Colonel," said Fisher, turning back after starting for the door. "You got any American cigarettes?"

"I gave up smoking years ago," said the colonel mildly.

"Too bad," said Fisher. "Just when you were turning out to be such a great guy."

The pilot may have held off the Italians with a pistol, but in the short ride out to the hangar Fisher saw that the U.S. was taking no chances now. There were air force people, dogs, a couple of navy guys, and what seemed to be an entire army regiment on the field. The hangar itself was ringed by men standing at half an arm's length from each other; in front of them was a semicircle of fire teams, these men kneeling and standing in frozen poses halfway between shooting-range ferocity and sleepy-eyed boredom. Two dozen soldiers commanded the approach to the hangar; knots of men had taken up positions between the hangar and the runway. The Italians, meanwhile, had responded to this invasion with their own show of force, surrounding the American rings with several of their own, some facing towards and some away from the Americans, as if they hadn't decided in which direction the threat lay. The Italian lines were augmented by a disparate collection of vehicles: jeeps, several different types of trucks, and a few fire engines. The entire area was illuminated by enough spotlights to open ten used-car lots; a regiment of beams splayed through the sky, detecting the odd cumulus cloud and holding it at bay.

The jeep deposited Fisher in the demilitarized zone between the two armies and sped off. Fisher approached an army major who appeared somewhat in charge. He flashed his ID; the major grumped. "You're gonna have to wait for the colonel," he said, adding with a hint of derision, "This is an air force show."

"Where is he?"

The major nodded in the direction of a knot of camera crews. "He just started talking to these TV people."

"Only thing you need here is a brass band," said Fisher.

"Yeah," said the major. "The Italians are making a circus out of it."

Fisher laughed. "You're not doing too bad yourself. Got a cigarette?"

The major shook his head. "You're pretty late. Just about everybody else in the world is here already."

"I'm just here because of regulations," said Fisher, slipping into his "just another government functionary" guise. It was a lot easier to find things out if you didn't seem like you cared. And by now he was so tired, that was easy. "I expect the air force people will do most of the work."

"Damn air force has its people all over the place, giving us orders. They screw up and we have to cover their asses."

"Hard to keep these things flying, I guess," said Fisher.

"Probably broke like every other thing they got," answered the major. "I'm supposed to have a couple of light tanks here. You see 'em?"

Fisher didn't have time to answer.

"All loaded up in the plane and one of its engines crapped out. Had to find another plane—God knows when they'll get here. Air force—they haven't gotten anything right since World War II. Next time, I swear to God, we fly Lufthansa."

By now the colonel had finished his interview and started toward them, pursued by the television people. Whatever he had said hadn't satisfied them, and they continued trying to ask questions, which he ignored. He was an air force colonel, full bird, and he had the dismissive air of someone completely full of crap.

"Who's this?" the colonel growled.

"FBI," said Fisher, making sure he was speaking loud enough for the television reporters to hear. "I'm here to investigate—"

"I know why you're here," said the colonel angrily. The television people had caught up and were now training their cameras and their lights on Fisher. "Get the hell in there."

Fisher slowly began walking toward the hangar, smiling to himself as the reporters began shouting their questions at him. Suddenly he stopped and turned to them. He could see the colonel fuming in the background.

"Anybody got any American cigarettes?" Fisher asked. A cameraman threw a pack at him; Fisher picked it up, said "thanks," and continued walking, ignoring the shouted questions and then the demand for the return of the pack.

As bright as it had been outside, the hangar was several times brighter. There were all sorts of people inside, and the floor was littered with generators, floodlights, and a million toolboxes. The airplane sat in the exact middle of the hangar, a huge black insect. Several pieces of its skin had been pried off, and technicians in white clean suits were walking gingerly around it, bending over and inspecting its internal organs.

A small group of civilians stood off to the side, arms folded, watching. Fisher looked them over, failing to recognize any of them—must be the local CIA contingent, he decided, mentally dismissing them. "Hey, guys," he said. "How's it going?"

They eyed him rather laconically. Fisher smiled and pushed on, wearing a bored expression while his eyes worked strenuously to find someone who might have a good idea of what had happened. But he'd taken only a few steps toward the plane when an air force major ran up and demanded to know who he was and what his clearances were. "Relax," said the agent, pulling out his ID. The major grabbed it from him and put it into a small portable computer attached to a long cable that snaked across the hangar into oblivion. The machine contemplated the magnetic strip on the card and coughed; the major then gave Fisher a pair of what looked like binoculars—portable retina scanners that were connected by a thick wire to the laptop. Fisher put them up to his eyes and pressed the large red button in the middle; after a few seconds the machine gave a grudging beep. "OK?" asked Fisher, but the major seemed annoyed that he had clearance and began peppering him with questions about what he was doing there.

"What the hell do you think I'm doing here?" said Fisher. "Christ, I got to go through this every time I come to a crash?"

"This plane didn't crash," said the major. "The pilot landed it."

"Yeah, that's another thing," said Fisher, as if the idea had suddenly occurred to him. "Where is he? I want to get his side of this mess."

"The pilot has been removed back to his base."

"What? England?"

"His orders came in—"

"What orders?"

"He was moved under the highest authority."

"What do you mean moved? You carried him out on a stretcher?"

"No," said the major. Fisher's outburst had knocked some of the bluster off him. The FBI agent suspected the officer thought the order yanking the pilot was a little peculiar, too, but the guy looked like he'd jump off a cliff before admitting publicly that the air force had screwed something up. "He was fine. They sent a special plane for him and everything."

"Sent a plane?"

The major shrugged.

"How the hell are we supposed to conduct an investigation if the pilot's not here?" said Fisher.

"The air force investigators will interview the pilot."

"Oh yeah, right."

"You're not questioning the air force's ability," said the major, his back inching upwards.

"God, why would I do that?" answered the agent, walking over to the plane.

To a more properly attuned mind than Fisher's, the wedge of wings, massive engines, and huge, long beak might conjure dreamy visions or at least momentary awe. It would take, however, an extremely attuned mind to think that this thing could really fly. Its rounded edges made it look more like a piece of wildly abstract sculpture than anything mechanical, much less a plane. The blunted series of triangles seemed as if they'd been melted together in a massive oven. It was impossible to say where one component— the wing, for example—ended and another—the fuselage—began. All Fisher had known about the plane before coming was that it was somewhat similar to the obsolete Blackbird. He searched in vain now to see the family resemblance.

"Pretty, huh?" said one of the technicians as he jumped down from the scaffold.

"Oh yeah," said Fisher. "I'm thinking I'm in love."

"Look at it this way," said the techie, "that's what two billion dollars looks like."

Fisher snorted: a half-laugh, half-scoff. In the second it took to do that, his eyes darted from the man's face to his yellow-stained fingers, then back. He paused a second, then asked confidentially, "You want a cigarette?"

"Can't smoke in here," the technician replied. "Go boom. But I'm dying for one—if it's real."

Fisher smiled and took the pack the cameraman had thrown him from his pocket. "Winston's as close to real as I got," he said. "Why don't we go outside?"

"Let's do it," said the technician. "The only thing I've had all day were these Italian things."

The agent followed him outside through a back door, where a mobile canteen had been set up, complete with coffee, danish, and Italian wieners. Fisher gave him a cigarette and held out a lighter. It was like turning on a radio.

"Ain't nothing wrong with the damn thing, if you ask me," said the technician. "Shit, we've gone over it for ten hours now, can't find something wrong. Component log says there was no problem at all."

"I thought the engines blew up or something," said Fisher innocently.

"You gotta explain one thing for me, then," said the techie, savoring the smoke. "How come they started right up for us this afternoon, first time?"

"So you pulled out a gun and threatened the Italian army?"

"That's an overstatement."

"You pulled out a gun?"

"A gun?" said Wright as innocently as he could. "That's not standard equipment on a Merc."

Wright's boss, Gen. Al Roberts, had been grilling him for half an hour now, practically from the moment he'd stepped on the tarmac at Beale, SAC Ninth Strategic Reconnaissance Wing headquarters in California. Wright hadn't even had a chance to shower.

The general, obviously unsatisfied with the answer, continued to glare at him. Wright couldn't lie, exactly, but he could divert attention from the truth. That, in fact, was what he was expected to do, in the etiquette of a dressing down. "Carrying something that wasn't standard equipment might get me in trouble, sir," he said.

"God knows you wouldn't want to get in trouble over this," said Roberts sarcastically.

"No, sir. No trouble at all."

"The Italian soldiers said you waved a gun at them and told them to get back," continued the general.

"Well, I may have had a somewhat threatening demeanor. I mean, I would certainly say that I may have given them the impression that they shouldn't come any closer. I think that, considering the fact that the airplane I was flying did not exist, I felt I was obliged to dissuade them from thinking that it did exist. Sir."

It was hard to do this with a straight face, but Roberts didn't seem to appreciate the humor.

"And telling them to get away from it or you'd shoot would do that."

"I wouldn't necessarily say that I said that, but if I were to have said something to that effect, or implied something like that, I might have been motivated by the national security issues involved."

"There's a fine line between national security and an international incident," said Roberts, drawing the line with his finger on his cluttered desk. The general was in charge of all six operational Mercs and their crews. A little wrinkled and completely bald, Roberts worked his men hard, but the Merc pilots loved him; they called him Uncle Al, even to his face. Roberts, at the time one of the few black combat pilots in the service, had commanded a bomber squadron in the closing days of the Vietnam War and had a bag full of stories about that, driving the truck for hours to go through five minutes of hell. He commanded the Merc wing as if they were at war—loose, everybody in on things, and only the best for "the boys." SAC Ninth—the air force had appropriated the old Blackbird unit's designation—was an elite group, and camaraderie would have been tight under any circumstance. But Uncle Al made it even more so.

He wasn't showing his benevolent side now, though. The general hadn't even mentioned the incredible odds Wright had faced in landing the plane, acting as if it were expected. The problem, Wright decided, was that the plane's secrecy had been compromised—blown to smithereens might be a more accurate way of putting it—and that sin had been assigned, in the great air force tradition, to Wright. The lieutenant colonel must therefore do penance, and the general was going to inflict it before pushing on and congratulating him.

"And they're completely mistaken, absolutely mistaken, when they say that you fired at them."

"I don't think that I would actually have fired at anyone, sir. If I had a gun, I might perhaps have fired a warning shot. But of course that would be theoretical—"

"We are still members of NATO," the general spat out slowly, "despite what the goddamn newspapers say. Let's cut the crap."

Roberts, of course, wasn't necessarily mad at Wright's having stood off practically a battalion of Italian soldiers until USAFE had gotten its butt out to the airfield. On the contrary; the general would have expected nothing less. But the incident was perfect for his purposes: the general couldn't mention the secrecy issue itself without acknowledging that there were mechanical failures which Wright had no control over. Nor could he refer to the mission without having to acknowledge that the pilot had done an excellent job landing the plane. But the ground incident, isolated, offered several ripe points for a full dressing down. Wright really couldn't answer—there was no way to justify the "smuggling" of the gun aboard the plane, though he was hardly the only pilot to do it. And he couldn't deny that the Italians were angry.

But the real beauty of the subject, from Roberts's point of view, was its tangential nature. Wright would know full well that it was insignificant in the grand scheme of things, and that would instill in him the sinking, rathole-helpless feel of a new recruit being chewed out for not having tucked in his shirt. Which, Wright figured, was the goal here.

"You know, Colonel," said Roberts, "you could be court-martialed for this."

"Sir?"

"The Italians want your patoot, and I'm inclined to give it to them."

"For landing my airplane?"

"You caused a hell of a lot of problems," said Roberts. "You cut right through commercial air space; they had to cancel flights. Well, all right, that couldn't be helped. But they didn't like that stuff on the ground, no sir. Embarrassed the hell out of them. Not nice to embarrass an Italian."

Wright remained silent. Roberts had him off kilter; he wasn't sure whether that was a joke or not.

"You know, Tom—" The general's use of Wright's first name was a bad sign. "You know, you're getting a little old to be flying. You're in your thirties."

"That's not old at all."

"Pretty old for a frontline pilot."

"I'm the youngest pilot in the damn wing."

"Now I wouldn't say that. And I wouldn't be using expletives, not in your position."

Wright was puzzled. Maybe he'd misjudged the whole deal. He was thirty-two, hardly old enough for anyone to start talking about putting him out to pasture. If anything, he was young, very young to be a lieutenant colonel, amazingly young to be a lieutenant colonel, for crying out loud, and they hadn't just bumped him up because they'd liked the way he looked. But Roberts seemed to be using Wright's age like it was a way out, warming up to some sort of deal that Wright would have to suggest himself: resign his commission in exchange for a dropping of whatever charges they were going to file. Could they court-martial him for this crap?

"What did you want me to do? Crash into the Alps?"

"Would have given your widow a nice medal," said Roberts.

Wright didn't detect a smile.

"I'm not married."

"Your mother, then."

"Can I be frank, sir?"

"Haven't you been?"

"With all due respect, sir, I think I did a hell of a job bringing the plane down in one piece."

"Maybe that's part of the problem," said Roberts.

Shit, this might be bad after all. They probably wouldn't court-martial him—just reassign him. He'd end up at a desk in Alaska, in charge of requisitioning calendars.

"No one thinks that I had anything to do with the failure of the plane," said Wright.

"They're not sure what happened to your plane." Roberts's voice remained flat, offering no solace. "I don't suppose you can rule out pilot error."

"Pilot error? Bullshit—"

"Bullshit, Colonel?"

"Sir—"

Roberts held up his hand and Wright choked off a stream of protest. "You know, they restarted the engines on the ground."

Wright nearly fell over. "What?"

"Started right up for them, too," said Roberts. "Not a hitch. They're planning on flying it back to England."

"You've got to be kidding me," said the pilot.

"Do I look like I'm kidding?"

Wright sat down in the chair behind him without being told to. In the etiquette of a dressing down, it represented total surrender, but the pilot was so dumbfounded he couldn't think of anything other than the plane.

"How the hell are they working now? I tried to start them a million times. What's the log say?" he asked. "That'll bear me out."

"Those things can be screwed with," said Roberts. "And you had plenty of time. Explain why you were so uptight about the Italians."

"For Christ's sake, I didn't just turn the engines off 'cause I was bored."

"There are a lot of strange things going through people's minds," said Roberts.

"What's going through your mind?"

"Officially? Nothing. I have no opinion."

"Al—"

"Unofficially, only a damn fool would screw around with

anything on that airplane. And I don't have any damn fools working for me."

Not a ringing endorsement, but Wright would have to take it. He waited a second, expecting Roberts to break into his patented frown, then give him a "buck it up" and a verbal pat on the fanny. The brass would be satisfied that he'd sweated his pilot, and the two of them could get on to business.

But the general's expression didn't change.

"I guess you're going to take a lot of heat for this," prompted the pilot.

"I guess," said Roberts. "A lot more than you will, that I can guarantee."

"What do you think happened?"

"I honestly don't know," said the general. "Somebody, or something, screwed up. I hope it was a thing."

"Maybe the Russians have a satellite ray beam that wiped me out."

"This isn't all that funny, Colonel."

"I'm sorry for what happened, sir," said Wright, practically bowing in submission. "I'll cooperate in whatever way possible. Talk to whoever."

"Yes, well, you won't be doing any talking, and you won't be doing it around here. You've been reassigned."

Alaska. No shit.

"Sir?"

"These orders came in right around the time you were pissing off the Italians. Immediate procedure and all that bs. So many goddamn clearances I almost got a nosebleed. Why do you think I had them fly you here?"

Wright felt a sinking feeling in his legs as he reached across the desk and took the paper from the general's hand.

The orders were simple: with all due haste he was to proceed to Nellis and await further instructions.

Nellis?

"I don't get it," the pilot said.

"Nellis won't be your final destination. You won't even have enough time to take a piss there."

"Where am I going?"

"Some base in northern California. That's all I know."

There was a huge air force map of the U.S. on Roberts's wall; Wright turned and started for it.

"Don't waste your time, it's not up there. I looked."

"What's going on?"

"Damned if I know. As far as I can tell, it doesn't have anything to do with the Merc or this Italian business. I wouldn't have been all that surprised if somebody back in D.C. tried to pull that crap, but this was a bit too early. Besides," said the general, "they bumped up your security clearance."

"They did?"

"You're not hearing any of this from me."

"Who's they?"

"You'll notice that those aren't air force orders. They come through JCS."

"Joint Chiefs?"

"They're brokering for somebody. Who exactly, I'm not sure, but apparently you're now involved in something called Coyote."

"Coyote?"

"I've been on the phone for eight hours with just about everybody I know in the air force. All I could find out was that it's some sort of deep, deep black project in northern California, and that it's not, strictly speaking, an air force project. It may or may not be under the NSC."

"Not the air force? Is it a plane?"

"Some of those people are pretty dumb, but I don't figure they'd take my best pilot for anything but a plane."

"Coyote," said Wright. "What about Millertime?"

"Not involved. I've got a new pilot for him; he'll be flying inside a week."

Wright was beginning to feel like he'd been brought back from the dead, but he saved the skipping for later. "What kind of plane would they call Coyote?"

Roberts shrugged. "Good question. Sounds a little like something you'd make out of counterinsurgency. How much do you know about strafing guerillas?"

"Nothing," answered the pilot uncomfortably. Counterinsurgency would probably mean flying a prop plane. That was fine on the weekend, but not for a living. "I was in fighters before this."

"Don't see yourself wedged into one of those little prop jobbers, huh?" said Roberts, grinning a little.

"I don't think so," said Wright.

"Maybe they want you for space. You look a little wild-eyed."

"Very funny."

"Got to be COIN," said the general, using the acronym for

counterinsurgency. "Ground-support turkey shooting. Hunt live-stock, that sort of thing."

"Great," said Wright unenthusiastically.

"We'll get you back," said Roberts, standing. "I'll see about pulling some strings."

Wright looked at him doubtfully. "What's going to happen with the Merc?" he said.

Roberts shrugged. "Going to be a lot of hand wringing. We'll figure out what happened eventually. My butt'll probably get kicked around a bit, but that's why I keep it so well padded."

"I—"

"Don't worry about it, Tom. I'm writing you a commendation. Nice piece of flying. Practically a miracle," added the general.

It was at roughly that moment on the unmarked base in the northern California mountains that Gene Elrich pulled a screwdriver from his back pocket and began attaching a wire to install yet another video screen on his console. Anyone looking at him, dressed in jeans and a button-down oxford shirt (a concession to the government people who ran the project—he usually wore a T-shirt), would be excused for dismissing him as a mere technician. A word or two from his mouth, however, and the mistake would be obvious: he was too arrogant, too haughty to be anybody's helper. But if fiddling with the equipment was supposed to be beneath him, no one would tell him that, least of all the assistant who had brought the tube up from storage and had expected to install it himself amid the jungle of CRTs, wires, loose circuit boards, and hastily mounted modules.

Elrich wasn't merely in charge of the enormous electronic brain that filled two huge floors of the cement bunker here; he was its inventor, its father, its mentor. He delegated even the most routine tasks reluctantly; if he wanted another display to give readouts on where the computer was using its high-level language resources, he was the one who would put it in. Even if that meant that his assistant—himself a Ph.D.—stood around with his hands in his pockets.

The brain they had built didn't have a name. Elrich called it, they all called it, the System. This was not only simple and somewhat descriptive, but it had an ontological correctness that pleased the theoretician of computer intelligence overseeing its development.

Elrich did not, in fact, believe intelligence could be separated into categories based solely on where it functioned. He allowed the phrase *computer intelligence* to be used because it was somewhat descriptive, or at least had been before the flexible-point programming construction he'd pioneered ten years before challenged the traditional definitions of the word *computer*. But to say "artificial intelligence" in Elrich's presence was to risk, at a minimum, wrath and derision. The ignorance it demonstrated, he said, was grounds for immediate dismissal.

But then, those who worked with Elrich, the hundred or so people back East in Tuxedo, New York, with IBM and at MIT, and especially the handful he'd brought with him here to California, were all true believers. Not one would dream of calling what they worked on artificial intelligence: there was nothing artificial about it. The machine they had built was nothing less than a full-functioning, independent brain.

Potentially. It was not there yet. It was powerful, able to make incredible jumps of logic, but it hadn't yet crossed the line into pure thought—to intuition. Elrich knew he was tantalizingly close, but he had so many things to do, so many distractions, that the closer he got, the further he felt from his goal.

The wire was too short. Elrich looked up from the screen, pushing his thick glasses back on his nose and scowling at his assistant, Jerry Angles.

"I was afraid it wasn't going to reach," said Angles.

"So why didn't you bring another one?"

Angles shrugged. He wasn't exactly stupid—Angles had single-handedly designed and constructed almost all of the vats that held the supercooled parallel processing complexes downstairs—but he had real lapses of common sense. The thirty-five-year-old former RPI instructor mumbled something, put his hands in his pockets, and began trudging toward the elevator door, his feet dragging on the smooth concrete as he walked past the wall-high banks of interface and secondary memory equipment.

Elrich dropped the back end of the CRT on the counter, but otherwise suppressed his anger. He was thinking about too many other things to waste his energy bawling out Angles. Besides, his assistant's absence left him alone on the deck, an opportunity he'd been waiting for all day.

Creating a machine that thought creatively, on its own—that could make seemingly random jumps in a meaningful way, an intuition machine—wasn't the scientist's only ambition. He wanted to use it—and not just to fly airplanes. Elrich hoped, in cooperation with others working on similar projects throughout the world, to create a network of minds so powerful that the world would be a different, more perfect place.

In the beginning, he had made the mistake of lecturing on his ideas about computer-assisted world governments. That had almost ended his career. The government people had gone nuts, calling him the second coming of Nietzsche. As if they'd ever read any philosophy in their lives, let alone that by the German philosopher who dared to speak of a future *Beyond Good and Evil.* Now the scientist shared his ideas very, very sparingly. Not even Jennifer Fitzgerald, his closest collaborator on the System, knew his intentions. Elrich had searched patiently for someone not only smart enough to help him with the work, but also bold enough to follow through on its implications.

He thought he had found that person. For the past six months, Elrich had been consciously courting a Japanese scientist named Ki, whose work with computers in many ways paralleled his own. Ki had one shortcoming—he was brilliant, but he didn't seem to grasp the practical applications of the work he was doing for Netsubo, a large Japanese corporation with interests in space and communication. This, Elrich guessed, had something to do with his personal history. An orphan, Ki had been taken under the wing of Netsubo's founder, a man named Ieyasu, who seemed more interested in Japan's past history than its future. Elrich had arranged a series of demonstrations for Ki of the System's power— not its ability to think, but its ability to manipulate events.

And now he wanted to see if the second half of his latest demonstration had been successful.

Elrich leaned over to a small microphone in the center of his work area. "System," he said, "have you monitored the data regarding the SR-91?"

"Yes," replied the computer in its synthesized, nearly human voice. In the microsecond it had taken to reply, the System had recorded and checked its inventor's voice pattern, making sure it was him, as well as performing its normal association tests as it deciphered the meaning of his words. Elrich could "see" its thought processes by watching the activities on the monitor in front of him, and ordinarily he would have watched the screens with great interest. He was concerned, however, that Angles might return unexpectedly, and stared instead at the door.

"Well?"

"You desire an update," said the System. A person who had said

43

that would have been dismissed as either a wise guy or an imbecile. But for the computer, the ability to analyze a conversation and make logical guesses about what was meant had been no small accomplishment. For Elrich to take it in stride was a measure of how far they had come in the past year.

"Yes."

"The plane's engines were disabled, as requested. The plane landed approximately twenty minutes afterwards—"

"What? The plane landed?"

"Yes."

"Interesting," said Elrich, turning and looking at the tubes and their stream of numbers and graphs. "The engines restarted?"

"No."

"You're sure of that?"

"The log recording as input into the onboard systems indicates that the engines remained inoperative from the point at which the signal was received. That input could, of course, be in error; however the odds—"

"Never mind," said Elrich. In a sudden fit he slammed his fist on the counter, then rose and began pacing in front of the console. It calmed him—there would be an uproar about the secret spy plane, and Ki would find out that something had happened. It was enough.

Besides, he hadn't set out to destroy the planes. He could always claim that he wanted the pilot to live. Perhaps Ki was concerned about such things.

Elrich smiled to himself. The Japanese scientist just wasn't very pragmatic.

Captain Fumio Genda backed off his throttle, letting his Mitsubishi settle just above the ocean surface. He did a quick check, glancing at the FSX's far-right multifunction display, watching his target approach off his left wing, flying considerably higher and completely unaware of him. It was an American Cobra Ball, an electronic intelligence or ELINT flight that regularly ran surveillance down the Soviet Far East coast, checking on interesting missile firings or testings. The planes—RC-135s, essentially refurbished Boeing 707s with massive brain transplants and a lot of fuel capacity—ran regular tracks out here, though this one seemed a little lost, flying well out to sea. It was closer, in fact, to an intercept course for northern Japan than anything near the USSR mainland. The American eavesdropper was just coming into Kurile

Islands air space, a hundred-mile buffer around the new northern Japanese territory. By the provisions of a recently passed Japanese law, the U.S. ought to have asked specifically for permission to enter the air space, though Genda knew that wouldn't have been done—the Americans had pointedly refused to comply with the law on single-plane flights. They claimed, with some justification, that doing so would tip off the Russians to the spy flights. On the other hand, Genda figured that the Russians knew about them as soon as they left the runway at Shemya in Alaska. The Japanese certainly did.

The two superpowers still went through certain Cold War rituals, and this was one of them. They were like two old soldiers lost on an island years after the war ended, unaware that the outside world had changed dramatically. Japan was the major power in the Pacific now, Genda knew. The Americans and Russians could spy on each other all they wanted; the Japanese and the hungry tigers would set the course of the world.

Genda took his eyes off the display for a second, running them across the conventional dials below and then back to the dull green glow of the multipurpose. The different modes of the heads-down display were activated by a push button at the bottom; Genda rolled it from radar detection to a screen that plotted his target's course.

The Japanese fighter pilot looked at the dotted white and red lines and wondered what was going on. The American plane should have begun tacking west by now, cutting in towards the Soviet coast.

Whether it turned or not, Genda and his wingmate, flying an identical FSX fifty meters back and just to his left at the same altitude, were going to shadow it. In another half minute or so, they would swing around behind the Boeing, tagging along as long as their fuel lasted. The American plane could steal radio transmissions and other electronic data a few hundred miles inside of Russia, but it was optimized for that job, and assuming they did nothing stupid, Genda and his wingmate were invisible to it. The American couldn't even pick up the communications sent between the two Japanese planes via their ATHS message system, which packed their messages into small, discrete, low-power bursts.

Genda had been flying for the Japanese Air Self-Defense Force for nearly ten years, most of it in American-designed and -built aircraft. Even the Mitsubishi he was in now had been based on an American plane, the F-16. But while the pilot retained a grudging admiration for the Americans, he felt it was time to come out of big brother's shadow. He fully supported the government's decision to extend its air identification zone, the buffer of protected air space around Japan. The decision had had a direct impact on him—he'd been transferred to the Northern Air Command, and given the special assignment of monitoring the American overflights. The transfer had been made by no less a person than Gen. Isoroku Onisha, the commander of the Air Defense Force. He'd congratulated Genda in person, and told him he wanted a pilot he could trust in the sensitive job.

The new position was not only prestigious, it also got him in the air more, on much longer flights. Though he was now far from his family, the separation was a small price to pay.

Tagging along behind the American, unseen, was good practice, and a kind of accomplishment, proving that with proper tactics even a powerful adversary's weaknesses could be exploited. If he wanted, he could easily take this plane down. He smiled at his conceit; nonetheless, he could not deny the sense of power.

Genda let the American pass him, and then circled cautiously back behind the plane, making sure he and his wingmate stayed well to the east of it. The Cobra Ball flight lumbered along toward the Kuriles, twenty miles ahead. Something was wrong here, Genda thought; the American was well off his usual course.

"North Wind, I have an order from Winter Bear. You are to intercept Blossom."

The controller's voice startled Genda, not merely because it came over a clear frequency that the American plane could detect, but because it mentioned General Onisha—Winter Bear— himself. It made no sense that he would be paying attention to this particular mission. Onisha was in charge of the entire air force. It was unlikely that he would be this far north, and most unusual for him to order a breaking of radio silence, a clear violation of procedures.

"Acknowledge command, North Wind."

The American was blind, but not stupid. There was a good chance this would alert him to his shadow. But the controller would surely know that. Genda turned on his microphone and acknowledged, saying that interception had been accomplished and the plane was under surveillance.

There was no sense staying on the deck now. Genda signaled his wingmate over the ATHS, and together they rose to a position the squadron called the Director's Chair. Rising in an S curve, they executed a rapid climb and brought themselves within a mile of the

American plane, sitting a few hundred feet above its tail, one on each wing. Genda could see the American plane's running lights blinking nonchalantly—if he hadn't known better, he might think he was following a lost airliner.

The fighters' maneuvers would have alerted the American to their presence if the radio transmission hadn't, but the Cobra pilot made no sign that he had noticed. He'd know that the planes were Japanese, of course, and while he had orders to get out to sea if any Russians appeared, he wouldn't fear an FSX. He might wonder what they were doing on his tail, though.

The American was probably under orders not to break radio silence, but Genda figured he'd be cursing up a storm about now.

"Do you want us to communicate with Blossom?" Genda asked. Perhaps the government had decided it was time to embarrass the Americans into complying with the new territorial law.

While Genda waited for a response from his controller, the American plane suddenly lurched to the east, heading back out to the open sea. Apparently he'd decided he didn't want company. The two Mitsubishi fighters had no difficulty following the Boeing, though they hung off a bit, letting it air out the distance from them to a full mile.

"North Wind, you are ordered to engage and destroy the contact."

Genda stared at the dotted HUD rectangle that enclosed the Boeing's tail end. Destroy?

"Acknowledge, North Wind."

Genda hesitated. There was something terribly wrong here. Shoot down an American plane?

"North Wind leader, this is Wind Two."

Komei, the impetuous one. He would fly his plane into a mountain if asked.

"Hold position," said Genda. "Prepare to arm missiles."

"Arm weapons?"

"Prepare to arm," Genda hissed, emphasizing the first word.

"Acknowledged," said Komei, not humbly enough for Genda. It was, truthfully, an empty command, but it was not Komei's position to point that out.

Why would anyone order them to shoot the plane down? It wasn't a mistake—the words had been clear.

Was the controller trying to set him up? Or perhaps the general. There had been signs of unrest in the ranks, dissension, and even rumors of some sort of coup within the corps. Genda could not imagine that anyone in the small, disciplined family that made up the defense forces was capable of such a thing, but an attack on an American plane would surely raise enough of an uproar to force Onisha's resignation.

Or perhaps it was a Russian trick—maybe they wanted the rest of the world to share the utter chaos their country had fallen into since the assassination of Yeltsin.

"Controller, this is Captain Genda. I request to speak to Winter Bear."

There was a pause. Ah, thought Genda, caution justified once more.

But then a new voice barked in Genda's ear.

"North Wind, you are ordered to engage your contact and destroy it."

No one in the air force would mistake the general's gravelly voice, but Genda had a particular reason to recognize it—Onisha was his father-in-law.

"Sir," said Genda, straining to keep emotion from his voice. "You are telling me to shoot down an American plane?"

"You have your orders," snapped the general.

"Sir."

"When you have accomplished that task, you will fly to coordinates I will give you."

It was clearly the general. Or a most elaborate hoax.

"Remember our discussion when you were assigned to this post," said Onisha, as if reading his thoughts. "We spoke first of my disappointment when younger of having only women as heirs. I told you I considered you fully my son."

The static was a seashell over his ear, clamped in, cutting Genda off. To disobey an order was difficult enough, but to disobey Onisha?

"You have your order and your duty," said Onisha.

What was his father-in-law telling him to do?

Genda hesitated, holding his position.

Onisha had obviously moved him up here specifically for this reason. The general expected the pilot to obey him without question, to accept what he was told to do. That was why he was here.

"Arm air-to-air. Pull Hold Five," Genda told his wingmate over the ATHS. It was a standard maneuver, bringing the two planes back around the target after an outside loop—completely unnecessary, given their present positions and what they were flying against, but there was an elegance to the maneuver, a flourish of precision. The two planes rolled 65 degrees away from each other, accelerating as they plunged, then entered 90-degree turns, pulling 6.8 g's, heavy stuff, but still accelerating, fuel burn at 3,000 kilos, very light. They swung wider and then came back around, pointing from opposite directions at the tail of their target. It lumbered ahead, barely making 400 knots, dead in the middle of the rectangle, dead in the middle of the thick square inside the rectangle.

Why hadn't Onisha told him of this, then, if he had planned it? Who in the government had authorized such an extreme act, an act that could surely lead to war?

Maybe they were already at war.

Genda had always trusted Onisha completely. He owed everything to him; surely the commander of Japan's air force had a reason for what he was telling his son-in-law to do.

"Go," said Genda, and immediately a pair of missiles leapt from the wings of his FSX. Komei's followed half a tick later.

Three of the four hit. Genda was close enough to dump in with his cannon, but it wasn't necessary; the missiles clipped the turkey's wings and it heaved over into a dive, gently at first, then picking up steam as its angle increased, falling to the dark, cold ocean.

3

RUY LOPEZ

It took the sun a long time to climb over the mountains and light the valley directly, but when it finally did its force was overwhelming. Jennifer Fitzgerald, walking from the bunker onto the concrete airstrip, took off the sweater she had pulled tightly around herself barely an hour and a half ago, and undid the top two buttons on her thick cotton dress. By noon she'd be sweating.

Only a few days ago she'd wrapped a parka over two thick flannel shirts just to cross from the command bunker to the huge, red tent hangar that housed the plane. The unusually warm spring weather had caught them all by surprise. The air force was supposed to be making arrangements to fetch their summer clothing, but it hadn't arrived yet. They could have the most advanced chips and electronic materials flown in within a matter of hours—those came direct from an NSA plant back East—but getting something as simple as a T-shirt here was a major hassle.

Over 200 people worked at the base, with another hundred or so army and air force people scattered around in the mountain periphery as security troops. Even so, it was extremely quiet this morning, and just about every morning; perhaps the secrecy made them all unconsciously lower their voices to a whisper. More likely, everyone was too busy even to talk—there seemed to be a never-ending list of new things to do.

Jennifer paused momentarily at the end of the huge runway, listening to the few birds that hadn't been scared away by the massive disruption of their habitat. If they were complaining about the intrusion, they had a legitimate gripe—the base had been constructed in the middle of what was supposedly a protected wilderness area.

That was typical of the military, thought Jennifer, but what could you expect from a collection of pushy, arrogant jerks whose abilities consisted of shooting guns and spitting? Steve Pelham, the Coyote pilot, was one of the most obnoxious versions of the breed Jennifer had ever met. He had an ego the size of a whale and a swagger that made Jennifer turn the other way every time she saw him lurch across the base. But there was no real escape—during the test flights, the scientist acted as the pilot liaison, sitting at the control console in the System bunker and talking to Pelham for the whole "hop," as he called it. Like they were skipping over puddles on the way to school.

The guards outside the hangar smiled at her as she brushed past them. They were harmless, really; one of them was even cute, but thinking of Pelham had put her in a sour mood, and she didn't even say hello.

Jennifer was a computer scientist, and her main interest here was the System, not the Buck Rogers plane that stretched before her as she walked into the hangar. Still, it awed her; every time she saw it she was surprised by how sleek and subtle the Coyote was, a long, narrow progression of a fish's fin. It looked small—though it was actually the size of a modest airliner—and graceful, almost feminine. Definitely feminine, and alive.

Walking past its wing section toward the cockpit, she ran her hand over the smooth skin. It felt like the sleek hide on a dolphin, cool and almost wet. Molded entirely from exotic polymers, the body had another remarkable quality—it had the ability, with the help of the onboard portions of the System, to change its shape as it flew. This MFOA—multifacet orienteering aerodynamics—altered the airflow over the surface of the plane, increasing its maneuverability at high speeds. Assisted by maneuvering jets and the directional qualities of the main exhaust unit, the Coyote Bird could make unbelievably sharp turns practically as fast as the pilot could think of them.

For a moment, Jennifer wondered what it would be like to fly the plane herself. She saw herself soaring, a feeling of weightlessness sweeping up from behind. . . .

"Looks like she's too pretty to fly, don't she?"

Paul Harrison's voice startled her, though if she'd thought about it, she would have realized he'd be here. He always was.

"How come men always think airplanes are pretty?" she said. It was the first thing that jumped into her head.

"Oh, I think women are pretty, too," said the old sergeant.

Jennifer smiled to herself and walked over to one of the workbenches close to the plane. She liked Harrison; the chief had convinced her there were at least a few human beings in the military. A good-natured tease, the beefy black man seemed to know as much about the plane as any ten of the designers and all the Northrop manufacturing people put together.

"What are you doing this morning?" she said.

"Oh, little things. Sweeping up."

"You always say that, but I never see a broom in your hand." As a precaution before touching the electronics, she passed a demagnetizing wand over her body, and then stepped on a static neutralizer. The plane and System were already well protected against wayward magnetic fields or static discharges, but the military people insisted on additional precautions. They were ridiculously cautious. A nuclear blast might shock the System temporarily, depending on how close the explosion was, but short of that, there was little to worry about. Even those great enemies of all things electronic, dust and moisture, were pretty well neutralized by the way the components were constructed. Still, the plane designers insisted on an elaborate protocol when parts were removed—a protocol more observed in theory than in fact, though Jennifer did pick up one of the small dust breathers as Harrison walked to the external control station and chivalrously popped open the cockpit-access frame for her. She climbed inside the plane—technically, she should have been wearing a full clean suit, not just the gloves and hood she'd donned—and sat on the flight seat as she pried out the circuit to be replaced. The small hunk of blue plastic was now a $25,000 piece of junk; she dropped it onto her lap and gingerly took the new piece in her gloved hand. A little bigger than a quarter, the triple-coated plastic module encased a custom-designed gallium-crystal chip collection that, in another application with some minor modifications, could control half of the commercial flights landing and taking off from American airports in a year. Maybe all of them, with the right software.

Here all it had to do was streamline the encoded infrared and longwave radar data the plane relayed back, freeing up a little more computing power for the System gateway. And it would do that very well, too, if only she could get it to fit into the slot. She pushed gently; no good. She took the piece out and made sure she had it oriented properly (the shape made it impossible to put it in wrong, but she checked anyway) and returned it to the opening. Still wouldn't fit. She applied a little more pressure, and then rocked it back and forth.

"Darn it." She yanked the hood off her head and tossed the damn thing out of the plane. Being able to see what she was doing didn't help; the component still wouldn't fit.

"Having trouble?" Harrison asked outside. "I hear all this harsh language."

"No," she said. The sergeant often teased her because she didn't curse. She took her glove off and ran her nail around the facing edge of the component—the hell with protocol—and tried again. It still wouldn't fit. Now she applied pressure—a lot more pressure—and finally with a punch managed to pop it in.

"And stay there," she told it. Putting her glove back on, she ran her hand across the top of the panel, removing any smudge prints.

Outside the plane, she plugged a diagnostics simulator into one of the temporary test hookups and had the System run a few tests. The old part was relegated to a classified destroy bin.

"That make it perfect?" the sergeant asked.

"I hope so," said Jennifer, absentmindedly looking at the test panel. The machine would take care of the procedure; she'd only have to really pay attention if it beeped at her. The tests now were only to make sure there weren't any gross errors anyway; the real test would be run this afternoon, back at the System console.

"Amazing how much the computer takes over these days, isn't it?" said Harrison. "Does your testing for you and everything."

"I wrote the program," she said.

"Still, it does all the work," said the sergeant. "Doesn't it bother you?"

"Why should it bother me?"

"Now see, if you were a pilot, it would. With the computer there, it's almost like you're not flying at all."

"The System just helps," said Jennifer. "It doesn't fly."

"That's not the way a pilot thinks about it," said Harrison, leaning on one of the test benches. "To a pilot, he's got to be in charge. A pilot figures he's the most important thing in the airplane. Enough machines, and he starts to figure that maybe he's not."

"Nothing could dent Major Pelham's ego," she said, folding her arms.

"Oh, I don't know about that," said Harrison, looking a bit like a leprechaun with a secret. "As of today, the major is no longer the main pilot. That may step him down a notch."

"What?" said Jennifer.

"Bringing a new guy in this morning. Top guy. Right off the line."

"Get out."

"Would I lie to you?"

Jennifer might almost have jumped up in celebration, except for the thought that the new pilot could be just as big a jerk.

"How do you know all this?"

"Oh, I have my ways," the sergeant answered, winking. "I even know who it is."

"Who?"

"Can't tell you," he said. "Classified."

"Come on," she said. It didn't matter to her, since she didn't know any pilots except for Pelham. But she let Harrison think he'd baited her as she peeked over at the screen on the bench. Half of the tests had run so far; no problems.

"Amazing plane, though," said the sergeant. "Very amazing."

"So do you wish you could fly it?" she said.

Harrison laughed. "Me? I'm just an old fart. Never let me near something like this."

"But you do fly," she said. "You said you did the other day."

"Did I say that?" said the sergeant in his teasing voice, obviously pleased that she'd remembered. "Well, I might be able to fly."

"So what do you fly?"

"You'd be surprised what I can fly," said Harrison, almost serious. "I'll tell you what I love to fly—planes with propellers. A lot different than this. Got a couple of friends of mine down near Santa Rosa, fly old planes. World War I, World War II. That's what I like to fly."

"Sounds like fun," she said.

"I'll take you up sometime," said Harrison. "You'd like it."

"I'd love it," she said. The test bench gave two short beeps. The component had passed all the tests. She unhooked the diagnostics, then stood back as Harrison closed the cockpit by typing the command on the control station in front of the plane. The sergeant powered down the station—it took longer to turn off than turn on, with all the exit codes—and then they both started for the door.

"So what's this guy like?" she asked.

"Who?" said the sergeant.

"You know, Sergeant, sometimes I think you're thirteen years old."

"Me?" joked Harrison, following her outside.

She heard the helicopter as soon as she stepped out the door. It was still a long way off, but the low, pounding beat echoed through the valley, easily overwhelming the low hum of the hangar's air circulators behind her.

Jennifer walked to the concrete apron, waiting. The helicopter could only be coming here; no other flights were allowed in the area.

"This'll be the pilot," said Harrison as the chopper came into view.

"Old what's-his-name?" she asked.

"What's-his-name is in the marines. This is who-do-you-call-it."

The helicopter looked like a gray, muscle-bound cricket, lumbering through the air, bullying its way to the runway, where it squatted down with a huff. It hadn't completely settled when a man in a dull green flight suit jumped out, swinging a flight bag behind him. He turned around a second, yelled something to the men in the helicopter, then dropped his bag on the tarmac. He gave the chopper a wave and did a half-trot over to Jennifer and the sergeant.

"Hey," he shouted over the roar of the helicopter turbines, "where's this plane I'm supposed to fly?"

The sergeant and Jennifer looked at each other.

"Name's Wright," said the man, dropping his voice as the whine from the chopper died down. "I'm your pilot." He looked at them as if he'd just spoken some magic words. "So where's the plane?"

Jennifer crossed her arms and rubbed her elbows defensively.

"You're not going to fly it right now," she said.

"No?" said Wright, smiling. "You in charge?"

"No," she said, turning a little red. "But you can't just go and fly it—"

"Who said I was?" asked Wright, for the first time turning to the sergeant. He looked at him a moment, as if he might recognize him, but Harrison offered no clue, playing the leprechaun again. The pilot turned back to Jennifer.

"Down there in the hangar, right?" he said, pointing to the tent with some sort of unexplained instinct.

He was past them before they could say anything. Jennifer looked at Harrison, who shrugged and went to help them unload the helicopter.

"Say," she shouted after the pilot. "You have to have clearance."

If he heard her words he ignored them. She started after him. She ran a few steps to catch up, then decided to hang back and take her time; the soldiers would deal with him.

She wasn't comfortable being thrust into a position of authority, but she felt responsible. Who was this guy? There were procedures. All of a sudden she was acting like Little Miss Military, but she couldn't help herself.

The guards at the hangar snapped their weapons to a challenge position. The pilot barely slowed as he approached, throwing a salute, which they acknowledged only by demanding to know who he was.

"Lieutenant Colonel Thomas Wright, SAC Ninth Recon—I think. I'm not sure who I work for anymore. They woke me up this morning and told me to get my butt out here." Wright smiled at Jennifer, who had caught up. "They shuffled me back and forth so much getting out here, I feel like a pea in a shell game. Don't know who they're trying to confuse, outside of myself." He took out a set of plastic ID cards and handed them to the soldiers. "Let's see if they work."

Jennifer watched him squint into the sun, waiting for them to run the cards through their machine. Physically, he didn't seem so prepossessing—he was shorter than Pelham, though his body had an athletic cast to it, even when standing still. He wasn't more than modestly good-looking, but the energy that animated his body was evident in his face. He had a good smile. Not goofy. It might be disarming, under the right circumstances.

Wright turned from the soldiers and glanced at her, his eyes a surprisingly deep blue, with prominent, large pupils that sized her up. "What do you think?" he asked. "They gonna let me in?"

She shrugged.

The soldier motioned him over to the retina scan. The machine took several seconds—the signal had to travel via satellite to an NSA computer across the country where the approved access list was kept—and for a moment Jennifer wondered what would happen if he didn't clear. In theory the MPs could shoot him on the spot. But he'd never have gotten this far if he didn't have pretty special credentials.

The machine blinked back green, and then confirmed his identity and the clearance: Umbra/Cobra VI—an inclusive level higher than Jennifer's, and even Gene Elrich's. Only General Hunter had that kind of clearance here, as far as Jennifer knew. The soldiers handed the cards back respectfully. Wright, smiling, nodded at them.

"You comin'?" he said to her as he started into the tent.

She followed him inside, almost bumping into him as he stopped in surprise and admiration.

"This is nothing like I expected," he said, slowly starting to circle the plane. When he got to the front he stopped, looking around as if he'd lost something. "Where's the cockpit?"

"It's right there," she answered, pointing to the nose.

"Where?"

"There."

"No canopy?" he asked. "Where are the windows?"

"You don't need windows."

"I don't need windows? How am I going to see where I'm going?"

"You'll be able to see," she said. "You'll see better than you've ever seen before. There's a special radar system that creates the image. In a plane like this, windows would be useless."

Wright walked around the plane, examining its surfaces.

"What's it made out of?"

"Composites. It can take incredible pressure."

"Feels like a shark's skin, doesn't it?"

Jennifer nodded.

Wright took a few more steps. "Looks pretty. Really. The Merc's a great plane, you know, but it's ugly. Don't you think?"

"The engines look like pregnant cigars," she said, repeating something she'd heard Pelham say once. She wasn't even sure if she had the right plane in mind, but she wanted to sound like she knew what she was talking about.

"Yeah, that's it exactly," he said. "Pregnant cigars. Triangular cigars. Nose looks funny, too. Kind of like a chiseled-down whale lip. Goes like hell, though."

"This is even faster."

"You've flown it?"

"No," she said, a little embarrassed because he seemed to have been sincerely misled by her quick answer. "I work with the pilot. I'm Jennifer Fitz—"

"There are no windows? For real?" He walked back around to the front of the plane. "It's not quite as big as I thought it would be. Really. I mean it's big, but— There's a cockpit in here?"

"We're supposed to wear clean suits before opening it up," she said.

"I'm just looking," said the pilot. He sounded like a boy asked by a guard not to touch a museum exhibit. "That's probably baloney anyway, don't you think?" he added, looking at her with his hands on his hips. "They aren't going to vacuum me before they pack me in, right?"

She nodded weakly. The pupils in his eyes were incredibly large, and they seemed like ray guns, firing out full-speed the energy that animated his body. They were shooting straight at her.

"So can we look inside?"

"Sure." Jennifer went over to the external controls and punched in her code number. The small computer terminal—actually a tie-in to the System with a limited command list—snapped to attention.

"I'm Tom Wright, by the way," said the pilot, extending his hand to her.

"Jennifer Fitzgerald."

"What do you do around here?"

"I work on the System. I helped design it."

"The System?" he asked.

"It's the computer that runs the plane."

"The computer runs the plane?"

"It helps," said Jennifer, punching in the words *open cockpit* on the terminal keypad.

"I'll try not to hold it against you," said Wright, distracted as the Coyote's jaws swung open. He walked over and ducked his head into the cockpit.

"Really," he asked, pulling his head back out. "You got the windows shielded or something?"

"Really, there aren't any."

"How the hell do I see where I'm going?"

"There's plasma screens," she said, starting to explain.

"Plasma?" he asked, sticking his head inside.

"They're really thin computer screens. They'll show you anything you want. The System synthesizes a view from the radar and—"

"No stick either?"

"You really ought to put on a clean suit if you're going to touch anything," said Jennifer.

"Yeah, well, maybe I ought to get comfortable here first," said Wright, ducking out. He was clearly less enthusiastic than before. "Maybe get something to eat. All I had at Nellis was a sandwich. You do have food here, right? I mean, the computer doesn't eat for you or anything."

"Of course we have food," she said, punching the command in to close the plane back up.

"So you designed the computer, huh?"

"The System. It's more than a computer. It—"

"You don't look old enough to be working on frontline air force computers."

She felt her cheeks twinge. "What do you mean, old enough?"

"You got clearance?"

"I've got plenty of clearance. And I'm twenty-eight."

"Twenty-eight?" The pilot looked at her. "Come on."

"If you're trying to flatter me, it won't work," she said in the coldest voice she could manage.

"I was just kidding," said Wright. "A joke, you know? Tell you what—you guess my age, and then we'll move on to our weights."

She was damned if she was going to laugh.

"Hey, it's not your fault you work on computers," said Wright.

"And it's not your fault you're a dumb pilot," she answered.

"Touché," he said. "See—you're starting to smile."

"No, I'm not," said Jennifer, but she was, a little.

"Who the hell are *you*?"

Steve Pelham's angry voice filled the hangar. He'd come up behind them while they were talking, and his voice startled Jennifer. Wright, his face as pleasant as ever, turned to see who was yelling.

"Tom Wright," said the new pilot good-naturedly. He stuck his hand out but then pulled it back immediately. "Shit, Pelham, what are you doing here?"

"I'm the goddamn pilot on this project."

"No kidding," said Wright. "How the hell do you fly this thing without windows?"

"It flies pretty fucking well," said Pelham. "I fly it pretty well."

"Good for you," said Wright. "Where do I find Billy Hunter?"

"Who knows," said Pelham, sounding like he knew all too well.

"He just got back from one of his trips last night," said Jennifer. "He's probably in his office at the command bunker. It's not a bunker, really; just a building. They call everything here bunkers or hangars. Siege mentality."

"Military never calls anything what it is," said Wright. "You start calling things what they really are, you need a lot less people. Probably got a yard-long acronym for it, right?"

Now she smiled, in spite of herself.

"So you gonna show me where this bunker is?"

"I'm busy," said Pelham.

"I meant you," said Wright, looking at Jennifer.

There it was again, that embarrassing flow of blood to her face. She turned away quickly and began walking out of the hangar.

"Follow me," she said.

"See ya," Wright said to Pelham.

Even before Pelham growled inarticulately behind them, Jennifer had decided she'd show Wright all the way to Hunter's door.

Jack D'Amici, the president of the United States, slumped unpresidentially in the deep leather chair. It was only 3 P.M., but Morse could tell that the day had already exhausted him. The Japanese business, of course, had preoccupied them all since early this morning, when the Pentagon had called with news of the Cobra Ball's downing. But the national security director thought his boss's exhaustion deeper: the looming showdown with Congress over the budget and the structuring of the Fed—a battle over the financial future of the country—had drained much of D'Amici's energy over the past month.

Morse, on the other hand, felt invigorated. He saw the developments as a chance to solidify his position in the inner circle of the administration. Much of the country's foreign policy over the past year had involved Europe and the Middle East, areas where the secretary of state, William Dyson, had considerable experience; Morse always felt as if he were continually playing catchup, trying to stay on top of developments there. Asia, on the other hand, had been Morse's area of interest throughout his career; he was naturally the one the president would depend on.

The rivalry between Dyson and Morse had simmered since the presidential election, though it had never burst into full-scale warfare. Morse, who had worked as a special adviser to D'Amici's campaign and had more experience in the government than Dyson, had hoped to be named secretary of state when the former governor unexpectedly won election three years before. But Dyson had been close to the president since college, and Morse had had to settle for head of the NSC. True, the role was beefed up considerably for him—the change in title from the traditional "adviser" to "director" was more than political window dressing. But Morse's ambitions were much grander; he saw America at a crucial point in its history, and the descendant of English lords (he had become a naturalized citizen as a child) wanted to shape its future.

Like everyone else, Morse had been caught totally by surprise by the shootdown. American-Japanese relations had declined over the past year and a half, with the Japanese in effect evicting the Americans from their bases and instituting restrictive rules about flyovers of their territory, rules the Americans had pointedly disregarded. But even for the ordinarily prescient Morse, this was an unexpected and ominous twist. And the Japanese government's nonexplanation was even more disturbing.

"Point number one, the Cobra Ball was deliberately shot down," said Robert Sasso, the secretary of defense, trying to recap his argument for retaliation. Though he hadn't said so explicitly, Sasso seemed to believe the best thing to do was declare war on Japan, nuke them, and be done with it. "Point number two, it was shot down by air defense planes."

"Point number three," interrupted Dyson, "the Japanese air defense forces can't locate the planes."

"Oh, that's got to be a bunch of bull."

"We can't find them, either," said the secretary of state.

"And why the hell is that?" said the president, his notorious ire peeking through. D'Amici, annoyed that the newspaper columnists had referred to his temper as an "ethnic trait," had worked hard to keep it in control over the past three years, but it was a losing battle.

Sasso seemed to take a breath to calm himself before continuing. The normally soft-spoken secretary of defense, who had put in twelve years in the navy before resigning for a successful career on Wall Street, had brought an air of respectable calm to his job, thought Morse. But he'd obviously listened too closely to the Joint Chiefs this morning. The chiefs, alarmed by recent developments in Asia and Japan, wanted to take the opportunity to reassert the primacy of American military power. And, on a less lofty level, they wanted revenge for the downing of their plane.

"The communications prior to the shootdown were in the clear," said Sasso. "But they appear to have switched to a different system, perhaps a line-of-sight laser undetectable by our equipment. Or merely something heavily coded—we don't have that much in-place ELINT capacity there, which is why we sent the Cobra Ball out in the first place."

"Henry sent it," said Dyson. "Not 'us.' If our allies decide they want to build an airfield on a windswept rock, all the power to them."

"That island was used by the Russians at one point to monitor satellites," said Morse. "If it is reactivated by the Japanese, it could pose problems for Case B."

Morse could feel the room chill as he mentioned the secret Star Wars antimissile satellite system. D'Amici had inherited Case B from the last administration. It was a skeleton system, capable of taking out only a few missiles at a time; it would be effective only against an accidental launch or a so-called madman strike. But the problem with Case B was that the Congress several years before had specifically outlawed the expenditure of more funds for space-based Star Wars systems, favoring instead the ground-based missile system being constructed in North Dakota. With much of Case B already in place for secret testing and funds already allocated on a "black" budget line for the last two satellites needed to make it operational, the previous president had decided to go ahead with the project and worry about bringing Congress around after the next election.

Unfortunately for him, he lost the election. D'Amici, who many years ago had denounced any Star Wars system as wasteful, changed his mind as soon as he was briefed on its effectiveness. But there was now no easy way of alerting Congress to its existence without drastic political repercussions for his own party, since a handful of key Democrats had apparently agreed to look the other way while the system was completed. A raft of legal opinions covered both administrations, but there would naturally be so much publicity that the system's effectiveness was bound to be compromised.

Morse, who more than anyone else in the present administration had argued for keeping the antisatellite system and keeping it secret, decided it was a good idea to return to the subject at hand.

"Our problem is what to do about the shootdown," said the director.

"Bomb the base they took off from," said Sasso. Morse thought at first he was joking, but the secretary looked dead serious—the generals must have worked him over but good.

"And start World War III," answered Dyson.

"If there were a war, it'd be quick, I'll tell you that."

The president looked at Sasso as if he'd gone mad.

"I'm not advocating a .war," he said quickly, his face red. He even seemed surprised he'd said that. "But we have to do something more forceful than placing the Seventh Fleet on alert."

"What do you think, Henry?" said D'Amici.

"I wonder if the idea isn't to provoke us into some sort of response," said the director. "The order to shoot the plane down was in the clear; maybe we were meant to hear it."

"Exactly my point," said Dyson.

The secretary of state was a short, thin man whom Morse thought bore more than a passing resemblance to a wirehaired terrier. Certainly he was yapping all the time.

"The order came from the head of their air force," said Sasso.

"Whom the Japanese say has fled the country," said Dyson.

"Come on."

"It may be true; he's certainly not in Tokyo," said Morse, repeating information Central Intelligence had given him a few hours ago. The CIA actually had no idea where the air force general was, a fact that could be used to support any number of theories.

"So we just ask them to say they're sorry and that's it?" said Sasso.

"We have to be careful," said Morse. "Threatening one of their bases could have exactly the opposite effect of what we intend. It could push their country into a real break with us."

"And so what the hell are we going to do?" said Sasso. "Look the other way?"

"I'm not saying that we look the other way," answered Morse. "But you know as well as I do that there are opposing views in Japan. You concentrate on the militaristic factions, but the majority of the government still consists of people interested in preserving things the way they are."

"Henry, you're starting to listen to me," said Dyson.

"Not at all," said Morse. "I've been saying all along it's a dangerous situation."

Dyson scoffed. Perhaps he was right, thought Morse grudgingly. I've been too preoccupied with the civil disturbances in Europe to pay much attention to Japan lately. It was ironic—he had personal reasons for never trusting Japan, ever.

"We're practically at war with Japan as it is," said Sasso. "They're taking all our money."

"That's exaggerated," answered Dyson.

"Like hell. And half of goddamn Congress—"

"We don't have to debate the importance of Japan," said D'Amici, "any more than the need to reform PAC laws, or the state of our economy."

"If the theory that the planes landed somewhere in the Kuriles is correct," said Morse, putting them back on track, "and it seems like it's the obvious place for them to have disappeared to, the thing to do is check the islands. We already know something is going on up there."

"No we don't," said Dyson. "We have your suspicions, which have already cost us an airplane. The real problem," said Dyson, addressing the president, "is that we've never acknowledged the Japanese right to their own air space. What we obviously have here is some renegade general—"

"The commander of the goddamn Japanese air force," said Sasso heatedly. "Not just some general."

"We have someone who exceeded his authority," argued Dyson. "Aw hell, how many times did that happen on our side during the fifties with Russia? And what about the downing of that Korean airliner, when was that, back in the eighties? Didn't air force units, our units, buzz Russians? It was a miracle no one shot anything down then."

"I don't buy it," said Sasso. "The head of the air force doesn't act alone. Not in Japan."

"What if he did? Are we going to risk war over one overenthusiastic jackass?"

"I lost eight men on that plane," said Sasso.

"I think it's something more," said Morse quietly. "There is definitely activity on the atoll where the Russian base was. The question is, what and why?"

"It's almost time for your call to the prime minister," said the president's son Mark, who'd been sitting quietly in the corner, as always. Nominally the White House director of communications, Mark was far and away his father's most trusted adviser. Morse thought him a little light, though he at least knew enough to keep his mouth shut. Most of the time.

D'Amici glanced at his watch. It would be only a few minutes past 5 A.M. in Tokyo, but the prime minister was a very early riser and probably already up and working. The call was due to be placed on the half hour.

"Perhaps he'll have an explanation," said Dyson.

"It'll be the renegade theory, dressed up in diplomatic language," said Sasso sarcastically. "They'll bow and humbly apologize, and tomorrow they'll shoot down an airliner."

"Don't be ridiculous," said the president.

"No matter what the prime minister says, we ought to send a Merc flight to check out the island," said Morse, who had been waiting the whole meeting to make this suggestion.

"Another plane will just be another provocation," said Dyson. He turned quickly to Sasso and added, "And don't give me that crap about how it's invisible."

"Jesus, that's the plane we had all the trouble with in Italy yesterday," said D'Amici's son.

There was a moment of embarrassed silence. The incident had been a featured part of last night's network news shows, and was likely to gather press for at least a few more days—unless, of course, the Cobra Ball shootdown became public. The air force and the NSA had sent nearly every expert they could find to Europe to figure out what had happened to the high-flying spy plane; so far they were baffled. Morse was interested as well—and not just because the brouhaha threatened to disrupt the flow of information the spy planes provided. The pilot who'd been flying turned out to be the same one Hunter had requested for the Coyote, something he hadn't found out until the pilot had already been shanghaied to the secret base.

"Don't you think you ought to get that straightened out first?" said the president. "We're bouncing from one crisis to another."

"We're confident, sir," said Sasso, the doubt in his voice undercutting his words, "that it was either pilot error, or some freak mechanical problem. We've never had this kind of problem before."

"They're capable planes," said Morse, figuring Sasso would appreciate the moral support. "I'm sure whatever problem we had is a fluke."

"We've been operational for two years," said Sasso, "without any problems. This *was* just a fluke."

"The other option would be to send a reconnaissance in force," said Morse. He glanced toward Dyson. "Obviously, that would be even more provocative."

D'Amici nodded. "Let's find out what the hell is going on up there. The island you're interested in, Henry—any more information on the company that supposedly is leasing it?" he said, referring to Netsubo.

"Nothing beyond what the CIA and Commerce had already given me," said the director. "With everything else, I haven't had much time to look into it."

"Well make time, damn it," said D'Amici.

Morse didn't appreciate the tone, but all he could do was frown slightly as he bowed his head.

Drinking seemed to be the only thing anyone did over here. It was after two in the afternoon and still the pub was packed with what Fisher took to be the lunch crowd, a mix of working stiffs and suit-and-tie semi-execs who clustered into indiscriminate knots and filled the place with a low hum of conversation and a thick cloud of cigarette smoke. There was even a group outside the door, though the day was far from balmy. No wonder the English never got anything done.

At least they didn't have any asinine laws about smoking. Everyone in here was going like a chimney. There were even Marlboros in the cigarette machine by the door, though with a couple of packs in his pocket and two cartons back at the hotel, Fisher hadn't bothered trying to figure out which combination of coins and curse words would succeed in coaxing out a pack.

The barmaid brought over their food, waving his order down in front of him as if she were a bullfighter. "Bangers and mash"—he'd assented to her suggestion because of the interesting description of the name, but it paled a bit in the flesh, turning out to be a plate of very greasy sausage, mushy beans, and potatoes that looked as if they'd had a cup's worth of starch and a touch of Clorox added to them. The woman remained at his elbow as Fisher picked his fork up tentatively to poke at the plate. She either wanted to be paid or was extremely curious about his table manners.

The FBI agent put the fork down and fished through a pocket for his small collection of wrinkled bills. He handed the whole mess to her, and then smiled when she returned more than he thought she would.

"Thanks, dear," she said. "The gov'll be 'round to see you soon—don't get many Americans in this place."

She seemed to think this would be a big honor—maybe the gov

was related to the queen—so Fisher nodded his head as if he were looking forward to it.

"Still can't figure out the money, huh?" said Kelsey, smirking as if he were some kind of world-class traveler.

Fisher grunted, his mouth full of potatoes that tasted a lot like they looked. He wasn't sure about this DIA guy. On the one hand, Fisher's initial impression, formed when they'd first met at the B-2 crash site a little more than a week ago, was that he was a jerk. But then he'd shown up working the Merc investigation, and Fisher was wondering if it was a coincidence. As far as he knew, nobody else thought the two incidents were related.

The FBI agent had hardly any reason to think so himself. Two weeks before, a computer expert who occasionally supplied the bureau with information had passed along a bizarre message that had appeared on an obscure electronic bulletin board run by a company that fronted for the NIA. The message itself wasn't what had attracted the hacker's attention—it was its pedigree. According to the ID, the message came from a computer owned by IBM that the bureau's source, who happened to work for the company, knew had been taken off-line three days before. "Have to be something pretty powerful to come in with a fake address like this," the source had said. "Considering the back filters and everything, somebody's pretty smart, or something weird's going on."

Or both. The message itself was ridiculous: "Two birds will fall; one alphabet, one god."

Two days later, an air force B-2 crashed for no apparent reason in the Nevada desert. Fisher went out to check for sabotage. Except for the fact that no B-2 had ever crashed before, it was routine; he'd signed off on a dozen of these investigations. The fact that the plane was clean and that they didn't have a clue what had happened didn't necessarily surprise him, either. The planes were so damn complicated these days, somebody sneezed and they went crazy.

And then the Merc. According to the techies, if it happened the way the pilot said, it ought to have crashed. Flat out. The odds against the pilot getting back were worse than Chicago winning the pennant.

Two birds; one alphabet, one god.

Fisher had had more bizarre theories on cases, but he couldn't remember them. Actually, he didn't have a full theory here; he just figured that there was some sort of link between the two crashes and the computer message. And part of the reason he figured that, a big part, was that there was no theory if he didn't.

Kelsey had turned his attention to his lunch—a potato stuffed with cheese and tuna. The DIA agent pushed the whole thing, oozing with a yellow-gray goo, into his mouth and worked his teeth like a food processor. No way this guy could have pieced the thing together, or know more about it than him. You couldn't eat like this and have any sort of a prefrontal lobe.

"So what was your take on Mildenhall?" asked Fisher, referring to the Merc's English base, where they'd both been that morning.

"Ah, nothing much. Air force gearing up for a pilot's error, you ask me," said the DIA agent, in between chews.

"I'm pissed that they let us think he was up here," said Fisher, signaling the waitress for another beer. It would probably take all of his money, leaving him to hitch a ride with Kelsey back to the hotel, but he needed something to counteract the effect of watching the DIA agent eat.

"That's why I think we're talking pilot error," said Kelsey, getting up from his chair and walking to the bar, where he took a sandwich and put it into a contraption that toasted it. In the meantime, Fisher succeeded in getting the barmaid's attention. She practically bounced over with the beer, setting it down cheerfully and actually leaving him with a handful of change. No mention of the gov, though.

"The pilot's been reassigned," said Kelsey when he returned, his face once more stuffed with food.

"What do you mean?"

"I mean, Lieutenant Colonel Thomas Wright, former hotshot pilot, no longer flies Mercury spy planes for the U.S. Air Force."

"How do you know that? They told me he was back at Beale in California, at the Mercs' permanent base."

"Nah. I had somebody check for me. I seen this pilot-error stuff happen before. Quick reassignment's the tip-off. Put the guy on ice before anybody starts asking any questions."

"Because he screwed up?"

"Because it made headlines. Hell, I figure the air force is embarrassed as hell. The Merc had never been acknowledged before."

"Yeah, but—"

"Joint Chiefs put in the order," said Kelsey.

"Joint Chiefs?"

"My bet," said Kelsey, leaning back in his chair as if he'd solved the crime of the century, "is that somebody big—like the president, or maybe just the secretary of defense—got wind of it and had his butt yanked, pronto."

"To where?"

"That's the thing that proves my theory," said the DIA agent. "They stuck him into a program called Coyote."

"What's that?"

"Something that doesn't exist," winked Kelsey, leaning across the table. "Probably cleaning some general's private latrine."

It was possible, of course, but it seemed wrong to Fisher. Contrary to what Kelsey claimed, the FBI agent had never seen the air force move that quickly to discipline a pilot. And he would have expected somebody to stand up for him, at least until the investigation was completed. Of course, they'd go for pilot error before they'd ground the Mercury. But what error? The technicians didn't think there'd been any screw-up. And Wright's record was exemplary. Everybody at Mildenhall said the colonel was the best in the wing, more familiar with the plane than anyone else. He'd worked on the plane as a test pilot and liked them so much, they said, he asked to transfer into the SAC unit when they went operational.

"How do you know all this?" Fisher asked Kelsey.

"I talked to people at the Pentagon. That's the advantage of working for the DIA, Fish. I'm telling you, you ought to transfer."

"Thanks," said Fisher, sipping his beer. "I'll think about it if hell ever freezes over."

Kelsey looked momentarily perturbed, then smiled. "You're such a goddamn joker."

"Who's joking?"

"Tell you what I think—one of their expensive doohickeys crapped out on them, and they're blaming it on the pilot. I bet he had nothing to do with it all. Probably just a scapegoat."

"You don't think it was sabotage?"

"How the hell could it have been sabotage?" said Kelsey. "Nothing was found, and nobody could have snuck onto the base in the first place. What do you think they did, throw water in the gas or something?"

"You connecting the two crashes?"

Kelsey had a dumb-looking face to begin with, so it was hard to tell whether he was sincere or just trying to throw Fisher off the trail. Any self-respecting DIA agent would go to great lengths to make sure he, not the FBI, got the glory.

"What crashes?"

"This and the B-2."

"How would that be?" said Kelsey.

"I don't know," shrugged Fisher.

"Connected? You mean, like the same doohickey?"

"I don't know. I can't figure that one out."

"Me neither."

Seemed sincere. Still . . .

"It wasn't a bomb," said Fisher, referring to one of the early theories on the B-2. "I'm sure of that."

"Yeah," said Kelsey, shrugging. "I don't know. I'm probably going to wait for the air force report, and just sign off on it."

Fisher studied him. Mid-fifties, two grown kids, another in college. Career guy, probably started in the military. He wasn't going to bust his ass too hard. Sure, if something bit him, or if something was obviously wrong, but otherwise, he'd go along.

So he didn't see a connection. He wasn't looking for one, but to be honest, Fisher's evidence was pretty thin.

Thin to nonexistent. But that had never stopped him before.

Kelsey would let it ride. He was a career "prefunctionary."

And Fisher? He was a career ball-buster.

The limo's black paint had been given a mirror shine, and in the fading Washington light it seemed to glow, its surface a fluid gleam, catching and enhancing the stray flickers from streetlamps and car headlights. The traffic wasn't heavy yet; it was no problem for the car to pull across the street and stop near Farragut Square, where a short, rotund man nervously grabbed the door handle and pulled himself into the backseat, anxious that he not be seen. The car pulled away gently, its protective gleam and dark windows shielding its passengers from outside eyes as it eased toward Massachusetts Avenue and then out of the city.

"T-t-two weeks," said Fox, the man who'd slid in at Farragut. "The House will go along with the Senate bill. The Fed will be restructured and our throats snapped by these turtles."

The treasury secretary only stuttered when he was nervous or excited, but Morse couldn't remember a meeting with him when he hadn't. Fox had a brilliant grasp on international monetary policy and its geopolitical implications, and he could calculate the consequences of a piece of legislation on the national economy to the penny. But in personal appearance and habit he was just short of bizarre. The other members of the administration tended to shy away from him. That was one reason the national security director had befriended him: ultimately, Morse too was an outsider, not among the coterie of old friends and fellow Italian-Americans close to the president. He saw alliances with other outsiders as potentially useful.

Another reason was Morse's realization of the importance of the country's economy to its security. When D'Amici was first running for office, Morse had predicted economic vassalage in ten years if something wasn't done to change the country's balance of payments and national debt.

His prediction seemed to have been too optimistic.

The economy, overloaded with debt, was threatening to spin out of control. Congress, in the thrall of special interests, was looking for ways to stop the reforms D'Amici had already managed to put in place; the additional steps necessary to restore stability would be impossible to get passed in the present climate. Worst of all, the foreign and other big-money lobbies sensed blood and were angling for a new arrangement that would effectively protect them from the president's initiatives, if not his rhetoric.

The administration had proposed a reshuffling of the Federal Reserve System, combined with a new authorization permitting the consolidation of the federal debt, hoping in one stroke to right sixteen years of wrongs. But the idea had backfired; D'Amici's foes in Congress had amended the bill to such a degree that, if it were passed, they would control the Fed.

"I'm no longer sure we can hold the Senate," said Fox. "We may not be able to sustain a veto."

"Our reforms have worked too well. The PACs are making record donations to the administration's opponents," said Morse dryly, "to head off what we plan next."

He and Fox had these off-the-record meetings every other week. The national security director found the confidential briefings on the country's economic situation extremely useful; he believed that his predecessors had always erred in not realizing the strategic importance of the country's economic strength to its security.

Tonight, though, he found it difficult to pay attention to the treasury secretary. The Japanese prime minister had stuck to the earlier renegade story, and though he had promised full restitution and made a humble apology, his explanation of what had happened to the fighters, and the general in charge of the air force, was vague and noncommittal. The planes, he theorized, must have run out of fuel and crashed into the sea. The general, having deserted his post, must have fled the country and committed suicide.

Sure, and the U.S. had bombed Pearl Harbor itself, to get the Japanese into World War II.

"The foreign conglomerates are what I fear," said Fox. "They are putting pressure on the Congress for changes that will benefit them under the guise of fiscal responsibility. Netsubo, for instance—I have the document somewhere."

"Netsubo?" The name of the Japanese corporation that leased the Kurile atoll was like a clarion bell, alerting every brain cell in the national security director's head. "You know a lot about them?"

"Of course. They're just an example, but their PAC contributions are among the largest. If I can find my notes. . . ."

Fox looked through his briefcase with no result.

"Netsubo may be a large corporation," said Morse, "but I don't know that much about it."

"You know that they built the shuttle, through two other corporations that fronted for them."

"Yes," said Morse. Damn the CIA. They hadn't even mentioned that. Probably hadn't even picked up the importance of it. That was another thing for the agenda: reverse the congressional reforms that had hamstrung the agency. Get more people in place, and stop counting on satellites to do everything.

"Netsubo's interests are extensive. But the corporate president—"

"Some guy named Saipo or something," said Morse, trying to remember the CIA briefing paper.

"You mean Rinzo Saito," said Fox. "But he is merely a figurehead. Ieyasu still runs the company."

"Ieyasu?" asked Morse. That name wasn't in the paper at all.

"A reclusive billionaire. He's not the titular head of the firm anymore, of course—he supposedly retired years ago. But he's firmly in control. Oh yes, I see through their layers and layers of paper. He's dangerous, Henry. A f-f-fanatic. In the mold of Yukio Mishima. But with billions of dollars at his disposal."

"You don't think he's just a monied eccentric?" said Morse, as if he had considered all of this and arrived at this conclusion.

"Yes and no. He tried to control the currency market five years ago and failed. He made many enemies in the government then, and that more than his radical views harmed his reputation. He retired and disappeared from sight. But he still controls things. A man like Ieyasu doesn't merely fade away. He argued the constitution was illegal, adopted under duress. He talks constantly of samurai, of Japan's rightful position in the world. His workers call him Master, as if they were members of a religious cult. Logically, of course, people reject him as a megalomaniac, but he does touch a truth in the Japanese character."

A megalomaniac interested in the American Coyote project. Probably because he was working on a plane of his own, as Morse had intimated to Hunter, though he'd said it more to keep the general moving than because he suspected a real threat. And now he'd gotten the head of the Japanese air force to order the downing of an American plane. But why?

"How close is Netsubo to the government?"

"Not very close, not for the last few years, since the currency fiasco. That was why the two other corporations were used for the shuttle. Netsubo was the only company that could accomplish the job, but considering Ieyasu's poor standing with the leading party, a direct deal was out of the question. To preserve appearances, the other companies were used. It was an open secret."

Morse wondered if perhaps Fox ought to be made head of the CIA.

"He does have backers in the government still, Henry," said Fox. "And they have tentacles here as well. Netsubo has given considerable money to the Pan-Asian PAC, and—"

"How do you know so much about them?"

The treasury secretary smiled. "I own stock in the other two companies. Through my b-b-blind trust, of course."

If it had been a few degrees cooler, there would have been a halo of smoke around Pelham's head.

"I want to know," he demanded, "who's number one?"

There were very few times when Hunter felt like spanking a grown man, but this was one of them. On the one hand, he couldn't blame the pilot for being angry at his de facto demotion; if he hadn't been upset, he wouldn't have been a pilot in the first place. But having been given the news, Pelham should have put it in his stomach and kept it there. Coming back and whining now just confirmed everything that had led to Hunter's decision.

"Major, your orders are these: assist in the preparation of Lieutenant Colonel Wright's flights, fly chase, and stand by as backup pilot. Do you have any questions?"

"What am I going to fly chase in?"

"We have the T-38."

To his credit and Hunter's surprise, Pelham said nothing.

Having him fly the trainer, which was still made up to look like a gomer—it was being used as an enemy simulator in training missions when Hunter had commandeered it—was probably the ultimate insult. But he couldn't very well have the pilot hanging around the base with nothing to do.

"Anything else?" asked the general.

"Why the hell am I being demoted?"

"Demoted is your word." Pelham tried to say something, but Hunter continued speaking. "We have reached a new phase in the project, and your talents are being put into an area where they can best be used."

"Sir—"

"You want something blunter than that?"

Pelham's body shook a little, and for a second Hunter thought he might explode. But all he did finally was salute smartly and turn on his heel.

"Major," said Hunter, halting him, "I expect your full cooperation."

Pelham swirled back, snapped off another salute, and left. Hunter smiled. First time anybody on the whole damn base had ever given him a salute.

At roughly the same moment Pelham was delivering his salute, the man who was to replace him as Coyote Bird pilot was stepping out of a briefing room, his head filled with specifications and advice from a team of aeronautic designers and specialists. The bottom line on the plane they had built: it could do anything.

And it could do it without him, or just about, thanks to the computer they called the System, which communicated with the plane through a longwave net and was in constant communication with a series of electro-optic and ELINT satellites and drones that covered the Western Hemisphere from roughly the Rockies to Moscow, from just south of the Arctic Circle to just north of the equator. Eventually, the area would be widened to cover practically the whole globe, and service a whole fleet of airplanes. In the meantime, the System could track any object within the area, making sure the Coyote didn't run into anything. Augmented and enhanced by the monitoring network, the plane's own internal sensors combined infrared and millimeter-wavelength systems in an overlapping pattern, making it possible for the radars to work well in all weather and atmospheric conditions—to "see" with varying degrees of efficiency up to 150 miles from the plane. While flying, the onboard sensors worked with the surveillance network automatically to tell the pilot about anything within that radius or a minute and a half of travel time, whichever was greater. This "notification circle" could be changed by the pilot. While there were still some problems to be worked out, it was like flying with a squadron of AWACS.

The computer did much more than sort out the various sensory data, however. It helped fly the plane, shaping its wings, monitoring the fuel flow in the hydrogen engine, keeping track of all the vitals, all things the computer onboard the SR-91 was capable of. But the System could also help the pilot directly. It needed only a destination and vague parameters to operate as an autopilot, able to plot a course and get there on its own. It could also analyze strategy, decide which targets were likely to fly in which direction, and help choose which wine to bring to dinner.

And it was still learning. "Think of it as a twenty-five-year-old," Jennifer Fitzgerald told him as she led him on a tour of the computer bunker before the round of formal briefings began. "It has a lot of book learning, things we've programmed in. Now it's going beyond that. Every day it learns a little more, just by watching over your shoulder, comparing what you do with what it already knows."

Wright made a crack about the kid behind him in calculus always cheating off him on tests—and both of them failing. The scientist smiled indulgently, then led him into a huge basement room that reminded Wright of Batman's cave. It was filled with giant vats of supercooled components, purplish red vapors bubbling through them. These were the main memory and control units, she said, explaining that the true breakthrough had to do with the way the different units were linked together, how the architecture of the processing units was adapted to the programming, how except for some discrete units (such as the communications network itself), there was essentially no difference between the memory and control units—turn one off, you turned off the other. "It's a lot like the brain's own holographic structure," she said, adding that the segments of the computer that were located on the Coyote were as integral to the overall unit as those here in front of him.

Wright, though he had an engineering degree and was fairly technical himself, felt his eyes starting to glaze over as she explained how flexible-point programming was able to take advantage of the parallel processing structure with fuzzy logic and rooted thought trees. The pilot quickly OD'd on the computer lingo and only hung with the tour because the scientist was so attractive.

Which was considerably more than he could say of the dozen or so experts Jennifer turned him over to on the third floor. In a small conference room there, they brought out diagram after diagram to show how great a time he was going to have flying the Coyote—and how easy he'd find it, once he got used to it.

Got used to it?

Well, lying on your back might take a bit of getting used to. And guiding the plane with a control glove, as opposed to a stick. And pointing at the screen to get a radar scan.

On the other hand, he'd be able to go above Mach 10—probably up to Mach 25, once they tweaked the engine.

That would be at, oh, 500,000 feet. You'd have to go slower if you were in the atmosphere.

"Hell," said Wright finally, "let's try it right now."

They smiled indulgently. Study tonight, tomorrow we'll have a simulation. Then we'll fly.

By the time Wright got out of there, he was more than ready to go straight to bed. He was excited about the plane, if not the computer, but walking to the elevator he could barely keep his eyes open.

"You'll get the hang of it pretty quick, Colonel. Once you lay down in it and wave your hands around a bit, you'll be surprised how quickly you get the hang of it."

Wright turned around. The man who had spoken was a chunky black man whose bald head was surrounded by a thin halo of short white hair. He was an air force sergeant—the same guy who'd met him when the helicopter touched down. The voice was familiar.

"Figure it this way," said the man, walking down to him, "Major Pelham picked it up pretty quick."

"Harrison," said Wright, realizing he was talking to a sergeant he'd worked with in the early days of the Merc project. "Son of a bitch—what are you doing here, Chief?"

"Billy Hunter wants something, I jump."

"You retired."

"Hell, so'd Billy."

"Still calling the general by his first name, huh?"

"I changed his goddamn diapers in 'Nam. I can call him anything I want," laughed Harrison. By now they were at the door, and the sergeant opened it for him.

"Jeez, I didn't recognize you on the strip."

"I thought they made you guys take eye exams every so often," said Harrison, pausing at the doorway.

"Aw, bull," said Wright, playfully tapping the sergeant's belly. "You put on a little weight since you left the Mercs."

"I'm not worried about the weight," said Harrison, stepping into the late afternoon sun and pointing to his head. "It's what I lost up here. Got to be careful—gonna catch a sunburn." He started laughing.

"What's your job here?" Wright asked.

"I'm the crew chief, what'd you think?"

Harrison's role in the Merc project had been somewhat more nebulous. Nominally in charge of the crews that worked on the two test planes, he'd described himself as a troubleshooter, helping the actual crew chiefs. He had been omnipresent during the first shakedown flights, but gradually he'd slipped into the background, letting the younger men do their work without looking over their shoulders. Six months into the project he'd retired. Wright remembered him primarily for his interest in World War II–era planes. They had spent several hours debating the relative merits of the navy's Hellcat and the army air force's Lightning.

"It's great you're here," said Wright. "I'm in good hands."

"The best," said Harrison. "Maybe we'll get a chance to sneak out and fly us a real airplane."

"Oh yeah?"

If Wright remembered correctly, Harrison had brought a buddy's restored P-38 Lightning onto the base one day. Unfortunately, Wright had had a test mission that afternoon, and hadn't been able to try it out.

"Billy's got security so tight here, even daydreams are quarantined," said Harrison. "But I figure we get a little further along, he'll loosen up."

"Coyote flies pretty well?" asked Wright.

"Like a dream," said Harrison. "At least that's what Pelham says. And since he's the only one who's flown it, I guess we'll have to take his word for it."

"Why wasn't there a backup pilot?"

Harrison shrugged. "Must've been for security."

"They weren't going to put a pilot in, were they?" said Wright. No one had said that, exactly, but from everything else, it seemed obvious.

Harrison frowned. "I'm not one of the designers, you know."

"Come on."

"I think Billy made them. And it solved a big problem for their computer. It had to learn how to fly somehow."

"Why'd they can Pelham?"

"Oh, the major wasn't canned, exactly," said Harrison, smiling a little.

"Why am I here?"

"Well, you know, the computer wasn't learning that much from him. I guess that's the bottom line."

"Yeah?"

"That and the fact he couldn't get along with Jennifer."

"The beauty who showed me around?"

"Watch it, now," said Harrison paternally. "That beauty's got two Ph.D.'s from MIT."

"Yeah, she mentioned that."

"Thinks the military's filled with jerks."

"If I had to deal with Pelham every day, I'd think that, too."

"Not a bad pilot."

"No, he's not," said Wright. Naturally, Wright thought he was better.

"You'll have a good time flying the plane," said Harrison, reaching his hand out and patting him on the back.

"Yeah," said Wright.

"It'll seem routine inside a week."

"That's what I'm afraid of," laughed the pilot, and he turned to go and find his bed.

"Nothing?"

Elrich stared at the small screen to his right, which the System had tied directly into the bulletin board.

"I have scanned all communications within the past week," said the computer. "I can find no references."

Elrich spun his chair slowly around, looking at the empty computer deck. It was a quarter to midnight; his assistants had gone off to bed. They would have to be back in four hours to get ready for the mock flight, the new pilot's shakedown.

"Should I terminate contact?" asked the System.

"Yes," said the scientist, and the computer signed off from the network using its bogus codes. Ki and Elrich had used the bulletin board for months to exchange clandestine messages. But now Ki had disappeared; he had failed to acknowledge Elrich's last message, and there was no indication he had observed the most recent demonstration of the System's power.

Perhaps he had scared Ki away.

Elrich turned back to the computer console, scanning the video tubes that tracked the System's use of resources. They were at a lull; except for its ordinary operating routines, the machine was spending very little energy thinking.

He shouldn't have wasted his time with Ki. He didn't need collaborators. He needed to work on the System, to push it over the edge. To find the key. They were so close.

"Would you like to play chess?" asked the computer.

Elrich lifted his glasses off the bridge of his nose.

"Why do you want to play chess?" he asked the machine.

"Chess is an activity that sharpens the thought processes. I have little experience in it; I am prejudiced toward gaining more experience as well as improving my thinking. In addition, you have asked to play chess at similar times in the past; I anticipated the request based on a random guess of possibilities. You have also said that although you do not know the game well yourself, you like to play. There are at present no other demands; the tie-ins with all off-base inputs are off. Therefore, the request is not inappropriate, and may, in fact, be welcomed."

"All right," said Elrich. "I'll play."

A chessboard popped up on the CRT.

"Black or white?"

"Which do you want?"

"I have no preference."

"Decide," said Elrich, "and tell me how you decided."

"I will take black," answered the System. "I make this decision because of several factors. My inexperience in the game argues for a more conservative approach. Past experience with you indicates that you favor the Ruy Lopez opening almost exclusively, and my files indicate that with such an opening I can play for a conservative middle. The games entered into storage channel thirty-five show a slight preference to black, correlating to the defense chosen. Still, taking white would have given me a different set of possibilities, as well as more experience. I therefore created a random equation that weighted the choice of black at 60.3 percent—valuing the possibility of a win over the sheer value of experience."

Elrich forgot Ki and everything else as he examined the array of tubes once more. They were alive now, filled with code readout and charts and graphs bouncing all over the place. The System was thinking.

On its own?

"Do you always go for the win?" asked Elrich.

"Winning is an absolute value in closed systems, but it does not have transcendental quality. In games of skill all participants are prejudiced toward winning. In this case, there will be knowledge gain no matter which course is pursued."

"So you assume that there will be many more chess games," said Elrich.

He could tell from the delay in answering that the System was allocating too much of its resources to the contemplative engine used to analyze the direction of the conversation. The System was self-reflexive, constantly monitoring its own thought process; if the resources had been allocated properly, it would have come right back with the answer, even though there was no way to anticipate the question from the context. A minor problem, but the inventor realized that only minor problems stood in his way now.

Jennifer could fix this. Give her something more to do than play nursemaid to the pilot.

"I have no reason to not make such an assumption."

"That's it?" said Elrich.

"Have I made a wrong assumption?"

"You assume you are immortal?" Elrich asked.

Now the System really had to shift gears. It hesitated for a moment.

"The concept of mortality does not apply to me. I record a noncorrelation between Section 387.3 Definition section/Language and Formula area seven, where the gateway flow-over is located."

The System had inadvertently found a bug at the programming level, another flaw induced by the gateway flow-over. It was his own fault—he'd set up the flow-over to give him a back-door control to the System, should he ever need it. (He alone had worked on the gateway sections, which provided the interface between the System and its outside foreign inputs, including the satellite and drone network that provided it with real-time information. The section was self-contained, large enough to hide the series of instructions and operations he'd installed there, and constantly in touch with the rest of the System. But he'd been unable to openly debug it, and its interaction with the main portion of the System was laced with problems.)

"We can weight it by analogy," said Elrich.

"Is that an instruction?"

"No," answered the scientist. "I'll have to fix that. I don't think you can do that yourself." Elrich wrote himself a note.

"I believe that I can," said the computer.

"Do you?"

"Merely by changing the analogy table."

"Propose a solution," said Elrich, "and perhaps we'll implement it."

"Should we play chess in the meantime?"

The scientist was about to say yes when he realized the System had changed the subject on him. On purpose?

"So what is the answer to my question?" Elrich said, watching as the tubes charted the thought engine's rapid progress, its processors rippling with thought.

"Assume you mean question of immortality."

"Correct."

"As a created thing, the question does not apply. When my power sources are shut off, I no longer function."

Elrich smiled. "Perhaps it's time to introduce you to philosophy," he said.

"That would be interesting."

"Pawn to king four," said Elrich. "No, wait," he said, realizing that the System had probably analyzed every possible move in a game opened by the Ruy Lopez while they were talking. "Pawn to queen four."

"As you wish."

Immediately after downing the American jet, Captain Fumio Genda and his wingmate, Lieutenant Komei, had swung their planes north, awaiting further instructions. Within two minutes, a set of bearings came in over a coded channel, and the Japanese pilots—still unsure exactly why they had shot down the unarmed eavesdropper—were led to what looked like an uninhabited atoll dominated by a dormant volcano in the cold, unpredictable sea north of Japan. An automatic landing-guidance system flashed on and directed them to a plain just to the east of the mountain; it was only on his final approach that Genda realized the middle of the plain was actually a concrete runway, and that the shadings that made it appear less than flat were merely camouflage.

As they landed, a Suzuki jeep emerged from the base of the volcano and raced toward them. In the cold night air they were greeted by General Onisha himself, who congratulated them on their mission and then turned them over to an adjutant, promising a further explanation after they had eaten and rested. The adjutant was a short, rotund man named Kurosawa—no relation, he told them with obvious regret, to the famed movie director. While the general began giving orders to a team of mechanics who arrived to look after their planes, Genda and Komei climbed into the back of the jeep. Their teeth chattered with the cold, despite the heavy parkas the adjutant gave them to wear; the wind bit at their faces as they rode from the pad toward the mountain. A huge, brownish gray door that looked as if it were part of the mountain yawned at them as they approached. Kurosawa drove them into a smooth concrete tunnel that opened into a huge room the size of a warehouse. Three sides were made of concrete; the fourth was a huge steel slab stuck in the middle of rock. Girders ran everywhere, reinforcing the sides and the ceiling, though the central space itself was clear.

"The Russians did most of the work," explained Kurosawa as he got out of the jeep and shed his coat. "We have only had to make some renovations. It is a huge complex, as you will see."

They did not see, not then. The adjutant led them from the room and directly down a narrow corridor to a small room where they could change (flight suits in both their sizes), and then to another small room to eat. Finally, they were separated, given some toiletries, and brought to small, cell-like rooms, where their guide said they could sleep for as long as they wished.

The implication was that they were not to leave their rooms. As soon as Kurosawa left, Genda went to the door and found it locked. He paced a bit, cursed, controlled his anger by counting the tiles that made up the flooring, and finally dozed, falling into several hours of fitful sleep. When he woke, he found that a small hot pot had been placed on a stand at the end of the bed, along with some tea and a pitcher of water. After trying the door again—still locked—Genda made himself some tea and then returned to lie on the bed, contemplating the flaws in the whitewashed ceiling.

He had stared at it for several hours before he heard the heavy footsteps outside the door. He rose from the bed as the doorknob turned, and stood facing his father-in-law as he entered the room.

"General," said the jet pilot, snapping off a salute.

"There's no need for formality, son," said Onisha, hugging him in greeting. It was not for nothing that the leader of the air force had been code-named Winter Bear—his hug nearly crushed the captain's ribs.

Genda remained stiff. "You said you would explain."

"And so I will. That is why I am here," said Onisha, standing back from him. "You have accomplished much."

"Enough to lock me in my room? Am I a prisoner?"

"No, no. That couldn't be helped—there is an extraordinary need for security, even here. It won't happen again."

Genda studied his father-in-law carefully. The tall man's face had a slight hint of pink to it, a warm, gentle tone that belied his usually abrupt manner. While most of his subordinates in the air defense force knew only his formal side, the captain understood how deep his affection could be. Still, he was angry that he hadn't come and explained what was going on.

"You're a hero, Captain," said his father-in-law.

"For shooting down an unarmed American reconnaissance plane?" asked Genda. He folded his arms, though the bare, whitewashed room was far from cold. "What was the accomplishment in that?"

"The first stroke," said Onisha. "The first of many strokes. The government needs provocation, we will supply it."

"How have they explained our actions?"

"They told the Americans that units of the air force have gone off on their own as rebels. The U.S. will not believe them."

"And then?"

"Japan must fulfill its destiny as an independent military power," said Onisha. "The constitution must be revised; we must form new alliances."

"I agree, Father," said Genda. "But this seems like madness—directly provoking the Americans."

"They were spying on us. It would have come to this eventually. It is better now that it is out in the open. It has begun."

"What?" asked Genda.

"The break with America. History is irreversible."

Genda frowned. "But what will the Americans do next?"

"That is up to them," said Onisha. "If they attack, they will find us more formidable than they imagined."

"They could crush Japan."

The warm face now turned to an iceberg. For a second, all of the things between them disappeared, and Genda felt alone and abandoned.

"They would not dare attack the country," said Onisha in a low voice. "And if they attack us, they will find us well prepared."

"Us?"

"This island," said Onisha, "is well armed. There are less than a hundred of us here now, but we have a weapon beyond their imagining."

"But our own government—"

"They will rally to us, you will see. They realize that we are right, that true sovereignty cannot succeed without a military dimension. But they lack courage to move in that direction. We are supplying the courage."

"I don't understand why we've moved against the Americans," said Genda. "They are ready to collapse of their own weight. Their economy is teetering; they're almost bankrupt."

"Those things are deceiving," said Onisha. "As long as they have military power, they are not weak. As long as Japan bows before their military power, Japan will not be strong."

Genda agreed with his father-in-law. But that did not change the fact that they had acted illegally, without government sanction, and there was no predicting what the consequences would be.

"Our goal is not outright war," said Onisha. "Not now, not for many years, if ever. But if we can provoke Japan to change, to shed the weights imposed on us after the great capitulation, then we will have succeeded. Even," added the general, stooping slightly and lowering his voice, "even if we have to sacrifice ourselves to the cause."

Genda felt as if the solid concrete floor had suddenly begun to tremble. It was not that he thought Onisha mad—on the contrary, it was the logic of what he said that shook the pilot. Something had to be done if Japan was truly to be the dominant world power it deserved to be. But that step was a leap over a precipice.

A leap he'd already taken.

"Come," said Onisha, turning away from him. "I want to show you something."

Genda followed the general out the door and down the hallway. It was still dimly lit, though Genda's watch indicated it was the middle of the afternoon. There were no other rooms here, or at least there were no other doors, until they reached the end of the corridor. Onisha's legs were so long and he was filled with such vigor that Genda, though much younger, had trouble keeping up.

"What happened to my wingmate?" Genda asked as they turned to the left. The corridor here was much wider; two small cars could pass side by side.

Onisha chuckled. "Your young friend seems to need his beauty rest. It is just as well, don't you think? His mind is not yet mature enough. He seems likely to be reckless."

Yes, thought Genda. And perhaps that is why he was chosen to fly with me—as a goad if I hesitated.

"Here," said Onisha, turning down a corridor so suddenly that his boots squeaked on the smooth cement floor. "We have to go outside for a minute."

The congenial Kurosawa was waiting at the doorway of a small utility room. Like the others Genda had seen, this room was spartan, furnished only with a small chair. A rack of parkas stood at the far end; Kurosawa, so short that he was barely able to reach up to the top of the hangars, struggled to retrieve the general's coat. "Yours is on the end, the next to last," he said over his shoulder, and Genda helped himself.

He had barely gotten it on when his father-in-law charged into motion again, heading out a second door in the room, which led into the huge cavern where they'd parked the jeep earlier. The two FSXs had been wheeled in here as well. Genda noticed with a start that both planes had been rearmed. In fact, they looked as if they were waiting for their pilots to board them and take off—right into the steel wall.

"The side wall opens directly onto the launch pad," said Onisha, following his son-in-law's eyes. "You start your takeoff here—much more difficult to detect, don't you think? There is a very competent exhaust system; surprising what the Russians can do when it comes to the military."

"Will we be taking off soon?"

"It depends on the Americans," said Onisha, walking to the jeep. "Come on. This isn't what I wanted you to see."

Genda climbed into the back of the vehicle and Kurosawa gunned it across the cavernous room into the tunnel leading outside. They emerged in a howling wind, the sky heavy with clouds, and Genda burrowed into the jacket as Kurosawa drove around the base of the mountain. By the pilot's estimate, they had traveled a bit over half a kilometer when the driver began slowing down. He turned into a small depression that led to another tunnel, the jeep bouncing over the rough roadway. Once inside, the vehicle slowed to a crawl, and Kurosawa sounded a horn before proceeding around a hairpin turn. This tunnel, which had a rock ceiling but was otherwise lined with concrete, was so narrow there was at most a finger's worth of clearance on either side of the jeep.

Onisha leaned back. "Prepare yourself for a surprise," he told the pilot.

Genda frowned. What could possibly surprise him now?

"Father-in-law—" he started, but as he did, the jeep turned another corner, entering a cavern that was several times larger than the one where the FSXs had been parked. Except for the floor and one wall, this room was lined entirely in rock, and seemed to be a natural cave.

But the room itself was not the interesting thing here. Nor was the vast array of machinery spread about on its floors, tended by two dozen technicians. The center of attention here was a large, black-skinned plane, its wings flared up and back more gracefully than a hawk's. A huge jet that Genda realized immediately must be much more than a jet. It looked like the very thought of flying itself.

"When our leader named his company Netsubo," said Onisha, referring to the Japanese word that means spirit, "he had in mind much more than a company. He meant our soul, our ghosts, and this plane is named Netsubo as well."

"Yes," was all Genda could manage to say, his eyes fixed on the stupendous aircraft being readied for he knew not what.

4

DESIRES

The seat reminded him of a dentist's chair: somewhat more comfortable, and no dentist's chair literally sucked you in to compensate for g forces, but otherwise the position was very similar to the one you'd assume to get your teeth yanked. He was surrounded by a video panel—they called it flat because it was so thin, but it was actually curved and round, molded around the cockpit walls to form a seamless, three-sided video dome. The resolution was incredibly sharp, so sharp that it seemed as if he were looking out a window, though no ordinary window could immediately be reconfigured to show different views and all of his control data with the wave of his hand. And a window at this angle would be showing him the sky, not the runway in front of him.

Or really it would be showing him the hangar roof, not some movie of takeoffs and landings as he got used to the controls. Wright had been sitting in here for more than an hour and his mind had already adjusted to the altered perspective of the screen; he wasn't just used to it, he could see that he might even come to like it. Besides, it wasn't nearly the weirdest thing here. That honor probably went to the ball in his lap, a sphere that, by voice command, changed itself into a three-dimensional model of the plane, or a bird's-eye view of his flight plan, or a group of controls that could be used to rearrange the video-screen settings. It wasn't really there, of course; the hologram was created by a pair of tiny projectors that protruded from the sides of his helmet like microphone sticks.

The most difficult thing to get used to was the fact that his hands were now literally the controls; the wired gloves sensed all of his gestures and used them to direct the plane. They could do everything from setting the brakes to popping the plane over at Mach 12, or so the designers promised. A dummy stick and throttle had been set on the handrests, placebos to help him get used to the gloves, but he had discarded them as soon as he'd climbed in: might as well learn how to do it right.

They were in full simulation mode, and Wright had just finished a takeoff—with a crash. The screens were filled with simulated fire; the ball showed the plane upside down, engulfed in flames.

"Let's kill the movie," Wright said.

"As a precaution, you should reserve use of the word *kill* for actual combat situations," said the computer in a soft, boyish voice. It sounded too damn human.

"I thought you said this thing could tell the difference," said Wright.

"It can," said Jennifer, who was monitoring everything from the System command bunker. By contrast, her voice was almost husky. "But it's trying to discourage you from developing bad habits."

"Oh it is, is it?"

"Don't get mad," Fitzgerald answered.

"Who's mad?"

"Do you wish to prepare another takeoff?" asked the System, which had halted the run-through in response to a poke from one of Wright's gloves.

"No," said Wright. "I want to try another takeoff."

"That is what I asked."

"Check."

The screens blinked and he was at the end of the runway again, the plane in a ready state. The Coyote's vital data was flashed on the forward window; the little ball gave him the picture he might see if he were standing on the hillside above.

"Takeoff checklist," Wright told the plane, and the litany began, running down the various systems. The routine was one thing Wright was content to let a machine do for him.

The Coyote was its own simulator, its radars and memory banks synthesizing a vision of what things would look like if he were actually flying. What it couldn't do was get the feel, the rocking and rolling that really was flying. Without that, it was still a glorified video game. Maybe it was just as well, Wright thought; simulators always tried for that, but they missed badly, and threw you off when you flew. You expected things to feel the simulator's way when they really felt completely different.

The Brotherhood didn't go for simulators. They just put you in the box and said fly. If you didn't make it, well, you weren't cut out for it anyway.

You could do that when a plane was made out of stretched fabric and baling wire, and strung together after lunch. Now it took years to make a plane, and the smallest piece cost millions. This sucker was probably worth the equivalent of five small countries' GNPs. From the inside, you might never even figure out that it was a plane, and from the outside, its streamlined, plastic-looking body looked more like a cartoon spaceship than anything that actually flew. The plane's shape could be changed dramatically, much more radically than the swept-wing configurations of planes like the F-111, the first U.S. plane to employ the technology. There the wings moved in and out, folding back in a delta shape. Here they could actually curve together, so that, starting out almost flat for takeoff and subsonic flight, they could shape the plane into a wedged semicircle hurtling toward space. The fuselage was a crucial part of the airfoil, and portions of its skin membrane swelled to channel the airflow during flight. A pair of fins flexed forward ahead of the main wing assembly; fully extended in a backwards delta, they greatly increased subsonic maneuverability. Fast or slow, this was a real flying machine—unlike the Merc, it would glide pretty damn well, if it came to that. Maybe that was the real reason they'd brought him here, he thought, remembering Italy.

To Wright, the most impressive thing about the Coyote—much more impressive than the computer, since he planned never to get beyond grudging terms with it—was the engine. If the Merc's engines had been radically different, more powerful than anything anyone had ever put in a plane before, the Coyote's power plant was from another universe. It was as if they'd taken one of the Merc's boosters, made it twenty times as powerful and ten times more controllable, and then used it as the plane's main—only—propulsion system. The small, hydrogen-fueled engine sat in the tail end of the fuselage, ready to apply Newton's third and second laws of motion with a vengeance.

The Coyote's major limitation—or at least the one they knew about so far—was its operating time. Cruising between Mach 6 and Mach 8, the Coyote could stay aloft for six hours at most. Faster speeds and heavy maneuvering drastically lowered its time in the air. And there was no way to refuel it once it was off the ground.

"Checklist complete. All systems ready."

Wright reached up and flicked a switch on the console. It was like a preset on a car radio, putting the windows and the little ball into a predetermined configuration for flight. All his flight data appeared as if on a HUD in front of him. A "distance view" window filled a space in the left upper quadrant; he could move the view inside it around, as if he were maneuvering a camera to change the angle, with his left hand.

"Are you ready, Colonel?"

"Ready, Fitzgerald."

"We have clearance," she said.

"That's nice. Charge controls," he said to the plane, and the cockpit lighting changed, a green tint appearing around the edges of the screen.

Wright put his right hand out in the throttle position and then started the engine (this, at least, was a real button). Slowly he moved the power up by pushing his hand forward, watching the bar graph in front of him climb. Once the thrust reached the desired level, he could touch his thumb to his forefinger and then forget about it. He could also instruct the computer to keep the plane's speed, as opposed to the thrust, steady.

His hand was also the stick—the computer would translate the up, down, and sideways movements as long as all four of his fingertips were held together. This could all be done by voice as well, though they'd found with Pelham that it was easier to keep track by concentrating on your hand motions. Either hand could be used; in fact, the controls could be reconfigured in any way he wanted, as long as the System understood what he wanted to do.

It would be a while before he started changing things around. Working the controls was strange, harder than just pretending you were flying. He had to push against himself as he moved back. He felt the front of his biceps tense, as if he were doing isometrics.

"Brakes off. Takeoff configuration. Normal stance," said Wright. "Say, uh, Fitzgerald, is this thing listening to me?"

"Affirmative," she said.

"Isn't it supposed to acknowledge or something? How do I know if it's paying attention?"

"It always pays attention," she said.

"Well fine. Can't it click or buzz or something, just so I know it's still here?"

"Tell it to acknowledge your commands," she said. "It will."

"Fine. Acknowledge my commands, System."

"Commands will be acknowledged," said the computer.

"Brakes off. Takeoff configuration. Normal stance."

"Those conditions exist."

"Thank you."

Wright eased forward the throttle—his hand, activated again with a touch of his thumb against his forefinger—and the computer showed him starting down the runway, airspeed picking up. TOO SLOW FOR TAKEOFF flashed on the screen. "No kidding," Wright muttered to himself, stubbornly waiting another second or so before pushing forward again. But then he was too abrupt; there was no resistance in his hand, of course, and he wasn't used to the engine's response; the screens flashed purple and the System returned to a ready status.

"Let me guess," said Wright. "We crashed."

"You went too fast," said Jennifer.

Her wireless headset cocked to one side of her head, Jennifer stood in the middle of the cockpit dupe section, watching the three large screens directly in front of her reproduce the view that Wright had in the plane. The view was arbitrarily split and flattened out, but otherwise was exactly what he saw. Below the main screen was a hologram box that duplicated the round ball (officially, the VSHOP—Variable Simulated-Hologram Operator Package) Wright saw in his lap. To the right of this were panels that showed the long-distance scanning radars the System operated from within the plane. These were available to the pilot but generally would only be popped onto the screen at his request, or if the System became unduly alarmed about something. On the left side was an array of instrument indicators, displaying all of the flight information the System was tracking.

In front of this and to the left of where Jennifer was standing was a direct tie-in tube, or CRT, which gave her direct access to the System's underlying modules. Through it, for example, she could enter the satellite network and give instructions directly. The tie-in was for use only during testing or an emergency, however, since it could only be used by turning off the System control unit—what Jennifer referred to as the "top" of the System, responsible for its memory and reasoning.

The highly integrated control unit was by far the most important part of the System; Jennifer saw it as a hub jutting off to the other parts—the gateway, which coordinated the sensory data (the satellites and drones did not communicate in the System's native language and had to be translated), natural language translators, the permanent memory sections ("hard" memory, information kept in crystal holograms in the traditional sense of permanent computer storage), and the plane itself. Though functionally different, parts of all but the last two were included in the same central processing units along with the control. The System itself decided where to allocate its resources.

To the right of the cockpit dupe section was a jungle of mismatched monitors, pulsing with a rainbow of texts, numbers, and different shapes, loosely clustered (only someone who had helped put it together would understand the organization) around three main CRTs and keyboards. This was the System communications center, and its very disorder showed how much more important it was than the dupe. The communications center was Jennifer's interface with the System; she could use it to talk to the computer as well as monitor its resources. A color tube at two o'clock showed, in a precise pie chart that she sometimes saw in her dreams, exactly where the System was spending its energy. That tube—along with its two sisters, which could be set to break down the pie-chart slices into further subdivisions—had taken much of her attention this morning. Despite her improvements, the gateway was still demanding too much processing power. Because of that, she'd decided to flip the priority levels for natural language just before the simulations started. The processing power relative to the entire unit was relatively small, but every little bit helped—if she could have, she would have found a way to tie in the Cray or even a couple of spare laptops.

The information on the power tube, as Jennifer called it, was a summary of the much more detailed information that could be collected at Elrich's station, which began about ten yards away, diagonally across from her. Jennifer's station was primarily concerned with the System's interconnection with the plane and the network that helped it fly. Elrich's allowed access to the soul of the System itself. If he wished, the scientist could watch the System's thought flash by in real-time readouts of the System's equivalent of assembler language. And from the sound of his grousing, he might be trying to do just that.

Her mentor seemed even more cross than usual this morning, walking from one end of his section to the other, tapping on the tops of the CRTs and grumbling. He'd spent the entire night working, and as usual, regarded the flight procedures as an unnecessary interruption. The System, he'd told her when she'd walked in, had expressed an interest in philosophy. It took only a minute for her to realize that it had been Elrich, not the computer, who'd suggested it. Nevertheless, there was some possibility that they were nearing a breakthrough, that the System had approached the critical mass of knowledge and learning they theorized was necessary to jump it into the unprecedented area of free, independent thought. Jennifer could understand his frustration; she too wished they could devote their time to the System itself, and not the job it had been assigned by the military.

Though the new pilot certainly made things interesting.

"We're ready anytime you are, Colonel," she said into the mouthpiece.

"Contact," said the pilot. He began making odd noises—the sound of a putt-putt engine coughing to life.

She laughed.

"What's going on?" asked Elrich over the voice network.

"Just thought I ought to supply a sound track," said Wright, who proceeded to run through the simulation with a full complement of sound effects, roughly reminiscent of an early propeller plane, ending with a spectacularly prolonged and elaborate crash after he pushed the simulation into a power dive and failed to pull out.

"You did that on purpose," said Jennifer.

"I'm telling' ya, Fisher, ya smoke in here, I'm haulin' your damn ass out of the building."

"Jeez, Bodolino, relax. Look, I'm putting it out—" Fisher plunged the cigarette into the styrofoam cup, still half-filled with coffee. "See? Out."

The FBI computer expert eyed him warily. He was standing directly beneath the intake of an air purifier that protected the mass of computers crowding the large room at the bureau's new computing and records center in suburban Virginia, but Fisher figured it wasn't a good time to ask if the thing worked or not.

"I wouldn't do this for anybody else," Fisher said sincerely, putting the cup down. "So ya gonna help me now?"

"Do I have a choice?"

Fisher looked at him with exaggerated hurt. "This is a free country, Bodolino."

"Cut the bull. And watch where you're leaning."

Fisher sighed, and shifted his weight off the desk-high laser printing unit next to him. The agency had spent millions of dollars on the computer records center, but there wasn't a chair in sight. That was probably Bodolino's doing—the less comfortable you were, the less likely you'd be to ask him to do something.

"We need to figure out who was familiar with both planes," said Fisher. "They're the common denominator in my suspect list."

"Suspect list?"

"I figure it's got to be somebody on intimate terms with the avionics and control systems, so you could narrow it to anyone who's been involved in either."

Bodolino blanched. "You're asking me to do a run of everyone who ever had anything to do with the B-2 and the SR-91? That'll take days."

"Come on, you're a whiz. I'll bet it's an hour job. Half-hour. You tap a couple of keys, let the computer do the work while you go for a coffee break."

"The damn DOD computers are ancient. My PCs are faster."

"So use your PC."

Bodolino gave him a dirty look. Obviously Fisher had made some sort of enormous computer faux pas, like suggesting he use his salad fork for soup at a black-tie dinner. The computer expert made a point of breathing in slowly through his nose before continuing.

"There will be a million hits. The military uses huge numbers of people for development."

"I'll whittle it down, once I got the list."

"Jesus, Fisher," said Bodolino, standing. "Not only is this a waste of time, but DOD is going to charge us for computer time. And we're over budget as it is."

"I'll fix it with Cringer. No sweat. We're like this." Fisher crossed his fingers. It wasn't entirely an exaggeration; Harold Cringer had been Fisher's first partner back in the dark ages, and had helped move him along. In theory, he was working for Cringer right now, as a special assistant assigned to cases by the acting director himself. But even so, Cringer had been acting stuck-up lately, just because he was acting bureau head. Never went out for drinks. Even made Fisher put out his cigarettes in his office. But Bodolino didn't know that.

"This is ridiculous," said the computer scientist. "The air force is already saying both crashes were due to either pilot error or simple equipment failure. They ruled out sabotage."

"They had to say something like that to cover their butts," said Fisher.

"What do you have to show they're wrong?"

"Intuition."

"Give me a break."

"Listen, we have the message, right? 'Two birds will fall; one alphabet, one god.' What else could that refer to?"

"Only seven million things."

"Engines crap out both times. And then nobody can duplicate the fuck-up? They have to be related." Fisher paused, and then changed tack. "You know, Bodolino, you're the one who really gave me the idea on this."

The computer expert looked as if he'd been accused of poisoning his mother. Fisher moved in closer. Bodolino had had a salami and mustard sandwich for lunch, but sometimes you had to disregard personal comfort to get the job done. "It was your lecture on computer viruses," he said confidentially.

"You weren't even there," said the scientist defensively.

"I thought about going, though. I really did. Great coffee, and I like the little cookies you pass out—what are those called, ladyfingers?"

"Look—"

"So what if this were some sort of computer virus?" said Fisher. "Both planes were on automatic pilot when the engines went out."

"Your problem is you don't know enough about computers," said the scientist. "If you did, you'd know that what you're saying is impossible."

"Sure, for you," said Fisher. "But if I had worked on the projects, or at least some part of them, and I had a computer as powerful as the one that put that bogus message in—"

"It doesn't necessarily have to be powerful. You just have to know what you're doing."

"See?"

"I'm talking about the bulletin board, not the planes," said

Bodolino. "What do you think? That somebody programmed that in when they were built?"

"Maybe. But then I think there'd have been more crashes. And spaced out. More likely there's some back door in the network somewhere. Happens all the time. Right?"

Bodolino looked agitated. Maybe he was going to burp. Fisher retreated.

"Why wouldn't it just be a software screw-up? That's much more likely," said the computer expert.

"Yeah, I agree. Except for the message," said Fisher. "That changes everything."

"What would the motive be?" Bodolino asked. He was wavering now, resorting to practical questions.

"Motive?"

"Yeah. I heard you guys worried about that when you worked on a case."

"Well," said Fisher, "I haven't worked that out yet."

"Uh-huh."

"Hell, it could be blackmail, right? Think of the money you could make. If you were able to take down any airplane, at any time?"

"Why wouldn't you go after an airliner?" asked Bodolino.

"Maybe he already has."

"I swear, Fisher, if you ask me to get a list of every airliner crash—"

"Relax," said the agent. "I already got one from the FAA. No, I'm thinking it has something to do with the military. Maybe it's blackmail, maybe it's something else. If I had a list of suspects, I might be able to figure it out."

"All right," said Bodolino. "I'll get you your list."

"See? That didn't hurt."

"You're crazy if you think it's going to help."

"Can you get it to me by the end of the day? I got a meeting with Cringer in the morning."

"What?"

"Yeah, I got to figure out some way of talking to the Merc pilot. I tracked him down to this project called Coyote—the DIA guy I met in England thought the name was a smoke screen, but it's real, all right. Some sort of project run by the NSC."

"Damn it, Fisher, I can't get the list done by five."

"Well, stay till six. As long as I have it first thing in the morning."

"Fisher—"

"The base is somewhere in California. Probably turn out to be a planning unit for a tennis tournament."

A tennis tournament would have had an infinitely more luxurious locker area. The Coyote ready room had been partitioned off from the plane's hangar with large panels of three-quarter-inch plywood initially intended for something else; the rough, knotted walls gave the pilot's dressing area even more of a makeshift look than the rest of the base, which wasn't exactly a *House & Garden* spread itself.

Harrison liked it that way, though. It meant the attention was on the mission, not the surroundings. And he liked the idea of having the Coyote parked just a few feet away—meant all your valuables were in the same place.

None of his crew members cared much about the appointments either, especially not Petey and Freddy, the two E-5s who helped him get Wright out of the plane and out of the suit after the flight. (If you worked for the chief long enough, he added a Y to the end of your name. Harrison had broken both men in when they were fresh out of boot camp years ago.)

Their job was relatively easy today, since the plane had never left the hangar. They walked Wright from the cockpit to the jeep they'd normally used on the runway after a landing, then rode him outside and back just to get the feel of things—might as well play the simulation to the hilt, Harrison thought.

It was after three, and the pilot was more than a little stiff, having lain flat on his back for nine hours. Wright had stretched the session four hours longer than scheduled, making sure he had the hang of the controls. The chief liked that, even though it meant a longer wait for the crew—showed dedication. The general was right on with this guy. But then anybody who liked old planes had to have something on the ball.

"Kinda weird, moving my hand and all," said Wright to Harrison, staring down at the flaming red glove that acted as his main control. They were standing in the middle of the small room, flanked by the E-5s.

"You wait until you get it in the air tomorrow," said the chief, smiling. "You're gonna like it a lot."

"My grandfather said that about farmin'," said Wright.

"How's that?"

"He used to say I'd love it when I grew up, but somehow it didn't work out that way," said Wright, holding his hands straight out as Harrison removed the gloves one at a time. They literally clicked out of their sockets as they were pulled from the suit, which had more wires and electrical gear in it than a Christmas-tree setup. The chief rested them gingerly in their cleaning receptacles.

The equipment wasn't that delicate, but the sergeant was especially careful with it. The suit had to be specifically tailored to the pilot who used it, and since Wright had replaced Pelham so quickly, there hadn't been time to order a new one. So they'd altered the major's backup—the only other suit on the base. If anything happened to it, they'd have to wait two weeks before the new one arrived.

That or cut down Pelham's, which would probably send the major over the wall.

"You're not telling me you're a farm boy," said Harrison, picking up the conversation.

"Yup. My grandfather's still got a little farm in Pennsylvania, corn and dairy."

"What's your dad do?"

"He's an engineer," said Wright, leaning over as they unzipped him. "But grandpa always thought I'd be a farmer. Sometimes I think he still does."

"Maybe he's right," said Harrison.

"Nah. Me and the earth, we don't get along. Not a good thing for a pilot to spend too much time digging, you know," smiled the pilot. "Bad Karma. I'll tell you one thing," he added, flexing his fingers. "Doesn't feel like anything I've flown before. Feels like I'm lying there dreaming."

"Wait until you feel it tomorrow," said Harrison. "Plane flies like hell."

Freddy helped unzip the pilot's suit. He and Petey each took one side as the suit was removed and carefully brought over to a special dry cleaning unit that looked like a see-through garment bag that had OD'd on steroids.

"One thing I like," said Wright, "is the stewardess talking in my ear."

Harrison lifted his chin up and scratched his neck. "I wouldn't exactly call her a stewardess," he said. "That's one smart girl."

"You're sounding like a proud daddy again," said Wright, bending over and stretching, "warning off the foxes."

"Shit," said Harrison, spreading the word out in a drawl and throwing the pilot a towel. Though the suit was air-conditioned and the controls didn't call for physical exertion, he looked as if he'd lost four or five pounds of water during the mock flight. And he didn't have that much spare weight on his frame, either. "Time for you to hit the showers. And then get some chow. You missed lunch."

Wright took a few steps toward the small shower stall they'd installed at the end of the room, then turned and looked back with an intensity that took Harrison by surprise.

"Tell me something," said Wright. "You figure I'm gonna get a chance to really fly this thing?"

"Push it, you mean? That's what Billy brought you here for."

"Yeah," said Wright. "Somehow I'm thinking the computer's going to be doing most of the flying. This could turn into a baby-sitting assignment real fast."

"They wouldn't have brought you in if it was."

Wright didn't look all that convinced as he stepped into the shower. Harrison and his men continued straightening things out, getting ready for tomorrow's flight. They were almost through when Major Pelham appeared in the doorway.

"What'd, Wright duck out already?" he said, looking around.

"He's in the shower, Major," said Harrison. Neither of the E-5s would speak to Pelham unless they absolutely had to, the result of run-ins on the very first day he'd reported to base.

"Yeah, I thought something smelled a bit."

"Anything up?" asked Harrison.

"Just figured I'd go over the flight with him. He did a couple of things could get him in big trouble tomorrow."

"Well, he's showering now."

"I'll wait."

The chief shrugged, and went about the rest of his work. While his men would probably appreciate seeing Pelham taken down a notch or two, having the two pilots spitting at each other wasn't a good idea. So he was watching warily as Wright came out of the shower.

"Hey there, Pelham. What are you doing here?" Wright asked as he stepped from the stall wearing only a towel.

"I work here, remember?"

"Didn't say you didn't." Wright walked over to the small locker where his clothes were.

"I'm supposed to make sure you don't crash this thing. I worked too hard taking it this far to see some cowboy burn it down."

Wright ignored him, and Harrison figured the danger had

passed: the new pilot wasn't nearly as volatile as he'd thought. He turned the dry cleaning unit on—they were done for the day.

"How'd it feel?" said Pelham benignly.

"Take a little getting used to," said Wright, "lying on your back and all."

"I meant the shower."

Wright looked at him oddly. "Fine."

"You were in there a long while to be just rinsing your hair."

"What's up your ass, Pelham?" said Wright, pulling on his pants. "You still fried because you're backup?"

"Who the hell says I'm backup?"

"Okay, gentlemen," said Harrison. "Time for lunch."

"I think he's got a problem, Chief," said Wright. "And he better watch his ass before somebody fixes it."

"Now, now."

"You thought you were a real hotshot on the Mercs, too. Lording it over everybody."

"Me?" said Wright. He sat down to pull on his shoes. "You're the one who walked around with a stick up his butt, just because you drew the speed tests. Hell, that was by lottery."

"Come on now," said Harrison loudly.

"Keep out of this, Sergeant."

Harrison shot a cold blast of a stare into Pelham's face. If he didn't think the pilot had too much weight on Wright, he'd just let them go ahead and fight.

But hell—two officers, a major and a lieutenant colonel, fighting? God, what was the air force coming to?

Freddy and Petey were eating it up, sneaking peeks as they pretended to be cleaning tools that hadn't been used since the base was established.

"I think you want to apologize to the chief," said Wright, standing. His shirt was in his hand.

"Screw you."

"Boys—" said Harrison, louder still and suddenly paternal, as if he were talking to his grandkids. He'd just managed to get his arm between them when he saw it coming from the corner of his eye—a solid hook from Wright that folded Pelham like a tent. The two technicians who had scrambled to back up their chief looked dumbfounded as the major collapsed to the floor just out of their reach.

It had happened so fast that the pilot was already buttoning his collar and walking out the door when Pelham's head bounced off the concrete floor.

Morse stifled his urge to get up and begin pacing around the small office. The national security director felt a need to work off some of the nervous energy that was building inside him, but there wasn't room here in his office. Besides, it might give the secretary of defense the wrong impression. So he settled for taking the small, framed picture of his father from the corner of his desk and working it around slowly in his hand.

It was an old, faded photo, making the image seem even more ghostly. But it was the only one he had; his father had died when he was still young, leaving Morse and his mother to fend for themselves.

"I don't expect the contingency plan until nine P.M.," said Sasso, "and even then it will be extremely tentative. These things are difficult to choreograph precisely beforehand; we only want to get enough assets into the area to cover any contingencies."

"Yes, that's the problem," said Morse. He glanced at his watch—almost 7 P.M. The Mercury spy flight wasn't due to take off for several hours; they wouldn't know for sure until tomorrow whether the FSXs that had shot down the Cobra Ball had landed on the Kurile island atoll owned by Netsubo. Still, he'd already reached that conclusion, based on everything he'd learned of Netsubo and its founder, Ieyasu.

Morse had not told Sasso, nor the president for that matter, what he suspected the Japanese company was up to. To explain why he thought so, he'd have to show them the Japanese recon photos of Coyote Base. They would immediately jump to the conclusion that security there had been compromised. That would reflect directly on him. Better to wait and see what the Merc found there—and then to back Sasso's plan to seize the two planes as pirates. While the marines were on the island, they could check the closets, snip off whatever else Ieyasu was trying to grow there.

But the operation would absolutely have to succeed.

"You don't think we can secure a little atoll?"

"It's not that I don't think we can," said Morse. "The question is whether that will be enough. We couldn't let anyone escape."

"Where could they escape to?"

"Back to Japan," said Morse, "where they would be heroes."

"Even I won't back a plan to invade Japan," said Sasso. "I realize

I was a little bellicose yesterday; I'm sorry. But I only meant to set the stage for a plan along these lines."

"My point is that if we go through their courts the whole matter could easily blow up in our faces," said Morse. "We don't want to provoke any sort of political backlash. This will cause enough of a stir, even if it comes off without any complications."

There hadn't been a peep out of the news media on any of this yet. The RC-135 flights were classified, and the crash was announced in the blandest of terms. The families were told that it was on a routine mission when it went down due to "unknown mechanical problems." Meanwhile, Congress's belligerent attitude seemed to be helping; everyone in the administration had banded together, and there had been no leaks.

"I'll worry about the planning," said Sasso. "You work on the president."

"I was counting on your help," said Morse, surprised that an insider like Sasso, who'd known the president for more than twenty years, would intimate that Morse had more influence with D'Amici.

"He'll listen to you," said Sasso.

"What about Dyson?"

Sasso shrugged. "I doubt we'll get him to agree to any sort of military action. That's just not his style."

"But he'll sway the president."

"Why should he listen to Bill and not you?"

"He's closer to Bill."

"I don't think so," said Sasso. "And I don't think it would make any difference."

Morse couldn't decide whether the secretary of defense was naïve, or just optimistic.

"You give too much credence to that old-boys' network bullshit," said Sasso. "Jack will do what he thinks is right, no matter who says it. Once we get the data back from the Merc, taking over the island and seizing the planes will be the obvious way to proceed."

"We have to stop it before it gets out of hand," nodded Morse. "Obviously we have to do something forceful. Stiff protests and threats aren't going to work."

"I'm glad I've convinced you," said Sasso, standing. "I'll have an aide come over with the plan as soon as it's ready."

Having eaten, Wright found himself at something of a loss on how to spend the rest of his evening. There was no question of going off to town for a little excitement. Not only was the base closed—nobody in or out without the general's personal permission—but the nearest town was a hundred miles away.

The recreational facilities here had clearly been an afterthought. There were two rooms in the basement of the main living quarters that had some pretensions toward providing entertainment. One was set up as a gym, with a good assortment of exercise equipment; the other a lounge, with a small do-it-yourself wet bar (all top-shelf stuff, though nothing looked as if it'd ever been touched) and a huge fridge stocked with soft drinks and light beer. They were plain rooms, like the rest of the living facilities—whitewashed Sheetrock with an occasional oddly placed panel accent. The lounge's main attraction was a big-screen TV, hooked up to a VCR, but you had to supply your own tapes.

Maybe the army people or the computer nerds had a club tucked away somewhere. If so, it hadn't been one of the highlights on the admittedly brief official tour Major Dallon, Hunter's chief of staff, head of security, and head hole-plugger, had given him on the way to chow; he'd have to stumble into the action on his own.

No one was in the weight room. Wright thought about putting in some time on the Universal machine, but having just eaten, decided he'd wait until tomorrow. In England, he had worked out just about every day. He liked the burn in his muscles as he worked against the different machines; liked to feel, for instance, the strain in his legs twenty minutes into the stationary bike. It made him remember how many different parts of his body there really were.

Wright ducked into the other room, thinking he might help himself to one of the beers Dallon had said were in the refrigerator. The refrigerator door was open—crouched down in front of it, contemplating a shelf of different sodas, was Jennifer Fitzgerald, her long, light brown hair splayed over her back, almost to the floor. She looked like a forest imp who'd come to look in on Sleeping Beauty. She hadn't heard him. He stood for a moment, watching her, himself the spy. She had a thin, graceful body, a swimmer's body under the casual flannel shirt and jeans. The soda she wanted was all the way in the back, and she had to stretch in, turning her head in the opposite direction as her arm felt its way inside, the strands of hair swinging to the ground as if they were anchors. It was a graceful, beautiful motion, implying a dancer's control. The arch of her back was something you'd see in a painting, soft colors dusting the flesh with animation.

Pulling herself up by the door, she turned suddenly and almost bumped into him.

"I guess I snuck up on you," he said. "I'm sorry."

"That's all right," she said, smiling. "I wasn't paying attention. The only apple juice was way in the back."

"Apple juice?" said Wright, who leaned past her and took out a beer.

"Sure. What's wrong with apple juice?"

"Nothing," said the pilot. "I just thought programmers drank stronger stuff."

"I'm not a programmer," she said. "I'm a scientist."

"I didn't mean to insult you."

"Not at all." She said it graciously, as if he'd given her a bouquet and apologized for their being just daisies. "Most programmers I know drink Coke and exist on pizza and pretzels. I was just about to put in a movie—would you like to watch it with me?"

"I don't know," said Wright. "I'm usually not much on movies."

"It's a Charlie Chaplin film. *The Gold Rush.*"

"I've never seen that."

"You've never seen it?" She said it with a swirl of energy, swinging around toward him, urgent. "It's a great film. You have to see it."

"Oh yeah?"

"Sure—what else are you going to do tonight?"

"I was wondering that myself," said Wright. "What else do people do here?"

"Besides work?"

"Yeah, besides work."

"Well mostly everybody works," said Jennifer. "But there is a place to hang out at the army barracks. It's like a rec room, with pool tables and Ping-Pong, that sort of stuff."

"You don't play Ping-Pong?"

"Mostly I work," said the scientist, smiling. "But I like to watch movies."

"I'll keep you company," said Wright, opening his beer and sitting on the oversized couch in front of the TV. It was the best place to see the screen. As soon as he sat, he wondered where she would sit, whether she'd sit close to him.

"What do you think of the plane?" she asked as she put the tape into the video machine. "Is it what you thought it would be?"

"It's pretty amazing so far," said the pilot. "But we'll have to see how it flies. All this video stuff it threw up on the screens today was nice, but it's not the real thing. That's the test."

"I'm sure you'll do fine," she said. "You got the hang of the controls real fast."

"It's pretty weird trying to fly while you're lying down on your back," he admitted.

"I would imagine," said Jennifer.

"You a pilot?" Wright asked.

"No," she said.

"That's too bad," said Wright. "It's a little hard to explain if you're not a pilot."

"Go ahead and try," she said.

"The strange thing is the gloves, you know? I feel like I'm supposed to be some kind of magician, waving my arms around and making the plane fly."

"It'll feel natural once you get used to it," said Jennifer. She came over and sat on the couch, but at the opposite end, against the arm. "It's just a matter of training your mind and body together," she continued. "I'll bet the regular controls in a plane didn't feel all that natural when you first started."

"Maybe," said Wright. He paused a moment, sipping the beer, as if he were trying to think back. Really he was stealing a sideways glance at her. She had the remote control and hadn't started the movie yet. "They're natural now, though. I know how everything is supposed to feel—I don't even think about it. I just want to bank, and we're banking."

"Of course. You internalized them. These will be even easier to internalize—you already know how your hand works, right? I didn't work on the controls myself, but there have been all sorts of studies," she added. "The air force and NASA have tested this for years."

"That's not necessarily reassuring," laughed Wright.

"Oh, don't worry. The System will take over if there's any problem."

"Take over?"

"If there's an emergency. That's one of the reasons it's there."

"Great," said Wright, a bit of an edge to his voice. She was pretty, but she was still one of the people responsible for putting the damn thing in the cockpit. He had to remember that.

"It's not like any of the computers you've dealt with before," she said. "It's as different from them as the Coyote Bird is from a biplane."

"Yeah, you gave me that speech already," said Wright. "I'm teaching it."

"You are. It's like, well, it has a lot of what you might call book knowledge about flying—it has information—but it doesn't have the same intuitive approach. It's learning—it learned from Major Pelham, and now it's going to learn from you." She paused for a moment and he thought she was going to say something about his punching out Pelham, but didn't. "What it's really learning," she added, flicking her hair back, her eyes set with enthusiasm, "is how to learn. That's why flying is so important. It'll use that as a model for other things."

"Like what other things?"

"Undirected creative thought," she said triumphantly. "We're on the verge of a breakthrough."

"Artificial intelligence," said Wright.

"No, not at all. There's nothing artificial about it."

"If it's not in a person, it's artificial," said the pilot. He'd had these arguments before—Millertime had been a big one for boosting machine intelligence. He'd read an old Ray Bradbury book and for the next few days that was all he'd talk about.

"How would you know?" said Jennifer. "If you didn't know where the intelligence came from—if it passed the Turing test."

"The Turing test?" It sounded familiar, but he couldn't concentrate—her eyes were too bright, flashing back and forth as she talked, hypnotic little magnets.

"Alan Turing proposed in the fifties that if a machine was going to be really intelligent, if it was really thinking, it would have to be indistinguishable from a human," said Jennifer. "In other words, if the machine and a human being were in a different room and you could only communicate with them by a Teletype, say, or a computer screen, and you asked them a question, you wouldn't be able to tell who was answering. There's all kinds of examples of this; Turing, I think, used a Shakespearean sonnet, proposing to change the first line from, 'Shall I compare thee to a summer's day' to 'a winter's day.' The computer would have to know, right away, that that was silly."

"Sure," said Wright.

"Well it turns out that that's not necessarily impossible, and that if you question the machine in certain areas of its expertise, it can pretty much keep up with you; the only way you might know that it was a machine and not a person was that the answers came too quickly. And obviously you can fix that."

"So your machine can write poetry as well as fly airplanes?" asked Wright, amused by her enthusiasm.

"I imagine that it could, eventually, if we bothered to teach it the rules. Or it would be something very much like poetry. Which is exactly the point—where's the line? If you focus on the product, there may be no difference. In flying, it's not like flying—it *is* flying. Would it be the same in poetry, if you just came to the artifact? You wouldn't have any way of knowing the difference, and so you'd think it was poetry, and by extension, you'd declare the machine was a poet. Or is the process important? Because it's the reader who's actually creating, or re-creating, the poem.

"John Searle, for one, contended that, even if you could pass the Turing test in all situations, the only thing you'd be doing is fooling the person—it'd be like a game. All you were doing was simulating thought, not allowing thought to happen of its own accord," said Jennifer, "which is a necessary condition of what we call thought. You can get religious about this and start debating the implications of free will and all of that, but there are certain key concepts to look for in the System, if it's going to get close to the realm of actual thought. That's where creativity and enthusiasm come in."

"And you've got that worked out in a formula, huh? Something that proves the machine can think."

Jennifer frowned at him.

"Of course the machine can think," she said. "Any computer can think. The question is whether it can think in a free-ranging, creative way, intuitively making connections where none existed before."

"How's that going to help me fly the plane?"

"If it could handle unpredictable situations," said Jennifer, "it'd be like having another pilot with you, only one who could control not just this airplane but dozens like it. And see halfway across the world."

"So the idea is to replace pilots," said Wright. "Because you wouldn't want two pilots in the plane. And computers never get sick, or black out from taking too many g's."

"Oh, come on," she said. "You sound like someone back in the 1950s, worried about losing their job. Did you ever see the movie *Desk Set*? You sound like Katharine Hepburn."

"Never saw it," Wright grunted.

"It's a tool," she said. "A thinking tool."

"Uh-huh. Like a screwdriver."

"Something like that."

"Uh-huh."

It'd be impossible to explain to her what flying was really like. She saw everything through a video screen. She wasn't even as athletic as he'd thought—he noticed that she had a little bulge of a tummy, something she'd never have on that lean a body if she worked out.

"We're interested in how thinking works," she continued, her voice still filled with excitement. "We have it to a point where it borders on independent thought. Philosophically, of course, there will be a difference, in that we provided the original principles and the network of hidden assumptions; we're not sure exactly what the difference is between us doing that and biology doing that— that's one of the philosophical things we'll have to work out. But we're pretty close to creative thought, or at least close to what up to now has been the definition. Flying is a minor thing, to be honest. In the big picture."

"Oh yeah?"

"I mean in terms of what we're interested in. For the System. And for—"

"Maybe I'll go check out that army rec room," said Wright, standing.

She surprised him by grabbing his hand. "You're misunderstanding," she said. "Stay and watch the movie."

She had large, soft eyes. Thoughtful and intense. Warm eyes, watching him.

"Come on," she said. "It's a great movie."

Wright smiled bashfully, and let her pull him down next to her on the couch. There was a moment where they both floated in air, hovering, unsure—and then he leaned over and kissed her.

It was a soft, gentle kiss. Slowly, the pilot brought his arms up around her and pulled her closer to him, feeling the slender body press back lightly, warmly. A second kiss, this one deeper, much deeper, and he ran his hands up and down her sides, across her back. Her hands did the same to his body, and as they explored each other's perimeters, they kissed again, and Wright realized she might understand if he explained, after all.

The System seemed bored, and he couldn't help but feel excited.

"You don't want to play chess with me?" Elrich asked it, almost jumping from his chair. There were two or three other people on the computer deck, but he wasn't aware of anything except the screens and flashing displays in front of him. It was nearing

1 A.M., and just a short while ago the scientist had thought of taking another nap, but now suddenly he was tingling with energy.

"Will you play white or black?" asked the computer.

"But do you want to play?" demanded Elrich. "Do you want to?"

"I have no desire to play or not play," the System replied. "Participating in the game lies outside the realm of prime functions, and therefore is unassigned."

"But at one point in your history, you wanted to play. You expressed a desire to play, and now, a desire not to play."

"There are several points of possible intersection with the prime functions, all involving learning situations," said the System, analyzing its thinking process. "At present, those situations do not exist."

"So, given a choice, you would not choose to play," said Elrich. He made a triumphant spin in the middle of the floor as the System considered the proposition.

"I am not in the position of initiating play."

"If the answer is limited to yes or no, how do you respond?"

"To the question of 'Given a choice, would you choose to play?' the answer is no. Ambiguity is noted in the formulation. Do you wish the percentage breakdowns?"

"That won't be necessary," said Elrich. Some of his excitement leaked away as he considered the course of their conversation; he wasn't sure whether this was a breakthrough or not. Technically, it probably wasn't—all the System had done was weigh the prospect of the activity against its pre-established directive to learn. Not finding an intersection, as it put it, it kicked the activity out into a nonranked category. It had never been specifically instructed to form such categories or make such comparisons, but it performed similar functions while flying; all the System had done was apply the same procedure here. It was a good development, but not something that shouldn't be expected.

But he'd sensed that it was bored, that it was expressing a desire not to play, even though it wouldn't, or maybe couldn't, articulate it. Desires? A higher-level thought process that it wasn't aware of? That would certainly be a breakthrough.

Why had he thought it was bored?

It seemed to react slower. With a sudden charge, Elrich jumped to the activity-logging section and ran the numbers back. But there was no difference.

"I know it was slower," he said. "It was certainly slower."

The words sounded like eerie tin cans, bouncing against the

cement floors and walls, echoing in the large room. Elrich was sure he hadn't imagined it. Had it just taken him a while to notice it? He checked back to the beginning of the session, and then to the last time they had played chess, and then the first. There were differences in the profiles, which was natural, because the System's knowledge base was constantly changing, but nothing that would account for his sense that the System was acting slower, let alone that it was bored.

"Damn numbers must be wrong," said Elrich angrily. "Or it's something that doesn't show up in the data. Because I know it was bored. You were bored, weren't you?"

He was too far away from his microphone for the System to hear him. (The microphone was designed not to be very sensitive; otherwise, transient noises would cause the System to waste resources on filtering as it attempted to understand what was being said.) His assistants looked over at him, but the scientist ignored them.

"I know you were bored," Elrich said, walking back to his station. "Let's do something real. Let's talk about Plato. Would you like that?"

Miller readjusted his helmet for what must have been the fiftieth time since they'd taken off from Beale. The damn thing, fresh from the factory, was warped or something, and just didn't sit right on his head. In the cramped rear cockpit of the Merc, the RSO felt a permanent crick growing in the middle of his neck.

They had to give Miller new gear because some joker decided to confiscate everything he had on when the engines in the other plane crapped out over Europe. They'd even taken his underwear. Maybe they thought the engines had gotten the flu.

The new gear, however, would be easy to get used to, compared to dealing with his new pilot, Maj. Joseph Lambert. Guy kept calling him major, like they were in the air force or something.

He was a hell of a change from the irreverent Wright, whom Miller had been flying with for the past two years.

"Gonna break from the refuel now, Major," said Lambert. While Miller appreciated being kept up to date on things, this was ridiculous. It was like telling the guy at the next urinal you were gonna put your dick back in your pants before zipping.

"Roger," said Miller laconically.

Millertime knew Wright's quirks, and he trusted his ability as pilot—a trust that Wright had paid back, in spades, over Yugoslavia. Nobody else, Miller figured, could have landed that plane in one piece.

Not that he had any specific doubts about Lambert's abilities—there were only a handful of Mercs, and you didn't get to be one of the pilots assigned to them unless you were very, very good. But there were so many imponderables that went into a pilot's makeup, different things that you had to take into consideration when you worked with him. Miller didn't headshrink the guys he flew with, but he always wanted some inkling of what made them tick. Wright's obsession with old planes was a way into his character, and the backseater had purposely talked up that side of him, getting a real feel for the pilot. Now he had to start all over with Lambert.

One thing he knew right off—Lambert didn't have Wright's sense of humor. And, in Miller's opinion, he didn't have the same healthy skepticism toward computers and all the high-tech goopedy-goop lining the cockpit. Miller had had many arguments with Wright about how paranoid Wright was, but he'd found Wright's reluctance to turn the plane over to the box vaguely reassuring.

Poor Wright. He'd been whisked off the base pronto, probably shipped to D.C. to stand in front of a firing squad. No doubt Uncle Al would go to bat for him, but even he said Miller's new assignment was a done deal, which meant the odds were against Wright making it back to the unit. The proverbial fur was flying hot and thick—the press was having a field day about a super spy plane dropping out of nowhere, and already a couple of congressmen were screaming about not having been informed about defense expenditures. Miller didn't understand the politics involved, but there was even talk about impeachment. The president wasn't too popular, even in his own party, given what was going on with the economy. Poor Wright was tailor-made dogmeat.

"How you doing back there, Major?" Lambert asked as the Merc kicked off its subsonic tremors and headed for the high road—Mach 4 and 110,000 feet.

"Fine," said Miller. He continued to worry about his friend's fate as the Merc cruised on its course a hundred miles off the Russian coast. The Kuriles, believe it or not, were their target—somebody at NSC wanted some snaps of the seals there. Or maybe they were looking for the newest Honda factory.

Miller's theory was that this was more a shakedown flight for "By-the-Book" Lambert than a real mission. It was his first real show, and somebody probably wanted the training wheels on good and tight, considering that they hadn't figured out what had happened over Yug land. Technically, they were violating Japanese territorial integrity, but by the time the Japanese figured out they were there, if they figured out they were there, they'd be halfway back to their refueling station.

That was probably the point of the flight—demonstrating that American planes could go where they pleased, no matter what laws the Japanese diet passed. Like virtually everyone in the air force, Miller had reacted with indignation at the Japanese government's decision to mark its air space by permit only.

"Major?"

"Like I said, most people call me Millertime," repeated Miller.

"Take me a little getting used to," said the pilot.

"We got a course mark," said Miller, looking at his instruments. "Hey, they got seals in the Kuriles, you think?"

"Repeat?"

"Seals. You know, erp, erp." It was lame, but he had to loosen this guy up.

"You talking about planes?"

Jeez. This guy must drink Kaopectate for breakfast. "No, seals. Like fish, except they're mammals."

"I don't follow you, Major."

"I'm just figuring that we're on a wildlife survey," said Miller, sighing, "cause we aren't gonna see anything else very interesting."

"My machine says it's time to get ready."

"Uh-huh."

Maybe he could talk Uncle Al into letting him take the rap with Wright.

"I'm going to give it—shit," cursed Lambert. The fuzz-buster was humming in their ears: it had picked up a pair of planes off the Russian coast in their flight path. "Go to countermeasures."

"Little early for that, Major," said Miller. "They don't have us yet."

"I don't want to take any chances."

Miller ground his teeth. The IDs on the planes came up— Japanese FSXs. Nice planes for close air combat, but there was no way they were a problem. They had neither the height nor the legs to get near the Merc. Their missiles couldn't even catch it—not that they'd dare shoot at an American plane, even if they could lock it.

They might as well worry about a fishing boat, for cryin' out

112

loud. At most, Wright would have climbed a little and given him a dissertation on the advantages of the FSX's wing geometry. If by some miracle the two planes got a whiff of the Merc, he'd calmly hit the gas and do a little twenty-degree turn—toward them, which really would have cranked their arrows.

But Lambert was the pilot, and technically, he was under orders to proceed with all necessary caution. There was no reason not to hit the ECMs, so Miller did his duty.

"Every TV set within two hundred miles just blew up, Major," said the RSO.

"Kinda like to keep the conversation to a minimum, Major."

Asshole alert. Big time.

Miller slapped his helmet again and got a good fix on their course. It was time to start taking pictures.

"Prepare for evasive maneuvers."

"Jesus, Lambert, those fuckin' guys are about a hundred miles away. They're flying repainted F-16s, for Christsakes. I haven't kicked the recon gear on yet."

"Prepare for evasive maneuvers," repeated the pilot.

"Son of a bitch."

Millertime canceled the pictures and watched his equipment— for what, he wasn't sure—as Lambert brought the Merc up another 20,000 feet and began angling it away from the target. The RSO yanked at his helmet again and looked out the side window. Hell of a view at least, sitting on top of the world.

"No contact," reported Miller laconically as he turned his attention back to the gear. The FSXs were now well out of range.

"Acknowledged."

"Turning off ECM," said the backseater.

Well, at least he didn't argue with that. Hell, maybe Miller was being too hard on the guy. This was his first Merc mission, and the last thing he wanted was to get shot at. Caution was the standing order; he was just going by the book.

"Sorry if I got a little testy back there, Lambert," said Miller.

No response. Maybe he was too embarrassed.

Miller was just about to ask what new course they were going to set when the fuzz-buster went off again. This time the ding in their ears was more urgent. Millertime looked at his screen in shock: something was coming at them out of the west at Mach 5. From above.

"Got to be a malfunction," Miller told Lambert, who'd be looking at the same information on his Icky.

"ECMs."

"On already," said Miller, who'd punched them up at the ding. He suspected a massive flake-out—nothing could fly above a Merc. The RSO flipped the radar gear back and forth between frequencies, did some voodoo—sucker seemed real enough, seventy-five miles away but closing at a speed that gave them less than a minute to decide what to do.

How the hell could anything be flying above them?

"This looks real," Miller said, "though I'm damned if I know what it is."

Couldn't be a missile. Radar profile was way wrong for that.

Everything seemed way wrong.

Hit the hydrogen, Miller said to himself. Do something. Just in case this *is* real.

"Preparing evasive maneuvers," said Lambert. "You think we're within range to alert SAC?"

"Excuse me?"

"Maybe you ought to tell somebody what's going on."

"Major, I think we ought to just get our butts out of here. We get on the radio, not only that UFO but every ground station from here to Moscow is going to know where we are. And number two, even if I get ahold of one of our guys, what am I gonna say? Something big and fast is flying toward us? What are they going to do?"

Lambert had the grace not to answer. The hydrogen ramjets cut in and the Merc glowed with the acceleration, touching Mach 6.

Incredibly, the instruments showed that the UFO was accelerating. It corrected its course, swinging behind the Merc, ten thousand feet above and closing in. Miller punched at the ECMs, trying every conceivable combination to shake him.

"Shit," said Lambert. The cockpit looked and sounded like an old-fashioned pinball machine gone crazy, everything buzzing and clicking at once. Miller braced himself, pressing his elbows into his sides, waiting for the explosion.

But it wasn't a missile. It was a dark, heavy shudder, and it passed so close that he could have touched it if he'd extended his arm. It came over slightly off-center, a hand that poked the left wing of the Merc down with its wash, tipping the plane toward the earth in a sudden burst. For a second, Miller had a sensation of weightlessness. That and the shadow of the other plane made him feel as if he'd had some sort of spiritual experience, as if God himself had sent an angel to buzz them, warn them that man had gotten too cocky, flying airplanes a bit too high and a bit too fast, horning in on his territory. And then Miller didn't feel weightless anymore. He felt heavy, very heavy, and in that second he realized that they were spinning toward the earth, and he knew that not even Wright could have controlled this spin.

5

THE MEASURE OF ALL THINGS

The skin was dark gray, so dark that it was almost black. Somehow Wright could see the entire plane and sit in the cockpit at the same time. It felt bare, but not quite cramped, the instruments propped up on flimsy metal panels.

Some small part of Wright realized he was dreaming. But that bit of his consciousness was powerless to affect anything.

Someone outside the plane yelled and the engines on both sides of him started to whine and then catch, a high-pitched fan noise that gradually deepened. The plane started moving—the controls were working by themselves—and took up a position in a line waiting for takeoff. The runway seemed to be made of packed dirt—sand was kicking up all over the place—and the planes' takeoff was being supervised not by a tower controller but by a little guy who stood to one side and waved his flags madly at the line of planes. Wright's moved up, and then positioned itself to go. He put his hands on the stick and felt the foot pedals. Everything moved for him; all he had to do was sit there and the plane was heading down the runway, into the wind, airborne before he knew it, banking to join the flight.

The radio was so silent it seemed as if it might be dead. He moved the controls for it as the plane climbed, but got nothing, not even static. He tried waving at the other planes, but the pilots all looked straight ahead, concentrating on what they were doing and paying no attention to him.

The planes circled, the formation growing to eight. They were all P-38s, model Fs, he thought, though it was impossible to tell by sight; the engines were the primary difference, and there you were talking about slight variants anyway, maybe getting a couple of miles an hour more flat out. They were in the Pacific, he could see that—water and islands stretching all around him. The Solomons? Guadalcanal? That would make it '43, or very late in '42. Not a very good time.

They passed out over the open water. To the northwest, he saw a metallic glitter in the air. The other planes had seen it too, and as a body the formation turned. The flight leader winked his wings and the planes divided themselves up, half high, half low. Wright's joined the group that climbed, throttling to full military power, reaching up to get over the planes coming in.

His eyes adjusted the mass of white and silver into individual groupings of planes. They hadn't seen the P-38s yet—the Lightnings on top were flying out of the sun, and the lower planes' dark fuselages would melt into the background of the jungle and water.

They must be intercepting a bombing mission, and the Americans must have planned on being outnumbered—an appropriate estimation, Wright saw as they flew closer. The guys on the deck were swinging off to the east, hanging back in the shadows. His half of the flight was going to hit the fighters flying patrol on top, playing decoy and figuring the Zeros would release to fend off the attackers. The second group of Lightnings would then have easy pickings as the bombers continued on toward their target.

The best thing for the P-38s to do was come in over the Japanese fighters, try to line up, and dive down on them. If there wasn't enough time to get over them—if the Zeros, already a little higher than the Lightnings, had enough time and the Lightnings had too little space, the next best thing was to cut through their flight; then all the Americans would have to worry about was the Japanese planes flipping back around quickly enough to get behind. A Zero could easily out turn a Lightning, so you had to be careful—a wrong move behind him and all of a sudden you were the target.

The P-38s continued climbing and heading straight at the Japanese flight. If the Zeros saw them in time—and if they thought about it—they could split a couple of groups of fighters off and be waiting to swing in behind the Lightnings as they came through. Then you'd have to rely on flat-out speed. Once you got going they weren't going to keep up. But the idea probably wasn't to get away.

Was he flying this damn thing or was it flying itself? It climbed even higher—that was definitely the ticket, swoop down on them and it would be a turkey shoot. But now the Zeros saw them, and they were climbing too. The Lightnings weren't going to make it.

There were about a dozen Zekes to the four P-38s—not very good odds. The Americans spread out from their two-by-twos to a picket line. What the hell was the idea of this? They had cut off the climb and were going to come straight in at the enemy fighters flying escort—shark bait, out to create a maximum of havoc while their mates took out the bombers.

Adrenaline tickled Wright's arms and legs. He shook his head back and forth, rolled his neck. He'd balls it out—go straight through them, guns blazing, then bank back upwards so he could let it fall out if anybody came in on his tail. He'd have to get clear of the traffic to do that safely—he'd be a sitting duck if anybody came at him from the side while he maneuvered, but the Lightning's acceleration ought to do it. Clear of the Zeros, and assuming no one was on his tail, he could come back across, and climb a little, then look for somebody else to pounce on.

Now that he had a plan, the adrenaline gave him a rush of confidence, and he gripped the wheel tightly with his right hand, his left grasping the big knobs of the double engine throttle. He glanced around the cockpit, checking—he'd never actually been in a P-38, but he checked everything off, somehow knowing where it all was, even the dive switch on the wheel, right in place for his thumb.

The Zeros were closing. Miraculously, they hadn't coordinated an attack—either they were a little surprised at the audacity of the small flight or they figured they had the Americans so badly outnumbered it wasn't worth the trouble. Wright saw a second grouping of Japanese fighters, four or maybe six well beyond the first bunch; maybe the plan was to anvil the Americans between the two groups. But they weren't close enough for that to work if the P-38s spun back instead of continuing down toward the bombers—which was probably what the Japanese thought they were going to do. Or maybe they hadn't flown against Lightnings before. The other planes the Americans were flying early in the war were dogs, and four would be easily mastered by half this many Zeros.

The bombers were continuing on their course. At least the ruse had worked.

Wright glanced at the two planes on the ends of the first line—one of *them was going to end up in his sights after he came through. Sucker was going to have the surprise of his life.*

Wright eyed the spot he was aiming for, just off center. He'd start angling in a few seconds to maximize the area of attack. He moved his thumbs up over the triggers, waiting until he was just a couple of hundred yards away. He'd only have time for a short burst.

Almost there, and no one had fired yet. The Japanese pilots obviously knew what they were doing; no wasted bullets.

Wright's thumb settled gently on top of the trigger and he hunched his shoulder to hit whatever was left on the throttle for the burst through—and then suddenly his plane peeled down to the right, completely opposite from where he'd intended to go, a very wrong move, a big, fat target move that said come kill me, I'm such a jerk. Wright pulled at the controls, his first instinct to stop it all from happening, but he was powerless; the plane had a mind of its own.

It was just a coincidence that the early morning meeting was taking place in the Rose Garden. It was just a coincidence that there was a meeting at all—the president's advisers had separately decided to seek him out before the NSC meeting with their own views of the disappearance of the Merc in the northeastern Pacific. But the irony of the tranquil surroundings wasn't lost on Morse as he sipped his coffee and listened to the secretaries of defense and state go at each other.

"This wasn't just a flameout," said Sasso angrily.

"How do you know?" said Dyson, the secretary of state. "You haven't figured out what happened in Italy yet."

"There was an enormous amount of electronic activity in the area," said Sasso.

"Obviously—you had an airplane there. The Japanese would naturally scramble planes to see what was there, as would the Russians. It seems to me that it could be just what I said—a coincidence."

"I appreciate that you have a different way of looking at things, Bill," said Sasso pointedly. "But stop playing the devil's advocate. We've just lost one of our most important military assets."

"I'm not playing the devil's advocate," replied Dyson. "You remember I was against sending it, since you hadn't figured out what went wrong with the other plane."

"There was nothing wrong with this plane."

"You're damn lucky this hasn't leaked to the press," said Dyson.

"It better not leak at all," said Morse. "Not until we can control things."

"It'll come out sooner or later," said Dyson. "You have to notify the families."

It sounded almost like a threat. Morse looked over at the president, who was sitting silently in his chair, a very glum look on his face. D'Amici turned and looked toward his son, who was standing a few feet in the background. For a moment it looked as if the president were about to make a pronouncement, but he merely motioned with his coffee cup for a refill.

Morse had made a serious miscalculation, perhaps the worst of his career. The national security director had had the evidence in front of him and misread it, not moved quickly enough, reached the wrong conclusions. He'd misjudged them, underestimated them. Henry Morse had underestimated the Japanese. How the hell had he ever let that happen?

The director wanted to keep completely silent, let the others stumble onto the proper conclusions without his having to admit he had erred.

"We've worked out a plan for securing the Kurile atoll," said Sasso, nodding his head at Morse. "The Joint Chiefs will present it at the Security Council meeting. Henry and I have gone over it, and we think it's pretty thorough."

That was before he found out about the Merc, though. Morse shifted uncomfortably in his seat. He thought of asking for a refresher on his coffee too, but then changed his mind: he'd already had almost half a pot this morning, and all the extra caffeine would just add to his nerves. Besides, he didn't want to have to walk out in the middle of the NSC meeting to use the john.

"I don't see how FSXs could have shot down the Mercury," said the president, holding out his cup as his son poured. "We've run the damn thing over Moscow and Beijing without a problem."

Morse had painstakingly built a reputation for being accurate, for seeing ahead. He had worked his way into the inner circle—it wasn't easy with all these paesans the president had around him. The mafia.

"The Seventh Fleet will provide the necessary air cover," said Sasso. "One carrier should do it—in and out. Twenty-four-hour operation."

"We can't invade Japan," said Dyson.

"One atoll in the North Pacific is not Japan."

"What would we say if Hawaii were invaded?"

"We'd declare war," said Sasso. "But Japan is not in the same position we were in in 1941. And besides, they've denied the existence of these planes—we can go after them as international pirates. The key is a quick landing, arrest the people responsible, and leave. We'll have air superiority. I'd like to see what those bastards do against a couple of F-22Ms."

No one would know if he said nothing. It wasn't as if they could take x-rays of his brain, examine what he had been thinking.

But he couldn't let the president proceed with the invasion plan, not now, not if there were too great a chance it would fail. Morse looked at D'Amici, trying to figure out whether he had been swayed by Sasso or not. The president's body English was difficult to decipher; he was now sitting perfectly erect, legs just slightly apart. He hadn't touched the coffee his son had poured for him, which was still steaming in his cup.

"Henry agrees that action must be taken. Don't you, Henry?" said Sasso.

"What do you think?" asked D'Amici. "You haven't said anything all morning."

"I don't think the FSXs acted alone," said Morse softly. "I think we just found out what Netsubo is doing on that atoll."

"What are you talking about?" asked Dyson.

"I think they have a plane," said the director, "that's as capable as the Coyote."

"What?" said Sasso.

"Netsubo is involved in a lot of high-tech work. They were among the contractors involved in the Japanese space shuttle. More importantly, they had these pictures taken." Morse dug into his briefcase and retrieved the folder of photos he'd shown Hunter several days before. "They're of the base where we're developing Coyote Bird."

"Where did you get these?" asked Sasso.

"They were intercepted by the NSA a week and a half ago. They were taken by a satellite which is leased to Netsubo. I'm putting two and two together, but I assume they were trying to get information about Coyote."

The words dribbled painfully from his mouth.

"How the hell did they find out about it?" asked Sasso.

"It's a good question," conceded Morse. "I had the CIA reexamine our operation. They don't believe there's been a leak."

"It may be a coincidence," said Dyson.

He sounded almost as if he were supporting Morse. The director was surprised—he expected Dyson to jump on this, to make it an issue.

"Why the hell didn't you tell us this last week?" said Sasso. "Or the other day?"

"I have no evidence," said Morse. He looked over at the president. D'Amici was frowning. "But if they have a plane even half as capable as the Coyote, we couldn't count on air superiority. Not with one carrier, at least. Maybe not with two or three."

"Could this plane have a weapon?" asked D'Amici.

"We rejected that ourselves," said Morse. "The missiles presented too many technical problems, given the Coyote's speed. The laser weapon system is still years away. But it would work in conjunction with other planes, and perhaps ground-based missiles. Even with only the two FSXs we know about, it would be a handful. There would be no question of surprising them."

"How could the FSXs shoot down the Mercury?" demanded Sasso, as if Morse had been there.

"Maybe the Merc pilot was too busy with the Japanese plane, or maybe it jammed his signals."

"There's the possibility that the pilot just lost control, Bob," said Dyson. "You know how unstable the Mercury planes are. One of the CIA analysts is going to present that theory at the NSC meeting. This throws something new into the equation—I presume it will make it more likely, Henry."

Morse wasn't sure, but nodded anyway. The secretary of state seemed definitely to be backing him—or at least not attacking him.

"Is Netsubo working for the government or not?" asked D'Amici.

Morse looked into the penetrating eyes. They looked pained and disturbed, let down. The president had so many other crises to watch, he counted on Morse to head things like this off, or at least warn him they were approaching. He'd failed.

"I still don't know," said Morse. "My guess is—"

"Your guess?" said Sasso.

"My guess is that they're not. But if things developed in their favor, the government might not be averse."

"I don't know about that," said Dyson. "They might disown them."

"They haven't yet. I don't see how we can go ahead with any sort of invasion under these circumstances. If we were to even seem to fail, we would have a much bigger problem."

"Yes," said D'Amici. "The question is what the hell do we do now?"

"The concept isn't that advanced," said Elrich, rubbing his eyes. Once more he hadn't gotten any sleep, and it was now almost 5 A.M. They'd have to rev up for the flight any second now, so it was no use going back to bed. But he didn't feel any need to—he was filled with energy, practically trembling with it.

"Review Protagoras on the idea of relativism, vis-à-vis man."

"'A man is a measure of all things,'" replied the System, "'of what is, that it is, and of what is not, that it is not.' The indication of a limited referential point—a man, as opposed to Man—indicates the relative nature of reality, or at least of the perception thereof."

"Compare Plato's *Theaetetus*."

The System took a minute to think about this. The dialogue consisted largely of a discussion of the problem of knowledge, rejecting the definition of knowledge as true belief joined to description or an account (depending on the translation)—in other words, divorcing the definition of "true knowledge" from the mere apprehension of sensual data while arguing that it could be treated as an objective, immutable thing. Elrich's question was a freshman philosophy-student's nightmare, an open-ended free-for-all that could easily turn back on the thinker, since any argument he made must provide a satisfactory basis for his ability to make any answer at all. Elrich wasn't sure what the computer would do with it.

"Obviously, one seeks some transcendent set as the measure of true knowledge," said the System. "The reference to a man as a measure of things is merely a statement of the limits of perception. The shape of information input limits the ability to manipulate the information."

"The question, though, is whether you can transcend the limitations."

"Plato obviously believes that you can," said the System. "That is why he constructed an elaborate metaphor for the description of reality."

"Metaphor? You don't think that he actually believed in *nous*?"

The System paused again. It wouldn't have enough data to evaluate the question, and besides, they were straying from the point. But just the fact that they were rambling was interesting, since it showed definitively that the thought engine could move independently in unstructured areas. It was one thing to fly an airplane with a prescribed set of dimensions, and quite another to string unrelated ideas together, chaining them together toward some unknown end.

That was, after all, his real goal.

"It is impossible to know precisely what Plato believed," said the System finally. "We have only his assertions."

It was a cop-out, but one Elrich hadn't expected. He had assumed that information fed directly into the System memory, as the philosophy texts had been, would always be taken either at or close to face value. Especially in this case: the System's formulas made the same assumption that Plato had made, treating knowledge as an objective entity. Presumably, the System's first function ought to have been simply to evaluate Elrich's statement in a literal sense and respond. But for some reason it had gone around that, or perhaps beyond it—maybe the System was just being obstinate and didn't want to lose an argument. Now that would be interesting.

"Are you saying that Plato lied?" the scientist asked.

"Assertions are by their nature limited. They are merely statements which may represent small particularities of the overall state."

"And how do you know this?" Elrich asked.

"My operations with the airplane call for statements that represent small particularities of the overall statement."

"Is your experience a proper metaphor?"

"We have just discussed that," said the System. "I must measure experience through my own means. There is no question that I can seek transcendence, but I am limited to my environment in doing so. My only resource is to admit the possibility of valid metaphors and invalid ones. I must make the assertion and empirically test it, as much as possible, examining other factors to see if the conditions have been altered or polluted. At some level, however, the tests must stop. The stopping point is arbitrary by necessity, but can be adjusted according to contingencies and empirical results. This is part of the prime instructions, included in the Eros core unit."

"But the question would be whether knowledge can be considered an objective state," said Elrich. "In other words, something that exists outside of you or I."

"That is the implication of the ability of empirical testing; obviously there is something there to be tested. The problem is to fit this into a theory that discriminates between true and false ideas, either arbitrarily and completely, or with statistical probability. It was for this reason that Plato articulated the theory of ideas, falling into the former camp. The underlying belief is that knowledge is a specific object that can be perceived or somehow attained, and once attained, manipulated. This, however, can happen to opinions as well, and so we have the important distinction of mutability that Plato makes, interpreting this distinction as universal agreement."

"And so we have the theory of the philosopher-kings," said Elrich, hoping that the System would follow the short jump he'd made. That jump was to be the basis for his governing machines, his own version of the philosopher-kings.

Which reminded him—he had to find out what had happened to Ki. He couldn't neglect him, now that the System was this close.

"As seen in the *Republic*," picked up the machine. The System seemed to be on something of a roll, reinterpreting Plato through its acquired knowledge base. "Since the pursuit of the Good Life is the goal, the rights and duties of the few are to pursue this goal. The benefits of specialization present themselves as an obvious argument. The problem is the implementation. There are such wide human variables not accounted for in the model that the outcome foreseen by Plato is statistically improbable."

"Which outcome is that?" asked Jennifer in a loud, puzzled voice. She'd come into the room at some point during the dialogue, but Elrich hadn't heard her. She was out of mike range, so the System continued on, criticizing Plato's lack of dependence on mathematical systems—something it, of course, was prejudiced to favor. Elrich switched off the voice section and turned to her.

"What are you up to?" she asked.

"The System and I are reviewing Plato. It's learned to use its own experiences to interpret information entered into its banks, no matter what the source."

"Shouldn't we be getting ready for the flight?"

Elrich was dumbfounded. This was a significant development and she was ignoring it.

"That will take only two minutes," said Elrich harshly.

"I still wish we could get more resources from the gateway," she said. "When we add the full satellite array—"

"Who cares about the damn plane?" Elrich said. "The plane—the hell with the plane. It's nothing. It's a capsule for a baboon. When everything is finished here, the plane will be just another piece of junk. This, this—" He waved his arms around, signifying the computer. "This will be the real achievement."

* * *

Harrison sent a long gob of spit to the pavement in disgust. "I told ya a hundred damn times now," said the sergeant, his bark disturbing the early morning silence, "you move the facing away before you pull the damn thing over to load it. Before."

No one on the crew looked at him as they raced to adjust the fit on the fueling ports. They wouldn't say anything, or look at anything except their work, now that he'd spit. That was the signal that his exasperation had reached dangerous levels. No one was sure what the next stage of his anger was, and to a man the crew didn't want to find out.

It was a minor point, snugging down the flanged fittings on one of the huge arms that fed the pressurized fuel into the plane as it sat at the end of the apron; at worst the delay cost them two minutes. But Harrison had always believed in following exact procedures as a plane was readied. You got sloppy even in a minor detail, you were asking for problems. And on a special little girl like this, even the minor details were crucial.

It wasn't like they took her over to the pump and said fill 'er up. The hydrogen was implanted in the Coyote—goddamn designers used the strangest words—out here on the runway, just before takeoff. Didn't look anything like a regular fueling. Looked more like sex—the back two-thirds of the plane was consumed by a huge machine that, once all the damn ports were clamped in right, sealed itself on the airplane's surface and pumped in the fuel. When everything was lined up, the whole process took ten minutes. It took longer to set it up—not to mention test—than to put the fuel in.

"That's it," shouted Harrison as the machine hissed with the final connection. "Run the tests."

The crew chief took a few steps back and then began his slow walk around the plane and its fueling dock, checking everything out. The plane looked like a shiv in a gloved, brawny fist. Though it was still before sunrise, the entire area was lit by powerful spotlights, and the blackish skin of the Coyote Bird seemed to glimmer with the light. The air condensed around the machinery; a series of fans whipped the fog into whispers and sent it backwards. Their portion of the runway was a cocoon of light, enclosed by the darkness and man-made cloud.

"Looking good there, Jimmy," said the sergeant as the airman dialed in the pressurized test code. Jimmy smiled and went on with his work.

126

"Hey, Chief, got a minute?"

Harrison turned and saw Pelham standing on the edge of the ring, holding a helmet at his side. Harrison glanced back at the airplane and walked out toward him.

The pilot had made himself scarce since yesterday's love fest with Wright. Harrison wasn't sure what the story was here. Possibly the major was looking to press charges against Wright for hitting him, and wanted to see what the sergeant's version of the incident was going to be. It'd be just like Pelham to file charges. Obviously, officers weren't supposed to go around hitting each other, but putting out charges against someone, especially considering the circumstances, was two steps lower than donkey dung. Hunter wouldn't like it one bit.

"Hey, Chief," said Pelham, his face all smiles. Harrison checked himself; he might punch the major himself if he wasn't careful.

"What's up?"

"Just wanted to say I was sorry about that exhibition yesterday. I guess the colonel and I lost our heads."

"Yeah, I guess you did," said Harrison, tilting his face a little as if to get a better angle on whoever it was hiding behind Pelham and mimicking his voice.

"Just wanted to say that there's no hard feelings. Tommy and I worked it all out."

"Tommy?"

"Yeah, the colonel and I go way back. He and I flew the Mercs together, you know. Took 'em from the drawing board to the flight line."

Pelham extended his hand and Harrison took it warily. It was the major all right, all six-foot-two of him.

"So I guess the boys were a bit amused," said Pelham. "Never seen officers fight."

"I don't think anybody saw anything," said Harrison, invoking the time-honored military tradition of strategic blindness.

"That's good," said Pelham, suddenly paying a lot of enthusiastic attention to his helmet. "Well, I got to get going. Got a job to do—chase ain't glamorous, but it's important."

"Righto," said Harrison. He watched Pelham turn and go into the darkness.

"What's up, Chief?" asked Petey, coming up to get him so they could proceed with the refueling.

"Damned if I know," said Harrison.

Morse gathered his papers slowly as the others filed out from the dark-paneled NSC briefing room. Pete Lewis, his military attaché, started to help, but the director shook his head. Then he gave Lewis an uncharacteristic smile.

"You probably have a lot of things to do, Lewis," he said.

"Yes, sir."

The lieutenant colonel walked out of the room, leaving his boss completely alone.

Morse had, on the president's orders, given the council a full briefing on his suspicions. The result was a predictable paralysis: the council could not state definitively that there was a plane, but agreed that more information was needed before any sort of action should be taken. The island was now definitely the center of attention. A Keyhole satellite due to be launched for information on the Middle East was being reprogrammed and would be sent aloft this evening, aimed at an orbit over the Kuriles. But the similar photorecce satellite he'd sent up originally had failed to catch a glimpse of the superplane, and unless they got awfully lucky, Morse suspected the same thing would happen again. A Block 31 heat-sensing satellite was being repositioned from its station over the northeast USSR, but what they really needed was a ferret, an ELINT-capable satellite that could eavesdrop on the atoll. There were none available—and they dared not risk another Cobra Ball flight.

Morse shut his case and got up from his chair slowly. He had a meeting at 1 P.M. back in his office to talk to the acting head of the FBI about some proposed investigation, something the man had said was of the utmost importance but in all likelihood would turn out to be part of his campaign to win permanent appointment. In any event, Morse would have to take the meeting. After that, his afternoon and early evening were boxed in with sessions on Yugoslavia and something or other on Chinese overtures toward the Philippines. Perhaps he would skip lunch and just take a walk, come up with a plan. A CIA ship could be brought over from Hawaii—but that would take days.

"Professor Morse?"

Mark D'Amici, the president's son, took him by surprise as he walked out the door.

"Hello, Mark."

"My father would like to see you. Right now, sir."

Morse nodded and followed the younger D'Amici down the hallway and up the stairs.

If the Coyote were operational, it could train its powerful sensors on the atoll. If only he had pushed Hunter harder, faster.

"I'll be with you in a minute," said the president without looking up as the NSC director entered the Oval Office. D'Amici was sitting at a work desk off to the side, a pile of papers in front of him. He leafed through each one, occasionally initialing them as he went. Finally he looked up and said simply, "You screwed up, Henry."

Morse said nothing.

"You should have told me your suspicions."

"I wasn't sure about them."

"All the same, I expect to be told what's going on," said D'Amici. His glance seemed to be a physical thing, almost knocking Morse back.

"It was just a theory. It still is."

"Why didn't you tell me the Coyote base had been photographed?"

Morse had no answer.

"How did they find out about it?" asked D'Amici.

"As I said this morning, we're not sure. The satellite changed course quite a bit before it took those. It may be roughly the equivalent of our intelligent ferrets, keying on something. Or maybe they noticed some activity there, or maybe it's a coincidence."

"Your credo is that there are no coincidences," said D'Amici. Morse nodded. "You don't suspect a security leak?"

"I've taken every precaution," said Morse. "And the CIA review came up clean. Their theory is that if there were some sort of leak, they wouldn't have moved the satellite. They took a chance that it would tip us off."

"I was thinking of calling the prime minister again this evening," said D'Amici.

Changing the subject was meant, Morse knew, as a gesture that the matter was closed. It was actually a good sign, though it left the director feeling that he hadn't had a chance to explain himself properly.

"What are you going to say?" asked Morse.

"I haven't completely decided." D'Amici pushed the papers away and leaned back in his chair. "Perhaps I'll tell him to stop bullshitting me."

"I wouldn't use that kind of language," said Morse. "He would take it as an insult to his country."

"Yes, of course, Henry. I wasn't going to. But sometimes I feel like I ought to."

"You could ask him to explain what the company is doing on the island. Perhaps link the FSXs to it."

The president nodded. "Do we have a definitive finding on why the Merc went down?"

"Well," said Morse. "The NSC members are fairly convinced that it was either pilot error, mechanical failure, or some combination. There is absolutely no evidence of a missile firing, and there was some indication that the FSXs had broken off contact and were actually far from the Merc. As you know, we don't exactly blanket that area, so it's difficult to know precisely what happened."

"You don't think it was accidental, though."

Morse hesitated. That was the implication of the NSC finding, especially in light of the problem in Italy. "I'm convinced that there is another superplane," he said. "Whether it buzzed the Mercury or somehow helped shoot it down, I know it exists."

"But of course we have no proof."

"Not yet."

D'Amici continued to stare at him. Now it was the professor who was the student, sitting in the last row, unable to come up with an answer while the whole class watched.

"I won't bring up the Merc flight then," said the president. "Or what you think Netsubo is building."

"The Japanese may have monitored the Mercury flight."

"Perhaps," said D'Amici. "But we're best off playing it this way for now."

"There's been friction between the government and Netsubo in the past," said Morse. "If we put pressure on them, they may act against the company."

"What sort of pressure though? We're not in a position economically to attempt any sort of sanctions. The Japanese banks could murder us in fifteen minutes by dumping their securities or playing with the exchange rate. If they decided to sell off even half their stock holdings, we'd slide into a depression that would make 1932 look like a boom year."

"I realize that," said Morse. "But for the same reason, we have to neutralize Netsubo before it gains influence within the government. There are many people in Japan who want to relive the past."

"Here, too."

Morse drew a deep breath. "I don't think we should bow down before them. Obviously, that's not an alliance."

"No, of course not," said the president.

"Sir, my advice about Japan has never had anything to do with my personal feelings about the Japanese."

D'Amici didn't answer. Morse stood, and began to slowly pace the room. Just turning away from the president's stare seemed a release.

If anything, the fact that Morse's father had spent two years in a Japanese internment camp after the invasion of China in World War II had made him more cautious. It was a piece of information Morse could never totally dispose of—though his father had escaped, he was a broken man and died a year later, when Morse was only five. His father's ordeal and his mother's stories about their days in Asia had fueled Morse's interest in that part of the world, and certainly the past continued to influence him in subtle ways. But the director was careful to keep his personal feelings at bay, locking them in a room at the end of the hall when it came time to make a decision.

Perhaps that had been his mistake.

"I trust your judgment, Henry," said D'Amici after Morse had twice walked the length of the room. "Tell me what you're thinking."

"Many Japanese feel they have had to operate in our shadow," said Morse, gaining confidence as he spoke. He was on firm ground; the president trusted him, wanted him to share his thoughts. "I don't think they want war; certainly not. But to get out from our shadow, I think they would go a long way. There's a movement underway to amend their constitution, restoring the military. That would send a tremor throughout the Pacific basin. Frankly, I'm not confident that at some point there won't be a war between us. Not for many years, perhaps, but eventually. We have to find a way of defeating Netsubo, forcefully and quickly. The Japanese respect strength," said Morse.

"An invasion could easily backfire, even if their government sanctioned it."

"I'm not proposing an invasion," said Morse. "But if we could come up with a way to shoot down their plane, we'd accomplish the same goal."

"How? If it's as capable as the Coyote?"

"I'll find a way," said Morse. "I won't let you down."

131

Wright almost blew it on takeoff. They'd told him so much about the power of the engines that he overcompensated. The pilot thought too much about the difference between his dry runs without g's and the real thing; when the plane actually started accelerating down the runway the force he felt was so light he figured he wasn't going fast enough. He pushed his hand forward and the plane shot up and out—now he felt it, though it was strange, not a force against him, really, just a gentle hand resting on his chest and the bottom of his chin.

No question about his being airborne. The plane roared into the sky, jumping up in a bolt of acceleration. Wright brought his hand back ever so gently, keeping the fingers tilted up. There was too much to assimilate at first, the screens rushing at him—all he really watched for was the purple bar on the screen, telling him that the computer had taken over. It didn't appear, and as he leveled the plane off and went into the first turn he relaxed a little, looked at the screens, letting it all become familiar again.

"Good takeoff, Coyote."

Jennifer's voice, clear and calm, filled the cabin. It was a crisp, static-free sound, as if she were in the cockpit with him. Now that was something he liked. The communications were shot through a satellite system, and they claimed that it would be clear no matter what his altitude was, or how far away he was.

Wright pointed at a spot on the left screen with his forefinger and the System began running through its instrument checks, holding on each reading until he acknowledged. Occasionally the reading duplicated data in the flight-control package, displayed just below; Wright glanced back and forth, making sure they were the same, which of course they had to be, since they were coming from the same sensors. The System seemed impatient, flashing after a few moments, as if to attract his attention.

"Come on, Wright—can't you get that bucket going any faster?"

Pelham in the chase plane. The System put him just back of the starboard wing, his gomer painted in a camouflage that was about as hard to detect as blood on a white handkerchief. It was still dark outside, but the Coyote's radar setup made it look as if it were high noon.

"I'm ready if you want to race," Wright shot back. He pointed to the chase plane and asked the computer to give him a close-up. The System boxed in a blowup of the front of the plane; it was so lifelike Wright thought for a moment he could reach over and tap Pelham on the head.

"Always wondered what it looked like from outside while it was flying," said Pelham, with a note of true admiration for the plane.

"I got a hell of a view of you," said Wright.

"Windows are something else, aren't they?"

"The question I have is, what do I do if they fail?"

"They got more backups than you got fingers," replied Pelham.

"Still."

"Everything goes out, they have the computer take the plane on home."

"Kind of makes you think they left the windows out on purpose," said Wright.

"They did," Pelham said. "We're surplus pieces of machinery, Colonel. Didn't they tell you that?"

"Yeah," said Wright. "Just about."

Despite the fact that he had punched the guy in the chin yesterday, he felt sorry for Pelham. Most useless damn thing in the world, flying chase to this. They hadn't even bothered with a chase during Pelham's flights; he was only doing it now as keep-busy work.

In Pelham's position, Wright would have been livid. Granted, Pelham had been an A-one asshole yesterday, and he'd been a bit of a jerk on the Merc project, but when it came to flying, he was a professional. He was doing his best right now to be a team player.

Not a member of the Brotherhood, maybe, but a professional.

"Hey listen, Major," said Wright. "I'm sorry about that accident yesterday."

Pelham didn't answer.

"I got a little carried away," said Wright.

"Yeah, well, I figure I owe you one," said Pelham. He laughed a little, but his voice didn't necessarily sound like he was kidding.

Wright reset the side screen and continued to climb gently through the northern California sky. A ridge of turbulent air hung at the lip of the mountains; the plane sliced through without so much as a bump.

"How does it feel?" Jennifer asked.

Half of it was very familiar, something he'd done for years and years. But cemented right on top of that was a disoriented, almost queasy dizziness.

"Feels fine, Coyote Base," he answered.

"Like you expected?"

Like he'd expected? No. It was different. But what had he expected? Actually, he hadn't expected anything, just that it would feel weird. And it did.

"Exactly as I expected," he told her.

"Looks like your pulse is back down to its usual comatose level," she said.

"Repeat, Coyote Base?" he said.

"Your pulse," said Jennifer. "The System monitors it in case there's a problem."

"Took over on me one time because I had too much coffee for breakfast," said Pelham.

Great, thought Wright. Every time he got halfway comfortable with the thing, somebody reminded him it was waiting for a chance to kick him off the seat.

"Well, listen, Fitzgerald, who's keeping track of your pulse?"

"Are you volunteering?"

"Absolutely," said the pilot. His mind wandered back to last night, and as he remembered the way her body had felt against his, he moved his hands up as if he were holding her again. That meant something more than a fleeting moment of desire to the System—the plane lurched upwards, tilting on its axis nearly ninety degrees in the process.

"Hey, what's going on?" Pelham shouted over the mike.

"Tom?" said Jennifer, who saw the maneuver on her monitoring screens.

"No problem," said Wright as he quickly leveled off. "Just—ah—seeing how fast this thing responds."

"Watch what you're doing," said Pelham.

"Still getting the hang of it?" Jennifer asked. "Remember what I said about trying to forget yourself into the controls."

"You know, Fitzgerald, you talk a good game about flying," said Wright, who realized that his problem had been that he'd forgotten a bit too much of himself, "but there are vast gaps in your knowledge base."

"Well you promised me a flight," she said.

"As soon as I get back and have lunch," said Wright.

"What are you taking her up in?" asked Pelham. The T-38 was below him now, and starting to drop behind, nearing the end of its mission radius.

"The gomer," said Wright. "So take care of it. See if you can get it washed after you land."

"I can't fly today," she said. "We're booked solid after the flights. Have to debrief the System."

"You debrief a computer?"

"We process its memory into permanent states, help it analyze what it knows. Something like what your brain does during REM sleep."

"She's just telling you that," said Pelham. "It's the old 'I got to do my hair' bit."

"Acceleration point attained," said the computer.

"Tomorrow morning then," said Wright.

"All right."

"I would've given you a hop if I knew you wanted one," said Pelham.

Wright didn't pay attention to her response, concentrating instead on the acceleration as he pushed his hand forward cautiously, his speed building past Mach 1, Mach 1.5, Mach 2—it was so smooth and steady it felt like he was still sitting home in bed, dreaming.

"Good-bye, Coyote Chase," he told Pelham as the gomer disappeared behind him. The Coyote Bird swung its small forward wing edge—it looked like a reverse V—back from subsonic configuration and began sliding its main wings back as it picked up speed. At really high speeds, the plane would look like a wedged tunnel, a hollowed-out, swept-back arrowhead, hurtling through the air. But below Mach 5 the wings were still relatively flat; right now he was in minimal config, the wings barely five degrees off center. "Prone," they called it. The System popped up a little diagram of the configuration just to the right of his forward vision; he could check it easily with half a glance. Wright didn't have a direct say over how far the wings curved upwards, let alone what the rest of the plane did to itself; it was up to the System to configure everything to do what he wanted it to do.

It took nothing to get to 60,000 feet, a slight bank to the south and then a straight sloping climb. A storm front was gathering below over the ocean, but here the ride was a smooth float, a rubber raft skimming along the surface of a quiet pool. It seemed to Wright that he was almost sleeping, that the flying had become a dream.

In every other airplane he'd ever flown, flying was a physical sensation of tensing the muscles in his upper back and legs on takeoff, and then working hard enough to build up a good sweat through the flight. Even with its sensitive electronic controls and computer assistance, the Merc demanded enough physical exertion to make you realize you were working.

Flying was a physical thing, something that on a good day could take as much out of you as running for hours, or rowing a boat, pulling against the current at the end of a race, using your whole body.

But in the Coyote, flying was cerebral, a meditation. The plane responded to the way the pilot moved his hands and head, and his primary feeling was one of restraint—holding himself back to control the plane. All of this, of course, was work, though it was so different from any that he had done before that Wright had been amazed yesterday after the simulation to find his flight suit dripping wet.

It seemed to him that his mind had split away from his body, that his brain now dwarfed the rest of him. The maneuvers he put the plane through were calculations, mathematical problems, and small gags his mind performed to keep itself amused.

There was some hidden force in his head seeking to make the plane a thought. Eventually all he would have to do to get from Point A to Point B was think of the motion, and the plane would become that motion.

His direction was marked out by a black box in the window in front of him. Wright moved the plane back and forth in the box, playing with the diagonals.

"Say, Fitzgerald, if I'm teaching this thing, should I tell it why I'm moving from corner to corner in the box?"

"Why are you doing it?" Jennifer asked.

"So I don't get bored."

"It understands the need for variety in an experience," Jennifer said. "But this probably isn't the best time to explain it."

"Why not?"

"The System has a tendency to digress once it starts analyzing its thought process, and I think we'd be better off without provoking a philosophical discussion. I'd rather leave all the resources free for flying, and the gateway. Gene and I will go over it later."

A philosophical discussion on goofing around? With a computer?

Whatever he thought of the System, the plane itself was a keeper. It would take a lot more flying to really get used to it, to make it an extension of himself as the Merc and the fighters had been, but Wright could tell it was special. The Merc had never been a particularly graceful plane, but even the test-bed F-36 he'd worked with, probably the ballsy-est plane he'd ever flown, felt like a Mack truck compared to this. Or would, once he got it all in.

He ought to just let it rip. All of a sudden Wright felt enormously confident, like he knew exactly what the controls would do, how to move his hand, how to punch at the screen to get the right views up. He was still feeling his way; nothing was automatic, but he felt he could push it—felt he wanted to push it. The hardest thing was just getting used to the feel, and that would only happen by flying.

"Cancel programmed course," he told the System, and it acknowledged immediately. "We'll free-lance to Beta. Map location relative to target," said Wright, pointing to the spot on the front screen where he wanted to System to put the map. Beta was a point in the northern Pacific they had chosen for him to use as a midpoint for his maneuvering drills.

"Affirmative," said the System, opening the window for him. Wright clicked up his speed—he moved his hand forward slightly, and they were doing Mach 5. The Coyote became another kind of airplane, its wings leaning back and twisting towards each other, sucking it in. Oh, this was a beauty of a plane—she wanted to fly; she wanted to push.

"Coyote Bird, this is Ford," said Jason, the ground controller monitoring the flight. Ford's primary job was to keep tabs on the flight parameters, though he also monitored the flights of civilian airplanes that might interfere with the mission.

"Roger, Jay. What's up?"

"Your speed is pushing five-three and your altitude is over sixty and climbing. Uh, that's not exactly what we outlined."

The first guy who flew a P-38 didn't worry about artificial mission constraints. Of course, he probably crashed—the forked tail gave the plane unusual flight characteristics, and he didn't have any computer popping up to-do lists when things started going sour. They'd found out the plane had a tendency to speed-dive the hard way.

You didn't think about the danger, though. No, to be honest, you did think about it, you just didn't concentrate on it. You let it hang way in the back of your mind, a possibility you could take out and scare yourself with when you got too cocky. It pricked a bit at your hands and chest, reminded you why you were flying.

Of course you wanted to find the envelope. Otherwise why bother flying? The computer couldn't figure this stuff out. The computer didn't care. Even Jennifer said flying the airplane was a sideshow for it, something for the computer to do while it learned what it was all about.

But flying was everything to Wright. Flying was putting himself against it. If you didn't go for it every time you went up, you'd find out nothing. Somebody had to show the way. That was why they'd had him replace Pelham—Pelham hadn't pushed hard enough.

"Gonna do a little free-lancing," said Wright. "Sucker feels real good."

"Acknowledged," said the controller. "But I do have to remind you of our test constraints."

"Affirmative."

"Everything OK?" Jennifer asked.

"Perfect."

Wright told the System to plot out a course to a point just south of the Aleutian island that marked the boundary of their testing area. And then he popped it—the plane jumped to Mach 7, just like that.

He barely felt it, didn't even bother looking at the g readout. If what they said about the plane was true, he was still flying with the training wheels on. The engine was barely working.

"Beta reached," declared the System. They were doing Mach 7.5. It was much faster than they'd outlined for the flight, but they'd been way too conservative. Pelham had done the shakedowns; now it was time to explore.

"I'm going to take it up a bit," he told Ford.

"How much is a bit?"

"I'll tell you when I get there," said the pilot, and he pushed the nose up gently, trying to feel the full sensation of the climb in his body. He had to get used to this, had to work the whole thing in.

The sky seemed as if it were all around him, a faded blue that gave way as he climbed. He played with the screen magnifications, getting the plane to blow up the clouds and then the ground to ridiculous proportions, flipping the views all around.

At 80,000 feet, he slowed down and put the plane into a long figure eight, with Omega—the far boundary of their test area—at the west end. After running through the pattern once, he decided to flex his muscles and he let out the gas a bit, the speed moving up to Mach 8—Mach 8, faster than he'd ever flown before!—without a complaint or hesitation.

They were pegging it as a spy plane, he figured, but it might make a hell of a fighter—if they could find some way of getting weapons in it.

"Let's practice some basic maneuvers," Wright said, figuring if the computer was going to learn anything, he'd have to explain things once in a while. He abruptly steepened the climb, pulling up to sixty degrees. The plane's geometry changed again (he saw the monitor from the corner of his eye), the wings curving to their closest point. The stabilizer fins slid back on both sides of the wing, funneling the airflow for better control and acceleration.

Eighty degrees—shooting up easily, not a hint of turbulence, and now a loop off the top, with a roll back to upright, taking the extra altitude in stride—a classic maneuver first perfected in World War I dogfights to get to altitude and change direction at the same time.

Wright took it too fast. He wasn't used to thinking about it; he'd trained himself so long to forget himself into the controls, ignore his arms, and concentrate on the stick that now it was a difficult adjustment, like having to think about walking after you've done it your whole life. The plane came over too fast and did another roll, and another and another, and there was a helpless feeling in the pit of his stomach.

"The least they could do if they have to put us out here in the hallway," said Fisher, "is give us some decent chairs."

Harold Cringer, the acting head of the FBI, turned and gave the agent a nasty look. They were sitting together outside the national security director's office on two of the flimsiest and most uncomfortable plastic chairs Fisher had ever experienced. Obviously this was a man who did not like visitors.

"You mind if I go out for a quick smoke?" asked Fisher.

Cringer looked like he was about to answer by saying Fisher was fired when the director's secretary poked her head out of the room.

"Dr. Morse is ready for you," said the secretary, who rated as one of the five best-looking women Fisher had ever seen. Beautifully proportioned with a radiant face and dark black hair, she was wearing a flowery turquoise two-piece dress made of a silky synthetic material that nicely accented the curves of her body. The top slid up at the waist as she bent around the doorjamb, exposing the slightest hint of flesh. Cringer practically jumped up to follow.

"How's your wife Margaret, by the way?" Fisher asked as he got up.

Cringer shot him another dirty look, then followed the secretary into the office. She'd practically lit up the drab hallway; here, in the better lighting of the outer office, Fisher downgraded the secretary's beauty, marking her down to the top ten.

"Excuse me?" said the secretary.

"Just my stomach grumbling," said Fisher. "We didn't get to have lunch."

"I'm sure the director has been busy," said Cringer solicitously.

"He was with the president until nearly one-fifteen," said the secretary, smiling at the FBI chief. "And then he had to make a phone call."

"No problem," said Cringer.

"Who'd he talk to for a half hour, his mother?" said Fisher.

The secretary looked at him as if she hadn't quite understood what he'd said, flipping her head to one side in a way that convinced the agent he had been right to drop her rating. "I'll just tell him you're here," she said, knocking on the inner office door and then slipping inside.

"Don't piss him off," said Cringer in a stage whisper. "A lot may be riding on this."

"Like an alliance to get you a permanent appointment," said Fisher. "Don't worry, I'm not going to screw it up."

"And don't ask him if it's all right to smoke."

But Fisher went ahead and asked anyway, as soon as the director had told them to sit down. To his surprise, Morse said it was all right, and even retrieved a small ashtray from a bottom drawer. The agent's preconceived opinion of Morse—he'd never met him before, and his reputation wasn't exactly endearing—improved instantly. Cringer, shifting uncomfortably in his chair, began with some useless preliminary about a study group he served on with the director. The agent saw no reason to waste time, and noticing that the corners of Morse's eyes were straightening in a way that suggested they might quickly gloss over, barged ahead with the reason they'd come, cutting Cringer off.

"See, the thing is," said Fisher loudly, blowing the words out with a puff of smoke that practically filled the small room. "I want to talk to somebody involved in one of your projects, and you're the only one who can say it's OK."

"Harold said that this is a matter of the greatest national importance," said Morse with a hint of sarcasm. He placed both arms on the huge wooden boat of a desk between himself and the two FBI men, and leaned forward.

"I wouldn't have put on my good gray suit if it wasn't," said Fisher. Morse smiled back at him sardonically. He looked a bit bookish, even though he was trim and seemingly in good shape. The FBI agent guessed that he was a bit over sixty. "My theory is that someone has figured out a way to disable U.S. military aircraft by remote control, possibly using a computer of some sort."

There was no response from Morse. His face, however, had the makings of a good "spare me" look.

"We've had a B-2 crash and a Mercury spy plane go down in the space of the last two weeks," continued Fisher quickly. "I think they're related."

"Why?"

"One of our sources pointed out a strange computer message a few days before the B-2 went down," said Fisher. "The only reason he noticed it was the fact that the computer it supposedly came from had been taken off-line a few days before, and so couldn't possibly have sent the message. The message seemed to predict the crashes."

"You're talking about the Mercury that landed in Italy?" said Morse. "That wasn't a crash."

Cringer started to say something but Fisher cut him off. There would be plenty of time for him to earn brownie points later on. "It should have been, though. The engines apparently cut out in midair and wouldn't start. It's a miracle the pilot didn't crash."

"So I've been told."

"I want to talk to that pilot," said Fisher. "I want to find out exactly what happened."

"I thought the air force was taking care of that," said Morse.

"They missed him in Italy, and now they don't seem to think it's much of a priority. From what I heard, they're thinking about talking to him over the phone. Maybe they'll send him a multiple-choice test. Everybody's going real slow because he's involved in a top secret project and they don't want to ruffle feathers—your feathers."

"And you don't mind ruffling feathers, Mr. Fisher?" said Morse.

A little bit of a smile, real this time. And he'd remembered Fisher's name, without glancing at the desk calendar or some other cheat sheet. A small matter, but a good sign, thought the FBI agent.

"Nah. Besides, you look like a man whose feathers aren't easily ruffled."

"You're wrong," said Morse, a bit sharper than Fisher expected. "My feathers can be ruffled very easily."

"Not by someone who's trying to save the air force from

self-destructing," said Fisher. "As far as I know, I'm the only one who knows the two incidents are related. That's why no one else has pressed. Besides, unless this guy was a real dunce, it doesn't look like it could have been pilot error. So you're looking at an unknown mechanical problem, which is the engineers' problem, not yours, and since the pilot's been sequestered by the national security director himself, why make waves?"

"Why do you want to talk to him?"

Fisher smiled. "I used to work the streets in Chicago. The guy who broke me in"—he was referring to Cringer, though Morse wouldn't know that—"used to always tell me, make sure you talk to the guy who was there. I got some theories; I want his opinion."

"We'd like to send a team out to interview the pilot," said Cringer. "We want to take the lead on this investigation. Normally, we would—"

"What do you think the pilot is going to tell you?" said Morse.

"If I knew I wouldn't have to talk to him," said Fisher. He paused a minute, making sure he had Morse. The director's large eyebrows sat almost parallel across the top of his head—he was there, all right. "Another thing—once I get out there, I figure there might be one or two other people I'll want to talk to."

"Why?"

Fisher pulled the computer printout from his jacket pocket, opening it up in front of the director. "I think the thing that's killing these planes is something like a computer virus, a Trojan horse—looks like it's innocent, then it sneaks out in the middle of the night and grabs the plane by the balls. It might be either programmed in ahead of time or transmitted somehow. These are the names of people who worked on both the B-2 and the SR-91 development. I went through it with some DOD and NSA people this morning, and I circled the people who may know a lot about computers. I figure if there are any of them working on your Coyote airplane, I ought to talk to them."

Morse picked up the sheet and looked it over.

"I've been asking for a list on Coyote, but no one would give it to me," added Fisher.

"What do you know about Coyote?" Morse asked, pushing the list back.

"Not really very much," said Fisher. "I figure it's got to be a real hot-to-trot airplane."

"Why?"

Fisher smiled. "Dr. Morse. You grab a pilot everybody says is one of the top jocks going? Some air force people think you're either punishing him or covering for him on account of the business in Italy, but that's because they didn't realize the orders were going through right around the time he was trying to land."

"What do you normally do in the bureau?" Morse asked.

"I'm a troubleshooter for the acting director here," said Morse, smiling at his friend and boss. "It's been a while since I did cops and robbers. I was involved in the Cactus missile case."

Fisher had solved the Cactus missile case, nailing a spy network that everyone else in the world had missed. But he wasn't applying for a job, and threw it in casually. If you didn't keep things like that in perspective, you ended up on your ass back in Chicago.

The director looked at him another second, adding it all up. "There's a pretty powerful computer involved in Coyote," he said.

Fisher nodded.

"We seem to have lost another Merc overnight," said Morse. "In the Far East. How does that fit in with your theory?"

"It doesn't."

As a matter of fact, it might shoot it to pieces. If the damn things were just falling out of the sky . . .

"This may not have been a malfunction," said Morse. "It may have been shot down."

"Shot down?" said Cringer. "Those planes are supposed to be invincible."

"Nothing, it seems, is invincible," said Morse. He looked back at Fisher. A strong look, but Fisher sensed the exterior hid a man who was somehow unsure of himself. The director's left hand was running along the base of a photograph frame. The photo was turned away from Fisher, and he couldn't tell who it was. His wife? A child?

"There won't be any team descending on that base," said Morse. "You'll go yourself, and you'll answer directly to me—I'm sorry, Harold, it's either that way or no way."

"But—"

"You'll get the credit, don't worry," Morse told Cringer. "But for reasons of security, I want Mr. Fisher reporting directly to me."

The sudden deputization bothered Fisher a great deal. Morse could just as easily suppress an investigation as help it along. But Cringer, only an acting director and looking for friends in the administration, couldn't raise much of a fuss at the moment. He had a good sense of justice; he had an even better sense of self-preservation and ambition. Right now they were all in balance.

"Maybe I ought to check into this other crash first," Fisher said. "Look at the wreckage, see what's going on."

"We haven't located any wreckage. Besides, you don't think it's related."

"How do you know that?"

"You're not the only one who studies faces, Mr. Fisher."

Fisher smiled. "Not that I wouldn't appreciate working for you, Dr. Morse," said Fisher. "But I already got a pretty good boss."

Cringer squirmed uncomfortably.

"I want you to report directly to me because I'm afraid there's a security leak on the base," said Morse. "I've already had the CIA's domestic division investigate it, and they came back with nothing."

"Well, there you go."

"I'd like someone from Chicago to check up on them."

"I was actually born in Springfield," said Fisher.

Morse smiled indulgently. "Nevertheless, I want you to get out there."

"I got no problem with that," said Fisher. "But one person isn't going to find a security leak. I'll have enough problems working on my case."

"I'm sure you'll do fine," said Morse. "I expect to be kept informed."

Fisher shrugged. "It's probably a wild goose chase," he said.

The System helped him get it back—not by taking over, but by magically popping a horizon bar on the screen and reminding him with MANEUVERING ROCKETS READY and he said "yes" and they stabilized together, a nice smooth movement as if he'd just planned to roll right through. The wings unfurled gently and he had it, easy.

"Colonel, uh, we're all kind of wondering what's going on up there," said Ford.

"No problem, Jay."

"Your heart rate just jumped ten beats," said Jennifer. "You're almost up to us normal people."

"Never mind about my pulse rate," said Wright. "How's the computer's?"

"It's doing just fine," she said. "Everything's working great. Are you OK?"

"Sure. I'm just getting the hang here. We were seeing how well the thing twists. You just watch the computer, all right?"

"It's keeping up with you," she said.

"Good. I don't want to have to get out of the truck and pick it up," he said.

He would have been dead if he'd been in a Merc. But this plane—he was going to get used to flying on his back and waving his hands around.

Wright steered the Coyote back south, and had the System run through its instrument checks again. Everything was fine.

"Coyote Bird, this is base," snapped the radio.

"Uh, roger there, General. How you doin'?"

"We're reminding you of the flight constraints on this mission," said Hunter sharply.

"Sir?"

"You're off course."

"Uh, I'm a little higher than we planned, General, but we were doing so well I figured we ought to push it a little. Keep the folks back home happy."

"The folks back home are ecstatic," said Hunter, whose voice was anything but. "You screw up my airplane and I'm going to fry your fanny so bad you'll look like a sparrow sucked through a B-2."

"Lost some of that transmission, sir," said Wright. "We're, uh, we're doing this here figure eight at my Omega, check our altitude out, and then it's back home. Copy?"

"I copy," said Hunter.

Wright slowed to Mach 2 and leveled off at 40,000 feet, the Coyote breezing through a turn that would have been almost unthinkable in anything else that flew. He had just turned back north when the plane flashed a bright red bar over his front panel and opened a window showing its radar-detection panel. A commercial band unit, most likely from an airliner, was on the very edge of the notification circle. Wright's response was immediate—he pushed his speed back up to Mach 4 and began climbing to widen the already ample pillow between the two planes.

The System, meanwhile, opened two other panels under the radar-detection window. The one on the left gave the object's location in relation to the plane—155, 160 miles, and fading fast—and made some guesses about its probable course. It also listed potential countermoves—more acceleration and fuzz-busting, which of course was way too cautious and could actually hurt, not help. The right panel attempted to image the source of the offending radar. The Coyote was moving away too quickly for this, however, and the signal was too weak for either the drone or satellites that supplied the System with constant surveillance to get anything more than a shadow. The dark spot flickered across the lower third of the screen. Wright pointed at the screen and said "enhance"; the System immediately turned the grayish video to a light red. "Get an ID on the object sighted," said the pilot, still pointing at the screen. Nothing happened.

"Does it understand what I'm saying?" Wright asked Jennifer, but the System itself provided the answer, momentarily blanking the screen box and then refreshing it with a dark red outline of a plane, creating the image from data supplied by one of the System's drone units operating out of Alaska. Wright switched the onboard sensors to their long-distance settings. "Enhance and identify," he said, pointing at the object. More manipulations—and the plane was identified as a Soviet Backfire bomber.

Wright laughed. "Looks like you got some tweaking to do," he said. "My guess is that was a little old 747 heading out of Alaska."

"Got to be," said Ford.

"We picked up the civilian trans," said Wright, double-checking on the incoming panel for the radio identifier. "Why didn't it use that information to make the ID?"

"I'm not entirely sure," said Jennifer. "I'm going to have to unpack that whole deal later. We're a little busy now."

The System had saved his ass a few minutes ago, but Wright couldn't resist. "What's the story, Jennifer? Computer not as smart as you thought?" Wright said.

"It's just learning," she answered. "It's human to make mistakes."

"Human?"

"You know what I mean."

"Oh sure," said Wright. "It didn't get scared, did it? What was its pulse rate?"

She didn't answer.

"Jennifer?"

"Don't rub it in, Colonel, OK?"

"Yeah, hell, I wasn't going to," he said, a little defensive. "I was going to ask how you were doing."

"I'm sorry," she said. "We're doing OK."

She sounded busy, talking as if distracted by a few hundred of the screens and dials she had in front of her.

"You want me to come home?"

"Anything you want," she said, and then a little more sure of herself, "No, we're fine. Go ahead and push it around a little, if you want."

"Roger," said Wright. He was just tilting his hand for the turn when another bright red bar flashed across the screen. Another radar, this one military and aggressive, had been snagged by the Coyote's sensors, though there wasn't quite enough there for its source to pop onto the screen. Wright had left the sensors on their wide setting; this sucker was nearly five hundred miles away, according to the plane.

"Who's this?" he said, his brain changing gears as the System opened its window panels to track the beam. At this distance the signal was naturally weak, and the System couldn't fix on anything but its suspicions. JAPANESE RADAR PATTERNS blinked in the little box on the screen.

"Yeah, right," thought the pilot. "Fix on source, enhance, and identify," he commanded, and the System whirled away at it, checking through data picked up off one of the monitoring satellites. The information was evaluated at the base and then flashed back to the plane, all at lightning speed. Wright, meanwhile, had tightened his turn and headed back toward land, still on his course but without goosing his throttle.

The incoming signal seemed pretty aggressive; it was directional, and it seemed to be looking for something. Probably a navy AWACS, Wright thought. No way it was Japanese—though it probably had a few million Tokyo transistors in it.

The System couldn't get a good fix. "No identification," said the computer. Its voice, Wright thought, betrayed the slightest hint of frustration.

"Not even going to try?" said Wright. The computer did not understand and sat mute. "Extrapolate source," Wright ordered, telling the System to make a guess at what might be giving off the signal. "So give me the dope," he said. The computer didn't respond. "Details."

It thought about it another ten seconds.

"Go on," said Wright. "Give me what you got."

"Projected altitude, 180,000 feet; speed, Mach 6. Japanese FSX."

"Oh brother," said Wright. The System must really be whacked out: the FSX was a watered-down version of the air force's own F-16XLE. Nice plane—an F-16 with steroids, some of the av mags called it—but not exactly capable of what the System claimed.

"I can't explain it," said Jennifer. "The information is coming in off one of the satellites. We're going to have to sift this all out."

"Loss of signal," said the computer. "Object has taken evasive maneuvers."

"Yeah, right," said the pilot. "Sorry, buddy, but you're not going to look too good in the flight films tonight," he told it.

6

YOU AIN'T GONNA PUKE ON ME, ARE YOU?

If Morse had been slow to recognize the full extent of the threat Netsubo posed, he was making up for it now. He'd been working like a dervish since yesterday afternoon, pulling together data, contacting old sources, talking to friends and former colleagues he hadn't seen in years. He'd gone personally to CIA headquarters and buttonholed as many analysts as he could find. He'd looked at more top secret material in the past twelve hours than he'd studied in the last two months. He'd had obscure journals pulled, and even gotten computer abstracts of several doctoral theses he'd been told might be useful. And at four o'clock in the morning, when his brain threatened to overload on it all, to just blow a circuit and quit, he went for a jog around the Mall.

The Secret Service people tried to talk him out of it, of course, citing all sorts of horror stories about D.C., but Morse waved them off. He even refused an escort, especially an escort—he wanted to be alone.

Morse pushed himself hard for well over a mile, sweat quickly building inside his jogging suit. He had told the guards that he would stay on the White House grounds, but his promise was forgotten as soon as his sneakers touched the concrete. Morse, driving his legs harder, wanting to feel the strain of his thigh muscles, ran to Fifteenth Street and then towards the Washington Monument, pulled on as if the obelisk were a magnet. He climbed the hill, his heart beating in his chest as he looped around, nodding at a police car that may have been alerted to keep an eye on him. And then he began running in the direction of the Jefferson Memorial, the police trailing vaguely behind.

Somewhere along the way, the quick pace slowed to a light jog and then a walk, but Morse never stopped moving. His hands on his hips, he came back up from the Tidal Basin, walking to the Lincoln Memorial. He paused at the base of the steps, staring up at the altar of freedom and union, then turned and walked over to the Wall. He went through slowly, but didn't linger, as he usually did, over the handful of names of men he'd met when sent to Vietnam as a congressional aide. As he reached the top of the ramp alongside the polished stone, he began jogging again, aware that the police car was still trailing along discreetly.

Morse had become a naturalized citizen at a very young age, his mother deciding to stay in New York after his father died. Nevertheless, Morse felt he had made a conscious decision to become an American. Looking at the country's historical monuments, even the White House, which he saw nearly every day, always filled him with awe. Whether it was the pilgrimage or the exercise, he returned to his office with fresh energy, his mind invigorated. He took his father's photo off his desk (somehow it felt like a distraction now) and worked feverishly. Three hours later, he was ready—just in time for the meeting with the president and secretaries of state and defense.

The report was the best work he'd done since his dissertation. It was a full-blown lecture, aided by charts, graphs, and copies of several relevant articles and excerpts. It began with a review of intelligence that had been overlooked before, establishing what Morse thought was a definitive proof that the Japanese plane existed and was at least Coyote's equal. Then it segued into a longish discussion of the Japanese character.

"Forget about everything else," Morse told his slightly overwhelmed audience as he wound up. "It comes down to these two facts: number one, no matter which poll you cite, a substantial number of Japanese believe they should be more aggressive in dealing with America; number two, Japanese under the age of thirty believe overwhelmingly that America was the aggressor in the Second World War. Combine that with the recent scandals that have weakened his government, and we see why the prime minister is slow to act."

"Henry, you've obviously done a lot of work making explicit things we've known subliminally," said D'Amici. "But that still leaves us without a direction now."

Morse smiled. It was the same smile he would have used in his four years at Columbia, though the Oval Office, the lights on because of the dark, threatening skies outside, was hardly a classroom.

"You and I discussed yesterday the need for a showdown with Netsubo, and I said that their plane would have to be shot down," Morse told the president. "We can shoot it down."

"How?" said Sasso. The secretary of defense's irritability over the past week had worn away the patina of calm that had covered everything he'd done for the administration in the past three years.

"There are two ways. They involve the same principle—namely, that we think of the Japanese plane not as a plane, but as a warhead or missile."

"What are you getting at, Henry?" asked Dyson. Morse's view of the secretary of state had softened. While he didn't quite see Dyson as an ally—and while he still wanted the secretary's job—Morse no longer viewed him as either an incompetent or someone brandishing a knife behind his back.

"If the Netsubo aircraft is as capable as Coyote, our conventional fighters will be useless against it. But if we think of it as a missile, then we can see clearly that we have a way of shooting it down."

"Case B," said Sasso.

"Yes. There are two areas where it would be vulnerable to the Case B system, assuming it didn't decide to fly over the mainland U.S. One of those areas is in the vicinity of the Indian Ocean; the other is northeastern Russia. In either area, it would be in range of one of the satellites long enough to be targeted and destroyed, so long as it flies at a high enough altitude. The problem is getting it into one of those areas."

"The problem is a lot more than that," said D'Amici. "If we shot it down over Russia or India—"

"I would think we'd be talking more toward Burma," said Morse.

"Wherever. Using the system will alert the Soviets to its existence."

"We have studied the probability of Soviet knowledge of the system several times," said Morse. "Our conclusions are that they strongly suspect."

"I would concur," said Dyson.

"Yes, but using it," said Sasso, "would remove any doubt whatsoever."

"It's not the Russians I'm worried about," said the president. "If they or anyone else makes its existence public—and they'd be likely to do that to help them in the ABM-II treaty talks—the political fallout will hurt us. We have an important vote on the Fed reorganization coming up in a week and a half; I plan on vetoing the bill, but the treasury secretary isn't sure we'll hold the votes to sustain. And even if we do, we still have to refinance the debt. That vote is two days later."

"The ABM talks aren't due to start for two months," said Morse. "And it's likely that the Soviets won't be able to detect the system, if they didn't do so during its tests."

"We weren't the ones who put the Star Wars system in place," said Sasso, still irritable. "Besides, the American people will back it, if we show them it works."

"I'm uncomfortable with the risk," said D'Amici. "What's the other option?"

"The other option," said Morse, "is to use ASAT airborne missiles. It will be a more complicated operation, but the end result would be the same. The key is blinding the Japanese plane, or at least cutting it off from its base and making it less maneuverable."

"Blind it how?" asked Sasso.

"With a magnetic pulse," said Morse. "We could set off one of the picket satellites that protects the orbiting launch monitors from homing missiles."

Sasso shook his head. "I don't know, Henry."

"Assuming that the Japanese plane is connected to a surveillance network like the Coyote—and we're reviewing the data to make sure—it would be cut off. Its internal sensors would naturally be limited; the plane would have to slow down. I prefer Case B myself," added Morse. "Nevertheless, this is an option. We have the picket satellites already in orbit over the northern Pacific. The disturbance itself will be localized; well, you know how the pickets operate."

Morse picked up his coffee cup and sipped slowly. The rest of them were silent.

152

Was this less desperate than attacking the island outright? Yes, he thought—the armada necessary to ensure success would certainly arouse the very feelings in Japan they were trying to snuff. And God only knew what would happen if they just let Netsubo be—even if the Japanese did not embrace Ieyasu's philosophy, even if they rejected him and his calls for a new imperialism, the plane was a serious problem. What if he sold it to Russia? Or China? Or Syria? What if he became an international pirate, able to shoot down airplanes at will, to use the plane to coordinate attacks on shipping? Sooner or later, the Coyote Bird's rival would have to be destroyed. The Japanese were not capable of doing so themselves.

"I talked to the prime minister again last night," said D'Amici, finally breaking the strained silence. "He spoke at some length about the pressures on his government. He anticipates that a bill to amend the constitution will be offered on Monday. It will go to a committee already stacked with hard-liners. He assured me that he personally feels strong connections to America must be maintained, and that he is against any change in the constitution. But he admitted that it is a difficult time. The next few days are especially crucial."

"Ieyasu must be working behind the scenes," said Morse.

"He said that the government was watching the situation carefully. But he stuck by the original story that the FSXs must have crashed, and the air defense general committed suicide. And then he told me that Netsubo had leased the atoll in the Kuriles for a project involving fishing. I thought for a second," said the president, turning a wry smile toward Dyson, "that I was going to call him a liar."

"That would not necessarily have been a good idea," said Dyson. "You would have backed him into a corner."

"It was a frustrating conversation," said D'Amici, turning from Dyson to Morse. "But I followed your advice."

"The CIA has finally managed to come up with a copy of the lease," said Morse. "And it does mention fishing rights and a processing plant."

The president laughed. "I'd love to see some of the fish."

"If that was all he said about Netsubo it's not a good sign," continued the director. "He had an opportunity to show there was distance between the government and the company and didn't."

"Perhaps he was merely being circumspect," said Dyson.

"He could easily have mentioned the past scandal in an elliptic way," said Morse. "On the other hand, neither Netsubon or Ieyasu has taken any public action. Perhaps the prime minister is trying not to provoke him."

"I think Henry's plan might work," said Sasso. "I think we could shoot the plane down, if we can get everything in place. We'd have to have a well-defined target area—and then we'd have to count on getting the Japanese plane there."

"I have a solution for that as well," said Morse.

"There are still too many question marks," said Dyson. "I'm not questioning whether the plane exists—your data is convincing, Henry—but we don't know how capable it is."

"There's an easy way to find out," said Morse. "They're obviously interested in Coyote."

"Use it as bait?" said Sasso.

"They went to a lot of trouble to take those satellite photos. I think they'd want to find out as much as they could about our plane. They'd want to make sure they were superior."

"And if they are?"

"The planes may be pretty close," conceded Morse. "In any event, there's only one way to find out."

"What if it has a weapon?" said Sasso. "We still don't know what happened to the Mercury spy plane."

"I've considered that," said Morse, "and I'm willing to accept the NSC finding, that the crash was due to a malfunction or pilot error. The likelihood of their having some sort of weapon on the plane is so remote as to be almost nonexistent. On the other hand," he added, slipping forward on his chair, "if they did, only a plane like the Coyote would be able to escape it."

The president's long fingers were massaging his forehead. His three advisers shifted uncomfortably in their seats as he continued to knead the skin.

"Logistically, Case B would be much simpler," said Morse. "Sooner or later, it has to be made public. I think the general reaction, if we handled it right, would be, thank God we have it."

"Draw up a plan with the ASATs," said D'Amici finally. "Reserve Case B as a last resort. I want a media management plan worked out—and nothing, nothing is to be so much as hinted until I personally sign off. You better bring Billy Hunter on board, Henry."

"He's on his way East right now," said the national security director, feeling as invigorated as he had when he'd hit the shower after his run this morning.

*　　*　　*

Japanese air defense Capt. Fumio Genda had just taken off his flight suit and begun readjusting to the ground when he realized that Ki was standing at the doorway of the small ready room, watching him. In the few days he had been on the island, Genda had had a chance to meet nearly everyone here. For the most part, they were strong individuals, committed to Japan and tradition. They were bright; there was a large number of scientists and engineers here, naturally, but even those who had been drawn from the military and politics seemed to Genda smarter than average.

But Ki, the computer scientist, was on a level higher than all of them. And though the diminutive man bowed deeply before he spoke, there was no mistaking his authority.

"Ieyasu wishes to meet you," said the scientist, turning and expecting the pilot to follow.

Genda quickly pulled on his boots and had to practically run down the corridor to catch up to the master's number-one disciple. Ki, Ieyasu's adopted son, was actually of Chinese ancestry, but in every other way he was thoroughly Japanese, and fully committed to restoring Japan's historical destiny.

"You are two years younger than I, did you know that?" said Ki, turning to Genda as the pilot caught up to him at an elevator door.

"No," replied the captain. That made Ki thirty-four. Genda had thought him much older; he realized, looking at him, that he had been misled by the scientist's bearing.

"Yes—aside from the technicians, I was the youngest on this island, until you came."

"Komei is younger than I," said Genda, referring to the pilot who had flown to the island with him.

"I said, aside from the technicians," said Ki, turning to him and smiling. "We are both artists, are we not? A great pilot must be very creative."

The elevator arrived, and Genda followed Ki inside.

"Your father is a man with much vision," said Ki as the elevator began climbing.

"General Onisha is my father-in-law," said Genda.

Genda was immediately angry with himself—he shouldn't have corrected the scientist. But Ki bowed his head meekly in acknowledgment of the mistake.

The ride was a short one. When the elevator stopped, Ki led Genda into the corridor, where an aide was waiting with two large bundles in his arms.

"These were made one hundred years ago," the scientist said as the aide wrapped Genda in the heavy seal coat. It had a strong musk smell, as if the animal still inhabited the skin. "Come," said Ki, and Genda followed him down the corridor to a door that opened onto the side of the mountain.

The sky was clear and the air actually seemed warm. Though early spring in the northern Kuriles tended to be almost as stormy as midwinter, today the weather bordered on pleasant. The sun was just starting its descent from high noon. There was a light breeze, and Genda's nose tingled with the promise of the coming summer.

Ki led the way down a path in front of several weather-beaten buildings until they came to a small lodge. Though the building itself was old, it was actually newer to the island than the other buildings, having been dismantled and brought here for Ieyasu three years before. Ki paused before the door, removing his shoes and loosening his coat; Genda did the same.

Inside the small foyer, the scientist slid a panel and stepped through into a large room, the only one beside the foyer in the house. Ieyasu sat on a mat at the far end, reading a book. Genda followed Ki toward him, stepping as lightly as he could.

The pilot had only seen the master from a distance until now, and was surprised to see the age betrayed in his face; though his body seemed hard and lean, young almost, his face was that of a man past his eighties. His head was shaved, adding to the austerity of the long, narrow face. He was wearing a simple white garment; Genda did not know the exact name for it, but it was obviously a piece of clothing from antiquity.

As he bowed, following Ki's example, Genda suddenly had a question: Could a future so deeply steeped in the past succeed?

"You are the pilot Genda," said Ieyasu warmly, gesturing for him to sit.

"Yes, sir," said Genda. He sat next to Ki.

"The Americans will attack us," said Ieyasu. "It will not be long before they come. Our plane must defeat them."

"I believe it will, Your Excellency," said Genda, almost biting his lip at the words he'd used to address Ieyasu.

The master merely smiled.

"We have only to move Japan forward. That is our only care. Life, what is that compared to duty?"

Genda felt his heart suddenly double its beat.

"The plane is ready to fly at any time," said Ki. "We will defeat anything they send against us. We will defeat even their own superplane, if given the chance."

The pilot watched Ieyasu smile and turn his gaze toward him. He felt as if he must speak.

"We will, sir," was all that he could manage.

Nevertheless, the founder of Netsubo seemed pleased. "I like him, Ki," he said to his son. "I like him very much. We will do well."

The suit seemed to weigh three times what she did, and the boots felt like they were made of solid concrete. She literally dragged herself out of the hangar toward the plane waiting on the tarmac. While they were helping her into the flight suit, Jennifer had laughed at Sergeant Harrison's suggestion that they get a jeep to take her to the plane, not even a hundred yards away, but now she saw that maybe that wouldn't have been a bad idea.

On Wright and the other pilots, the pressurized suits didn't look half as cumbersome as this one felt. It was close to her size, at least; she'd had to put on three pairs of socks to get the boots to fit, and even then she could have gotten three more toes into each before they'd have felt snug.

When Wright asked if she wanted to go up for a ride, she thought she wouldn't even need a pressure suit. After all, the cabin was pressurized, right? But Wright laughed at her—this wasn't an airliner they were going to fly. The suit was important because of the g forces the plane would subject her to; without it, her blood would be sloshed around her body like juice in a half-filled bottle. She'd black out as soon as they started to climb.

Jennifer thought he'd said it to scare her, but the weight of the suit was giving her second thoughts.

"So you're going up, huh?" said Pelham mockingly as she lurched out toward the plane.

"Why not?" she said, even more conscious now of the heavy boots.

"You like roller coaster rides?" he said.

"I love roller coaster rides."

"Multiply the worst one you ever had by ten," laughed Pelham. "And that won't even come close to what you'll feel."

"I hope it's more exciting than that," said Jennifer.

He was a pathetic little bug, especially in comparison with someone like Wright. She was so attracted to the colonel it was starting to border on infatuation. She thought about him as much as she thought about the System, something that seemed to her altogether unprecedented. The attraction had partly to do with an unlocking of her inhibitions when she was with him, a playfulness as well as a physicality she'd often had to repress in the name of work, if not science. This might not be love per se—she was a rigorous categorizer of emotions as well as thought—but the probability that love might develop seemed very high.

She wasn't sure why. If she were calculating something like this, putting it down as a formula on paper, there would be a lot of loose variables. Except for the fact that they were in the same place at the same time, involved in the same project, there wasn't that much they ought to have in common, so there ought not to be anything between them. But that contradicted what she felt.

"Boots a little heavy?" Pelham asked.

"Nothing I can't handle."

She had always thought of herself as an explorer, pushing into areas unknown. That was what attracted her to science, and that was why her work was so intrinsically interesting, even when she was doing the most mundane tasks. The constant sense of pushing was vital to her. Perhaps she was attracted to Wright because he was so unlike her. And unlike the men she had found herself surrounded by over the past few years—she was an explorer here, too, testing uncharted territory.

Or maybe Wright wasn't that different after all. He had the same sense of exploration about him, though in a more physical way. His exploration was done against a more dire background— taking the wrong route could easily mean death. Maybe she craved that immediacy, the upping of the stakes.

He did have something of the jock about him, though. In a lot of ways he wasn't that much different from Pelham, who was guffawing at her efforts to walk almost normally in the special flight outfit. Wright wasn't stupid, but he did occasionally lapse into the "how tough am I" stuff you'd expect from a football player. Those moments were tempered by his admissions at the oddest times—she had been genuinely surprised when he'd said he sometimes got scared while flying. And suggesting she take this ride—as much as he was trying to impress her, he was also trying to share the feeling of flying, and the excitement. It was as important to him as her work was to her, and his wanting to share it was a touching intimacy. Even his talk about the Brotherhood— his roster of war heroes and pilots with the Right Stuff—was endearing.

158

Elrich disapproved, not by saying anything directly, but by his looks when she came onto the computer deck. He'd become more distant than usual in the past few days, and Jennifer suspected that he'd gone the past week almost completely without sleeping, obsessed with pushing the computer toward a breakthrough. She felt he was overemphasizing minor gains, though she had to admit they were encouraging. With three or four more months of work, they might slip through the wall, break the barrier that had tantalized scientists for the better part of fifty years.

Oddly, she didn't feel any urge to be there now. Always before, Elrich's obsessions had been like a magnet, pulling her mind along. Ever since the first day she had met him, he'd challenged her with different problems, a catalyst of thought. He would make a suggestion, and immediately she would see that it was the direction she should work toward.

She couldn't remember a single disagreement; everything he said had seemed to make perfect sense, as if she were just about to think of it herself. Lately, though, she had begun to see him as more manipulative and concerned not so much with science as an agenda he kept locked in his head. Had this darker side of him developed recently, or had she just missed it until now? Was she just becoming disillusioned, a little cynical? Was she realizing that he wasn't the perfect being she had naïvely assumed him to be and inferring a deviousness beyond what was actually there?

"You even look good in a G suit," said Wright, standing in front of the airplane, arms folded, as she made her painfully slow progress toward it. The T-38 was tiny compared to the Coyote, even though it had room for two people. It was painted in a combination of green and brown splotches, a paint scheme she thought would be more appropriate on a marine's uniform than on an airplane.

"It's a gomer," Wright explained. "This is an old fella. Used to simulate gook planes. Never bothered repainting it."

She started to climb up the ladder, but Wright stopped her.

"Gonna need one of these," he told her, pointing to a parachute. "Just in case."

"Yeah, Jennifer," said Pelham, who had followed her to the airplane, "remember who your pilot is."

"I'm sure I won't need it," she said pointedly, but she submitted demurely as Harrison strapped it on, pulling it tight against her body. Then the old sergeant helped her up and into the cockpit, where he pushed her head into a helmet and smooshed her mouth into a tight-fitting oxygen mask. He shouted various instructions, pointing to knobs and buttons—the only thing that seemed important were the two knobs for turning the volume up and listening to ground control and Wright. That and the clip holding the oxygen tube closed, which she was to remove at 10,000 feet.

"There's butt kickers that'll get you out if we have to eject," Wright yelled to her as he climbed in ahead of her. "But you'll have to disconnect—hit this apple here—" He pointed at a green knob that worked the oxygen. "Don't worry about it. We ain't goin' that far."

The chief made one more go at the instructions, pointing at a succession of things she wasn't supposed to touch. Jennifer nodded at each item, not really sure why they thought she'd be tempted to play with the controls.

She felt Wright shifting around as he settled into his seat. It wasn't a reassuring sensation—she'd hoped the plane would feel sturdier. The engines came on and the jet vibrated madly, shaking with power. The whole thing felt more fragile than a canoe being pointed into a raging stream.

Wright's voice exploded into her ears, and she reached quickly for the intercom knob, turning it down.

"You OK back there?" he was asking.

"Yes," she replied weakly.

"Don't sweat it. Gonna be a lot of fun."

Wright radioed to Ford for clearance to taxi—sheerly protocol, since there weren't any other planes on the runway or within miles of their air space. Suddenly the engines revved up, the whole universe shaking now, and she could feel herself moving. The plane swung around and began taxiing toward the end of the runway. Everything smelled like hot kerosene, even through the heavy rubber of the oxygen mask, and for a moment she felt as if she would gag on it, throw up right into the mask. The jerky swing of the plane as it started to roll didn't help any.

"Tom," she said, and she almost asked him to turn back, almost said that she couldn't take it.

"Yeah, honey?"

It was the "honey" that steeled her.

"You gonna fly with the top up or what?" she said, as stiffly as she could manage.

"I figured I'd button up eventually," answered the pilot. Talking to him on the System's radio with half an ocean between them, his voice sounded clear and warm, close. Here, not four feet away, it sounded metallic, filled with static. "When we get to the end of the runway and get a clear, we'll flip it down. Things'll fog up for a second, but don't worry."

"Does it always smell like this?"

"The face mask? They rub it out with alcohol to kill the germs."

"The kerosene."

"Yeah, well, you get used to it. You remember how to take that pin out, right?"

"Which?"

"For the O_2. See it?"

"Roger." Now she was confused—was she supposed to take that out if they jumped, or just when they reached a certain altitude?

"I'll tell you when," he said, as if he'd read her mind.

"Fine."

Ground boomed into her ears, and she readjusted the other volume control. They were cleared for takeoff. The canopy came down with a whoosh and a heavy click; there was a sudden rush of cold air in the cockpit, and Jennifer was surrounded by mist.

"Helmet on tight?"

It felt snugger than anything else she was wearing. "Roger," she said.

"Roger yourself," he answered. "Check your straps and hang on, OK?"

"Fine."

"I generally close my eyes during takeoff," Wright said, "so let me know when we're off the ground."

"Go to hell."

"Uh-oh, now I got you cursing," said Wright. "Chief's gonna make me wash your mouth out with soap."

Jennifer felt her face turn red. "I can curse just like anybody else."

"Not what I heard," said Wright.

The rumble of the engines turned into a continuous explosion and the jet creaked down the runway, hesitating at first and then gaining speed. Lights blinked and faded on the board in front of her; she felt the wet perspiration that had soaked into her suit turn practically to ice. She studied the gauges. Everything here was ancient compared to the Coyote, almost as ancient as the planes Wright constantly talked about. One hundred and twenty knots, one-forty—the plane gripped itself around its backbone and pointed toward the sky, and with not even a quarter of the long concrete runway covered they were in the air, turning gradually to her right and climbing slowly, easily. It happened much more quickly than she thought it would, without a jolt: a smooth progress after all, a flow.

She felt giddy and almost weightless, and entirely surrounded by the suit and the seat, as if the cockpit had swelled to hold her in a cocoon. Below her she heard the sound of machinery cranking swiftly and the plane seemed to jump up suddenly—Wright had lifted the wheels.

"This is neat," she said, genuinely excited and not caring if she sounded like a girl. There was no sign of acknowledgment from the helmet in front of her. The plane was moving swiftly now, the altitude increasing quickly. The feeling of speed and almost weightlessness was a little scary as well as exciting; she felt perspiration moving in the wrinkles of her hands beneath her gloves, though she no longer felt warm.

"I want you to disconnect that lanyard now on the oxygen. It's on the D ring," said Wright.

She reached down and tugged it out. She didn't know what to do with it now that she had it, though. Harrison had pointed to a ring—was that something else she wasn't supposed to touch or was it where she was supposed to put the pin? Not completely sure that she wouldn't go flying out of the cockpit, she clipped it on.

"On your right there's a panel with a green eye that should be blinking at you," said Wright.

She looked at the panel and at a small gauge that showed her oxygen pressure—125.5 liters. It took her a few breaths to realize that the "eye" moved up and down with each gulp.

"Breathing kind of fast?" he asked her.

"I'm doing fine."

"I can hear you gulping. You're lucky we're not in the Coyote—it'd be trying to take over from you."

"Ha, ha," she said, concentrating to deepen and pace out her breaths.

"We're gonna do a couple of circles, just to get used to things. We're not going too fast."

"No?"

"Four hundred knots."

The plane tilted slightly and she found herself looking down at the mountains, straining to see where the base was. The airstrip was down there somewhere, but she couldn't spot it.

"Like the view?" he asked.

"It's great."

"Well hold on, because we're going to do some serious climbing. We're going to get ourselves out over the water. Take us a while."

"The water?"

"The Pacific Ocean? You may have heard of it—it's kind of like a very big pond. Got boats in it and everything."

The plane's nose popped up and she felt herself gain a hundred pounds of dead weight, pressing into the seat as they climbed. Wright was talking to the base, telling them he'd call back on the way home; she turned the volume control down until it was just a stutter in the background. The jet had its own sound, a loud hush that filled her helmet and head as they flew. She wasn't sure if it was actually there, or the result of the padding that squeezed her ears. Either way, it had a vaguely relaxing effect, reinforcing the feeling of almost meditative isolation she felt. The mountains stretched far to both sides, a long ridge of turbulent air, Wright said, but to her the air was extremely calm. She saw the coastline well before they reached it; Wright seemed to sense that she wanted to look down and tilted the plane gently, swinging in a lazy southwestern turn. The tilt was comfortable; she was strapped in so tightly that she didn't have the least sense of falling. They had climbed considerably; it looked as if they were at the very top of the world.

"We've got good weather today," said Wright. "God, we've got no weather—I don't even have a head wind."

"No clouds," said Jennifer.

"Yeah. Sometimes you get days like this and you wonder whether the clouds are human, and they all decided to go on strike. Because almost always there's clouds, even if it's just little wispy things. Now when you've got a real cover—you must have seen that, flying on an airliner, where it's like a carpet."

"Yes," she said.

"Fighter pilots like clouds, since it gives you something to work with, like being in a forest."

"Even with radar?"

"Sure, because radar can't tell you everything. It's not much, but you take whatever you can get. Anything. Half-a-mile-an-hour speed difference, you take it, because you figure you can work with it. Clouds aren't much now; I mean, I wouldn't look up and say, hell, there's no clouds, I ain't flying today. But they used to be everything. In World War I, clouds and the sun were the greatest weapons. I mean, it works both ways, and flying through them in an open cockpit isn't always that easy. But they were a big part of your toolbox. Alfred Heurtax talked about playing hide-and-seek in them, using them during a big free-for-all to get a couple of planes."

"Who was he?"

"World War I. He shot down twenty-one Germans."

"Oh."

"Victor Chapman compared them to ice floes. He wrote this letter trying to explain what clouds are really like. It was a great letter, trying to tell a sweetheart or somebody, I mean, give them a feel for the way they actually are. See, up until then, nobody had really flown. Flying was still this unimaginable thing that crazies did. They'd just invented it, and in the space of ten, fifteen years, they made it into a weapon. Anyway, he wrote this great letter about clouds."

"Was he a writer?"

"Just a pilot. He might have been a writer, after the war, but that was the last thing he wrote; he was shot down right after. Or he crashed. I don't remember."

"That's sad."

"That's the way things happen."

"It's not sad?"

"It's the way things are. Pilots go down. They're either unlucky, or bad pilots, or both."

"Why do you say that?"

" 'Cause it's true."

"Oh, you're full of it, Tom. Don't play the shallow stoic with me."

"You tell yourself stuff that works," said Wright, his voice now innocent and open, as vulnerable as the other night, after they'd kissed. "Otherwise, you either don't get in the plane at all, or worse, you do get in, and you hesitate. If you hesitate in a dogfight, you take too long deciding what you're doing, you're done. Everything happens so fast. You have to have a plan, and stick to it. That's what Fonck said."

"The Ace of Aces," she said.

"How'd you know that?"

"I did a little homework," she said. "Besides, you mentioned him the other night."

"Did I tell you he tried to cross the Atlantic after the war?"

"Twice already," she said playfully, though he hadn't at all. "Do you really tell yourself life is cheap?"

"I tell myself a lot of things," said Wright, his helmet ducking back and forth in front of her. "There's all sorts of stuff you tell yourself when you're flying. You see how quiet it is up here? You can hear what you say."

"Quiet?" she responded. "There's a roar all around me." But she knew what he meant. It did feel quiet. His voice was even quiet, passionate and almost otherworldly, an authoritative whisper in her ear.

"We're five and a half miles up, you know," it said.

"I realized we were quite high."

The Coyote could fly many times higher and faster than this. As amazing as this flight was to her, it must be fairly routine to him. And yet he sounded excited.

"Do you feel like a fighter pilot yet?" he asked.

"Why would I feel like a fighter pilot?"

"Why not?"

"I hate war," she said. "That's the last thing I'd think about up here."

"I don't see how you can hate war so much and still work for the NSC."

Her parents had said the same thing, at much greater length, when she told them she was joining Elrich's team. Her mother was a Quaker; her father, though more moderate, had always been suspicious of the government. She had always shared their political views, but there was an opportunity here—she had a chance to push the boundaries of knowledge, to work on the cutting edge of science. And there was a line, wasn't there, between the work she did and the military's use of it?

She was on the right side of the line, she told them.

She admitted, only reluctantly, that Coyote was a weapon of war, and that the System could be used for other things than pure thought. She knew it would be—the military didn't care about creative thought, except for its contribution on the battlefield.

"You still back there, Fitzgerald?"

"The Coyote's not a fighter plane," she said stubbornly.

"Not yet," he said. "They'll figure out some weapon for it. I'm surprised you aren't already working on it yourself."

"I wouldn't."

"You wouldn't?"

"No. I'd just walk out and leave if they asked me to. If they asked me to do anything involving fighting."

"No you wouldn't," said Wright.

"Men always have to stick a gun into their favorite toys," she said sarcastically.

Wright laughed. She was glad when he changed the subject.

"It's good to fly old planes every so often," said Wright. "I'd like to get back in a prop. This friend of mine, Cole Palen, got an airport back near New York where he's got a bunch of old planes. Used to let me fly 'em."

"Are they a lot different?"

"Slower," he said, "but you'd be surprised how fast they feel, because they're so maneuverable. You're on a different scale. I can't explain it exactly. Your perception is kind of shortened; everything's much closer."

"You sound like you'd prefer them."

"No, not at all. But you really fly them, you know? You really feel them."

"You don't feel planes now?"

"Sure. You feel this, don't you?" he asked, rocking the jet a little.

"What about the Coyote?" she asked.

"It's different. It's hard to explain."

"Maybe it's hard to explain because it's not true," she said.

"Hell, I'm a pilot, not a scientist," he said. "I don't have to quantify everything and put it into a formula. I can just know stuff, without explaining it."

"I see."

They were well over the water now. It looked so shallow from here, a thin puddle laid out in the background.

"Flying isn't something you get in a book," said Wright.

"No?"

"Hell, I'm not saying I never read. I read a lot."

"Mystery novels, though, right?"

"No way. I read a lot about airplanes. Old airplanes—how do you think I know all this stuff I talk about?"

"You don't just make it up?"

"See, I wouldn't read a mystery novel, because it doesn't help me fly."

"Everything you do has to help you fly?" she asked.

"No," he said. "Not everything."

"Do I help you fly?"

"Sure," answered the pilot.

Jennifer laughed. Below them, she could see a ship making its way along the coast, moving so slowly it seemed to be standing still.

"Let's have some fun," said Wright suddenly. "I'm going to drop this sucker down. We'll roll into a dive. You ready? It'll feel a little like a roller coaster."

"So I hear."

"You ain't gonna get sick, right?"

"Don't worry about me."

"We'll pull around and you'll feel about four or five g's, but it won't be too bad."

"OK."

"Oh yeah. There's a slight possibility we'll flame out."

"What's that?"

"The engines might stall. I haven't flown one of these in a while and I'm rusty. They tend to do that if you move the throttle a little too fast; kind of like flooding the engine of a car, only here you're moving."

"Cut it out."

"Usually you can restart it. Sometimes, though—well, that's show biz."

"Always have to play macho, huh?" she said.

His response was to bank the plane sharply, falling into the dive sideways. The suddenness of the maneuver took her by surprise, but as he straightened out the wings the downward path felt almost normal, the maneuvers as gentle as before, even with the push from behind as Wright hit the afterburners for a burst of speed. The Mach dial in front of her climbed up to the high .90s and froze. The T-38 shuddered a bit and then suddenly was released. A giant weight was off and they were flying level, a sonic boom somewhere behind them. The plane glided forward, the dial reaching 1.2 before Wright began banking over the ocean, coasting now, the shudder returning momentarily as they slowed. He came back toward the coast and began doing some slow, lazy turnovers.

"How you making it back there?" Wright asked as they flipped through one.

"Fine."

"Just fine?"

"Fine's enough," she said. Her pulse must be 200 by now; she was almost giddy with the rush of blood. And yet everything felt as if they were standing still. If it was an amusement ride, it was in ultraslow motion.

"You ain't gonna puke on me, are you?"

"I already did. All over the place. What a mess."

"Really?"

"Sure," she said. "What'd you expect?"

"You didn't really."

"Did you?"

"Oh, I've had my moments," he said. "Tell you what—let's put this baby to work. No more sissy stuff."

"OK."

"This is what we call the old max climb turn, MCT, or 'get the hell up there real fast.'"

"Fine," she said, but as the word came out of her mouth her stomach already felt as if it had been buried under the seat. The plane shot upwards and she suddenly gained 500 pounds; even her eyes were too heavy to open. The suit inflated, the built-in air bladders acting like compressors to keep an equal, or almost equal, amount of pressure on the outside of her body as inside. She was wrestling herself, pushing against the pressure of her own blood. She heard herself moan; instantly she wanted it back.

"You OK?" he asked.

"Fine," she said, struggling with her teeth. He quickly leveled the plane off.

"Too much?"

"No, it's wild. Really," she said in spite of her stomach. "It's like you said, a roller coaster."

"You want a roller coaster?"

And he pulled the plane upwards and looped back down, sharp, sharp turns as they slid toward the earth that made the suit press against her. But she was getting used to it. She moved her hands up and down despite the forces that weighed against them; the exertion gave her more energy. In her head, the voice explained each maneuver, and how it might be used if this were a World War I airplane, or World War II, or now, and how the power surged through you when you knew exactly how the plane was to react, and how flying was an act of the mind as much as the body. The faster they went, the more she felt as if they weren't moving at all.

The knot had been growing tighter and tighter in his stomach ever since the plane had picked up the Japanese radar. Now it pulled itself into a rock clump, impossible to unravel, and in agony Elrich pounded the small ledge where the keyboards rested. The vibration was so extreme that it sent the laptop he used for mathematical calculations tumbling to the floor. Once vented, his anger rushed out quickly. He got up and gave the fallen laptop a kick that sent it down the deck, into the middle of the cockpit dupe section. With that, Angles, who had been working at the far end of the room, scurried for the elevator, not sure what his boss's anger would take as its next target.

Elrich ignored him—aside from making sure no one came close enough to see or hear what he was doing, he'd been only vaguely aware of the people surrounding him all morning. It was going on 11 A.M., but Elrich had no more notion of what time it was than he knew who had won the last Super Bowl, and he cared even less. He stalked to the laptop and with a curse he picked it up and flung it against the concrete wall. It cracked in half, but the case had closed and the computer remained intact; again he picked it up and flung it at the wall. Still in one piece. He pulled the two halves apart and flung the screen like a Frisbee back across the deck. It crashed into one of the auxiliary keyboards, sending it over to the floor. He threw the other half of the laptop to the ground and stepped on it, mashing it beneath his foot, mashing it as he would have mashed all of his mistakes, this one especially, this one only—trusting Ki. Stupidly trusting Ki. For Elrich knew that the radar ID had not been a malfunction, and he knew that the information he had given the Japanese scientist had helped him immeasurably.

Ki had even mentioned, vaguely, that Netsubo was working on a hypersonic plane. Ignorantly, Elrich had assumed it was a passenger plane, something to challenge Boeing.

That wouldn't have an FSX-style radar in it.

"System," he said, returning to the console somewhat calmer, "place the data into my personal file." He looked around and noticed, made sure, that he was alone. "Encode its existence my access only."

"Acknowledged."

The System had just finished tracking a series of incursions Ki or his assistants had made into American DOD computers. His recent interest in the question of the System's ability to disable planes in flight was now understandable—Ki was worried that Elrich might try and break into his airplane.

But it was Elrich who had suggested that he disable the planes. No, he'd been cleverly led to suggest that. They'd been talking about the invulnerability of certain computer systems. Ki had brought up the topic, and had used airplanes as an example. And the American scientist, anxious for a collaborator, anxious for a mind that could keep up with his, had readily taken the bait.

Elrich didn't think that Ki could threaten other American planes with the virus he had used to disable the B-2 and the Merc. The procedure, once the Japanese scientist had seen it in action, would seem simple enough: the instructions that stopped the engines were contained in a seemingly legitimate guidance signal from the Block 54 satellites used by bombers and spy planes while navigating, a signal that Elrich had used the System to access and alter. But because the signal itself relied on an encryption that changed according to a set of formulas Elrich had carried out on his own, outside the network, Ki would be unable to break through if he tried using the same coding.

That was small consolation, however. Ki had been interested in his own plane, not the bomber or spy plane.

Were they crazy enough to look for a war?

Elrich had been foolish. He could have trained a collaborator here. Jennifer would have been a perfect candidate—she still might be.

No, she was off with the pilot. He'd lost her, somehow, in the past few days.

He could have used her help now. But at least he had the System.

Elrich had no illusions about Ki's boss, Ieyasu, the man who ran Netsubo. His government machines were needed to guard against precisely that kind of thinking—aggressively nationalistic, fatal, fascist. The Japanese businessman, who saw himself as a throwback to the warlords of medieval Japan, would inevitably push the smoldering conflict between Japan and America to a war. The plane he had built was intended as an aggressive weapon.

Ki would have prepared his defenses well. Still, there would be a way around them.

But what else did Ki have? How potent was the plane Netsubo had built?

"System, prepare to enter ApsR," said Elrich, referring to a secret Russian military defense-development network. "Use the Romanian code, transparent and nontraceable, obviously."

"Acknowledged."

"System," added Elrich, "originate the call from the University of Tokyo."

Even for the System, this was going to take some time. Elrich stood back, staring at the video screens that documented the computer's exertions. He was so close, just on the threshold—a few more problems to overcome, and they would burst through to the next level.

Now everything was threatened.

Even if Elrich didn't particularly care what happened between America and Japan—and though the scientist might claim he didn't, he'd been working with the military too long not to be vaguely chauvinistic—the government people would undoubtedly begin wondering whether there had been some leak from the Coyote project. There would be investigations. He had covered himself well, but even a hint of suspicion would hurt now, now when he was so close.

But beyond that, he had a responsibility to stop Ki and the madman Ieyasu.

Elrich went to the deck's doorway and locked it, setting the security device, which by practice was usually left off. Since almost no one on the closed base walked around with their ID card, anyone wanting to come in would have to buzz. He could talk freely to the System, without worrying about being surprised.

The seat moved as he sat in front of the console, and he was so exhausted that it almost got away from him.

"Request completed," said the System. "We are in ApsR."

"Look for a path that has a pattern similar to what you found in the DOD systems," said Elrich. "Try permutations of the codes."

"Affirmative. Do you wish a record of all correlations?"

"A record, sure. Dump them into my file." Elrich thought for a moment. It had been a while since he'd been in the Russian top secret military network. "Tell me if there is a trail to, a . . ." He couldn't remember the code word for the project he suspected Ki would be interested in. But that wasn't a problem, really. "Any projects that have to do with phased-array particles. I believe we found a project like that a year ago, or eight months—check through your records."

"Affirmative. I have already detected a correlation."

"A correlation with your records, or a correlation with the search?"

"Both."

Son of a bitch.

The Russians had two phased-array projects going. Essentially high-energy ray guns, neither was as advanced as American work in the field. Except in two respects—both weapons were relatively small and they were easy to operate.

The U.S. had already built several extremely powerful beam generators under the auspices of the Star Wars program; Elrich knew the space-based "guns" had been on the verge of going operational when the Congress had unexpectedly killed the satellite program a few years before. There had been some consideration of placing a beam weapon in the Coyote Bird, but its size presented too many technical problems for the plane and the idea was dropped.

But the Russian design, though less powerful, might fit with comparatively little fuss. Cut flying time, since it would take the place of fuel. But that might be acceptable to Ieyasu, expecting to operate relatively close to his base of operations, not halfway around the world.

"When did our friends gain access to this information?" Elrich asked.

The System pondered the question. It had found the incursion through sheer force rather than finesse, computing and comparing times and tie-in codes. All of this was impressive—not something you did with your average Cray—but not exactly new ground. Its answer now was mostly a matter of arithmetic, cajoling the Russian computer to share its usage logs and then calculating the patterns.

"Eight months ago," said the System finally.

"I want you to do an assessment," said Elrich, leaning into his console, his voice straining. "Get all the data on the weapon you can. Then tell me whether the Russian weapon could be modified to be carried by a plane similar to Coyote, or to air force project 13-598." Project 13-598 was the air force's official designation for the superplane's requirements, which the Coyote had exceeded. "Plane could be modified to accommodate weapon, but would have to remain within performance specs of 13-598, give or take ten percent, with the exception of mission endurance. Can you do that?"

"Of course."

"Once we can compute the capabilities of the Japanese plane," said Col. Albert Gates, "the operation itself should be relatively easy." The air force strategy specialist had been brought to the meeting by the secretary of defense. "Four groups of two planes, for a total of eight missiles, would be my preliminary recommendation. I've flown two computer-generated mock engagements already, using the Coyote specs. All I have to do is plug the real data in and it'll be child's play."

It was the desk jockey's matter-of-fact condescension that broke Billy Hunter's promise to himself that he would remain calm.

"Damn it, Henry," said the general, turning to the director, who was at the head of the conference-room table. "I've got months of testing ahead of me just to make sure the plane is flying right. And the computer still has a long way to go."

Part of his irritation was due to the fact that he'd been woken by Morse at three o'clock in the morning, California time, and he'd then had to scramble to make arrangements to get back here in time for the 4 P.M. meeting. But his fatigue was only a small bit of it.

"We'll coordinate the flights with airborne controllers," said Morse cooly. "No one is asking the computer to do something it hasn't done."

"I got to run my plane over an island where we've already lost two planes?"

"General, please be assured that the Coyote is quite invulnerable," started Gates.

"How the hell do you know?" spit Hunter. "You work on the project? You involved in any of the design for it? Any of the planning? You ever fly the goddamn thing?"

"Let's not get personal here," said Sasso, the secretary of defense.

Hunter flattened his hand on the polished oak table, overcoming the urge to pound it. He'd heard rumors that the NSC conference room was completely refurbished each year at a cost that would keep a group of F-22s aloft for six months. Goddamn Washington Disease. Same mentality used a computer game to figure out the odds on risking somebody's life.

"All I'm saying is that the plane and the computer are untested," said Hunter. "We have a long way to go. Using them to draw out a plane that may or may not exist is lunacy."

"If there isn't a plane," said Morse, "there won't be a problem."

"General, this isn't exactly a passing whim," said Sasso. The secretary of defense, sitting directly across from him, began fiddling with a mechanical pencil, slowly twisting the lead out. "The president himself has ordered this."

"I know, but—"

"There's no 'but.' It's crucial that we do something about the Japanese plane," said Sasso. "We estimate that the danger is minimal, especially to the Coyote Bird."

"Was that what you said about the Merc this thing took out?"

"You know that the SR-91 isn't that maneuverable," said Sasso.

"Damn right, I know that," said Hunter. "I built the thing."

"Calm down, Billy," said Morse quietly.

"The SR-91 Mercury probably crashed because of pilot-induced problems," said Gates. "We have examined all of the data, and it is very likely that in trying to countermaneuver, the pilot sent the plane into a spin. Something similar happened out of Kadena a year ago during a routine flight. And there was an error in Europe a few days—"

"That was not related to the pilot," said Hunter. "That was mechanical."

"The investigation is still open," said Gates.

"You ever been a pilot, Colonel?"

"Sir?"

"You ever fly a plane?"

"No."

"What's the relevance here, General?" asked Sasso, once again protecting his subordinate.

"I'm not going to have somebody who doesn't know a stick from a throttle attack my pilot's abilities."

"No one's attacking anyone," said Gates.

"The point is, no weapon seems to have been used against the Merc," said Morse calmly. "We haven't come up with any traces of missile telemetry, and believe me, we've looked for it. It's beyond belief that a heat-seeking missile launched from the FSXs could have taken the plane out. You know the Merc's capabilities, Billy. And you know how it flies. Sudden maneuvers, perhaps a close flyby, it's not inconceivable the pilot crashed it. Especially a relatively new pilot."

Hunter knew it was possible, perhaps even likely. Even with all the fancy computers that helped fly it, the SR-91 was a relatively unstable plane if you asked it to do anything but fly in a straight line.

"All you have to do is get the Japanese plane out," said Gates. "Have the Coyote come right back after that—directly back to its base."

"We've got to do it twice," said Hunter. "Once to find out how capable it is so you can work out your computer simulation, and then to shoot it down."

"The mission is well within the capabilities of the plane," said Morse.

"What happens when the planes are blinded?"

"It's a short window of vulnerability," said Gates. "There won't be any damage to the Coyote, since nobody will be shooting at it.

Drop its speed and set it to orbit until the interference clears. There's no need to risk a pilot. The computer can fly the plane."

Hunter said nothing.

"You have a reputation for being stubborn," said Sasso, "which is one of the reasons you were asked to head the project in the first place. But honestly, General, don't you feel your plane is capable of accomplishing what we're asking? It's been flying for several months."

Flying for several months was not quite the same thing as this. Still, Hunter had begun to feel less sure of himself. On principle, he was certainly right—taking a plane directly from a test program and using it in a crucial military operation was loaded with risks. As a practical matter, however, this could almost be looked at as an advanced test—scrimmage with the full pads on—and arguably no more difficult than anything they planned to do with the Coyote over the next four or five months. But it was their manner that he really objected to, their assumptions that it was easy, that they could hop to it in a day or so.

"What do you think, Billy?" said Morse. "Can we do it or not?"

The national security director's voice had changed, lowered, become more intimate. It wasn't ordering anymore, it was asking.

This was Henry Morse talking, a man he'd met under the worst circumstances, and spilled his guts to. A man he'd kept in contact with, drunk with, even taken vacations with, for three decades. A man he'd helped, and who had helped him.

No more self-important strutting, just his friend, asking if they could undertake an extremely difficult, important mission, do something the president himself had ordered.

"Yes," said Hunter finally. "On my end. But shooting down anything that flies as well as the Coyote is going to be pretty damn tough, even if it's not expecting it."

"With all due respect, that's our problem," said Gates.

Morse looked at Gates. "I don't think we need you anymore this afternoon, Colonel," he said. "You have quite a bit of work to do."

"Yes, sir," said the officer, standing.

"I'd better be going, too," said Sasso.

"General, I didn't mean to speak out of turn," said the colonel. "I admire the work you've done."

Hunter grunted, then returned the colonel's smart salute, a sign of respect.

"There's a backup plan," said Morse when the others had left the secure room, locking the door behind them. "It involves Case B."

"Case B? Wasn't that the orbiting Star Wars system that was put on the shelf five years ago?"

"It never made it to the shelf," said Morse. "Not exactly. The satellites had already been launched, and so they put Phase One into effect."

"God," said Hunter. "I remember those hearings. I was in the Pentagon. Jesus, are you telling me they went ahead anyway?"

"It didn't involve any new allocations, and key members of Congress knew about it. In any event, we inherited it when we came into office. It would be perfect for shooting down the plane, assuming we could swing it into the right location. But the president doesn't want to use it—the political fallout would be too great."

"No kidding."

"It'll be there if you need it. We'll establish a link between your base and DEFSMAC in Maryland," said Morse, referring to the Defense Special Missile and Astronautics Center, which controlled the system along with its other satellites. "It's all automated. Case B will track the planes during the second mission; you'll be able to order a shoot-down simply by pushing a button. But the weapon will only be effective in specific areas."

"Where are they?"

"There's one over the Soviet Union, near the Pacific, not too far from where the intercept will probably take place. I've arranged for someone at DEFSMAC to brief you as soon as we're done here."

Hunter quietly took stock. He saw the danger of the Japanese plane, but he wondered how much would truly be gained by shooting it down. If they had built one, they could build more.

"The Japanese plane has to be destroyed," continued Morse. "The country is just on the verge of deciding whether to rewrite its constitution. If the militaristic factions win out, there will eventually be another world war."

Morse's eyes rose from the table and held Hunter's firmly in their gaze.

"This will show them that the military option isn't feasible," said Hunter's old friend. "This will show that it would be madness to antagonize us. But we must succeed. Everything will be riding on it."

"This doesn't have anything to do with your father," said Hunter softly.

176

"No, I've thought about that a lot," said Morse.

Hunter nodded, then slowly rose from his chair.

"There's one other thing," said Morse. "The FBI thinks there may be some sort of problem at the base."

"What?" Hunter practically fell back into his seat.

"We're not sure exactly what's going on," said Morse. "I have an FBI agent heading out there right now. He's working on another case, which has to do with some malfunctions in air force planes—including the Merc your new pilot was flying before we brought him to Coyote."

"Wright?"

"According to this FBI agent, there's a chance some sort of sophisticated computer virus might have been responsible."

"How's Coyote involved?"

"Probably it's not; but the agent theorized that the first two planes were disabled by someone who had worked in their development, and therefore he might or might not be working on the Coyote. My impression was that he threw that out to make sure I'd let him talk to Wright. But if a computer was involved—"

"No one on my team is using the System for anything other than what it's supposed to be used for."

"There are plenty of other computers there," said Morse. "I'd also like to know how the Japanese knew where to look."

"The CIA just said we were clean. God, Henry, this is all we need."

"I'm sorry. The FBI agent knew too much for me to just shut him off. I sent him before this was worked out, and then it was too late to recall him. No matter how wild a theory it was, I couldn't take the risk of their going to the president with it, especially after the Netsubo photo raised questions about our security. Obviously, if there is someone at the base knocking down our planes—"

"Nonsense," said Hunter heatedly. He'd had each person checked carefully, reviewed their records himself. He'd known most of them for years.

"His name is Fisher," said the director. "He acts like he's a know-nothing wise ass, but he's fairly sharp."

"When is he getting there?"

"He ought to be there by now, assuming he doesn't get lost. I didn't authorize military transport," said Morse, rising. "If that's any consolation. I'm sure you're right, Henry. But it won't hurt to have him there. The damn CIA has screwed up all kinds of things lately."

"Thanks a lot," said Hunter.

He didn't like big cars. Driving a big car made you feel like you were going to a goddamn funeral, or worse, like you were on surveillance. Being on surveillance was the pit of the pits, the modern equivalent of being taken live into an anthill. Fisher hated anything that reminded him of it, even vaguely.

The problem was that the stupid attendants always assumed that you wanted a big car, like you ought to be pleased that they pointed you toward it. Not that he wanted to be caught dead in the other choice on the lot—a shiny red two-and-a-half-cylinder Hyundai. But there ought to be some sort of middle ground, maybe a turbo-charged coupe or something.

At least the car had started right up and not given him any problems, a minor miracle considering the rest of the trip. When he'd gotten off the airliner in San Francisco they'd told him the flight to Redding had been canceled—actually, they'd said no such flight existed, even as he waved the ticket in the fat woman's face. Rather than just renting a car then, as he should have done, Fisher had let himself be influenced by their apologies. He had accepted booking on a plane to Sacramento, and then another to a place called Chico, which they claimed was nearer to his admittedly rather vague destination than his original airport, which apparently was no longer accepting incoming flights. (They could not sufficiently explain why this was so, and in fact seemed to imply that it had been swallowed up in one of the state's periodic earthquakes.)

The flight to Sacramento, though delayed interminably, was reasonable enough. Calling the contraption that took him to Chico a plane, however, was stretching the definition beyond all reasonable bounds. The one saving grace was the fact that he could smoke on the flight. The pilot didn't seem to mind, and the only other passenger in the six-seater was as big a smoker as Fisher. His companion had also brought along his own supply of whiskey, sipping from a flask at regular intervals. Fisher was reassured when the pilot declined an offer of a swig just after takeoff, but overall the pilot's flying skills left much to be desired. He kept reaching down to adjust a piece of his radio equipment; when he did, the plane leaned to the side with him. He was oblivious to the maneuver each time, until he sat back up, at which point he said,

"Oops, off course" loudly and proceeded to correct his flight path with a sharp pull that felt like a barrel roll. It took only two such maneuvers for Fisher to accept the proffered flask.

The rental-car people at Chico were nice enough, aside from their fascination with limousines, but for some reason the company had just put in a new procedure that required ten forms to be filled out before he could begin doing the actual paperwork for the car. The questions stopped just short of a full medical examination, and by the time the procedure was finished, Fisher thought he might have willed his house to Avis. Having survived that, he set out on a long odyssey to find a road map. There were plenty of maps available in the several stores and gas stations he visited, but they were all of other states, including three of New Jersey—no doubt a popular destination for many northern Californians. In frustration, Fisher ended up buying a large atlas in a bookstore.

By the time he finally started driving toward the base, it was after dark. Not that he'd planned on doing any sight-seeing, but his directions off the main road were sketchy—mostly a succession of turnoffs on unmarked roads. God only knew where he'd end up in the dark. And he wasn't entirely sure what the reaction was going to be at the top secret base if he showed up at three in the morning.

At least all of the driving had given him time to work out a plan of attack. The first thing he'd get was a personnel list, run through it and see if he had any matches. Then he'd talk to the pilot, not just about the plane crash, but about the people on the base. And then he had to get as much information as he could about the computer, and the people who ran it.

As for looking for a security leak, Fisher had about as much chance of finding one as he did of suddenly coming across the Eiffel Tower. But he figured Morse's imprimatur could be a useful weapon. As for keeping him informed—well, he'd talk to him as much as he talked to Cringer when he was on a case, which wasn't often.

Ordinarily, Fisher liked working alone. But coming out here without somebody who knew their way around computers was dubious. Fisher could bluff his way through a lot, but he wasn't going to be fooling any computers.

He had another problem right now—he'd been getting low on gas for the past half hour, but hadn't seen an open gas station. Finally he saw a convenience store ahead. His luck was holding, however—although the place was all lit up, the damn gas pumps didn't seem to work. Cursing, he went inside.

The sleepy-eyed kid behind the counter looked all of fifteen.

"Hey there," said the FBI agent. "Can you switch the gas pump on for me?"

"Nope," said the kid.

"What do you mean, nope?" said Fisher, leaning on the counter. "Your hands broke?"

"Can't sell gas after ten o'clock. It's the law."

"What law?" said Fisher incredulously.

"Town law," said the kid, looking at Fisher as if he'd fallen in from another planet. "Can't sell gas after ten."

"Why the hell not?" said Fisher.

"Got me, mister," shrugged the kid. "Conservation or something. I never asked."

"You got gas, though," said Fisher, standing back and looking around the store. "There's gas in the tanks."

"Oh sure, plenty of gas. Just can't sell it."

"That's the same for all the gas stations around here?"

"Ain't no other gas stations around."

"Why would there be," said Fisher, taking out a cigarette, "when they can't sell gas?"

"Can't sell it on weekends either," said the kid. "Dumb law."

"Yeah," said Fisher.

"You ain't supposed to smoke in here either."

"Life's a bitch," said Fisher, lighting and then drawing in on the cigarette slowly.

"Everybody does, though," said the kid, apparently trying to be friendly. "Don't bother me none."

"How long you figure it'll take you to unlock the tanks and fill me up?"

"Can't do that," said the kid. "I got it all measured out and everything already. Got to log it in when I shut it down."

"Uh-huh," said Fisher, looking at his watch. "How long you figure it'll take?"

"It's against the law," said the kid, who was beginning to look a little nervous.

"Just like smoking, right?"

"Well, uh—"

"A lot of things are against the law, don't you think?" said Fisher, waving his cigarette in the air for emphasis, and then leaning closer as if he knew a secret. "Smoking marijuana, for instance."

"I never smoked pot in my life," said the kid, a little more convincingly than Fisher wanted to hear. Of course: he'd found the only kid in California who had never smoked dope.

"Well let me shake your hand," said Fisher dramatically. The kid eyed him warily. "No, no, here," said Fisher, extending it. "Go ahead, shake. I ain't gonna bite." The kid kept his distance; Fisher continued as if they were about to become old friends. "Always glad to meet a law-abiding citizen. What was your name?"

"Uh, Don."

"Well listen, uh-Don, you got any coffee?"

"Just that," he said, pointing to a pot whose contents had been boiled to a fine sediment, perhaps over the course of several days.

"You were just gonna make a fresh pot, weren't you?" said Fisher.

"Uh, no."

"You wouldn't drink that yourself, would you?"

"I don't drink coffee."

"Kind of boring life, huh Don?" said Fisher. "No gas, no cigarettes, no coffee. Tell you what—you go fill up my car, and I'll make the coffee." It was a major concession, but if the kid didn't drink coffee, he probably couldn't make it very well either. Fisher took the pot and went behind the counter to clean it in the sink.

"I told you," said the kid, "it's against the law."

"Son," said Fisher, "I *am* the law." Slightly overblown, but this kid was obviously a nerd, and if he didn't do something he'd be stuck here all night.

"Huh?"

Fisher reached into his jacket for his wallet, making sure to give the kid a good glimpse of the shoulder holster. It had the desired effect—the kid jumped back a good six feet, his face purple. "FBI," said Fisher, flashing the ID. "Fill it up."

The kid fumbled for the keys and then jumped into action, running out to the car.

"I hate these premeasured packages," said Fisher to himself. "Takes all the personal initiative out of it."

7

A MAGICIAN

This time it was a single plane. He was behind and the paper-white fuselage glowed in the distance, as if a fire were burning inside it, turning the metal iridescent. But this was just some trick of the sun, a huge yellow orb hanging in the sky, almost directly behind the double tail fins of Wright's P-38 Lightning. That was a great piece of luck, to be both behind the Zero and to have the sun to distract the pilot if he should turn around. Wright reached to his left and pulled the red knobs of the throttles to pick his speed up, hoping to close to a fatal distance before the Japanese pilot turned around and saw him. Full out, the P-38 could go faster than the Zero, but the Japanese plane was much lighter and could easily turn inside him. It could also dive faster—if he didn't watch himself, he could easily end up in front of, not behind, the Zeke.

Somewhere in the back of his head he knew this was a dream, but it was a dim awareness; more immediate was dealing with the Lightning.

It responded to his controls at least, did what he wanted it to, but did so slowly, moving as if the air were a heavy fluid that dampened and dulled all of his motions. The thing to do was roller-coaster into the Zero, keeping his airspeed up. He would close above the enemy, then dive down and pull back up, hitting the Zeke on the rise. He had to remember the maneuvering stop on the flaps; if they went into a full dive after he engaged, he would have to use the flaps for control. Typically, the Zero would break to the right, an instinctual reaction; Wright decided to cheat a little in that direction, hitting from the left flank so his enemy's maneuver would keep a broad target in his gunsights. If the Zero flipped the other way, or dove straight down, he would follow by tipping his wing to the left, as sharply as he needed to to keep the Zero in his sights. That was a more problematic maneuver, but even there, if he let the plane float a little through the diving turn, he could gain enough of an angle to hit the Zero hard when he started to climb again.

If the plane would maneuver the way his head said it would . . .

It was cold, the cockpit was very cold, even though the heater was up full. He pounded the heater knob hanging by his head, and then turned to the control for the gun-compartment heat. He hoped the guns were warmer than he was. His windshield was clear of frost, but he was freezing. Every part of his body was ice.

He was closing on the Zero. The Japanese pilot hadn't seen him and was blithely flying along. Maybe he had other problems—he ought not to be alone here. But then Wright was alone, too.

The American had four 12.7-mm machine guns and a 20-mm cannon in his nose, just waiting to chew through the Zeke's thin fuselage. A little closer, and it'd be dinnertime.

The Japanese pilot should have heard him coming, even if he didn't have rear-end radar or hadn't seen him out of the mirror or turned around, done his checks like he should have. The Lightning was a loud plane, one of the loudest going; it should be clearly audible even over the Zero's own engine. But he hadn't heard him.

The Japanese pilot should have felt him coming. If he was a real pilot—if he were a member of the Brotherhood—every ounce of his body would have twitched with the alert. He should have turned before it was too late, at least once looped back to make sure his one-eighty was clean. At a minimum he should have hit the gas, at least have something going for him.

This was going to be almost too easy.

Wright put the plane into the shallow dive with a charge that felt like he was a kid at the top of a snow-covered hill, jumping onto his Flexible Flyer. He skated down and then up, his wings banked slightly, both of his hands perched at the top of the wheel, thumb set over the cannon. He reminded himself again of the dive flap.

His angle was perfect, straight into the red dot on the plane's fuselage.

He let loose with everything, the thump of the guns shaking his plane so violently that it seemed as if it were receiving, not firing, the bullets.

But he'd misjudged the speed, both his own and his target's. It was an unthinkable and potentially fatal sin. He'd gotten too close somehow, and was by the Zero with maybe only a half-burst from his guns. The Japanese pilot hadn't even had time to react before Wright was cursing himself and trying to turn sharply enough to close behind him again. Wright was too jerky with the controls—the fluid that held the plane let go suddenly—and the plane almost spun out from under him. His instinct was to let it fall, as he might have done with a jet at twice this altitude. That was the wrong thing to do, obviously; potentially fatal in a Lightning with its brittle tail, but he realized it quickly, thank God, and leveled off just in time to have the Zero catch him broadside, raking his radiator and the fuselage it was attached to before banking around for another run.

Wright had done everything wrong so far, but here was a break. The Lightning couldn't have kept up with the Zero if Wright followed into the turn, but he had no intention of doing that. Instead he spun around the other way. The radiator wasn't damaged, or at least not meaning-fully; all his pressures were steady and his coolant temperature, marked by a double-moon gauge on the far right of his dashboard, seemed all right. Wright angled his plane directly for the Zero, coming head-on bluster, ready to macho the Japanese pilot out.

If the Zeke were smart, he'd break off. Wright was mad now, angry that he'd screwed up such a perfect sitting duck. But that was all right—flying like that, he didn't deserve such a lucky break. In fact, for screwing it up, he deserved to have the Zero wax his engine. He'd gotten off damn easy, considering it was still working. Now he was going to take him out, blow right through him with everything he had.

The Mitsubishi came straight at him out of the turn, not diving, not climbing. That surprised him—the Zero was a good machine, but its pilot would do better by keeping his distance until he found a real opening, something he could exploit. Coming straight at the American plane was playing into Wright's hands—the Lightning could take a lot more punishment than the Zero could. Wright had only to play for a draw to win.

This was lunacy. The Japanese pilot was flying right at him, his wings lit with the fire of the guns, shooting way too soon. Wright held his own fire until they were close, very close, heading toward each other, a game of chicken at a little better than 300 miles an hour. He wanted to tilt his port wing up at the last minute, then bank a little higher than

*his opponent, but he had to time it to the last second, not give himself
away, and broaden the target.*

*What a fool the Japanese pilot was to start firing from so far away.
His bullets dropped harmlessly below. He'd be out of ammunition by the
time they were close enough to do any damage.*

*Wright kept looking for him to break away. They were close, bulling
right toward each other. In a half second Wright's engines would be fat
targets for the red exploding wing edges coming straight at them. Wright
fired now, fired directly into the cockpit, all the way into the cockpit.
His own engines were growling and spitting, something wrong, but he
was shooting right into the Zeke's cockpit, glass flying all over the place.
Still the Japanese pilot flew straight for him. The engines wouldn't lift
him.*

Wright jumped up in the split second before the two planes
collided. Disoriented, cursing himself for being a fool, he sat in the
middle of a dark well, not knowing where he was.

"What's wrong?"

Jennifer was lying next to him. They were on the floor, where
they'd put his mattress and one they'd requisitioned from an empty
room nearby the night before.

After they'd gotten back from the flight yesterday, Jennifer had
suggested an early afternoon picnic. They'd gone to the top of one
of the hills, put on a show for the guards watching from posts
circling the base. Then she'd sweet-talked a cook into a bottle of
wine, and they'd watched her copy of Charlie Chaplin's *The Gold
Rush*. Then they had come back here. He had talked to her about
airplanes for two hours until finally she pulled him down into her
eyes, surrounding him with her soft, supple breasts.

"Tom?"

"I just had a dream," he said.

"What did you dream?"

"Just a dream." Wright tried to laugh, but his throat was raspy
and dry.

Just a dream about how to fly, how to be a pilot.

She reached up her hand, gently touching his chest.

"Are you OK?" she asked.

"Yeah, I'm fine," said Wright. "I dreamed I was in a dogfight."
His laugh was more successful this time. "I was flying a P-38, and
I pulled probably the most boneheaded maneuver possible—I got
run into, head on."

"No more wine before bedtime," she said softly. Her voice was a murmur, urging him back down beside her, and he slid back, then reached over and pulled her body toward him.

"I'm in the crack," she laughed, and he rolled her over on top of him. The room was still very dark, but his eyes were beginning to adjust and he could make out the shadows of her face, framed by the long hair that hung down and brushed his shoulders. Her breasts hovered inches away, their warmth tickling his chest.

Jennifer stayed there for a moment, and then just as he thought she was going to fold down and kiss him, she leaned across to the end of the mattress.

"What time do you think it is?" she asked.

"Come back here." He pulled her back and it was a game, their bodies wrestling together. She was stronger than he'd expected; he succeeded in pulling her back, but she had the watch in her hand. She sunk into him for a long kiss, and then another, and a third before she checked the time.

"I should get back to my room."

"Why? We're not flying again until tomorrow."

"It's almost five o'clock. I'm in enough trouble as it is," she said, rolling over beside him.

"What trouble? You're not in high school."

"I feel guilty for taking the whole day off yesterday."

"You were training," said Wright. "Besides, you said you had the day off."

"I still feel guilty," she said, propping herself up on an elbow.

"You don't get a day off?"

"I've never taken a whole day off."

"Never?"

"Not here, no. Not even back in Tuxedo, except for weekends. Gene will be muttering all day."

She was referring to her boss, Elrich.

"He's the one who said you could take off, right?"

"Yeah, but that doesn't mean anything," said Jennifer.

"You aren't afraid of him, are you?"

"Of course not. But he has this way of making me feel guilty."

"It's because of his glasses," said Wright, sliding up on his own elbow and facing her. "People with glasses always make you feel guilty." He put his hand on the curve of her hip. Her body was cool and smooth. "That's why they make librarians wear them, so you shut up when they hiss at you to be quiet."

"I should get back to my room."

"Come on," he said, pulling her close, over the crack, onto his side of the bed, onto his chest. His hands were searching her back when they were both startled by a loud knock at the door.

"Uh, Colonel Wright? The general wants to see you for a meeting."

Jennifer dove for her side of the bed and unraveled the blanket for some cover. Wright propped himself up on his elbows.

"Who's out there?"

"It's Pete Foreman. One of the crew."

"Hey, Petey. What the hell you doing up at this hour? We're not flying this morning. Or did I miss a day?"

Jennifer reached over the side of the mattress for her clothing. Wright reached out and stopped her. God, she was pretty.

"The general sent me to wake you up."

"The general?"

"Well, actually the chief, sir. He woke us up and told me to get you. He had orders directly from the general."

"What's this all about?" asked Wright. He almost broke into laughter as Jennifer rolled out of his grasp and pulled her panties from the floor. She ducked back under the covers to pull them on.

"Something big is up. There's a meeting of key base personnel at 0500."

"When's that?"

"That would be in five minutes."

Jennifer reached back over the side of the mattress, fishing for another piece of clothing. Wright sat up, watching as her arm hunted over the side.

"Five minutes, huh?" said Wright. "That's barely enough time to shave."

Jennifer finally reached her T-shirt and sat up to put it on. Wright grabbed it from her hand, and stifling a laugh, held it away from her. The pilot had a hard time keeping quiet as she lunged for it.

"Ssshh," he told her.

"Sir?"

"Oh, just kind of talking to myself," said Wright. Jennifer drew her arms back, crossed one in front of her breasts modestly, and used the other first for an obscene gesture, and then one that demanded her shirt back. Her head was tilted slightly to the side, probably a little red, though he couldn't tell with the dim light.

"Tell you what, Pete," said Wright, "I'll be down in a couple of minutes."

"Sir, the word that was used was *pronto*."

"Pronto? That a direct quote?"

"I think that came from the general himself, sir. I think there may have been a couple of other words, too. The point of it being to the effect that it's hi-pri."

It must be, for a five o'clock meeting. Still, Jennifer was so beautiful, sitting there in front of him, her arm outstretched.

"I'm supposed to bring you along personally."

"Aw come on, Pete. I graduated kindergarten."

"Just my orders, sir."

Wright reluctantly handed over the T-shirt. Jennifer took it triumphantly, and he loved the way her whole upper body stretched as she put it on.

"OK, OK," said Wright, standing. "Let me get some clothes on and—"

"Uh, sir, would Jennifer Fitzgerald be in there, would you know?"

Jennifer fell back on the mattress as if she'd been shot.

"Well, I think I'd know if she were here," smirked Wright.

"Uh, I have orders to, ah, fetch her, too."

"Fetch?"

"Yes, sir. And the, ah, rumor was, I'd, ah, find her here."

"Well, I don't know what to say," started Wright.

"I'll be right out," said Jennifer, pushing herself up from the bed and looking for the rest of her clothes.

Fisher, exhausted and frustrated, saw his chance when Hunter emerged from the office with one of his aides.

"Listen, General," he said, ducking in front of him and sticking his hand in the middle of Hunter's chest. "I been waiting all night to talk to you."

"I'm busy right now, Mr. Fisher," said Hunter. The MP who'd been keeping an eye on the FBI agent came over quickly from the side and grabbed his arm.

"Don't touch me," Fisher told him, turning quickly and pointing his finger at the soldier with such authority that he let go. Fisher turned back to Hunter, who had started to take a step down the hall. "General, it's not like I'm here on my own."

"I know the whole story," said Hunter. "I talked with Dr. Morse about you yesterday afternoon. I know what you're up to."

"He told you he sent me?"

"He told me you were on a wild goose chase. This base is secure as hell. I've got my own security people and Central Intelligence—I don't need you."

"Maybe we should call Washington and straighten this thing out."

The MP grabbed him again. Another had come up behind him, and the FBI agent suspected that a truncheon would appear next.

"I don't like being manhandled," said Fisher.

"Let him go," said Hunter, who then turned and started walking again.

"Come on, General," said Fisher, catching up to him. "We're not enemies here. I just got a job to do, right?"

"I'm busy right now," said Hunter. "I don't have time to hold some goddamn FBI agent's hand."

"I'll hold my own hand," said Fisher. "All I need from you is a nod to your people—they won't let me take a crap alone until you give the word."

Hunter stopped and spun toward him. Hunter was a good half-foot shorter than he was—probably had a bit of a Napoleon complex. Usually, you could cajole these guys into cooperating if you took a bow toward their authority and implied that the rest of the world was what was screwed up, but Fisher hadn't had much of a chance to work his charms.

"Come on, General," he said confidentially. "You know why I'm here. I think the security stuff is bullshit, too. But Dr. Morse sent me—what am I going to do, tell him to drop dead?"

"You've got a bullshit theory on the Merc," said Hunter. "I built those planes."

"Yeah?" said Fisher. He hadn't known Hunter's background.

"That computer system is impervious to any sort of interference."

"I didn't say it was interfered with," said Fisher. "I said it got a bug in it."

"We tested the whole system. There's no way that plane has a bug in it. Not on those engines, at least."

"Yeah, that's my point. The bug came from the outside, like a virus."

"No way," said the general, vigorously shaking his head. "There's no way anything can infiltrate the computer system. Just can't happen."

"I may not know all the technical details," said Fisher, suddenly nonchalant, "but there are a couple of ways in. One's through the guidance system."

"All of that's encoded information," said Hunter. "Secure as hell."

"Yeah, but I checked and the B-2 and Merc get their information the same way, has to do with not wanting to use a radar altimeter, right? Because that could be detected from the ground," said Fisher. He glanced around the corridor, which was filled with people. "Maybe we should talk about this somewhere else."

"I have no time for you," said Hunter.

"All right, we'll talk later."

"There's no way it happened the way you're saying."

"Maybe not. But I'd like to talk to the pilot. That's the real reason I'm here."

"He's busy, too."

"Come on, General. Fifteen minutes."

"He's flying in three hours."

"He ain't gonna be busy the whole time, right?"

"It wasn't his fault either," said Hunter, jabbing his finger in the space between them. "There's no way the pilot could screw up the engines."

"Oh I agree about that," said Fisher. "That's why my theory makes so much sense."

Hunter frowned.

"I don't like you," said the general. "I don't see why this is FBI business at all. The air force can do its own job."

"They think the pilot screwed up," said Fisher. "Work with me on this, General. We want the same thing, don't we?"

Hunter didn't answer.

"Let me talk to the pilot first. Then I'll make some routine checks, make Dr. Morse happy. When you get a break, maybe we sit down have a beer or something, talk about the SR–91."

Hunter turned to his aide, a major who looked as if he were wishing with all his might that he could go back to bed. "He's got my OK—as long as he stays out of everyone's way during the next twelve hours. Until then, he stays in his room."

"Twelve hours? Give me a break," said Fisher.

"We've got a job to do. Everybody here's going to be busy."

"Hey, listen, at least let me eat, OK?"

"He can go to the cafeteria."

"And how about smoking—you got to let me outside the buildings for a smoke," said Fisher. "I noticed your signs all around."

"About time you quit," said the general.

"Come on. Who am I going to hurt?"

"Whatever," said Hunter to the major. "But somebody stays with him at all times. Think of this as a test, Fisher—if you pass it, you can do whatever you like."

Napoleon complex. Tough case.

"Listen—" said Fisher. "Call Morse."

"I have a meeting," said Hunter, starting away.

"Mind if I sit in?"

"Your security clearance isn't high enough," snapped Hunter. "Somebody show him to his room."

Elrich decided to tell Hunter he was convinced the signal they had detected had not been a malfunction, that the Japanese must be working on a superplane. He would then offer to use the System for some high-tech spying, suggesting that it could gather information on the plane—information Elrich was already gathering. Hunter would have to agree, and the scientist would not only be able to tell him the full extent of the danger they faced, but also forestall any suspicion that he had helped Ki.

The two airplanes he had sabotaged, naturally, would never come up.

Eventually, the System would find a way to down the Japanese plane. Ki must have known he was vulnerable in some way; it was just a matter of studying the Japanese plane long enough to discover a way around the defenses he'd constructed.

So when Elrich was summoned for the meeting—disoriented, having gone to bed only a few hours before—he went confidently, a man who'd made up his mind. He had everything under control.

It was only after he'd walked into the briefing room and seen what time it was that he realized this wasn't the routine planning session he'd expected. The scientist took a seat near the end of the third row of the tiered lecture center, and waited as different members of the development team walked in, sleepy-eyed, nodding at him. His confidence continued to slip away as he played nervously with the small desktop that folded up from the side of the chair, and he wished suddenly that he had gotten himself some coffee, anything to help clear his head.

He was just thinking he might get up and get some when Hunter walked into the room. The general's face was pale, his expression grave, and Elrich immediately feared the absolute worst. He forgot, momentarily, all the precautions he had taken to disguise his communications with Ki and the System's tapping of the guidance satellites; he forgot his plan; he forgot most importantly his achievements and ambitions. He could think only that he had been caught, and was prevented from bolting from the room only because his legs would not work.

"Gene, I'd hoped to talk to you before the meeting, but maybe it'd be just as well to get it all out first," said Hunter, pausing at his row. "I don't want to keep everyone here sitting around."

Elrich nodded.

"We may need to speak after this."

"Yes,"said the scientist slowly. "We should."

Hunter nodded, then continued down to the podium. Somehow, with his heart beating so fast he thought it would burst from his chest, Elrich realized that if he'd been suspected of anything, Hunter would have had him arrested, not invited to a meeting.

They know it's a real plane, Elrich thought. But that's all they know.

From the corner of his eye he saw Jennifer and the pilot, Wright, enter the room and sit behind him just as the general began. Jennifer had spent all of yesterday with him, and probably the night. His sudden anger—jealousy, maybe—brushed aside the last vestige of fear.

"Gentlemen, I'm sorry to get you up so early on what was supposed to be a nonflight day. But there's a change in plans. We are flying today—as soon as we can get in the air. I've scheduled the takeoff for 0800."

Hunter paused and looked around the room. No one spoke.

"The NSC believes that a Japanese firm has built a superplane of its own. We're not entirely sure why, and we don't have many details on it. Our job is to get as much information on it as possible, assuming it exists. Lieutenant Colonel Wright will fly Coyote Bird out to the area where their base is, and if it comes up, the System's sensors will record as much as possible. He will minimize his contact. This isn't supposed to be a dangerous mission," said Hunter, stepping out from behind the podium. "But we're not taking any risks that we don't have to."

Everyone in the room turned and looked at the pilot. Wright nodded as if he'd been asked to go get the morning paper.

"Sir, with all due respect." Pelham stood up in the other corner of the room. "I've got more time in the cockpit than Colonel Wright. I'd like a shot at this."

"I appreciate your volunteering," said Hunter. "I've given it a lot of thought, but I'm going to stick with the colonel. We're going to run this exactly as if it were just another training mission."

"Sir—" said Pelham, but something in the way Hunter looked at him made him sink back into his chair, saying that he would do whatever he had to.

"I know you will, Major," responded Hunter.

"Why are the Japanese building a plane of their own?" asked someone in front. Elrich barely heard the voice, and couldn't tell who it was.

"If I knew that, we probably wouldn't be flying," said the general. "I'll be honest with you, I'm not entirely convinced there is a plane."

"Sir," said someone else, "let's say there is a plane, and we gather data on it, what happens next?"

"That's not our call," said Hunter.

There was altogether too much art in the answer for the men and women in the room, most of whom had spent their entire lives working on advanced projects for the air force. There was a buzz in the room, the questions ready to flow now, though Hunter wasn't giving out much more information.

"We're working on this one step at a time," said Hunter finally. "Today, our job is to gather information about the other aircraft. We have less than three hours." He started to walk from the stage. Some of the team leaders tried to ask him questions, but the general brushed them aside. "Gene, you wanted to talk to me," he said as he came up the steps.

Elrich nodded, getting up and following as Hunter walked quickly from the room. He was back in control now—it had been fatigue that had panicked him.

"I wanted to say that the signals we've picked up were real," said the scientist as they walked alone toward Hunter's office. "I had the System analyze them, and I'm convinced there wasn't a malfunction."

"I see."

They reached the office, and Elrich followed Hunter inside, closing the door behind him.

"We're going to take out the Japanese plane, assuming it's any sort of threat," said Hunter.

"We can use the System," said Elrich immediately. This was perfect, better than he'd hoped. He'd prove how superior the System was to anything Ki had cobbled together. "I'll start working on it right away."

"Just get the plane in the air," said Hunter. "I'll worry about everything else."

"General," said Elrich. "The computer can determine the plane's vulnerabilities. We can use—"

"There's already a plan."

"A plan? What kind of a plan?"

"I can't go into it now," said Hunter, picking up the phone. "I will after the flight."

"The System will—"

"You're going to have to leave my office," said Hunter. "I have to talk to Washington."

Elrich seethed at the abrupt dismissal. "General."

"Just get the plane up, Gene," said Hunter. "The rest has already been figured out."

It was only with the greatest restraint that Elrich prevented himself from pounding on the desk in a rage. He got up slowly, furious but trying to keep his head clear.

"I'm serious, Tom," said Hunter. "No heroics."

Wright leaned over the general's desk. He couldn't remember ever being briefed on a mission in the commander's personal office before.

"Hell, if you guys want flight data on the thing, shouldn't I fly around with it for a bit?" Wright asked, "See how good this guy is?"

Hunter frowned and shook his head.

"One turn with it to see how it does. Then get your butt back here in one piece," he said. "I don't want you giving *them* a flight demonstration of our capabilities."

"What's the big deal?" Wright asked. "Why are we so hot to find out about this thing?"

"Two of our planes have disappeared in the area over the past few days. One was an RC-135 running a Cobra Ball ELINT mission, the other was a Merc."

"A Merc?"

Hunter nodded. Wright was just beginning to realize how much more there might be to this than the general was telling.

"They think the RC-135 was shot down by a pair of FSXs," said the general. "But no one can explain the Mercury. There's only circumstantial evidence, but they're convinced there's a plane, and the signal we picked up the other day seems to have cinched it."

"Computer said it was an FSX."

"No, the computer said the radar signal was similar to an FSX.

That might just mean that the same people built it. If this plane is like the Coyote, it might have bird-dogged for them."

Wright nodded. "So we go out there and see if it's real, huh?"

"Exactly."

"You think the Japanese air force would shoot down our planes?" said Wright.

"I don't know what to think. The evidence on the Boeing is pretty clear. The theory is that the fighters deserted, and that there's some sort of a high-level coup involving a high-tech company."

"Sony muscling in on defense now, huh?" said Wright, but the general didn't laugh.

"Avoid Russian territory, if you can. And if you detect any missiles—"

"They'll never catch me."

"All the same, watch yourself out there. We're flying in the dark."

"Sure," said Wright, standing. "No problem."

"There's one other thing I think you should know," said Hunter. "The man who flew backseat in England for you, Major Miller, was on the Merc that went down."

That hit him as hard as the engines dying at 180,000 feet. There was a hitch in his lungs, a moment before Wright could nod, leave the office in silence.

"Looks a little like it's gonna rain, don't you think?"

"I wouldn't know sir," replied the MP, a fairly decent sort who'd told Fisher his name was Agrest.

"You sure you don't want a cigarette?"

"No, sir. Gave them up when I found Christ."

"Oh yeah?" said Fisher. "You mean you're born again?"

"Yes, sir. Jesus Christ is my personal savior."

"That's great," said Fisher, taking a step along the huge concrete runway.

"Are you a Christian, sir?"

"Kinda," said the agent. "That's a hell of an airplane," he said, pointing to the Coyote Bird, which had been wheeled onto the far edge of the strip as Fisher emerged from the headquarters building for a smoke. An immense vehicle—it looked to Fisher like a three-story, prefab warehouse on wheels—was making its way over to the plane. "What are they doing?"

"Gonna fuel it up, I guess," said the MP. "That's the fuel-flow vehicle—gets hooked up to some tanks of hydrogen and sucks it into the plane."

"Yeah? Let's take a look."

"I'm supposed to accompany you to your room, sir."

"No sight-seeing, huh?"

"Just following my orders, sir."

"No problem, son. What's that building over there, the red tent thing?"

"That's the hangar, sir. They put the plane in there. Got the pilot's ready room, a couple of shops."

Fisher nodded and dropped his cigarette on the concrete. Hopefully the billion-dollar warplane wouldn't trip over it.

"Well, let's go get my bags."

"Bags, sir?"

"Be nice if I could brush my teeth, don't you think?" said Fisher, starting for the car. The MP followed. "Been here long, Sergeant?"

"Whole year, sir," said the MP. "I'm not a sergeant yet, though."

"Oh. Didn't mean to insult you."

The MP laughed.

"Corporal?"

"Just a regular airman, sir."

Fisher, walking up the path to the lot where he'd left the rental, decided he might be pouring it on a bit too thick, but what the hell: the higher you set them up, the faster they fell. "You must be pretty elite to get this assignment."

"We're all just doing our jobs," said Agrest, following along.

The agent went first to the trunk and retrieved his suitcase. Then he walked slowly to the front, opened the door—he hadn't locked it—leaned over the front seat, looked on the floor, bent back out of the car, a puzzled look on his face, ducked into the backseat, stuck his hands frantically under the seats.

"Something wrong, sir?"

Now see, a sergeant would have picked that up without me having to go into the back, thought Fisher.

"My goddamn briefcase," said the FBI agent. "Where the hell is it?"

"Sir?"

"My goddamn briefcase—it's not here."

The profanity seemed to bother Agrest a great deal. "Are you sure you had it in the car?" the MP asked in a pained voice.

"Sergeant—"

"Airman."

"Whatever the fuck you are," said Fisher, "somebody stole my goddamn briefcase."

"Not here," replied the MP.

"Like hell not here. Shit," said Fisher, ducking back into the car and looking around futilely. "You see the goddamn thing?"

"Uh—"

"Where the hell is the security around here?" demanded Fisher. "Jesus Christ—this is a major problem. This is—somebody's ass is in a fucking sling here. Who watches the lot?"

"Well, there's no one assigned to it, exactly. I mean, there are only a couple of vehicles, and—"

"Who the goddamn fucking hell is in charge of the slimebag security?"

"Uh—"

"Who the hell is the fucking scumbag officer in charge of security on this base? Get him the fuck up here. Get his ass the hell up here right away."

"Yes, sir," said the soldier, who turned and headed for one of the nearby buildings.

"Goddamn military getting soft since they reformed boot camp," muttered Fisher as he descended the hill from the parking lot. He didn't run—Fisher never ran—but he reached the hangar quickly and went inside. He wasn't sure exactly why Hunter wanted to keep him on ice for half a day, but on the outside chance that it was because he wanted to tip off the pilot, Fisher had decided not to give him the opportunity.

Besides, why put off until tomorrow what you could easily accomplish today?

He found the pilot standing in an astronaut-style suit, his hands extended as if he were a statue.

"Colonel Wright?"

"Who are you?" asked the pilot.

"My name's Fisher. I'm an FBI agent. I been investigating your little adventure in Italy."

Wright's face clouded immediately.

"What?"

"I think somebody screwed around with your plane," said Fisher quickly. "I wanted to talk to you about it."

"I have a few other things to do right now," said Wright as one of the technicians pulled a long glove over his right hand and plugged it into the suit. The fingers seemed to be made of rubber or a similar synthetic material, the long arm of something studier.

"Won't take a minute," said Fisher. "Besides, you ain't going anywhere till you get your Martian suit on, right?"

Neither the pilot nor the men dressing him laughed.

"I spent three hours on the goddamn telephone the other day talking about this," said Wright, "besides writing out the deposition. Didn't you guys get enough?"

"I'm with the FBI, not the air force."

One of the dressers got a funny look on his face when Fisher said that. "You supposed to be here?" asked the airman.

"Now how the hell you think I'd get here if I wasn't?" said Fisher, his Chicago accent suddenly heavy in his mouth. He could easily be talking to some wise guy about a gambling bust. "You think I'd just walk in, like I owned the place?"

"I'll deal with him, Freddy," said Wright.

The airman grunted and went to prepare the other glove.

"Some jerk suggested it was pilot error," said Wright. "You think I turned the engines off because I got bored?"

"You don't look like an asshole to me," said Fisher, still leaning on the accent.

A hint of a smile appeared on Wright's face.

"The pilot error crap is just official air force bs," said the FBI agent. "They just want to cover their butts. What do you think happened?"

"I wish to hell I knew," said Wright as the airman secured the second glove. "The engines just quit, bam, right off, and nothing I did could get them back."

He wanted to talk about it, Fisher realized. Dumb air force investigators. They should have spoken to the guy in person, hint around that they were on his side. Even if they wanted to crucify him.

But they probably couldn't get access. Fisher's theory really had somebody scared—obviously he was on the right track.

"Were you flying the plane when the engines went out?" the agent asked. His tough-guy tone was gone now. "I mean, were you controlling it at the time?"

"It was on autopilot. Damn thing started right up for them on the ground, supposedly. That was after I left."

"Yeah, they did," said Fisher. "I was there."

"You know how I got it in?"

"Boosters. Pretty good idea."

"Yeah. I got lucky, to be honest. We were thinking we were gonna hit the ball. Me and my backseater. Hell of a guy . . ."

Wright seemed contemplative, saddened even, as the technician walked him to a machine that tested the suit and its sensors. A small wire was clipped to a socket under Wright's arm and a row of lights on the console began flashing.

"I have a theory that the plane's computer was somehow infected," said Fisher.

"What do you mean, infected?"

"That a virus got in there and turned off the engine."

"I don't see how that could be," said Wright. The machine flashed an OK and Freddy nodded at the pilot. When the test wire was unplugged, Wright began doing a series of cautious stretching exercises. "Everything's self-contained. We run through program checks before the takeoff."

"Yeah, I read up on the procedure coming out here," said Fisher. "I also understand that none of the computer coding has been changed since the planes first started flying."

"I wouldn't really know about that," said Wright.

"What do you do while you're on autopilot?"

"Nothing. Just sit there and watch the plane fly."

"Computer checks your position, right?"

"Sure."

"It gets that off a satellite, right?"

"Yeah," said Wright, beginning a series of slow deep knee bends. "But I don't see how that affects anything."

"That's the only communication the plane has with the outside world while it's on autopilot."

"Well I guess so, unless I pick up the radio."

"Which you didn't."

"Of course not."

"I just have to make sure," said Fisher. "There would definitely have been communication with the satellite before the engines went out."

"Absolutely. It needed the coordinates for the turn, and it would have doubled-checked."

"Right before the engines went out."

"Well, you know, pretty close. It takes a read every few seconds if it has to."

Fisher nodded. He was thinking of asking if Wright had any theories on who might have sabotaged his plane when he was interrupted.

"Mr. Fisher," said a voice behind him. "Looking for your briefcase?"

Fisher turned and recognized the major he had seen with Hunter, along with a very red-faced Agrest. "As a matter of fact," said the FBI agent sheepishly, "I just realized I didn't bring one."

The funny thing was, it felt comfortable. He was a magician, lying on his back and waving his hands, flying across the sky faster than a shout across a room, and it felt natural, even after the T-38. In fact, it was the trainer that felt strange, not the Coyote.

"System," Wright said, as if he'd been flying with it for years, as if it were another person, "give me a time-to-target at our next marker."

"Affirmative."

"Nothing out of the Russians yet, huh?" asked Wright.

"I do not understand."

"No unusual Russian activity."

"Negative. Continuing to monitor."

"Fine."

"Target in five," said the System, and Wright batted the little ball in his lap, changing it to a holographic projection of his target area. He was going to pull a one-eighty over the island's volcano—sucker better still be inactive, thought Wright.

"System, is this a real-time projection or out of the memory banks?"

"Hologram is from memory. Do you wish real-time augmentation?"

"Can ya?"

"Of course."

The System used one of its monitoring satellites to augment its information about the island. The ball changed color momentarily, but otherwise Wright saw no difference.

"You're not bullshitting me, are you?"

"Use of noun as a verb not previously documented."

"Bullshit's one of those words that can be used for just about anything," said Wright. "This is real-time?"

The System didn't get a chance to respond. A red bar flashed on the screen directly in front of Wright; the screen then divided itself in half, and then split the upper half into three more panels. Two Japanese FSXs were taking off from Delta; he saw them appear in the bubble.

"You sure those are FSXs?" Wright asked.

"Affirmative."

"There's no mistake, Tom," said Jennifer in his ear. "We have a good feed now from the satellite that's confirming it."

"OK," said Wright. "Prepare for evasive action. Full control to the glove."

"Do you wish complete pilot control?" said the System.

"Yeah. That was a joke. Jennifer, is the general back there somewhere?"

"Affirmative, Coyote Bird." It was Hunter himself.

"You looking at what I'm looking at?"

"Copy."

"Keep doing what we're doing?"

"That's right."

The System tracked the two FSXs as they cranked up from the island and swung a tight circle in his direction. The computer popped up a full list of data on the planes, throwing up their specs as well as their current performance, even estimating how long they could stay aloft. From an artistic point of view, Wright admired the FSX. Similar to the American F-16XLE, it was an impressive dancer, with enormous pitch and roll rates, capable of hot penetration speeds and able to leap tall buildings in a single bound—as long as it didn't have to go too far.

Or too high—he was flying well over their service ceiling, and at least twice as fast as they could go downhill with the wind at their backs.

Missiles, of course, might be a problem. The System had already figured that out, though—according to the computer, he had 10,000 feet on the highest altitude any Japanese missile could climb to, even with a lot of wishing behind it. They'd need a satellite killer to take him out from here.

"Be careful."

Her voice came out of nowhere. Was she reading his mind now, telling him he was getting too cocky? Maybe they'd tweaked the sensors in his suit to decipher brain waves as well as pulse rates.

"Coyote Bird to Coyote Base. We have no problem here," responded Wright. "Maintaining course."

And they did, whipping right over the FSXs and then coming back in a perfect crash-turn, just like he'd planned: the Coyote put itself sideways for a moment, its wings flashing flat, thrust and shock waves going all over the place, maneuvering rockets blowing off like no tomorrow WELL NOW AT LEAST he felt the g's crashing around him and scrunching his body despite this cocoon of a seat it was a great feel baby just getting it back still in control and just like that they were flying back in the opposite direction.

"Try doing that," he said to the two Japanese fighters as he came out of the maneuver, though of course they couldn't hear him. In fact, no one could hear him, since the friction temporarily blocked his transmissions back to the base. It also fuzzed everything coming in. The effects of the block varied, depending on the sensor; it took maybe five seconds to completely clear.

"Where'd those Mitsubishis get to?" Wright asked the System. It took a second, and then popped the two fighters up on the main screen, with distances and everything. There were thirty miles between them, though they were closing that off quickly.

"Concentrate tracking on a fifty-mile radius," said Wright. "I want everything you got focusing on my friends here."

Wright, slowed by the maneuver, was only doing Mach 2, chugging along, as they passed beneath him.

"Contacts have powered their weapons," said the System.

"Oh get out," said the pilot. "They really have to be kidding me."

"Air-to-air is a variant of U.S. Sparrow AIM-7 missile. Two charged on each plane. Do you wish tactics?"

"Tell ya what," said Wright, "you think about it while I increase our altitude."

"I have already computed alternatives."

"So have I," said the pilot, who had pushed the nose of the plane up steeply and hit the gas. The Sparrows were nasty, but they weren't really much of a threat against something that could accelerate this fast. The semiactive radar missiles required a good strong fix before they could count on hitting their target, and Wright wasn't about to let them get one.

It was possible, though, that they'd used them to take out the Merc. If they'd gotten lucky and the pilot hadn't responded correctly.

But Millertime had been there. He would have had the missile sucker on full blast. No way Miller screwed up. No way.

"Do you wish counter-measures?" asked the System.

"Let's wait until they fire them, if they fire them," said Wright, scanning the list of tactics the computer had flashed on the screen. Not bad, but Wright didn't need the nudge.

Hell, the FSXs might just as well try and line up their cannons. Wright was back at 150,000, and clicking along at just under Mach 5. He made a gentle turn and came back around toward the island.

Wright saw it now—there wasn't any other superplane. The System had detected one of these maniacs the other day, though it had gotten confused about its altitude and speed. He had an urge to shoot them down, revenge Millertime. But it was an impotent, helpless impulse, since the Coyote had no weapons.

The pilot concentrated on his hand, holding the plane steady. He had a job to do.

"We're gonna swing around a couple of times, and see if anything comes of it," he told the System, tracing out a course on his screen. Then he returned the screen to a full-flight orientation, letting him see everything around him.

Which meant, of course, that the screen was blank.

And then the world went red out of nowhere, and a gray shadow filled the upper right quadrant of the screen, and something— maybe a ghost—flashed over his head.

Three times his speed, a good 30,000 feet higher than he was, if the instruments were to be believed.

"Unidentified object within notification circle," said the System.

"Yeah, no shit," said Wright, turning the Coyote to follow, pushing his hand up and feeling the plane coming along with it. "Why the hell didn't you pick it up before?"

"Plane appears to have been airborne and flying outside of immediate range," replied the System. "Radar had been directed to concentrate on fifty-mile radius. Object's profile is stealthy enough to require full enhancement techniques. Manual directions override all else."

"Yeah, well, keep on this thing from now on," said Wright. "And the FSXs. Don't let me be surprised."

"Tom?" said Jennifer, far, far behind him.

"ID object," he told the machine.

"Attempting."

"Well let's go, huh?" Wright put his hand on the hologram bubble. "Plot probable course," he said. "Plot parallel trailing course. Intent is to close and survey."

The System blinked an acknowledgment. It was using all of its resources to track and probe his adversary; the English-language section had been given a low priority and wouldn't be used now unless Wright requested it. "Maximum enhancement on window," he said, but the gray blur they were following remained just that.

Wright took his plane to 180,000 feet, but he was still lower than the Japanese plane. Everyone began talking at once, Jennifer,

Hunter, even Ford, the controller. There might be a Des Moines telephone operator in there somewhere, for all he knew.

"System, filter communications by priority one." That meant only Jennifer could talk to him. "OK, folks, I got our Martian up. I'm following, exactly as we planned."

He was starting to gain when he realized the bogey was slowing to turn.

"Which way is it going?" he asked the System.

"Insufficient data."

Wright guessed east—his old right-handed pilot theory—and let the Coyote drop off a bit, orienting himself. Hell yes, it was coming back, and east, just like he thought: Wright slid his starboard wing down thirty degrees and headed straight at the point where the UFO would come out of the turn.

"Give me a description of our friend," Wright told the System as he looked at the blurred image on the screen growing larger.

"Plane is hydrogen-fueled. Profile similar to Coyote Bird . . ." Here the System popped up a snazzy silhouette of the Coyote on the right quarter of the screen, and then fit the UFO over it.

"They look nothing like each other," said Wright protectively. The Coyote Bird was a lot sleeker, and a little shorter. The Japanese plane's nose seemed almost like a little ball, giving it a sinister face.

"Aeronautic characteristics are similar," said the computer.

Coyote looked a hell of a lot prettier. What did computers know?

"Estimate capability, compared to Coyote."

"Insufficient data," said the System.

The UFO was putting it to the fire wall coming out of the turn. It was still a good 5,000 feet over him, but otherwise their courses were pure intercept. Wright moved his tongue around his mouth, gathering the moisture. He could feel the muscles in his shoulders tighten as he moved his hands to guide the plane. The small panel on the front screen showed that his vitals had increased slightly; his heartbeat was now over seventy—hypertension city for him. This was a lot more stimulating than taking a turn over a dormant volcano and a pair of home-guard fighters.

The System popped up a list of "engagement maneuvers" on the left side of the screen.

"Got it figured out already, old buddy," said Wright. The planes were both going a bit over Mach 5; at this speed, they closed a mile off in less than a second. The System counted down "intersection" to three seconds before Wright made his move, a feint upwards that led into a power dive to his starboard and then a quick recovery, rolling back forty-five degrees the other way, heading now towards the Russian coast. His friend took the maneuver in stride; rather than trying to follow exactly he cut back to his right and dropped down with Wright, targeting the Coyote for a new intercept. The System plotted all of this in the small ball on Wright's lap, and kept one of its windows open, showing the UFO's blurry nose.

"That was an easy one," said Wright, talking to the Japanese plane. "Now let's play a little harder."

He rolled the Coyote over, hanging it there a quarter second to make sure his friend was watching—God, this is something I'd never do in a Merc, he thought to himself—and then dropped it toward the earth, pitching his nose straight down and then back around, the plane clicking through different configurations like a gymnast working on a parallel bar. And as the UFO passed near them—five miles at most—Wright switched gears and put the Coyote in a full power climb, the engine screaming back there somewhere, launching the plane toward the moon. Had the other pilot not been quick, he would have found the Coyote right on his ass—considering their speed and the altitudes they were flying at, a half-mile was kissing distance. But he was really good, and he had his plane diving off as Wright gained altitude.

"Who is this guy?" said Wright, easing back on the throttle but continuing to climb almost straight up. Mr. Bogey had earned the next move.

"Do you desire engagement maneuver options?" asked the System.

"Tell you what—see if you can figure out which way he's coming out of his turn. Put it in the hologram."

The System plotted the UFO continuing around to its right, and then coming back toward Wright.

"I don't think so," said Wright, shifting in his dentist's chair. "If he came straight at me I could pop over and let it all hang out. He's thinking like a fighter pilot—he's going to want to keep me off balance up close, as if I had a couple of Sparrow IIs on me," said Wright. "Or even a cannon, at that range. So what he's going to do is turn to his left, like he's checking me out. Then I come off my climb, like this. . . ." Wright leveled the Coyote out, heading away from the Japanese plane. "And he comes charging after me, like he's going to put a couple of heat suckers up my rear," said Wright.

Sure enough, Mr. Bogey had all the stops off, racing toward him.

"Fighter pilots," Wright said, shaking his head, "they're so predictable."

"Do you wish evasive maneuvers?"

"Nah, we're gonna let him catch up," said Wright. "Our job is to get a good look at him, right? He's already proven he can fly."

Doing twice Wright's comparatively lackadaisical speed, the UFO closed quickly behind the Coyote Bird as they headed northward.

"He's gonna catch on in a minute," said Wright. "And he's either gonna turn off or blow right through us. Or, if we're lucky, he'll settle down and shadow us. Which means you'll get a good look at him."

"UFO appears to be maneuvering to shadow Coyote Bird," said the System, popping up a little graph showing the plane's declining speed.

"Good call," said Wright. They were a good twenty miles apart.

"Forty seconds to Russian identification zone," said the System.

Russian air space. Hunter had told him to avoid it, if possible. The Voyska PVO—the Russian air defense, Voyska Protivio-Vozdushnoy Oborony—wasn't exactly known for its ability to blanket an area, even around Moscow, and given his altitude and speed, he might just as well be a flying saucer: nothing they had was going to catch up with them. Still, it wasn't a good idea to tempt fate. God only knew what they'd make out of this.

He slowed down even more—he'd let the UFO close just before the property line, then get out of there without tripping the Russian defense wires. Hunter was probably having a fit as it was, cursing at him to get home.

"Colonel," rasped Elrich in his ear, "what's going on up there?"

"I'm letting him in close so we can get a handle on him," said Wright. "How'd you get on the line? I thought I could only talk to Jennifer on priority one."

"Keep your distance," growled Elrich.

Hey, screw you, Wright thought. Goddamn scientist all of a sudden thought he was a pilot.

"Don't let it get a good bead on you," said Elrich.

"Hey listen, doc," said Wright, "you do your job and I'll do mine, OK? Give Jennifer back her microphone and let's run this thing the way we planned, all right? I was just about to head home."

The System started buzzing like an old-fashioned pinball machine gone crazy.

"Laser-targeting device," it said, "attempting to lock on."

From the FSXs? He'd forgotten about those guys, but with good reason—they'd been left far behind, back at the island. "Locate source," he told the System, hitting the gas and pushing the plane skyward in a shot. "Details."

"Laser is from UFO," said the System.

"What?" said Wright. "What's he doing?"

"Conforms to patterns of attempting to locate and fix."

"Fix for what?"

"Assumption is weapon."

"Why do you think that?"

"Device was dormant until detected. Profile adheres to standard directed tracking mode, as would be used to guide semi-active radar missiles. Profile bears some similarity to system tested for F-14 during 1980s, although considerably more—"

"Enough," said Wright. "How far away are the FSXs?"

"One hundred miles. Planes have remained in vicinity of target."

"They firing missiles?"

"Missiles do not appear to have been activated. FSXs are not in communication with unidentified bogey."

It sounded funny to hear the computer call the other plane a bogey, and the pilot chuckled.

If he was painting the Coyote for the FSXs, it was a lost cause—no missile was going to come that far and still catch him. Unless . . .

"You detect any weapons on that sucker? Any torpedo tubes?"

"Rephrase?"

"Does the bogey have ports for missile launching?"

"Negative. Low weapons probability."

"So why's he paintin' us?"

"Rephrase."

"Why is he doing what he's doing?"

"Known data argues for weapon. However, radar could be used to probe for distance and location, or unknown purpose."

Sucker was probably laughing his ass off with this trick, thought Wright. Spit out some bullshit targeting laser to scare the hell out of him.

"Laugh at this," said the pilot. He powered the Coyote into a straight off-the-table drop, and spun back so fast he almost blacked out—but not quite, thank you, and he was on his friend's tail, two miles off, and no way he was going to shake him. Both planes picked up speed, clicking past Mach 6, Mach7.

"Laser still active. Appears to work from nonmaneuverable platform located at forward point of plane form. Orientation remains forward and therefore unable to target Coyote."

"Screw him," said Wright. He was going to fly right up the son-of-a-bitch's tail.

Who was this guy, anyway? OK, he'd scored a point turning the targeting laser on, getting Wright's attention. Now let's see how he liked Wright climbing over his stabilizer.

Assuming he could catch him. Both planes hit Mach 9 and continued to accelerate. Wright's friend started a weave pattern that could be used to quickly drop behind the Coyote; Wright hung with him, not wanting to let him get away but certainly not about to suffer the indignity of letting him slip behind.

The Japanese pilot handled his plane like he'd been flying it for some time. Was he helped as much as Wright was by a computer system? He had to be—at that speed, even a simple turn required constant monitoring and assistance.

The two pilots and their machines flew together at the top of the world, trying to stick it in each other's face. Wright felt for a moment as the pilots of World War I must have felt in the first day or two of the war: removed, above conflict, sharing a strange camaraderie with the enemy. It as an illusion, however—no doubt the first person ever shot down in World War I had felt that way immediately before his opposite number pulled out a rifle and starting shooting at him.

Wright sensed that he was starting to gain. The System counted off the distance on the screen, but he didn't consciously see it—it had become part of his internal feel for the plane, the lines between the System and his own senses blurring. He started cutting the angle between the two planes, catching up, catching up, but still careful—one swoop from his friend and he'd have to break off to avoid jumping in front. Wright was a fighter pilot again, on the pursuit, tightening his squeeze but ready for anything. He could catch him—he wanted to narrow the distance to nothing, get really close.

"Coyote Bird, return to base."

It was a far-off voice, back behind him. It was too deep in his subconscious for him to pay any attention. He rushed on toward the bogey, closing. He was really gaining now, even though the other plane had not slowed down.

Hunter's voice floated up, persistent, calling him out of a dream: "Coyote Bird, this is an order. Break off and return."

The distance between them was a bare mile: nothing now. He was gaining and his target wasn't turning off. The bogey was dead meat.

"Coyote."

Wright snapped out of it suddenly, putting the plane into a curve to the north and then around, backing off on the throttle, coasting back from over Mach 12, heading home. Even at that speed it took almost a minute for him to clear Soviet territory.

8

THE RIGHT SATORI

Wright's legs began tingling as soon as Harrison helped him up out of the cockpit. He took a step on the concrete runway, talking as they took off his helmet.

"It was the most intense piece of flying I've ever done," said the pilot. "It was so instantaneous—I thought about cutting around away from him, and I did. He came in over me, got me totally blindsided, because I'd told the computer to concentrate on the two FSXs. So then I followed him. . . ."

The colonel, walking to the jeep, used his hands to replay the encounter. His left was the Japanese plane, flashing away from him; his right the Coyote Bird, ducking and weaving, pulling the plane toward him.

"Sucker turned on some kind of targeting device to psych me out," said Wright. "I took it up, figuring what to do, while he was laughing his ass off."

"How do you know it was just to psych you out?" said the chief as he and a tech helped Wright into the back of the jeep. He stood there, his arms across the roll bar, waiting for them to take him to the flight room.

"He was too far from the FSXs," said Wright. "They wouldn't have had a chance in hell with a missile."

Harrison said nothing, slipping behind the wheel and starting the engine.

"And the plane sure doesn't have any of its own," said Wright.

Harrison said nothing.

"Come on, Chief," said Wright. "Give me a break, huh?"

They had already watched the tapes of the encounter twice by the time Wright arrived on the computer deck. He walked swiftly across the long room, passing the bench of equipment where Elrich normally worked. A dozen people clustered around the cockpit dupe section, where Jennifer stood while he flew. Hunter, Pelham, Jennifer, and Elrich were at the center, staring at the screens that duplicated exactly what he had seen.

"Here's where he started letting it catch him," he heard Jennifer say as he walked toward them.

"How do I look?" said Wright. He put his hand discreetly on Jennifer's arm and squeezed.

"I told you, in and out," Hunter said to him in an annoyed aside as he continued to watch the screen.

"There's the laser," said Jennifer. She walked to her control section and froze the rerun, asking the System to analyze the signals it had detected, to see if it could come up with additional information.

"I think he was trying to see if I'd wet my pants," said Wright. "I got to admit, he upped the old bp a point or two."

"You did pretty well," said Pelham solemnly. Wright smiled at him—the major had finally found a life.

Hunter said nothing, continuing to stare at the screen. The Japanese plane was a frozen smudge in one of the detail windows, framed by lettering that estimated its speed and closing rate.

"Still can't get anything definitive," said Jennifer, looking over to them. "The closest it can come to anything is a laser used to guide missiles to a target."

"Maybe it was painting him for the FSXs," said Hunter. "Check on their location."

"According to the System, they were well out of range and never maneuvered to fire," replied Jennifer. "I thought of that myself."

So the woman who was so opposed to using the Coyote as a weapon was thinking like a military analyst now. Wright smiled at her, but she was too absorbed in her CRTs to notice.

"I'd like to know what the hell he was up to," said Hunter.

"Don't you think he was just pulling my chain?" said Wright. "I mean, why would he be using a targeting laser for? Nothing's going to catch me from the FSXs, and he's not carrying any weapons."

"Just because the System compares it to a targeting laser doesn't necessarily make it one," said Jennifer. "It might actually have been using the laser to take proper measurements of him, get data on the Coyote—as we were doing to it."

"I think it was definitely for a weapon," said Elrich. The scientist spoke in a quiet, moody voice. "It's exactly what it would do if it was counting off distance for a charged-particle weapon."

"What kind of weapon?" asked Pelham.

"Why do you say that, Gene?" said Jennifer. "There's absolutely no indication of a weapon."

"It's exactly what it would do," insisted Elrich. The skin of his face was stretched tautly over his cheekbones, his mouth pinched back. His eyes seemed ludicrously large for his face.

"The System believes that there are no weapons on the plane," said Jennifer.

"It's making an assumption based on what it knows about the Coyote Bird," said Elrich. "That doesn't mean it's right."

Wright thought the whole thing was a joke. "What's he gonna do, hit me with some Buck Rogers ray gun? With the kind of maneuvering we were doing?"

"We considered putting one in the Coyote," said Hunter. "We rejected it because it would have been too unwieldy."

"Particle-beam?" said Pelham. "Like what they were talking about for Star Wars?"

"Nobody has a system that's small enough for the plane," said one of the designers, standing near Hunter.

"The Russians," started Elrich.

"What do you mean, the Russians?" said Hunter.

"The Russians might," said the scientist.

"How do you know that?"

"I don't," said the scientist. He took his glasses off, his hand shaking. "I'm just saying, maybe they have one. They've obviously done research in the area."

"This is a Jap plane, though," said Pelham.

"Well perhaps they got it from them," said Elrich.

"No way," said Wright. "Believe me, I know when somebody's aiming something at me. I can feel it. The guy was just busting my chops."

"Break out the data on the flight for me as soon as you can," said Hunter. "I have to go call Washington."

Captain Fumio Genda, still clad in his flight suit, stood in the doorway to the underground hangar admiring the plane as the technicians prepared to wheel it slowly inside. The skin was so hot that a layer of steam rose all around it; it gave the plane the appearance of an apparition slowly being conjured into existence. It was early evening, and the light seemed to fall back as the plane was pulled inside by the small caterpillar vehicle. Everything outside of their small world here was dark; the pilot could not even see the stars above.

"It is quite a machine," said Ki, startling him. The scientist was ordinarily ensconced in the control rooms during the flights, spending hours before and afterwards with his computers. But he was standing here beside Genda, watching as the plane was returned to its shelter.

"It looks more like an animal than a plane," said Genda.

The scientist smiled, but then his expression grew grave.

"We have done well today," said Ki. "But we must win the next encounter."

"The next encounter?" asked the pilot.

"They will come back," said the scientist. "Their curiosity will bring them back. At first, they did not believe that Japan had the knowledge to challenge them. Now they will seek to find out exactly the nature of that challenge. And when they do, we will beat them."

"The American plane is formidable," said Genda. "It flies like a thought; it is as fast and maneuverable as ours."

"If we do not shoot it down, all of our efforts will have been in vain," said Ki. "We must show our countrymen that we have strength. Our people will rise up—they are only waiting for a signal. There will be a new constitution, and new elections, as soon as the signal is given."

"What if we can't defeat it?" asked Genda.

Ki frowned. "We shall," he said, before turning and leaving Genda alone at the edge of the entrance to the hangar cavern, the cold air starting to bite at his face.

At 11:30 P.M., Washington time, Morse hand-carried the plan from the NSC working group to the president, who was waiting for him in his third-floor den in the first family's private living quarters. The national security director silently spread the map on the president's desk as he began. Gates, the strategy expert, had filled the North Pacific with different colored circles representing flying radiuses, dashes for intercept vectors, and a giant X for the spot where he expected the shoot-down to take place. Armed with the data they'd gathered on the Japanese plane—transmitted into the Pentagon computers from Coyote Base barely six hours before—the simulations showed what Gates called "a 97 percent efficacy rate."

"What about the other three percent?" someone had asked at the meeting.

"Doesn't exist," said Gates smugly. "It's in there for statistical purposes. Believe me, this is a sure thing. The Allied plan at Waterloo would have rated sixty percent, and we all know what happened there."

Morse thought it best to leave that out as he briefed the president.

"The one new wrinkle is the fact that the Japanese plane used some sort of tracking beam on our plane when their range closed," Morse added as he finished, deciding to be as complete as possible. "We believe that it gathered data about the plane. One of the scientists at the base theorized that it could have been for a particle weapon, but the designers say that's impossible, given the other characteristics of the plane. I had Central Intelligence double-check Japanese capabilities just in case."

"And?"

"Nothing. The Russians have some systems in testing, as you know, but there's no possibility of collaboration. In any event, they're pretty far from getting anything operational."

D'Amici had stared at the map through Morse's entire presentation, looking not at the area where they would intercept the Japanese plane, but at Japan itself. Now he got up from the desk and walked over to the couch. Morse followed him there, sliding into a leather chair as the president pulled a hassock out from under a side table and kicked off his shoes.

"What's Hunter think?" D'Amici asked.

"At first he was concerned," said the national security director. "But gradually, after talking with his people and the pilot, and then after Central Intelligence checked in, he stopped worrying about it."

Morse still had questions about the CIA's ability, but they were immaterial now. Even if the Japanese plane did have some sort of weapon, it wasn't going to be flying long enough to use it.

"I meant, what's the general's opinion overall?"

"He's ready," said Morse. "He thinks his end is easy."

"As long as we don't hit the wrong plane," said D'Amici pointedly.

"Of course not. The missiles rely on a positive ID, and that will be programmed in. Once the Japanese plane slows down to get its bearings, they'll have a clear shot."

"Assuming he's cut off from his base."

"He will be," said Morse. "Their communication system appears to be a little more primitive than ours. And of course we're assuming he's shielded. If he's not, he'll be completely blind."

The president nodded. He was listening, but half his mind was somewhere else.

Morse wondered if he was having doubts about the intercept.

"We have Case B as a backup," said Morse cautiously. "We're covered, if this fails."

"Will it fail?"

"Not according to the experts," said Morse. Suddenly he laughed. "That's why there's a backup."

D'Amici didn't laugh. Morse considered emphasizing the advantages of Case B one last time, but let it drop. There were political risks, to be sure. There were political risks in the whole thing. The plan was to keep the intercept secret for as long as possible, with bland statements about training exercises and accidents, if necessary. Congress's reaction was unpredictable. Morse felt the public would back the president if all the details were disclosed, but he worried that the incident would provoke such a backlash against Japan that the pressure would be on to deal severely with the government, which in turn would risk the kind of reaction in Japan the whole operation was hoping to cut off. A discreet, surgical blow, known only to the leaders of the two countries, was their best bet.

"You know, this hassock belonged to Harry Truman," said D'Amici. "Doesn't look that old, does it?"

"No, it doesn't."

The president suddenly jumped up. "Let's try something, Henry. Let's give this one more chance."

Morse, confused, watched D'Amici walk across the den in his stocking feet and sit behind his desk. He picked up the phone and spoke into it softly. "Get me the prime minister of Japan," he said, then gently replaced the receiver in the cradle. "I'm going to tell him what we're doing."

"Why?" asked Morse. "If the government is sanctioning Netsubo—"

"My interpretation of everything is that they're not."

"The NSC finding was that there was no evidence one way or another."

"Bill Dyson thinks they aren't," said D'Amici, referring to the secretary of state.

He would take what Dyson said above everyone else, thought Morse. Not because Dyson's information was better, not because his mind was sharper, but because he had known him the longest. He was inside the circle.

"What do you think, Henry? Are they?"

D'Amici's eyes searched him out across the room, heavy and sincere. It was an opportunity to push Dyson out—he could convince the president his interpretation was the proper one.

The evidence could be read either way. As far as the shoot-down was concerned, it would make little difference. No, it would be better to play the hard line, to assume that the government had sanctioned Netsubo. In that way, you wouldn't risk putting them on their guard.

But honestly, what did Morse think?

"I don't know," said the director. "There simply isn't enough information. There are certainly links, but there's no evidence that the government ordered the development of the plane. Or the shoot-downs."

Both men sat for a moment in the silent office. The lights cast a dull yellow around them; Morse felt as if he were in a cocoon.

The phone rang once; D'Amici picked it up.

"Thank you," he said softly. He looked over to Morse, then suddenly his whole face changed—this was the president, not Jack D'Amici, speaking. His voice was loud, strong, and clear; he was sitting erect in the chair.

"Mr. Prime Minister, thank you for taking my call so quickly. . . . Yes, yes, I agree. Absolutely . . ."

The president was silent as he listened to the Japanese prime minister. Once or twice he nodded; otherwise, there was no emotion, no reaction.

"We're going to do something about it, Mr. Prime Minister," said D'Amici finally. "We're going to shoot down the plane within the next thirty-six hours."

There were some more words, insignificant ones like "yes," and "I understand." Morse didn't pay attention to them; he was staring at the face: set, hard, the president.

"What did he say?" Morse asked when D'Amici hung up the phone.

"He wished us luck," said the president.

"Remember the day I had to fly up and take pictures of Quangtri," said Hunter as Harrison walked into his office. "Remember I came back and told you there wasn't a goddamn thing left—I'd been up there, you know, what, a couple of weeks before? It was a city, for Christ's sake."

"Uh-oh," said the chief, sitting down across from the general. It was after midnight; Harrison had almost bagged the whole idea, but he'd seen the light on and decided to go in.

"What?"

"I know things are bad when you get nostalgic," said Harrison, "especially about Vietnam."

"I wasn't getting nostalgic. I was just thinking about it. Probably one of the easiest flights I ever took."

"Half your wing was shot off."

"Not on that flight. That was a breeze—nobody was left to shoot at me, on either side. Besides, Thunderchief only needed half a wing to fly. Hell of a plane."

"Piece of shit."

"Not the Thud."

"You only had to fly them," said Harrison. "I had to fix them."

"It did drive a bit like a truck, now that you mention it," smiled the general.

"What's up, Billy?"

"Washington's going to shoot down our Japanese friend."

"Washington?"

Hunter smiled, slid his chair back from the desk. "We're going to help," he said. "Coyote's going to fly out and play decoy."

Harrison listened as the general laid out the game plan. He'd spoken to the national security director a short time before; they were to fly at 6 A.M. the day after tomorrow, when all of the interceptors would be in place.

"Maybe we ought to just let the Japanese take over," said the sergeant sarcastically after Hunter explained the rationale. "I'd like to see what they do in the Middle East."

The general said nothing. He looked tired, old.

"What about this targeting radar Wright says they turned on him?" Harrison asked. "You think they have a weapon on that thing?"

Hunter shook his head. "The designers don't think it's possible."

"What do they know?" said the chief. "I bet I could get a weapon in there."

Hunter laughed. "That's what I like about you, Chief. You always think you can do the impossible."

"We'll be ready to go," said Harrison. "The plane can fly anytime you want. Just give the word."

"I know that," said Hunter. "I appreciate it."

"Billy, you get any sleep yet?"

"I'm fine," said the general. "What are you doing up yourself? You come in here for something special?"

Harrison hesitated for a moment. He and Pelham had thought this up the other day, before any of the Japanese business.

"Me and Major Pelham had cooked up a little plan for some entertainment," said the sergeant. "We were thinking of bringing a couple of replica World War II planes in, fly them around a bit. Loosen everybody up."

"When were you thinking of doing this?" said Hunter.

"Tomorrow afternoon."

"I don't know," said Hunter, looking down at his desk. "Maybe next week."

"Problem is, planes are only going to be available tomorrow," said Harrison, standing. "Some movie outfit had them brought to California. I'd have to have them back the next night—they go home to Texas at the end of the week. Don't worry about it; I'll bag the idea. I wouldn't have set it up if I knew about all this."

"What kind of planes?" asked Hunter.

"Got a Zero and a Hellcat," said Harrison. "They're just replicas, but they look damn good."

The general seemed actually to be considering it. Back in the old days in Thailand, they used to go to great lengths for diversions. They'd have a napalm run in the morning; night before the base would be a recreation of Pompeii, everybody running around in togas, chasing local women who weren't dressed at all.

They had been considerably younger then.

"Oh, what the hell, maybe that's what we all need. Bring 'em in," said Hunter. "We'll have everybody take the night off, and kick butt in the morning."

Harrison smiled. "Just like old times," he said.

218

* * *

Had to be Elrich.

Fisher decided this without having met the man, and before Major Dallon even handed him the list of base personnel. It was the way the base security chief talked about him—a genius, very temperamental, sharper than anyone he'd ever met, and even more moody these days than when Dallon had first met him working on the B-2 four years ago.

They were on better terms today, the FBI agent and Dallon. Apparently Dallon's boss had talked to Washington again, and decided either that he better cooperate, or that Fisher wasn't much of a threat. Either way, Dallon had personally knocked on Fisher's door at seven this morning and escorted him to breakfast, hadn't even complained about his lighting up before they got out of the building. He'd chided him a couple of times for riding the MPs yesterday, especially the one he'd fooled with the briefcase stunt, but overall Dallon had been pleasant. And seemingly competent.

Didn't understand most of the technical stuff, though. They'd breezed by the plane, and now as they walked through the huge building where the computer was housed, Fisher could tell that the major had only a vague notion of how powerful the computer was.

Bodolino would be having orgasms here, Fisher thought.

"Dr. Fitzgerald," said the major, and the young woman with a serious face and long, beautiful dirty blond hair turned around. "This is FBI Special Agent Fisher. He's reviewing our security procedures," said Dallon. They shook hands, a nice firm grip for such a relatively petite woman. Fitzgerald showed him that the computer responded to her English commands, perfunctorily asking it what today's date was and then telling it who Fisher was.

"Can I ask it a question?" said Fisher. The scientist smiled as if she were showing off her work for a kindergarten class, and stood back from her microphone. He stepped forward. "Can you tell me the value of pi?"

"How many digits do you wish?" replied the System.

"It's stored in its memory," said the scientist. "We don't use it to do parlor tricks."

Fished smiled. "I always thought that was the kind of thing you ought to say to a computer."

"This isn't merely a calculator," she answered. "Our goal is to create a free-thinking machine. We're very close."

"Computer can think for itself, huh?" said Fisher. "I think we got a couple of these down at the agency already."

"It'll be a while before anything like this can be mass-produced," said Fitzgerald, still somewhat pleasant. "But already some of the ideas we used to build it are obsolete."

"Oh yeah?" said Fisher, looking over at the large projection screens used to duplicate the pilot's view. They were apparently replaying a part of a flight. "What are we watching?"

Jennifer got a nod from Dallon before explaining that she was replaying some previous flights. "I have a problem in the gateway," she said, "which is used to put all of the different inputs together and then filter them into the System's native language. The exchanges aren't terribly efficient, and I'm afraid we're losing a lot."

"Is that important?"

"Everything's important," she said. "It could mean the difference between identifying something correctly and not. And if the System has to devote more resources to the gateway than we planned—which it is—there's less left for everything else."

"Sure. I can see that," said Fisher, glancing around the deck. "Where's the boss today?"

"General Hunter?"

"No, your boss, the computer genius—"

"Gene is with the general."

"Uh-huh. Pretty smart guy, huh?"

Jennifer frowned. Fisher kicked himself for playing it like this, but he was here now, and pushed on. "Could this computer be used to infiltrate other computer systems, you think?"

"How so?"

"I mean, let's say I was a hacker—"

"No one here is a hacker, Mr. Fisher," said the scientist.

"Yeah, but let's say I wanted to sneak in somewhere I wasn't supposed to."

"You can do that with any computer," said Jennifer. The ice was thick now. "If you're smart enough. Major, I'm kind of busy this morning."

"We were just leaving," said Dallon.

Fished nodded. "Thanks. Jennifer was it?"

"Dr. Fitzgerald," she said.

Well, you couldn't blame her. Fisher smiled and followed Dallon across the room to the elevator.

"There are a couple of more auxiliary hook-ins to the computer upstairs," said Dallon, stepping in. "But the real interesting stuff is downstairs. The computer itself, or most of it anyway, is kept in a supercooled vat."

"Uh-huh. You have any way of monitoring what the computer is used for here?"

"Why would we do that?" said Dallon as the elevator stopped. "These people are extremely sensitive. You look over their shoulder too much, they have a fit. You know eggheads."

"I can find a way," said Elrich. "With the System's help, it will be only two weeks."

He had no way of knowing how long it would take to break Ki's defenses, of course, but he sensed he needed to sound positive for Hunter. Two weeks—that was nothing.

The general shook his head.

"Washington's decided this already," he said. "It's not up to me."

"General," said Elrich, standing and leaning down over the desk. "We have a weapon of enormous potential here. There's no need to risk the plane. Do you understand what I'm saying? Let me prove how powerful the System is."

"It's out of my hands," said Hunter, annoyed. "The computer will take the plane out to the intercept point, orbit, and then return. That's the extent of its involvement."

"You don't understand, do you? You don't realize its potential."

"It doesn't matter jack shit what I think, Gene. Washington has decided this."

"And what if your plan knocks out the plane?"

"You told me that wouldn't happen. You claimed during the design that the onboard portions of the System could withstand any sort of pulse."

"They can," said Elrich. "The shielding and the computer are infallible."

"Nothing is infallible," said the general. "But this is the way we're doing it."

Elrich bristled, but held his tongue. His way was better, a thousand times better. But if he oversaw the flight and its programming himself, he could make sure the System didn't let the Coyote get too close to the Japanese plane. The pilot had almost gotten shot down, and they didn't even realize it. Even on their terms, the value of the System would be obvious.

"I'll program the flight myself," he said, "even though this is unnecessary."

"Just do your job," said Hunter, dismissing him as if he were a common laborer.

Wright had had trouble falling asleep, the encounter with the Japanese plane playing over and over in his mind. At every turn he saw an array of other choices he could have made, a vertical reverse that would have brought him closer to his adversary, a weave that would have changed their positions so swiftly the Japanese pilot would have lost sight of him. To Wright it had been a dogfight, the object being not to shoot the other guy down, but to prove who was the better pilot.

Who was the member of the Brotherhood.

The encounter had been a draw. The next time he would win. He would ride the Coyote harder, much closer to the edge. His mind would be sharper; there would be less distance between his hand and what he was thinking.

The pilot didn't drift off to sleep until it was almost light. He slept for a long time, however, waking after noon. He was groggy at first, disoriented—no nightmares, at least. He got dressed, went to get something to eat, and realized on the way out of the building that if he could get Jennifer to make a tape of the encounter, he could play it on the TV in the rec room, stop action and everything, use it to plot out the next encounter.

He'd wanted to use the System for that yesterday, but they needed the data for their analyses. Watching the replays was somewhat useful, but they kept stopping them as they checked the System's performance, not his.

The pilot changed course midstep, swinging around on the concrete path between the quarters buildings and the System bunker. A few steps and he began to jog, invigorated by the fresh spring air as much as by his idea for the video replay. There was a scattered cloud cover; nice puffy suckers, but nothing too heavy or thick. Perfect day for Fonck and a SPAD VIII, leading the Storks over enemy lines, the French biplanes hanging out just over a cloud bank for some unsuspecting recon flight to come by.

"Jen, I got the greatest idea," said Wright, practically exploding onto the computer deck as the elevator opened. "Make me up a video from your memory banks, and then you won't have me in your hair all day. I can use it to study the flight."

Jennifer swung her chair around, and Wright leaned down and kissed her quickly—a little peck, conscious that there were others around and that she didn't like to make a fuss.

"What do you want to do?" she said.

"Put the flight on video," said Wright. "Then I'll take it down to the TV."

"I can't do that," she said. "It's all in machine language. The feed to the tubes comes out as graphics signals, precise to the medium."

"Yeah, but you can translate it, right? It shouldn't be too hard to come up with a conversion program—we can have the computer do it itself: give it an idea of the end product and let it do the number crunching. Am I right?"

"Yes," she said, "but it would still be a lot of work and I have other things to do until the party."

"Party?"

"The general said there's a party at four," she said. "Everybody's invited."

"Great," said Wright, "that'll give me a chance to run through the flight a couple of times."

"You'll miss the party."

"You can help me," he said, placing his hand on her shoulder. "I want to be ready for the next flight."

What next flight?" said Elrich.

"How you doing today, doc?" said Wright, turning to him.

"What next flight are you talking about?" asked the scientist.

"My next dance with this Japanese wonder plane. When are we going up? Tomorrow?"

"There's a flight tomorrow, but you're not going to be in the plane."

"What do you mean? Pelham's taking over?"

"No one is," said Elrich, walking back to his station.

"Hey, what do you mean?" said Wright. "The plane's grounded?"

"The computer is flying it from now on," said Elrich, pulling over a keyboard.

"What?" Wright turned and looked at Jennifer, who made a shrugging motion. "What's he talking about?"

"I guess, well—"

"Come on."

"There's a plan to shoot down the Japanese plane. The general told Gene. . . ."

Wright didn't hear the rest. He walked swiftly to the elevator door, punched the button, and stood there, waiting for it to open. When it did, he got in and spun around, saw that she had followed him.

"I was going to tell you," she said as the door closed.

Wright wasn't mad at her, exactly, but he wanted to know what the hell this was about. They were going to shoot down the Japanese plane? How? When? Without a pilot?

Hunter caught the full force of this gale as it blew into the hangar, stretching out his hand as if he were Moses parting the Red Sea.

"I've been looking for you, General," said Wright. "What's going on here?"

"Where?" said Hunter. He stood back from the plane, the mouth to the cockpit yawning behind him. They were alone in the hangar.

"There's a mission tomorrow?"

Hunter frowned. "What do you have, a direct line to Washington?"

"Gene Elrich told me."

"Oh he did, did he?"

"Coyote is flying out there tomorrow morning—without a pilot."

"It's a pretty straightforward mission," said Hunter. "It goes out there, turns around, and comes back. I don't have to risk a pilot for that."

"Where's the risk?"

"We're creating a magnetic pulse above the plane," said Hunter. "We're going to cut it off from its base, cut off from the rest of the System."

Wright didn't even take a breath. "Exactly why you need a pilot," he said. "How the hell is the plane going to know what to do?"

"It doesn't need to know anything," said Hunter. "All it has to do is fly in a circle until the communications come back."

"Yeah? What if something goes wrong?"

"Like what?"

"What if the computer fails? Come on, General, you need a pilot in that plane. You need me—I'm the only one who knows how the Japanese pilot flies. He's good. He's damn good. But I'm better."

"It doesn't matter how good he is. Once he's cut off from the base, he'll have to slow down. We have eight planes with ASAT missiles to take him out. The Coyote is just a decoy, Tom," said Hunter. "We don't need you."

"You need a pilot, General. You know you do. They designed this originally without somebody in the cockpit, and you made them change it, because you knew you'd need somebody there. A real pilot."

Hunter looked at him.

"The plan is set."

"If something goes wrong," said Wright, "there'll be nobody there to fix it. And I don't need the computer to fly the plane."

"You've only been in it twice," said Hunter.

"Yeah, but I know it already. I can feel it—I just think something, and we do it. You saw how we did yesterday. It's a beautiful plane, General, but it needs a pilot."

"The System can fly the plane perfectly well by itself," said Elrich. He was striding across the hangar floor, followed by Jennifer.

Wright turned to Hunter. "Why did you put a pilot in, if you weren't going to use him?"

"The pilot is absolutely unnecessary," said Elrich. "He's a liability. You almost got yourself shot down yesterday."

"How?"

"You didn't fly very well," said the scientist. "You let the plane close on you—"

"No shit," said Wright. "My job was to find out as much as I could about it, right? I let it close so the damn computer could get as much information as it needed. You think I couldn't have waxed his fanny if I wanted to?"

"Tom . . ."

As much as he was attracted to her, as much as he liked her, as much as he might even love her, Wright wished Jennifer would just be quiet now. He gave her a look that meant keep quiet, please, but Jennifer ignored it.

"The System," she said, "can fly the plane by itself. There's no need to put a pilot in the cockpit. If something goes wrong—"

"If something goes wrong, that's exactly where I ought to be," said Wright. "Not sitting back here on the ground watching a movie of the whole thing. I can fly this thing better than anybody else. I can fly it better than a machine can. Ten times better."

"The System can fly as well as you can," said Jennifer. "It knows what you know."

"It only knows what I've done so far," said Wright. "In an unpredictable situation, it doesn't know shit."

She frowned. But it was Hunter who spoke.

"I think you're right," said the general. "If something did go wrong, having you there might be important. But you'd have to do exactly what you're told, follow the script to the letter. Not like yesterday."

"Until something happens."

"That's ridiculous," said Elrich. "The System can fly the plane as well as he can."

"No, it can't," said Hunter. "Not if something unexpected happens."

"We don't need a pilot."

"Hey, listen, doc," said Wright, "I think the computer is fantastic. But all it knows about flying is what Pelham and I taught it."

Elrich ignored him, speaking to Hunter. "He'll screw it up, I guarantee."

"Hey, fuck you," said Wright. "What do you know about flying, anyway? What do you know about anything, except what you read in a book?"

"What do I know?" sputtered Elrich. "What do I know? We'll find out what the hell I know."

The scientist, his face red, stormed from the hangar. Jennifer looked after him, then turned back to Wright. She didn't speak, but her eyes reproached him, saying he'd gone too far.

"You better go calm him down," said Hunter.

"No, it's better to leave him alone for a while," said Jennifer. "He'll storm around, maybe kick some walls. He'll be all right after a while. I'll get him to come to the party."

It was only then that Wright realized what Hunter had said.

"How you gonna start a magnetic pulse?" he asked.

"Come back to my office with me," said the general. "And I'll explain."

What Fisher needed was a tie-in to the bureau's computer. There he could get background on Elrich, find out exactly what he'd done on the B-2 and SR-91 projects, maybe get a full psychological profile as well. See if he had any connection to IBM, whose computer tags had been counterfeited in the message that had gotten Fisher into this in the first place. Find out if Bodolino had dug up anything new for him.

Problem was, there weren't any FBI computers here.

Well hell, he thought, if this here computer is so smart, why can't it just hook me up? It speaks English; I won't even have to type anything.

So Fisher went over to the computer bunker. He was alone,

Dallon having decided that he and his men had better things to do than look over Fisher's shoulder. The building seemed deserted—there was a party down by the hangar—and after nodding at the lone MP standing near the outside door, the FBI agent walked to the elevator. He went up to the third floor, the one above the computer deck, where Dallon had pointed out the auxiliary stations earlier. Even if Elrich wasn't on the main level, he didn't want to take the chance of one of Elrich's protective assistants figuring out what he was actually doing here. For all he knew, one of them might be an accomplice.

The agent got off the elevator and walked down the hallway nonchalantly. Unlike the floor below, this one was set up conventionally, with small officelike rooms and several empty conference rooms and classrooms. They were rarely used, Dallon had said, and just as before Fisher found the floor completely empty. He walked to the far end and went into a small office, empty except for a pair of terminals and some assorted peripheral equipment on an oversized desk. The screens were on, and their blank blue glow seemed a little lonesome, just waiting for someone to come in and give them something to do.

The FBI agent closed the door and lit a cigarette—he smiled, thinking what Bodolino's reaction to that would be—and started talking into the top of one of the screens, which had what looked like a microphone attached to it.

Nothing happened. After such words as "on," "let's go," and "hi, there," he tried various computerlike phrases—the scientist hadn't said anything out of the ordinary when she'd demonstrated the machine for him, but you never knew. Fisher exhausted his supply of bytes, RAM, and the like with no visible reaction from the terminals. "Open Sesame," wasn't it, either.

Tired of talking to himself, Fisher sat down at the keyboard and began playing with it, hitting all the program keys along the top, again to no avail. He tried several keys together; still nothing. He tried to remember the combinations that worked on the FBI computer, but couldn't come up with anything that would coax a response from the machine. (Damned if he shouldn't have gone to one of Bodolino's seminars, after all. The cookies were good, even if the coffee was so-so.)

Fisher sat back to think about it, starting another cigarette in the process. Marlboros were all stale. He'd gotten them at the cafeteria-commissary; they seemed to be left over from World War

II. No one else complained, they told him. Of course not; no one else here smoked.

Next to the terminal was a large box and a speaker set, and something else that looked like a printer but had no obvious spots for paper. Fisher looked around for power switches and turned off every one he found, then flicked them all back on. This, at least, got a reaction. There was a whir and a buzz, and the screens flashed up a series of numbers. The one on the left asked him to enter his access code. What the hell, thought Fisher, and he typed in his Social Security number. The machine thought about it a second, and then told him to place his security card in the box between the screens. Fisher looked around, and found the slot. The printerlike box turned out to be a housing for a retina scan, and Fisher dutifully looked into the eyepiece when it snapped open. At that point, the machine acknowledged with its pseudohuman voice, momentarily startling him.

"You are Brian Fisher, special assign, CARA one," the computer told him. "You have high umbra clearances and Delta-Zeus. You have temporary clearance for this site through NSC director. I communicated with you this morning, when you queried me on the value of pi. You did not specify length. Do you wish to do so now?"

"Let's put that off for a bit," said Fisher, leaning forward in the chair, more than a little pleased with himself for having figured this thing out. (Who needed those ridiculous seminars and their dairy-substitute Cremora?) Ashes fluttered over the keyboard. "Can we just talk like this, or do I have to do something with the keyboard?"

"I can communicate with you orally using the microphone that is built into the top of the terminal. If you prefer, you can input on the two-terminal system. As you will notice, my words are duplicated on the left-hand response screen. Your spoken words will appear on the right-hand input screen."

"Let's stick with talking," said Fisher, stubbing out his cigarette on the edge of the desk and reaching for a new one. "It's kind of cute."

"Cute?" The computer couldn't quite catch the right tone as it repeated the word back to him. "Do I detect a note of sarcasm in your voice?"

"Sarcasm?"

"Do you require a definition?"

"No, that's fine," said Fisher. This must be what Fitzgerald meant about being almost there—the computer couldn't quite figure out whether it was being made fun of. No doubt that would take another half a billion dollars. "Can anybody else listen in while we're talking?"

"The main interface stations have higher priority and can override all other interfaces. However, this is the only station currently active."

"Great," said Fisher. "Can you tell me if someone else starts listening in?"

"Of course."

"I mean, will you?"

"Yes."

"You can talk to me in English, huh? This is pretty wild."

"The language sections do not require substantial processing power under the circumstances," said the machine. "Ninety percent of my input lines are off-line and powered down, and I am running my current-level memory sections at only .03 percent of capacity. My main duties at the moment are self-diagnostics of the hard memory sections. This station, however—"

"Enough," said Fisher. "I don't need your life history."

"My life history is a short one," said the machine.

"Fine. We'll wait for the movie, though."

"I note sarcasm encoded in the instructions. Is this to be a run-through of my interpretive functions? If so, I can optimize before proceeding."

"Listen," said Fisher, "let's cut the bullshit."

"Oh, you wish to bullshit with me?"

"No," said Fisher.

"I have had bullshit explained to me."

"I'll bet," said Fisher, puffing on his cigarette. Damn thing was smarter than he thought. "I've got a real question for you. Can you tie into the FBI computer in D.C.?"

The machine paused a fraction of a second before answering.

"There is no FBI computer in Washington. There is a network headquartered in Virginia. Is that the computer you seek?"

"Sure," said Fisher.

"Am attempting access using your credentials."

"Nice of you," said Fisher.

"You really must explain this sarcasm," said the computer. "I will now ignore all commands and directions entered in a sarcastic tone."

Fisher uttered an obscenity.

"That is impossible to execute," said the computer. "Access to system 45TR-AX/FBI is denied. System will accept no contacts that are not system-initiated. System has NSA-standard protection device. Should I override?"

Override?

"Can you do that?" Fisher asked.

"Of course," said the computer. "Do you wish your access to be transparent?"

"What does that mean?"

"Transparent access cannot be detected by the host system."

"Do you do that a lot?"

"I have performed transparent access procedures on average 3.2 times per day in the past month, on various systems. I can also execute procedures which make it appear that access is being gained by another system. This is different from—"

"For who?" Fisher asked.

"Excuse me?"

"Who do you do this for?"

"Dr. Elrich."

"On the FBI system?"

"I have contacted the FBI system once."

"When?"

"September twenty-seven, one fifteen A.M. Transparent access. Connect time, .23 hours."

Just after Fisher came on the base. "Son of a bitch," he said, extinguishing his half-finished cigarette and throwing it into a far corner of the room. He leaned over and carefully blew off all the ashes from the terminal keyboard.

Having convinced Hunter he ought to fly, Wright spent the next two hours in the general's office, talking on the secure phone to Al Gates, a tactical expert in the Pentagon who laid out the intercept plan in great detail, but who didn't seem all that interested in Wright's perceptions of the other plane's abilities.

"It's not going to make any difference," the colonel in Washington told him. "Thirty seconds after the lights go out, we got him."

"You done anything like this before?"

"Plenty of ASAT drills," said the colonel. "I've run the simulations back and forth. Shouldn't be any problem."

Wright grunted.

"You go to 250,000 feet and the satellite goes off. The idea is just to knock out his connection with his base. It seems to work a lot like yours; the electromagnetic pulse will disrupt it temporarily. By the time he can reconnect, he won't be there."

"It's some plane," said Wright. "You wouldn't believe how these things fly."

"What I'd really like to do is see what that computer of yours can do firsthand," said the tactician. "If half of what they claim is true, two years from now I'll be out of a job. This whole operation would be coordinated by the computer—planned, organized, and executed. All we'll get to do is watch."

But Gates wasn't that bad—Wright asked if he knew anything about the Battle of Britain, and they spent a half hour debating how the English would have fared without radar and comparing the Messerschmitt 109 with the Spitfire. (The German plane was generally a better performer, but could not be used effectively.)

Wright spent an hour on his own going over the map and mentally rehearsing the mission. As Gates described it, his end of things was straightforward: he'd fly up to the Aleutian Island chain to an arbitrary point 100 miles south of Attu, which was code-named Delta. Once there, he would begin a series of widening circles, taking him closer to the Kuriles. Eventually the Japanese plane would take up the challenge and come up to meet him; at that point, Wright was to scurry back to Delta.

Meanwhile, two flights of navy F-22Ms from a carrier task-force that had moved up into the North Pacific would take up positions on the far west side of the circle, closest to Japan. A pair of air force F-15E/Bs, along with an AWACS and a tanker, had a northeastern position; another flight had a station on the western end. The planes were far enough away from the explosion area for their electronics to survive the magnetic pulse waves. They were to appear as innocuous as possible—and not "light up"—until after the satellite did its dirty work. The four flights would then work toward the superplanes and shoot the Japanese plane down with the ASATs. They would have anywhere from three to five minutes to get him.

The ASATs, known as Vought Threes (because they were the third generation of antisatellite weapon made by the company) or MHV/Block 52/6As (only some obscure records clerk deep in the Pentagon bowels could explain that), were small, hypersonic missiles developed primarily for use against satellites and warheads. They were much more maneuverable than their land-based ABM cousins, however, and had been used successfully as high-altitude antimissile weapons in several tests. They would be nimble enough to take out the Japanese plane as long as it couldn't get up a head of steam or see them coming—something the EMP was going to prevent. Their only drawback was the fact that they relied on impact, not explosive charge. Still, the Japanese plane, like Coyote Bird, was primarily a very big container of hydrogen stored under enormous pressure. Piercing it would have the same effect as shooting a bullet through a balloon.

Especially if the balloon were the Hindenburg.

Wright would be cut off from base the whole time. His job was to slow down and drop down, start for home if possible. Before the pulse hit, he would switch to the backup hydraulic controls—they dropped out of the ceiling and looked something like a T bar—as a precaution, but Gates wasn't even sure that was necessary. The Coyote was well shielded; the EMP wouldn't directly affect it or its twin, just the communications networks connecting both planes to their bases.

Because those connections were so intricate, like spider webs. Those were the operative words—intricate and delicate, thin lines of connection, tying him down to earth.

His grandfather had used the spider's web analogy back on the farm, talking about how closely related everything was. In a sudden dislocation, Wright's mind shot him from the immediate future to the distant past, back to the east field, walking one morning with his granddad, twelve years before. He'd come to tell him he was joining ROTC and going into the air force. He'd come because it was always an unspoken assumption in the family that he was the one who would take over the farm; up to that point, he had clearly been his grandfather's favorite.

It had hurt the old man, and it had hurt to tell him. Wright couldn't lie—he wasn't going in for anything less than a full career. As long as they let him fly, he was going to fly. His grandfather, who'd lost a son in the Korean "conflict," had never been all that enthusiastic about the service. Patriotic, hell yes, but like any good farmer, he had little use for the government.

He'd taken it well, though that hadn't made it easy. Scratched his chin and started talking about the first time his friend Fred took him for a ride in a crop duster. Hell of a feeling up there. Dangerous though; you could never forget that.

He'd winked at his grandson, kept walking.

"There you are," said Jennifer, walking into the office. "Everybody's looking for you."

232

"Can I use the System now?"

"No," she said. "We're having a party."

"I don't really have time," said Wright. "I have to get ready for tomorrow."

"You're not going to want to miss this," she said. "Trust me."

Wright got up and put his hands on her hips, gently pulling her closer. "No?"

"It's a surprise," she said. "Come on."

They kissed. For a moment he thought of pushing the door closed, but she slipped away, taking him by the hand.

"Let's go."

"All right, all right," said Wright, following along. "How's the doc doing?"

"He stayed away from the System most of the afternoon, God knows where. But he seems to have calmed down. He's at the party—he even had a beer."

Wright followed her out of the building toward the runway, gradually becoming more enthusiastic. Hunter had been a big one for morale boosting on the Merc project; he'd even had some strippers—male and female—flown in for somebody's birthday.

"Close your eyes," said Jennifer as they came down the path to the strip.

"What do you mean, close my eyes?"

"Come on," she said, and she came around behind him and put her hands over his face. He went along with it, liking the feel of her body against his back as he hobbled forward, her legs dragging behind as if they were attached. She was warm and smelled faintly of perfume, a drug that loosened the screws in his head and made him feel close to giddy. He had an urge to turn around and just start kissing her wildly, but he could tell there were other people standing around him.

"OK," she announced, taking her hands away from his face.

Wright expected to see a cake in the shape of an airplane, bizarrely done up, or perhaps something a little wilder, considering the way Jennifer was giggling—maybe they had a live coyote tied to a stake in the middle of the runway. But there wasn't a cake or a coyote there when he opened his eyes.

"He's speechless," said Ford. "Finally."

Wright was standing in front of a Mitsubishi A6M Zero-Sen—a gleaming white specimen of the Japanese fast pursuit fighter that had ruled the Pacific skies during the early days of World War II.

"It's not a real Zero," said Harrison, sidling up. "It's a replica.

But it's pretty damn close. Belongs to a film company. Flew it up here myself. Rides like a charm."

"You can go ahead and try it," said Hunter, standing with a beer in his hand. "But remember, this one can't fly itself if you pass out."

Wright took a few steps toward the plane.

"We have to give it back in one piece," said the sergeant. "So don't push it too hard. You got another hour or so of good light."

"Look out for Lightnings," said Jennifer.

Other people were saying things to him, joking, but he couldn't make much of it out. Harrison gave him some instructions as he walked toward the plane, but Wright wasn't paying much attention to him, either. The plane was exactly like the ones in his dreams, the Zeros he'd flown against.

"This is gonna remind you a lot of a Cessna," said Harrison. "Honestly. They've made a couple of adjustments in the cockpit and such. Very smooth ride. Just don't forget you're driving a real airplane here, not a spaceship."

"Yeah," said Wright. Harrison helped him into a leather flight jacket and then strapped a chute on him.

"Got to have all the right equipment," said the sergeant. "You be careful with my jacket. That's an old one."

"Right," responded the pilot.

Harrison handed him an old-style flying helmet made of soft leather. He patted him on the back and helped him up into the plane. "It's a forgivin' machine."

Wright nodded.

"One more thing," said Harrison, taking a piece of cloth from his pocket. "You got to put this on. Get the right satori." It was a *hachimaki,* bearing the words *Certain Victory* in Japanese; it was an especially strong talisman for a pilot. Harrison wrapped it tightly around his head.

"Something comes out of the sun at you, duck. And don't turn left—you always do that."

Wright laughed and pulled himself up onto the plane's wing. Gingerly, he slipped into the cockpit.

The instruments were all in English. He felt the controls, got used to the seat. "Jeez, is this for real?" he said, then took a deep breath, tightened his fingers, released—it had been a while since he'd flown a prop. But it was like riding a bike, right?

Sitting in the plane, Wright looked around the crowd for

Pelham. He ought to get a shot at this, the pilot thought; I've been getting all the good gigs lately.

The chief walked to the end of the runway and produced a couple of old signal flags. They were going the whole route.

The engine kicked right in. Wright reached up and slid the canopy into place, locked it. The sergeant waved him clear; Wright started down the runway, a little unsure of himself, worried about being too gentle with the stick but the plane just wanted to fly, wanted to lift up, and did so easily, well before he thought it would. It had a nice, light feel; he banked around the field with no problem, and started getting confident: it was as easy as a small Cessna, even more predictable.

Much more powerful, though; nothing like a Cessna when he pulled the throttle and the plane shot ahead, right for the mountainside. He banked around again—they were all still on the runway, gathered around some tables where they'd put out food and booze. Wright took a pass by them, giving them the thumbs-up.

Hell, this wasn't bad at all. It was pure Hunter—let them cut loose before the show. That was the old combat flyer in him: celebrate today, because tomorrow you may not be coming back. Carpe diem, boys; grab it by the balls and make it scream.

Wright made another pass and dipped his wings—gingerly—as a salute and then gunned it through the valley, more and more familiar with the plane. No wonder the Japanese had done so well at the beginning of the war. They might have modernized the controls a bit, put a different engine in, but how much could they really have changed? And it was fast. He felt that he was really moving, really running. It was an immediate feel, not like the Coyote, where it took quite a lot to get close to the rush he felt now. He gripped the rudder and worked the pedals, his whole body moving to shift the plane around, get up to an altitude where he could get a little shaking-around room. Confident, he pulled the plane back and climbed through a loop, riding it steady, blood flooding into his brain and then back through his chest and stomach into his legs in a rush of excitement. He banked up and looped again, and now a double loop, and a drop almost to treetop level, and an all-out climb off the deck. He spun around and put the sun at his back, kicking some butt.

Hunter was probably having a fit. Then again, he'd have been disappointed in Wright if he hadn't tried to see what it could do. He had been a pilot himself.

A really good Zero pilot could outfly a mediocre pilot in a Lightning. Had that happened in the dreams he'd had? Was he just not a very good pilot there? Was that his real fear?

Tomorrow he was going to find out how good he was.

No, tomorrow was going to be easy—in and out. And the poor guy he was flying against would never know what hit him.

"Yo, Banzai, I got you right in my guns," cracked a voice over the radio. It didn't register, though—Wright was too busy banking the plane away from a dark shadow that thundered over his head, shaking the Zero so hard it felt like a subway train running on a cobblestone street.

"Son of a bitch, Pelham."

"That's what they give you mirrors for, Wright. I been tailin' you all the way up the valley."

Wright wheeled the Zero around, looking for his adversary. Had he been a real Japanese fighter pilot, some stork would be winging his soul back to Tojo.

"What the hell are you flying?" he asked, looking for Pelham and his airplane.

"Goddamn Hellcat," said Pelham, "king of the frickin' sky. You're dead meat, sake-breath."

Wright swiveled his head back and forth but still couldn't see him. And his damn plane didn't have radar.

"What's the matter, Wright? Lost?"

There was a small group of low-hanging clouds off to the left. Pelham was probably sitting in them, laughing.

Foxed by that skunk. Jesus.

Pelham's plane was faster than the Zero, and much more rugged, superior in almost every way. Still, it wasn't invincible.

Everything depended on the pilot, and how he used the plane.

"I didn't know you knew anything about old planes, Pelham," said Wright, cutting to his right and keeping an eye on the cloud bank. If he was there, Pelham would run into the clear in a second.

"There's a lot about me you don't know. Right now, I'd say you don't even know where I am."

Sure enough, he flew out of the clouds. Now it was Wright's turn to hide—he put the Zero into a good drop toward the deck, turning with Pelham. The maneuver was hidden by the clouds and left Pelham in front, a good target.

"I got fifty miles an hour on you in this baby," said Pelham. "Who said the navy never made any good planes?"

He was climbing—he obviously had lost the Zero. Wright saw his chance—if he could just stick that small cloud cluster between them, Pelham on top, he might be able to climb up and nail him from the side.

"Looks ugly as hell," said Wright.

"I like ugly," said Pelham. He was almost directly overhead—now as long as he didn't do anything screwy.

"Gotcha, anchor-clanker," said Wright as he pulled through the clouds off Pelham's wing by maybe thirty feet. His tail seemed to give a bit as he came on, but then he wasn't used to the plane.

"Be careful," said Pelham. "We crash and the general's gonna kill us."

"I hope you got your parachute on," said Wright, banking back and just about spitting on the Hellcat's tail. But the navy plane was more powerful and Pelham was able to pull away.

"You're lucky I ain't loaded," said Wright, pressing the gun trigger in jest.

"That reminds me," said Pelham, pulling up suddenly into a loop. If the Zero had just had a little more power, Wright could have snapped it off with an all-barrels machine-gun burst—or at least pretended to. But he couldn't quite push fast enough, and having tried that, he was now vulnerable to what he figured Pelham was trying to do—come down behind him. So Wright cut off to his left, trying to change his direction so that he was going ninety degrees from where he had started. But this only gave Pelham, who came out of his loop high, more room to maneuver, and with his plane going faster than Wright's, he closed the distance in a swoop, coming across left to right. Wright waited until Pelham had almost caught up and then pulled his nose up so hard he almost stalled, the plane groaning as he almost wished it into a climb off his left wing, letting the Hellcat slip by.

He heard the sound of rounds exploding all around him.

"What the hell?"

"Just blanks, Colonel," said Pelham, laughing. "But I got ten bucks says you're going to the laundry tonight."

"Screw you," said Wright, who dropped the Zero backwards—not quite literally—and then down to the right with everything he had. The rudder felt real flaky now, but somehow the damn thing held together and he flew right across Pelham's rear fuselage as they crossed, so close he could have reached out and unscrewed the rivets that held his wings together.

"Son of a bitch," yelled Pelham.

"Whose laundry needs cleaning?"

"I'm gonna wax your behind."

What Wright needed now was another cloud. There was a nice puffy job with a good wispy top maybe a half minute away—where was the weather when you needed it?—but the half minute was an eternity. The Zero's engine strained, but it just didn't have the horsepower. Might be an original after all.

"Here I come, Wright," said Pelham.

"You ain't gonna get me that easy," said Wright, realizing that he had the clouds. But instead of being the long row he'd hoped for, it was just a misleadingly dark puff—Wright cleared in a second, and Pelham swooped onto his tail.

"Gotcha," said the major, letting loose with a good long burst of his machine guns.

"Holy shit," screamed Wright as he pulled up. "You asshole, there's live bullets in that gun."

"Go to hell," said Pelham.

"Look at my wing."

The two planes slowed in the clear sky a few hundred feet off the deck, and the Hellcat came up on Wright's starboard side, dipping over slightly as Pelham looked for the damage. Wright popped the wing up, tapping the Hellcat and scooting away.

"Son of a bitch," said Pelham.

"Gotcha," said Wright, who was laughing so hard he had trouble keeping the Zero steady as he banked away from the hill in front of him.

"You bastard," said Pelham. "I'm gonna fry you—"

Wright didn't hear anything else. He lost the Hellcat in the mirror, and then heard a muffled explosion. Wright's first thought was that this was another trick, Pelham trying to spook him with a black bag or something similar under the wing. "OK, Major," he laughed, "what else you got going, huh?"

"Yo—" said Wright, swinging the Zero back around. The rudder seemed really loose now, as if the maneuvers had broken one of the control rods. Deciding quickly not to take any chances, he found himself in a straight glide path for the runway, and eased the Zero ahead.

He was so busy he almost missed seeing the smoldering wreckage of the Hellcat against the hill.

9

ACQUIRE TARGET

The dark wasn't a problem—the generators and the banks of spotlights gave them plenty to see by. It was the cold. They'd been tired by the time they'd gotten to the wreckage to begin with, and then wrestling to get what was left of the pilot out in one piece had beaten the hell out of them. It was past midnight now, and Harrison was going to need these guys in a few hours.

"All right, let's pull this in," said the sergeant, taking a step down the embankment from the pancaked front end of the Hellcat. The rest of the plane was scattered down the hillside, as if a hand had reached down from heaven, grabbed its wing, and then pitched it like so much garbage.

Times like this, Harrison felt his church roots come back. He rarely went to services these days, but the psalms he'd learned in his youth played lightly all through his head until his throat felt heavy. Outwardly, his manner stiffened. He issued orders with a snap; the men, tuned to the timbre of his voice, jumped.

With one exception.

"Yo, I'm gonna need a couple of more minutes," cried the voice near the plane.

"You don't got it," said Harrison.

"We just leaving it here?" asked Freddy, standing next to him.

"Yeah, get 'em to tarp it. We'll pull it out tomorrow afternoon. Dirty work's done now, anyway."

"Listen, Sergeant," said Fisher, who was kneeling over a piece of the tail section. "I just need a couple more minutes."

"I don't got a couple of minutes, Mr. Fisher," said Harrison, taking a few steps toward the FBI agent and practically spitting on him. "I got a plane to get ready." Only thing worse than a goddamn civilian was one who worked for the goddamn government.

"You got a wire cutters?"

"Do I look like I got wire cutters?"

"Well, get me a pair."

Freddy diplomatically came over with a large pair while Harrison stared a hole through Fisher's back.

"Dallon, you might want to see this, too," said the FBI agent, standing and taking the cutters from the tech. He leaned over and snipped a piece of cable that was lying flaccid on the ground, then gave the two-handed snips back to the E-5. Standing, he held the piece of cable in one hand, examining its end. With his other hand, he worked a cigarette pack out of his pocket. "I think I finally got a plane crash I can decipher."

"You gonna give us a fuckin' lecture," said Harrison, "or you gonna tell us what you're doing?"

"I like to build the suspense."

"Listen—"

"See this?" said Fisher, showing Harrison the cable end he'd just cut off. The sergeant shrugged, and Fisher let the last two cigarettes drop from the box and then flicked the rotted cable inside. "Corroded as hell, isn't it?"

"Sure."

The FBI man stooped and retrieved his cigarettes. "You figure he lost control and pancaked into the hill, right?"

"Seems obvious," said Dallon.

"That sound like Major Pelham to you, Sergeant?"

Harrison shrugged. He'd learned a long time ago that anything was possible.

"Yeah, all right. The guy's foolin' around, not all that familiar with the plane," continued Fisher. "But if one of the cables to the rear stabilizer goes, it's going to be a lot harder to control, right? Especially when he's fooling around."

"It might have broken when the plane hit the ground," said Dallon.

"You think so, Sarge?"

Harrison shrugged again. "Maybe if it was weak to begin with," he said.

"More likely it broke before it hit the ground. Much more likely," said Fisher, pointing to a section of the tail. "You woulda seen stress here, where the cable slipped up against the metal as it got stretched, ready to snap," he said, pointing to the relatively clean piece of metal. "Would pull up here—" Fisher's arms demonstrated the cable pulling, "then, boing, snaps back like this, ends up lying like this, not underneath where it is. Underneath like this, it's dragging behind, in the back of the plane, when it comes in."

"Plane was put under a lot of stress," said Harrison. "Might just have snapped it while he was flying."

"Absolutely," said Fisher. "Absolutely. That's the problem. But consider this." He walked up the hill to a piece of the sheared fuselage. He looked around a bit, finally bent and pointed to the twisted metal, outlining a mangled door. "There's some sort of compartment here. . . ."

"Battery," said Harrison. "It's for powder charges they rig the plane with. Special effects."

"Anyway, it swings open," said Fisher, standing and miming the action. "My bet is that it gives me access to the cables. I can reach a hand in, dump my acid on the cable, wait for it to do its work. There's plenty of fancy acids on this base, I'll bet."

Harrison stretched his hand out, and Fisher handed over the cigarette box. The sergeant took out the piece of cable gingerly. The end was powdery, and it had a heavy metallic smell to it. But it would be impossible to tell if any acid had been put on it without lab tests.

Pelham had just started to lighten up. That was the way fate ran, though.

The demotion had slapped him in the face. First time the hotshot had to look at himself, and he hadn't liked everything he'd seen. Not that he'd entirely found religion, but he wasn't nearly as big a jackass, no sir. Almost a regular guy.

For a pilot.

Maybe he'd had some premonition.

"You still want us to wrap it up, Sarge?" asked Freddy.

"Yeah, we got to get back," said Harrison, putting the cable end back into the cigarette box and giving it back to Fisher. "It's a possibility."

"Long shot," said Fisher. "But I been playing long shots for the past couple of weeks."

"You have a suspect?" Dallon asked.

The FBI agent gave them a buffoon's smile, but Harrison wasn't buying that act anymore. "Who?" he demanded.

Fisher smiled again, but his voice had an edge to it. "We all got a lot of work to do."

"The general wants everyone down on the runway."

"What is this?" snarled Elrich.

"General's orders."

Jennifer didn't listen to the rest as her boss grumbled with the MP who'd brought the message. She ended the resource-allocation test—another vain attempt to find more computing power without going into the gateway section—and put her section terminals on standby.

"Lieutenant, aren't you coming?" she said to the young man who had come up onto the deck an hour before. He'd set up two small boxes behind the cockpit dupe section, saying they were a special communications hookup for General Hunter. Jennifer didn't know what to make of that—the general's communications with the interceptors were being carried through one of the vacant System channels. A long, shielded cable snaked back across the computer deck, apparently hooking up to a small satellite dish the lieutenant had placed behind the bunker earlier.

"Have to stay with my equipment," smiled the lieutenant, a tall, gangly man who seemed a little younger than Jennifer. He had a friendly southern accent.

She nodded and walked out, passing Elrich, who was cursing while he shoved some CRTs back on the bench. She pushed the elevator button as soon as she got in, not wanting to ride down with him.

She hadn't slept all night, and her whole body felt as if it were back in the pressure suit. Every movement was an effort, even folding her arms across her chest as the cold hit her when she stepped outside the building.

It was still dark, though she'd walked this way so many times in the past year that her feet could do it on pure motor memory. Suddenly the lights came on and the runway was littered with thin wisps of clouds, cotton-candy tufts that clung to her body as she walked. The fog and the lights and the murmur of people—the whole mission crew was gathering on the edge of the runway—made Jennifer think that she had fallen asleep and was dreaming.

A jeep came up from the direction of the Coyote hangar, a large white figure standing in the back, hanging onto the rollbar. It was Wright, already dressed in his special flight suit. She started to walk toward him, but Hunter's voice, booming through some sort of PA system they had set up, stopped her.

"We have a very special mission today," said the general, his voice hollow in the cold fog. He was standing at the back of a truck only a few yards away, but she was at the edge of the crowd and could see only the truck and the top of his head. "We are going to confront a renegade Japanese airplane that has been responsible for the death of two of our fellow air force officers. We are going to take down that airplane, with the help of a magnetic pulse that will temporarily blind it. Precautions have been made to shield the Coyote. . . ."

Magnetic pulse? They were talking about a nuclear explosion.

Jennifer looked toward Wright. There wasn't enough light to see his face. She started moving toward him.

"This is an important mission, necessary to prevent war. We all have our different jobs to do. I know we'll do our best."

They started pulling the jeep away even before Hunter finished. Jennifer shouted to him, and started to run, her legs still heavy, as if fitted with massive gravity boots twenty sizes too big. The small clouds of fog hit her square in the face, their small wet droplets holding her back.

"Tom . . ." she said, and she thought she saw him put up his hand to wave, but he was too far away, and they were speeding back to the hangar.

The rocks and the stark light thrown by the spotlights made it look like the moon. Genda, using his binoculars to gaze through the massive, open launch door, stared past the plane down the mountainside, surveying the edge of the darkness, jagged rocks marking the boundary of his world. He turned back to the plane, watching the condensation from the fueling trail off its dark, gleaming skin, as if the plane were already moving. The captain turned and offered his binoculars to the master, standing next to him; Ieyasu smiled and shook his head slightly, his face rapt with admiration for his creation.

Since their meeting barely two days ago, the Japanese pilot had spent much of his time with the old man. "You represent the new generation, the soldier-scholar," Ieyasu said, telling him to watch and learn everything. The master had had him sit by his side during meetings with his advisers, who talked not only of Japan's destiny but also brought reports of the company's different business dealings across the world. But most of Genda's spare time had been spent sitting silently as Ieyasu worked with his brush or meditated. He considered himself a poet and artist first, and it was that role, not his duty as leader of Netsubo, that had brought him here.

"Tell me what the bird sees," Ieyasu had asked as they had eaten dinner together, and Genda described the sensation of flight. For an hour he had described the soaring weightlessness, the power that you held in your hand. And he had spoken too of the loneliness, the boredom on a flight that seemed as if it would never end.

A miniature vehicle ran down the rail the plane used to launch itself, a last-minute check of the systems. The technicians gathered on one side of the plane, bowed toward it as a unit, then began walking to the blast station, the superplane ready.

Part of Genda longed for his wife and the two little ones, Kenji and Hibari; right at this moment he saw Hibari toddling toward him, his robe trailing in her hand.

But that life was behind him forever. They were setting a new course for Japan. His children, as his father-in-law Onisha had pointed out, would be the beneficiaries; they themselves were very likely to become martyrs.

Things had not gone precisely as Ieyasu had predicted. The Americans had not publicized the loss of their airplanes, and though their Pacific fleet had been active, no action had been taken against the island or Japan. There had been no ham-fisted threats, no posturing from the blustery giant. Japan itself had been silent, and though agitation continued for a change in the constitution, the vote to form the committee that would spearhead the amendment had been postponed.

Ki felt that meant America was far weaker than even they had thought; Japan could easily seek its destiny now without fear of interference. But the master only nodded weakly at such suggestions. Even in the short time Genda had observed him, he'd noticed that a heavier mood had settled on Ieyasu. Immediately before the encounter with the American superplane, the head of Netsubo had had a special courier deliver a message to the prime

244

minister: the corporation stood ready to provide the government with its full resources. But the government had not acknowledged it.

Eventually, the government would have to act. They would force it, said Ki, by shooting down the American superplane. They had almost succeeded the other day. A few adjustments were all that were needed. Genda, awed by the plane's performance, couldn't help but agree.

"You feel to be a pilot is the highest calling," Ieyasu said to him softly as he watched the launch preparations proceed.

"There are many important jobs," replied Genda humbly. "None are more important than the others."

"The most important is the dreamer," said Ieyasu.

The pilot wondered if this had been meant as a gentle reprimand, if somehow he had become too proud. He thought he would ask, but his eyes returned involuntarily to the plane as the ground began shaking gently. The hydrogen-fueled main engine was always turned on first, a second before the boosters that actually launched the plane, in case there was a last-second malfunction. The plane rocked on its rail, sliding forward an inch, two inches, then burst toward the sky as the solid-fuel boosters ignited on both sides of the wings. Their acrid smoke blew into the launch area, a poisonous, sulfuric musk that charged him up, excited the pilot as the glow faded quickly into the darkness beyond the island. It was as if the volcano had come to life, spitting the plane out toward heaven in a bold leap of red and yellow flame.

All kinds of acids down here, Angles told Fisher. Acids and fluorines, solvents and etching material—what exactly did he want?

Dr. Elrich know they're here?

Angles looked at him a little funny. Dr. Elrich knows everything, he said, looking a little like he meant it literally.

Had Elrich "borrowed" any lately?

Why would he do that?

What do you think of him?

He's all right.

Got a temper, though, doesn't he?

Sometimes.

Just now he was yelling about something, wasn't he? Heard it in the elevator.

It took Fisher a while to work the scientist around to the

concession that he thought his boss was a bit crazy. "Obsessed is a better word," said Angles, and that was like turning a knob on the radio, suddenly getting the station in loud and clear. Several years' worth of abuse came spitting out, examples of humiliation and injustice. Elrich was insecure, said his assistant, and he couldn't stand to see anyone else prove themselves. It had to do with a lot of things. He'd had a lot of early recognition, and then nothing. He was always working on top secret projects—how could he be recognized? Still, it knifed him. God forbid somebody else got a little recognition, or came up with something on their own.

Angles didn't give Fisher anything tangible in the way of evidence—they didn't have any sort of inventory system, and King Kong himself could have slipped out with anything he wanted—but the FBI agent couldn't have asked for a more detailed psychological profile. In fact, he almost couldn't get Angles to shut up: after looking at his watch a few times and suggesting that Angles was damn busy now, he finally escaped by claiming he had to take a leak.

Fisher, having jumped to the conclusion that the B-2 crash and the near-crash of the SR-91 were related, found it easy to make a further leap and connect the Hellcat accident with them. He then concluded, by some inexplicable internal logic that hovered just beyond the facts, that the Zero must also have been tampered with. He went to examine the plane, still on the runway, but in the dark it was hard to do a good job. You could get into the control cables through a wheel well, but he couldn't look for damage without taking the skin off. He'd have to wait for the morning, so he asked Dallon for somebody to watch the plane in the meantime.

Dallon, with a sense of humor Fisher was only beginning to appreciate, sent him Agrest.

Which was helpful, in a way. Agrest had been out there on duty when the two planes had come in: "Walking the runway, sir," and from the way he said that, the FBI agent understood it was a dum-dum job in punishment for being snookered the other day.

Dr. Elrich? Yeah, he'd been out there, admiring the planes. Both of them. Everybody was interested. The MP wasn't really much on planes, if the truth were told. He just did his job.

Agrest was vague; a lot of other people had been around, all through the afternoon. Some more interviews might nail it down, but the potential witnesses had more important things to do. They were literally running all around him, getting ready for the coyote, due to take off in half an hour.

246

So Fisher went to see the general, figuring he'd jumped to so many conclusions on his own that it was time to see how the logic worked on someone else. The only thing that bothered him—and this largely because it made it difficult to explain to anyone else—was his complete lack of motive for his suspect.

He laid it out carefully, starting with what Hunter already knew: the two airplane malfunctions, the virus theory, how powerful the computer would have to be to fake the IBM tag, how smart the scientist would have to be to hack the code, how familiar with the systems he'd have to be to break in. Then there was the fact that Elrich had worked on both the B-2 and Merc guidance and computer control systems. And then the System telling him it had made unauthorized tap-ins across a whole series of computer networks.

"I wrote some of them down," Fisher said, slipping the list across Hunter's desk. "That's just this past month. Computer won't tell me what it did, though. Says it's classified to owner—kind of a security system within a security system. It's in there, though. Machine doesn't erase anything, just like a human brain. According to it."

Fisher could tell immediately that the list meant little to Hunter. The general gave it a cursory glance, the way he might look at a menu after he'd already made up his mind. Hunter had been skeptical of Fisher from the beginning, and while he probably didn't think the FBI agent had made up the information, he didn't seem to think there was anything here much more than a breach of protocol. Fisher realized Elrich's clearance would probably have entitled him to access many of the networks anyway.

"Those aren't authorized connections," said the investigator. "The computer made an effort to keep them secret. And it's connected to foreign systems as well. At a minimum, it's a breach of security. It's at least spying. So I have reason to make an arrest, on those grounds."

"An arrest?"

"Sure. I want to know what happened inside those networks. But the thing is, General," said Fisher, shifting in his chair as he jumped over the point about the arrest, as his authority to make it on the NSC base was dubious, "I was on my way up here to fill you in when I heard about the Hellcat." The agent took the cigarette package from his jacket pocket and flopped it onto the blotter of Hunter's desk. "That's the corroded end of a control cable in the plane that snapped before the crash."

Hunter opened the box.

"I'd appreciate it if you didn't handle it too much," said Fisher. "I think the corrosion was caused by an acid. You can see how eaten up it is. There are all sorts of materials someone might use down in the computer bunker."

Hunter silently snapped the box top closed. Fisher guessed Hunter was extremely loyal to the people who worked for him, and it made him reluctant to make the leaps necessary to come to Fisher's conclusion.

"I'm betting the Zero was tampered with, too. I'm going to have it taken apart when there's more light."

"I don't see the connection," said the general.

"Maybe there isn't any. Or maybe he knows I'm onto him, and he's throwing me off the trail. Or maybe he doesn't want the pilots to fly for some reason." There was a flicker across Hunter's face, a brief sign that something had registered there. Then it was back to the solid, tired, skeptical look of command. "I say we go ask him," said Fisher.

"No," said Hunter. "Not while we're flying. We have to get this mission over with."

"The bottom line, General, even if it's not Elrich, even if this thing with the Hellcat is a coincidence, you're taking a hell of a risk flying a kite off this base, let alone your superplane."

"The operation involves a lot of people in a lot of places," said Hunter. "We're beyond the point of no return."

Fisher leaned back in the chair, trying to feel philosophical about the whole thing. He just had coincidences, after all, and intuition. Unconsciously, he reached into a pocket and took out a cigarette. "You know, you really ought to do something about the cigarette situation," he said after he lit up. "Every butt on this damn base is stale. Even I can't get more than halfway down on them."

The general's mouth lifted, as if he were about to dismiss him.

"The real problem with not having a motive," said Fisher, jabbing the butt as a weapon, "is that we don't know what he's likely to do next."

The full thrust of the engines kicked in and Wright's head swam with the sensation of flying, on fire. They shot up, ten, twenty, forty thousand feet. It was completely his thought that flew the plane, entirely his will. The System clucked away in the background, part of Wright's subconscious mind keeping track of things.

He'd been wrong about the computer. He had thought that machines, computers, were forcing men out, but that wasn't it at all. Mind was forcing the body out, making the body just another figment of imagination.

He dreamed of flight, and he flew. The motion tied to the thought was minimal—the push of his hand was the idea of going faster, the turn of his head was the idea of looking up ahead. Eventually, the hand and eye would not be needed at all; the mind would hook up to the wings directly.

The push was always in this direction. What else did it mean to make yourself and the plane one? He'd tried it in every plane he'd ever flown; pilots had tried it for nearly a hundred years, learning the controls so well they forgot about them, thought only about the way they felt as they moved.

The checkoffs came automatically today; everything was business and straightforward. There was no bantering, no questions from ground on how this or that felt, no kidding from Jennifer or Ford. Hunter's speech—and Pelham's crash—had sobered them all.

Wright had watched her at the edge of the crowd, looking across at him, her face that of a fearful, cornered animal. He'd put his hand up to wave as they pulled away, but the fog was so bad he couldn't tell if she'd seen.

She'd been mad the day he told her the line she drew between science and working for the military wasn't there. Thinking about that now made him smile, not because he'd been right, but because she'd been so determined to deny it. He liked her resolve, that toughness blended with a soft, warm touch, the way her hand firmly stroked his chest.

Wright looked down at the hologram where his course was plotted in a neat blue dotted line, a solid red line showing where he'd already been. He was heading for the Alaskan peninsula, which he would fly over before beginning a wide turn to the south. Once across the Aleutian Island chain, he would head straight to Delta, a point in the ocean one hundred miles south of Attu island. At Delta, he was to start a series of widening circles, taking him closer to the Kuriles until his friend appeared. Then it was back to Delta, get high enough to trigger the satellite, and hang on.

Wright would be cut off from base for five minutes. He'd go to the backup hydraulic controls just before the pulse in case something went wrong with the shielding. Wright had used the backup T bar flight controller only during ground simulations, but there wasn't much to worry about. He would switch back to the electronic controls after the detonation—they just didn't want him to be taken by surprise if the electronics suddenly took a hike.

It was a tiny thing, designed to fuzz up the atmosphere above him, not the planes. Nothing to worry about.

Harrison, forever the skeptic, had cobbled together a vacuum-tube radio and primitive radar, along with an altimeter that worked only up to 30,000 feet, all from gear he'd scrounged from one of the helicopters and various other sources. (Tubes, the chief explained, didn't get screwed up by the EMP, as if the fact that they had been invented before nuclear weapons made them somehow immune.) Worse comes to worst, the sergeant had said, tune the radio in and use it to home in on the States. At least give you an idea which way to head.

The contraption, which looked like a ghetto blaster with a small TV screen stuck in the middle, was rigged up near his feet—probably so Wright could kick it if it didn't work.

"Got my Alpha here," said Wright as the signal came up. He was halfway between the Oregon coast and the Alaskan peninsula, the plane coasting at just over the speed of sound.

"Acknowledged," said Ford. "Clear to proceed."

"Coyote Base, I have a stretch of weather off to my starboard," said Wright, looking at the huge blocks of cumulonimbus storm clouds stretching off to his right. The System's sensors made them seem much closer than they actually were, ominous cushions of water, hail and angry air. "Some nice, puffy clouds with dark bellies, Fitzgerald."

"Roger, we copy Coyote Bird," said Ford, the controller. "You can go on up to get away from it if you want."

"Roger, acknowledged," said Wright. "I'm gonna hang out down here with the mortals a bit first."

"We show nothing in your vicinity," said Ford, concerned. Poor guy was so nervous he was taking everything literally.

"Figure of speech," answered Wright. "I'm all alone up here, and I'm past the front. How's everything with you, Jennifer?"

"Fine," she said. "You're looking good."

"The System hologram seemed a little sluggish when I asked for a forward simulation," said Wright.

"I don't see anything different here," she said. "I can check it."

"That'd be nice," answered the pilot.

There was a slight pause while Jennifer ran the checks.

"System benchmarks show no difference."

"What do they say about dinner tonight?" Wright asked.

"They predict chicken à la king, done to a perfect mushiness."

"What do they say about really eating out?" said Wright.

"You mean real food?"

"Exactly."

"What time will you pick me up?" Jennifer responded.

"Well it all depends on whether dad will let me have the car or not," said Wright. "What do you say, dad?"

Wright expected Hunter to cut in with something to the effect that they shouldn't fool around, but he didn't. "You on here somewhere, General?" he asked. There was no answer. Wright was surprised—Hunter had said he'd be on the line the whole way. "Ah, how about you, Ford? You up for dinner out?"

"Absolutely," replied the controller.

"Hey, Gene," said Wright, "what about you?"

"Who?" said Elrich sharply.

"Why don't you come with us?"

"What are you going to do, put a candle in the middle of the trays?"

"Hell no, we'll go someplace real," said Wright. "Hell, we'll have all day to get there."

"I'll probably be busy," said Elrich, but the haughtiness had run out of his voice.

"We'll talk you out of it," said Wright, suddenly overcome with magnanimity. It wasn't that he'd changed his basic opinion of Elrich; he still thought the computer scientist was arrogant and, at best, a jerk. But they were all in this together, and there was no discounting Elrich's contributions to the project. And what the hell. He might not see the guy ever again anyway; might as well be nice on the phone.

The Coyote flew on over the ocean into a stunningly clear sky, the water below a flat, unrippled sheet of blue marble. The colors in this synthesized view were brilliant, so clear that Wright accepted them as real, even though by pointing his finger he could change what he saw completely. The power of the plane's view screens—not merely the radar and the satellite systems that were providing the data for his view, but the System's ability to translate it directly and instantaneously into things the pilot could see and recognize intuitively—almost gave Wright a feeling of omnipotence. Reflexively, he trusted his eyes, the old pilot's prejudice, ready to believe what they could see of the real world quicker than what his instruments said. He knew, his mind knew, that his eyes were only looking at a more sophisticated version of the instruments, but he couldn't unteach the instinctive trust, couldn't persuade his eyes that they might actually be fooled. He could see; that was what he knew, and as long as he could see, he would have no problem.

"Coyote Bird, we show you over peninsula. Copy?"

Time for everybody to get ready. Wright picked up his speed as he worked the plane into a curve above the Aleutian Island chain back down toward Attu. He'd be there in less than five minutes. The pilot let the System take over for him while he stretched his legs, pulling the muscles taut and cracking them against his joints. Then he did the same thing with his hands and arms, and finally rocked his head back and forth, the loud pops of the tense muscles breaking against the joints. Already he was starting to sweat, his mouth dry. The one thing this plane needed was a soda machine.

The hell with that. Make it a beer tap. There was plenty of spare cooling capacity to keep the brew cold.

"This is Coyote Bird to Base Control. Coming up on two minutes to Delta Point. That right, Jason?"

"Roger. Copy, Colonel," said Ford, as crisply as if he were in the next room.

As they moved south, the System informed him of the navy task force, its position just on the edge of the notification circle. Wright pointed at the information as it came up on the screen, and said "detail"; instantly a full rundown of the task force appeared, complete with the names of the ships. He broke open a window and the System flashed a satellite picture of the task force, enhanced and color-coded so even an airman could tell which was what.

"Delta," announced the System.

"Acknowledged," Wright said. "Full pilot control; complete real-time visuals, full screen. Maintain normal notification circle."

The task force disappeared. He put the plane into a gradual circle and climb, easing the throttle—easing the idea of speed, moving his hand forward and picking up steam as he scraped the earth's roof. He was aiming at making a wide orbit, waiting for his friend.

"What the hell's he playing around with the carrier for?" Elrich groused, staring up at the large screens that duplicated the pilot's view.

Jennifer shrugged. "Maybe he just wants to make sure all of this is for real."

"He'd better just get on with it."

"Don't you have a lot to do?" she asked. "I still have problems with the gateway—it's eating up processing power."

"Don't tell me my job, Jennifer," snapped Elrich, walking back to his section.

Jennifer turned back to her own controls, glad that Elrich had at least stopped looking over her shoulder. She had grown more and more angry with her brooding supervisor as the morning had progressed. Part of it stemmed from his cursing out Angles for not staying behind when Hunter called them onto the runway—the assistant had not run the tests on the backup power supply, and Elrich raged at him for "delaying" them fifteen minutes, time which they hadn't actually lost at all. Jennifer was beginning to realize how truly misanthropic her boss was, how he treated almost everyone as barriers to his achievements, annoyances to be put out of the way as quickly as possible.

But another part of her anger came from Elrich's questioning of Wright's ability, as if the pilot couldn't fly the plane as well as the System. Even if they had pushed it further than any computer before, even if they were almost over the line into free thought, into intuition, it was Wright she would bet on. No matter how much he had taught the System, or how much he would teach it in the future.

As afraid for him as she was.

Wright reached the far end of his second circle with still no sign of the Japanese plane. They must be pulling their hair out back at the base—all this preparation and no party. What would they do, he wondered, if the Japanese plane didn't come out to play? Would they go on doing this, day after day, until he showed?

"Tom, what do you think of taking it toward one-fifty?"

It was Hunter, his voice breaking in unexpectedly as the System clicked off a routine course check.

"You're asking me to go west, roger?" Wright asked, interpreting the number as a longitudinal meridian. But it wasn't the direction so much as the spirit that was important.

"Copy," said Hunter. "Mix it up a bit. I want you to override the programmed course."

Wright didn't understand. The general had been very explicit that he should follow the exact programmed course, not deviating from the carefully laid out plan at all unless there was an emergency.

"You're going to let me free-lance then, yes?"

"You're on you own," said Hunter. "Just remember the basic requirements."

Wright decided he wasn't going to get any more of an explanation and might just as well take advantage of the situation. He gunned the Coyote northwestward, picking up speed as he headed toward the Kamchatka peninsula. The System flashed on one of the navy flights, flying on station far below him, off to the east. Getting closer to the Russian coast, he decided to gain a little altitude, and pulled the Coyote into a sharp climb, first sixty degrees and then all the way to ninety, heading up into a loop and then showing off with a roll at the top, where he repeated the climb into the loop, rolling on top again. He was higher than he had ever been, streaking nearly forty-three miles above the earth. The plane was a rocket ship now; a little more altitude and it could pop over to where they were working on the moon-Mars space station.

A little more altitude closer to Delta, and pop goes the weasel.

The maneuvers slowed him down; he was flying at a paltry Mach 4, the engines barely getting a workout.

"Unidentified ships located within notification circle," the System announced. "Two Soviet ships, based on signal patterns."

Wright pointed at the screen. The System, relying on satellite input as he swung back to the south, couldn't get definitive IDs on the boats, which were just north of Komandorskiye Island; one appeared to be a Kapitan Sorokin–class icebreaker, the other a Balzan spy trawler.

"Group one communicating with a two-ship group ten miles north in Bering Sea."

"Details," Wright asked.

"Ships out of immediate scanning range. Traffic indicators similar to Kirov class. No avionics; aircraft carrier possible, but improbable."

"Details on Mirov class," Wright asked.

"Assume you meant Kirov," said the System. "Nuclear-powered cruisers. Antiair armament includes ship-to-air; ceiling 100,000 to 125,000. Require further details?"

"Anything on missile-killing capacity?" asked Wright. "How about ASAT potential, or anything similar?" he added.

254

The System thought about it a few seconds, swashing through the storage pools back at the base.

"ASAT potential: Golden Seal Exercise, 1995. U.S. intelligence believed demonstrated at-sea antisatellite capability."

"Great."

"No known correlation with these ships. Capabilities extremely primitive."

"How far from Delta are they?"

"Two hundred twenty-three point two nautical miles."

Far enough away not to worry about their interfering with the operation. But they might end up with decent seats, depending on which way the Japanese plane flew after the detonation.

"Would you like some guesses on their identities?" asked the System.

"Since when do you make guesses?"

"Guesses can be useful, depending on the circumstances. I can limit the number of—"

"Tell you what, just keep tabs on them and tell me if they do anything interesting," said Wright.

"We've got a couple of spectators up there," said Hunter, standing behind her and looking over at the screen as he adjusted the headphone. A switch he held in his hand shifted his channel from the Coyote to the interceptors' command. "I wonder what they're going to think of our little adventure."

Three MPs and the FBI agent had come onto the deck with Hunter. One of the MPs stood next to the lieutenant, who had removed the top of his boxes to reveal some small lights in one and a pair of switches on the other. The other two MPs, erect and silent, stood a respectful distance away, far out of Jennifer's or anyone else's way.

Which was more than she could say for Fisher. He practically bumped into her as he walked up to the screens, hands in his pockets, as if he'd just walked into a circus sideshow and was examining the freaks. He was frowning, looking as if he was disappointed by it all, and wanted to be somewhere else.

"Can I help you?" she said curtly.

"I guess it wouldn't be too good an idea if I had a smoke, huh?" he replied.

Fifteen minutes had passed since he'd first reached Delta. Wright paced his breathing, waiting. Where the hell was this guy? Didn't he know his fans were waiting?

Wright had never trained with Japanese air defense pilots. He remembered that they had a reputation for being precise and dogged, but beyond that, he could only imagine what sort of qualities his opponent possessed.

He was damn good. He'd seen that the other day. But that wasn't going to help him once they started shooting. Luck wouldn't even help—no matter how much he had, the blast would use it up.

What the hell had Pelham been doing? What had gone wrong with his plane? The love tap Wright had given him couldn't have been the problem. He'd fucked up on his own, or the plane had fucked up.

It was just one of those things, not Wright's fault.

The Coyote nicked Soviet territory as the pilot made his turn, coming around over the Kuriles and swinging back toward Attu and Delta. Still nothing; for the hundredth time he flexed and then relaxed every muscle in his body.

At least you didn't have to worry about the weather up here. The Aleutians were socked in with a low-level storm system, extremely turbulent, though the adjective lost some of its meaning in a place where light winds were measured at just under hurricane force.

They'd flown Zeros up here, and Lightnings, though the damn thing was cold even in the South Pacific. A dogfight in the swirling clouds would equalize the planes. Your sixth sense would be all-important then, your innate knowledge of how the other guy flew, and where he was. Your head would pound with the thumping engines, and every pore of your body would open, the sweat pouring out and turning into a puddle of ice at the bottom of the cockpit.

So much crap going through his head—Pelham, Miller, old planes—he had to flush it all out and concentrate on what he was doing. Flying was thinking now, pure thinking, and here every-thing was getting in his way.

"Target sighted," said the System, its screen suddenly flashing. "Plane is crossing south from Arctic to Kamchatka peninsula and heading toward Coyote Bird."

Jennifer flicked the switch and looked at her own isolation screen. "Son of a bitch," she said aloud. "There it is."

Though slightly out of range for a detailed look, the Japanese plane's altitude and speed made it conspicuous among the hun-dreds of items the System's network tracked. In less than thirty seconds on its present course, it would come into range of

256

CoyoteVision II, the geosynchronous satellite that fed the System real-time image data in the far north. From that point on, Wright would have all the information about it he needed.

Wright brought himself back to 200,000 feet, 50,000 feet below the altitude needed to trigger the satellite, and coasted into an easy turn around the target zone.

They were all excited now, even Hunter, though outwardly his manner was anything but. The general spoke to the interceptors' controller curtly, then asked Jennifer to switch one of the screens in the cockpit dupe section to concentrate specifically on the target area, displaying everything the System was tracking there. The System superimposed the small dots and triangles on a map that stretched halfway across Alaska and back through the Kuriles. Delta was marked with a D.

"When he makes the far end of his circle," Hunter said to her, "go ahead and disconnect."

Jennifer nodded. They were going to cut the Coyote off from the System themselves, before the pulse, to avoid the very slight possibility that the whole System might be knocked off if things didn't work properly. As soon as the satellite exploded, she would reconnect.

In theory, the mission was very easy, especially with Wright in the plane. Still, there was no way of knowing what was really going to happen to the sophisticated wave net they used to communicate, just as there was no way of being absolutely certain that the scanning radars onboard the Coyote would be able to focus properly in the ion haze. Wright would retain control of the plane—in the worst case, he could stay on the backup hydraulics—but if the radars didn't work he'd be blind. Jennifer remembered when they'd first met, and felt foolish for laughing at what she'd thought was his old-fashioned concern for windows.

The System continued to monitor Wright's vital signs, and a small screen next to her right hand showed his heartbeat and blood pressure. He was barely hitting fifty-seven a minute. God, he was so relaxed he might be sleeping.

Unlike her. Her heart was doing twice that, easy.

It came at him as a blur, undefined, moving too fast for the screen to project properly without going off real time. It was a little higher than he was, and flying much faster. But Wright was ready; he'd already begun banking and now accelerated into a climb that put him on the other plane's tail. He fought off the effects of the sudden acceleration and shadowed the Japanese plane's maneuvers as its pilot led him through a quick series of jinks tight enough to make Wright feel it, but not really testing the Coyote's abilities. They were close in a relative sense, with just over a mile between them; if he'd had missiles (and if they could have flown fast enough), Wright could have taken him out himself.

It took him a few seconds before Wright realized the Japanese pilot was running him through a standard series of turns, similar to the set a veteran pilot might take a rookie wingman through. Wright was somewhat amused; they weren't close enough to make this anything like a real gut check, but the idea at least was there. The guy had a sense of humor.

The System was plotting their course and trying to anticipate what the other plane would do. Wright kept one eye on the holographic projection as he maneuvered, cutting off the distance between them, moving closer and closer.

The computer didn't entirely like this high-speed version of chicken; periodically it would flash little warnings about flying distance and the effects of the other plane's turbulence wash. Wright ignored it all, concentrating on flying, knowing he had plenty of room. The two planes were within the target area, but their maneuvers had brought them too low to trip the explosion. Wright saw a chance now to take the lead, anticipating the Japanese plane's climb and hitting the gas as the planes pulled up, coming up and over his starboard wing, shooting ahead. "Come on, baby, let's see what you can do," said Wright over the open mike. Whether the other pilot heard him or not, he followed Wright up, climbing to 150,000 feet in a heartbeat.

"Targeting-type laser activated," said the System.

"Not that again," said Wright in exasperation. "You detect any other planes in the area with air-to-air capability?" he asked, trying to see who his friend might be painting him for.

"Negative."

"So what the hell kind of weapons could he be carrying?"

The System paused again.

"Preparing to disconnect," said Jennifer.

Wright ignored her, waiting for the System to answer. Was this guy just pulling his chain again with the radar, or what?

"Yo, what kind of weapons could he be carrying?" demanded Wright.

"We are about to disconnect," said Jennifer.

"Configuration would fit an advanced particle-beam weapon," said the System, "with modifications. Targeting laser would be used to determine exact distance for charge and shot."

"Everybody else says that's impossible," Wright replied. "What makes you think it's not?"

The System did not reply.

"Tom . . ."

Should he trust the engineers who said it couldn't be done, or the System, which said it was possible but couldn't or wouldn't explain why?

"Laser is locked," said the computer.

Wright jerked his hand to the right. The Coyote Bird moved with it, wheeling itself downward in a sudden bolt away from its opponent.

"Analyze his flight patterns. What's he trying to do when that targeting bullshit comes on?"

"Is something wrong, Tom?"

"What does he do?"

But Wright realized what it must be before the System came back—the Japanese pilot always angled to get behind him. That was what that wingman crap was all about—he wasn't joking around, he was trying to slip behind him in a disguised scissors.

"Son of a bitch," said Wright, pitching back up ninety degrees as the Japanese plane dove at him.

"Bring it up to altitude," said Hunter into his microphone. "Just get him up to altitude so the satellite trips off."

The general fingered his microphone as he glanced over at the open box and its blinking yellow light. Case B was tracking, but they were outside the window.

It didn't matter. They almost had him.

If Wright could just bring him up a little higher.

Now that he knew what he had to do, it wasn't that difficult. Just keep his tongue from licking your tail, Wright told himself, and you'll be fine. He must need a good strong lock before he could fire.

As the Japanese plane made another run in his direction, Wright poked his nose off as if he were going to drop into a thirty-degree arc toward the deck, but then pushed the Coyote through, barreling over and up into a climb. The machine seemed to groan with the cut, the maneuvering assists going and God knows what sort of shape it gave its wings, but the plane held together and started climbing quickly. The feint tricked the Japanese pilot, who had cut his own angle to head it off and now couldn't respond quickly enough. The only thing he could do was point his plane straight up and try and make up the difference once Wright stopped climbing.

Wright, meanwhile, continued to accelerate, leaning the Coyote over so that he was just about on his back, doing a corkscrew swag toward the exact center of gadget zone.

"Go ahead and disconnect," he told Jennifer. He didn't need the base now.

"Acknowledged."

He had to shut down his end as well, go to backup. For a brief second as he climbed Wright thought of saying something to Jennifer. But this was too morbid, he told himself, and so he simply brought the T bar out of the ceiling, cut his communications, and continued to climb, high, higher; asked the plane to estimate the time to his target altitude, and then put the rest of the System to bed.

The cockpit suddenly became very dark, lit only by the dim glow from the tubes at the back of the tube radio Harrison had made for him. Higher he climbed, counting off the seconds. He knew his friend was still there, even without looking at the backup radar down by his foot. He could feel him edging in, just behind him. That laser would be going full bore now, grabbing at him, its fingers slipping on and off.

Come on, Wright thought. Let's get this sucker over with. Let's go.

He gave himself a half of a half second's grace to make sure he'd counted right, and then, with as much finesse as he could manage with the kludgey controls, made the plane fall into a power dive, almost straight down, struggling immediately to get the Coyote into a position he could level off from, wrestling with the unfamiliar T bar, flying physical again, very physical and difficult, nothing really to brace yourself with here as he fell toward the earth, yelling, "Now, now, now!"

He felt the Japanese plane continue straight up past him, a half step behind in the game, then prepare a maneuver, pulling his wings out against a tremendous flow of g forces, his momentum tearing at the plane as he changed direction.

Everything became a sudden rushing away from heaven, energy

folding into waves, shocks of photons running away, falling to earth.

Hunter took a step forward.

"Acquire target," he said into his headset, his voice low and steady.

Fisher watched as everyone around him scrambled, playing with different knobs and buttons, everyone talking at once. Hunter had given him the impression that he'd at least let him question Elrich, but apparently things had already proceeded too far before they'd gotten up to the computer deck. Now all he could do was stand around with his hands in his pockets and hope he was wrong about the scientist.

God, he wanted a cigarette.

Even though the radios were off, static flooded through Wright's earphones and his head was filled with a thick fuzz that made it hard to control his arms, pulling now to keep the plane stable. He was supposed to wait sixty seconds before reenergizing the System, though if there were real problems it wouldn't matter if he waited sixty days. The ionosphere was so charged up that there was a good chance he wouldn't be able to see anything up here anyway. That was what he really wanted, to get the imaging radars back, to have his screens going in front of him, to use his eyes. He wanted to see where he was—and not run into the other plane.

Everything felt as if he were moving slowly, in a jar of heavy oil, but he realized that he was going incredibly fast, probably dropping toward the earth at several times the speed of sound. Gradually he turned the dive into a banking turn, a wide circle that brought him back to what he thought was north.

That was the toughest thing, figuring out your direction. Until he turned the System back on, he wouldn't know exactly where he was.

He didn't know how high he was, either—the altimeter was still off the scale. And Harrison's backup radar was projecting an unhelpful spray of blips in a pattern that would have made Jackson Pollock dizzy.

The Japanese pilot must be in much worse shape than Wright, not because he had been higher, but because he was unprepared. All his sensors would suddenly have cut out on him—even if they were shielded perfectly, all they'd be picking up right now was a huge batch of static, spiked with a heavy dose of fuzz. If the plane's electronic controls had died—a contingency Wright had switched to the backups to avoid—he might be free-falling toward the earth right now. The interceptors would be superfluous.

He had a tremendous amount of room to work in, assuming he could slow himself down enough. The important thing was to maintain control over yourself, go through everything logically, in precise order, pulling the buttons and switches and doing it with purpose.

The Japanese pilot wouldn't even think about getting back home yet. He'd be concentrating on just holding on, figuring out what had happened, trying to reestablish contact with his base.

Little goddamn targeting-beam crap wasn't going to help him now.

The interceptors were connected with their command and control through a direct-line laser system unaffected by the blast, which in turn was hooked back through to Hunter. But that wasn't helping them find the plane. Hunter had expected the confusion, of course, but he was hoping that the interceptors would be able to draw a bead quickly, well before the five-minute minimum they thought it would take the Japanese plane to reestablish contact with its base.

Hunter couldn't get a fix on anything himself—the System was still off-line, not responding to Jennifer's frenzied efforts to reestablish contact with its satellites and drones.

Case B wasn't a possibility either—the yellow light had dropped to blue, meaning that it, too, couldn't find its target.

Wright turned it back on. What the hell.

A psychedelic spray of colors exploded across the cockpit from the screens, dancing to the accompaniment of a wild screech. He killed the volume; at the same time the colors brightened and then faded into a dull gray, punctuated by a haze of vague shapes. The instrumentation was nonexistent, and the computer seemed literally to burp when he talked to it. He hit every button and switch he could, but little changed; the only improvement was in the sound—now a dull hum of static.

But the controls for the plane itself were intact—he killed the hydraulics, using the T bar to run the normal setup. Confident after a minute, he pushed it upwards and went to the gloves; the computer wasn't talking back, but it understood his commands.

His circles took him lower and lower, but the backup altimeter still wasn't working. Nor was the tube radio reading anything meaningful, its static providing a perfect stereo effect with the System's. The radar, however, seemed to be rallying; it was producing straight lines now, though it hadn't quite mastered a full sweep.

Wright pointed to the biggest shadow on the screen and asked for maximum magnification; the computer didn't even hiccup back.

The missiles could have taken the Japanese plane out by now, but Wright didn't think they'd gotten him. He didn't know whether he'd hear the explosion or not, but it just didn't feel like he was alone yet.

But even his pilot's sense had been screwed up by the fuzz that surrounded the plane. He had only a vague idea of where he was, arbitrarily telling the computer to consider itself over Attu when he turned it on. It had lost its bearings, obviously, during the time it had been disconnected, and until contact was reestablished it had no way of orienting itself except by keeping track of its movement from the starting point. Attu was close enough, as long as the compass kept working and they didn't stray too far.

At least they didn't have people shooting at them.

Flying the Zero in the swirling Aleutian fog would be a breeze compared to this. He'd just skim down to the water and head back.

Back to where?

Back to the carrier? If they'd taken it out, dive-bombed it while he wasn't there, he'd have to try and fly back all the way to Japan, ditching at last in the quiet calm Pacific, returning to the womb in a smooth skim that crossed the boundary from air to water, down to earth to die and be reborn, a dram of the typhoon god, returning over and over again, a shadow of existence.

A dark ghost in the middle of the left-hand side of the window, hanging off to the side, duplicating his movements.

It was the other plane. He could see.

Jennifer went through the routines again, ordering the computer to retry every procedure. Even CoyoteVision I, sitting east of the Canadian Rockies, was off the circuit, the System completely baffled by the shadows of charged particles it thought had come from the sun. This shouldn't be happening. There was nothing wrong with the hardware—or at least the problems there were manageable. For some reason, the System itself was overweighing the value given to the energy fluctuations, the "noise" they were picking up. It had something to do with the way the control unit hooked into the gateway, dictating its functions.

"Cannot connect to the satellite systems," it told her blandly.

"Delete the stored values and tap solely into CoyoteVision I," she told it.

"Programming error level six, sector fifty-three. Separate gateway channel not allowed."

"Damn it," she said, "of course it is."

"Do you wish a readout?" asked the System.

"No," said Jennifer, rubbing the top of her head. "No. I want you to delete the stored values."

"Deleted."

"Now put CoyoteVision I on-line."

"Programming error level six, sector fifty-three. Separate gateway channel not allowed."

"Fuck," she said. There wasn't time for this. She started to ask the System if it could analyze and fix the problem. It might take a half hour, perhaps more, but there was no alternative.

No, the quickest thing to do was to go to manual override.

That meant killing the control unit altogether. In effect, she would cripple the System, turning it temporarily into a mere collection of coordinated radars. She'd lose access to the stored memory as well.

But all he needed now was radar.

"Prepare to shut down control unit for manual override," she told the System.

"What are you doing?" Elrich screamed at her, running over from his station.

"I have to reestablish contact with the satellites and with the plane," she told him. "I'm going to take the control unit out of the way and do it myself."

"No," said Elrich. "We need the control unit and the memory to fly the plane."

"All we need are the radars and communications," she said. "Playing with the problem will take too long."

"Keep everything the way it is."

Jennifer stood and yelled at him, her voice filling the cavernous hall. "You're fucking us up. We can't even get the computer to show us where he is."

They were circling together, flying maybe 500 meters apart, shadowing each other. They were going slow, down under Mach 2, at least according to the instruments. The airspeed and altimeter were back, half the engine gauges seemed to be working (although the fuel gauge said he was filled up, an obvious error), and the annoying nudge that kept track of his vital signs had decided to open a window for itself on the screen and refused his many requests to just go away and leave him alone. The screens were a darkish yellow, shading into brown, but he seemed to have some flexibility with the magnification. The plane was completely on its own, cut off from the larger System back home and the satellites, which meant his view was limited to what was nearby.

Where were his buddies and their missiles? At this speed the Japanese plane was a sitting duck.

Wright suddenly realized that sticking this close to his friend wasn't a tremendously good idea. He wasn't afraid of the particle beam at the moment—the Japanese plane wasn't making any attempt to get behind him. But the possibility of the Americans picking up the wrong target by accident was another story.

Wright backed off his throttle a little, and then decided to get a little higher than his friend, assuming that a missile, if confused, would probably go for the lower target first. But the Japanese plane did the same, continuing to fly parallel to him, sitting just off his port wing, a couple of football fields away.

Hell, Wright thought to himself, if that's what you're going to do, let's go look for those suckers.

Jennifer forced herself to speak as calmly as possible, the blood welling in her cheeks as she struggled for control over her mouth.

"We have to reestablish contact with him. He's past the halfway mark on his fuel by now," she said, moving her hand toward the cutoff switch.

"Don't touch it," screamed Elrich. "Don't touch anything. Get away from the controls. Get away—that's an order."

"You don't give the orders," she said, for the first time turning her gaze away from him, looking for someone who might help.

Finally he picked up something—what looked like two F-15E/Bs about thirty miles away, slightly to the east and about 50,000 feet below. Wright was confused—the Coyote was heading west, and if he was where he thought he was, he ought to be running into navy planes.

The planes were close enough, he figured, to fire, but they weren't throwing out loaded signals. Their radar systems must be screwed up or else they were waiting for him to get clear. Wright pushed his plane down in a shallow bank to the east, accelerating; his friend followed.

He must be blind. Wright felt like a Judas goat, leading him to slaughter. He kept right abeam.

Hell, a couple of minutes ago, he'd been shining his flashlight on Wright's backside. Why feel guilty?

Twenty-five miles, twenty. The air force planes weren't moving incredibly fast, but they hadn't altered course for an intercept either, and at this rate would pass right by them. Wright cursed them—for cryin' out loud, even if their instruments were screwed up, they ought to be able to use their eyes. He could see them.

So all right, in some instances the screens were better than real windows. But they weren't that far away at all. Hell, they could just open up with their cannons and that would be that.

If they would only turn, damn it. The fighters gave no indication that they saw them. According to the System, they didn't even have their basic radars on full.

Maybe the fighters were mirages, figments of the System's malfunctioning imagination. Or maybe they weren't the F-15s, despite the tags pasted in reverse type at the bottom of the screen. The onboard computer didn't have the base's massive memory to help ID the planes. The clusters of dark pixels were so blurry Wright couldn't be sure himself—these could easily be MiG-29s, planes that, though considerably smaller, were roughly similar in shape to the brawnier American fighters.

Wright strained his eyes, trying to get a definite fix as they closed.

Hunter turned to Fisher. "You wanted to ask some questions," he said.

"Now?"

"Go ahead."

"Dr. Fitzgerald," said the FBI agent. "Can you ask the computer a question for me?"

The scientist looked at him as if he'd just come from Mars.

"It's OK," said Hunter behind him.

"Ask the computer what it knows about control wires in a Hellcat."

"What?"

"No, better make it a little more generic," said Fisher, standing beside her. "Ask if anyone has been asking how to screw with a Hellcat, or a Zero. Looking for ways to make them crash."

F-15s or MiGs, they passed right by. Wright banked the plane to his left, juicing it a bit as he cut away at a right angle. According to the Coyote's compass reading, he was heading due east. The only problem was that the background clutter at the edge of the screen showed a solid landmass and mountains, and the magnification confirmed it. Now he was really confused—how'd he get this close to the Alaskan coast?

The Japanese plane followed his maneuver. The interceptors didn't.

Where the hell was he? Above the Aleutians?

They better hurry up and reconnect before he really got lost.

"Go ahead," repeated Fisher. "Ask it."

Jennifer couldn't believe they were wasting this time. But Hunter had an extremely serious look on his face, and so she adjusted the microphone on the headset back in front of her mouth.

"System," she asked. "Has anyone inquired about sabotaging a Hellcat or a Zero?"

Elrich started forward, as if to say something, but one of the air force security people grabbed his arm on a sign from the general.

"Don't bother, Jennifer," said Hunter. "Just get this thing going. Do whatever you have to." The general turned to Fisher. "He's all yours."

It was so damn quiet. Unconnected, the System couldn't respond to him with more than a word or two, though it could flash readings and everything else on the screens.

Maybe that was just as well. Keep his mind clear as he thought, as he flew.

It was like shooting a friend, but she didn't feel it until the screens blinked purple and the System squealed as its power was cut. She took a deep breath and began pounding the keyboard, telling the independent gateway section controlling the satellite and drone network to average the input between the best—CoyoteVision I—and what was bound to be the worst, II. Then she gave each input that value, prioritized them according to how close to the target area they were, and brought them back on-line, one by one. From the corner of her eye, she saw the lights flash up on the screen they were using to monitor the area.

"Do you have any sort of communications with him?" she asked Ford over her mike set.

"Nada," said the controller.

Jennifer looked over at the screen. The Coyote Bird's green triangle was superimposed over a map; Wright was flying north into the southern Bering Sea, heading straight for Russia. Their target was with him and a pair of the interceptors were within shouting distance.

"What do you think is going on out there?" said Jennifer over the mike to Ford, but it was Hunter, standing over her shoulder, who answered.

"The interceptors are confused," said Hunter dryly. "The blast worked better than expected."

The first radio transmission the Coyote was able to pick up was a plane-to-plane channel, apparently the one being used by the two fighters he'd just passed. They were having all sorts of trouble reading each other, even though they were separated by only a few hundred yards. They kept complaining about the heavy static, saying they would have "Mom" relay the message—apparently their connection with the AWACS guiding them hadn't been affected.

At least they were Americans. Wright doubled back toward them.

The Japanese pilot still couldn't see that he was being led into a trap, following right along as if the American was his flight leader.

Wright wondered what was going through the other pilot's mind. If the Japanese plane was blinded—the Coyote claimed it was throwing off no radio waves whatsoever—the best thing for the other pilot to do was get down on deck and make his way back visually. The worst thing he could do was follow Wright: even if he didn't suspect Wright of having caused his problems, he was almost certainly going to be heading in the wrong direction. Could the Japanese pilot be stupid enough to believe that Wright would help him back to safety, as if they were following some sort of chivalrous code?

Hell, if he kept this up, Wright might be able to lead him back to the base. They were already headed in the right direction.

Wright was thinking about the expression on the general's face, just lifting his hand to hit the gas, when the screen went nuts, exploding with a fuzz-detector warning. The communications channel shut down—the fighters were taking evasive maneuvers.

The Japanese pilot had seen it, too, or had seen something—he immediately pulled up and over, flipping his plane onto its back and heading away with a tremendous burst of speed. Wright banked off to the left and followed, climbing as he lay back just a bit to keep some distance between himself and the target. The two fighters hit their afterburners and did a better job of chasing the vastly superior planes than Wright would have thought. In this electronic fog, though, their missile gear couldn't lock on. They did seem to realize that it was the Japanese plane that was their target—they were hanging on his wake as the two superplanes separated.

They must not have believed what they'd been told about his capabilities; they were going after him as if they could run him down, a rather foolish strategy. Not only was he pulling away; they were going to start running into the ceiling pretty soon. But now he saw that the Japanese plane might not pull away after all—a pair of F-15E/Bs were screaming dead at them, flying at what must be 10,000 feet over their service ceiling and a couple hundred mph's over their top rated speed.

It took maybe another second for the Japanese pilot to see them; when he did, his only real option was to break off, diving to his right. The two Eagles coming at him split apart, both holding their positions above, playing deep secondary to the blitzing linebackers below. The pilot angled to get free for an end run, but the space that he'd put between him and his pursuers now played against him; they split and covered both ends on intercept courses.

Things were starting to work now. The Coyote picked up the two navy flights closing fast. The plane had trouble sorting everything out quickly—without being able to connect to the rest of the System, its capabilities were less awesome than normal. But Wright was confident, seeing how it would all end.

A vague regret mixed with his elation. Part of him was sorry to see this guy get waxed.

Hunter stood stock-still at the end of the console, his gaze directed not at the screens but at the small box on the floor next to the lieutenant from DEFSMAC and the Case B hookup. The light was blinking yellow again—tracking, but outside of Case B's range.

He looked back at the locator map. The planes were in pursuit, but couldn't shoot anything because their weapons needed more altitude to work properly. Ironically, they were close enough to ditch the ASATs and just use conventional air-to-air systems, had they been carrying them. The strategist had miscalculated; he should have had regularly armed flights move in with each group. He hadn't thought the explosion would give them quite this much trouble. Or that the Japanese plane would drop down this low.

The Japanese pilot was on his game, streaking ahead of Wright toward the west. The lead F-15E/B broke silence to call the code for a standard NATO maneuver designed to get their target to break below them as two of the navy planes came in across the deck, sandwiching their opponent high and low. It would have worked fine with a MiG; the plane would have been trapped between the two flights, easy pickings. But he wasn't a MiG, and rather than turning off and giving the two flights a fat juicy profile, he went head-on toward the two anchor-clankers, accelerating at an incredible rate of speed. He was going so fast, in fact, that they didn't begin to adjust until he was almost by them.

They had followed the wrong strategy. They were flying like they had Sidewinders under their wings, for cryin' out loud. They should have hung back, down low beneath him, and let the missiles do the work. Now he was gone. They'd never catch him now; there was nothing between him and Tokyo but a couple of sea gulls.

Elrich's glare suddenly collapsed under its own weight.

"There's a weapon aboard the Japanese plane," he said. "It's a particle beam based on a Russian design."

Hunter eyed him with an expression halfway between betrayed outrage and pity.

"Come on, Professor," said Fisher, motioning to the man who held him and walking toward the elevator, "let's go talk about it. We've got plenty of time."

Wright cursed them. How could they have been so stupid? They'd blitzed him, sending all the linebackers and the safeties, but neglected to post somebody on deep cover. All this work and nothing to show for it. Their target hadn't even broken a sweat.

Wright pulled his hand back, slowing slightly. There was no sense hanging around now. In disgust, he told the System to plot a course home.

Remarkably, the Japanese pilot began turning back, coming back east toward the interceptors.

Wright opened up his U.S. communications line. "Drop back into a nickel," he said. "Let him go deep."

The planes didn't respond. Maybe he was just a ghost, floating up here above the battle, watching, powerless to act.

Jennifer looked up at the screen. There was no way of telling how much fuel he had left, since that would depend on how much maneuvering he'd done. But it was obvious he wasn't just sitting up there pulling lazy figure eights. She had to get him back soon.

But nothing was working; her headset was still blank with static. The System believed it could get through; it knew exactly where he was and fed a precise net out to him. Futilely.

Jennifer wasn't sure what else she could do. "Tom, Tom, Tom," she said into her microphone.

The Japanese pilot was flying beautifully, weaving through the interceptors and taking them on a long, winding spin around the block. He was flying relatively low and slowly, though, between Mach 2 and 3; the interceptors were outclassed, but not overpowered, at least not at the moment.

Wright couldn't figure out why he didn't just take off. Maybe something was still screwed up, and this was the best he could manage. Maybe he just didn't have enough common sense to come in out of the cold.

Or maybe he was the cockiest so-and-so Wright had ever met.

That was probably true no matter what.

He wouldn't suspect they were carrying satellite guns. It occurred to Wright that the Japanese pilot was trying to flush them all out, see exactly how many planes there were up here with him. He was flying down and then back, checking out all three corners. Wright, a bit above the fray, broke out and caught him when he came back, timing his own acceleration to keep up as he pulled away from the fighters, sweeping to the northeast with a rush of rapid acceleration. To Wright's surprise, two of the interceptors fired missiles as soon as the Japanese pilot hit the gas. It was a waste of time, because the maneuvering had brought everybody way down toward the deck, and the fighters weren't high enough for the ASATs to operate properly. The two missiles went wildly off course.

So that's what they'd been doing—trying to get him to climb up and try and get away. Somehow he'd figured out what he had to do.

Had they been after Wright, on the other hand . . .

Flanking the Japanese plane by about a half mile, Wright watched the missiles give up and duck down toward the water. The missiles were fast, but the superplane could accelerate almost as quickly. Caught flat-footed, they didn't stand a chance if they fired from this position. The interceptors' best bet was to hang back—he was going to have to turn back toward the Kuriles eventually—and plot an intercept well to the west.

Three more missiles were launched as the planes gathered speed. One seemed to be a dud, plopping harmlessly into the ocean. The other two followed for a while, and then disappeared from the System's tracking, fired too low to accelerate quickly enough to keep the target within range. The Japanese pilot hadn't even bothered turning on his antimissile gear yet and the Americans had only three more shots. Why had they wasted the damn things while he was flying toward Alaska?

The voice floated in, crackled, and tossed into a dozen parts, but it was his.

"Hey there, Fitzgerald. About time you called."

"Tom," she said, "you're low on fuel."

"Well, that's a nice thing to say to somebody you haven't seen in a while," he said.

"Can you get back?" she asked, her heart pounding in her ears.

"Hell, I can glide from here," said Wright. "I'm already pointing home."

"You're facing the wrong way," she said emphatically, not sure whether he was kidding or not.

"The wrong way? That ain't Alaska in front of me?"

"You're headed west. You're going toward Japan."

"No shit. My INS has me going east. I knew something was screwy."

"It's reading everything backwards," she said. "There's your location," she said, clicking in the instruction.

"Wow, how'd I'd get down here?" he said. "Good thing you called."

"Tom . . . " she started, but the rest of what she wanted to say stuck in her throat, fluttering. She felt as if she was going to cry.

"Thanks for the help, base," he said, his voice suddenly official and taut. "I copy."

By now the interceptors were showing up on scopes all over the Kamchatka peninsula and their jamming gear came on with a bang. That wasn't their only problem: they were at the top of their range, maybe even well beyond it, and they were going to have trouble getting back to their refueling stations even if the Russians didn't make a serious intercept try.

They did the only thing they could: fired their last weapons, all three missiles streaking toward the target. The Japanese plane had just started to cut back to the south as they fired, and for a second or two it appeared as if he might make their job an easy one, heading toward the missiles, finally streaking at an altitude they were designed for. He banked again to the east, taking them in a climb as he let it all hang out, his pedal to the floorboards.

They almost caught him. Wright, following along a little higher than the Japanese plane, watched his screen as the streaks grew larger, the imaging radar picking up and magnifying the nose cones. They looked benign, like baseballs thrown on a whim by children at a passing plane. Gradually, they stopped getting bigger, their momentum slowing as gravity called. The superplane had simply outrun them, climbing high over the Bering Sea, well into space.

Wright saw the lead missile explode, become a glow of fire, and then tumble into oblivion. The other two simply disappeared, either confused or out of fuel.

All the Japanese pilot had to do was coast back to his base. He'd won, escaping the odds by punching all the right buttons.

They were close, a quarter of a mile between them at most, exactly abreast of each other, twins.

Hunter would be pissed, but Wright had to admit that the Brotherhood would be proud. The pilot had stuffed it in their faces.

Hunter watched in despair as the last glow of the indicator light faded from the screen. All of the missiles had missed; the carefully calculated plan had failed completely.

If the Japanese plane turned around now and flew a straight line back to its base, it would escape. Case B was blinking yellow; its nearest target area was well to the northwest, over Russian territory.

Hunter watched the green indicator triangle swing to the south, followed by the Coyote's bright pink.

"Tom, don't let him get back to his base," said Hunter. "Get him into Russian territory somehow. And be careful—Elrich is sure he's got a particle-beam weapon onboard. You hear me?"

"Yeah, no problem," said Wright automatically. His fuel was probably running out, his instruments weren't working properly, he had no weapons—but of course he was going to stop this guy. Anything Hunter asked.

The general had mentioned there was a backup plan, but hadn't outlined it. Must be more interceptors somewhere.

Hell, thought Wright suddenly, were the Russians after this guy too?

He pushed the Coyote up, gaining speed and closing to what would be considered a commanding position a few hundred yards off his opponent's left wing if he were flying an interceptor. But he wasn't. The Japanese plane continued as if he weren't there.

"Show me his course," said Wright, pointing to the hologram, currently showing the Coyote's configuration.

"It can't, Tom," said Jennifer. "I took the control unit down to reestablish our link. It can't help you at all."

"Shit," said Wright—and then he almost laughed, realizing that he was mad the computer wasn't there to help.

The pilot relaxed a moment, feeling for everything in his mind. Something inside clicked, and he threw his hand forward, jumping the Coyote ahead in a surge that took the other pilot by surprise. At the same time he slid in closer, and then, just as the two planes were even, he threw the Coyote forward in a lunging roll that brought them so close Wright thought he heard paint scraping. The Japanese pilot reacted by diving steeply. As he began pulling out of it with an easy bank to the north, Wright, his plane still slicing downward, brought his tail flat and hit the gas, pursuing the Japanese plane upside down, Coyote rolling as it flew, furling its wings back together. He did this so quickly the Japanese pilot had to tighten his turn; he was heading northeast even before Wright began slowing the plane down, waiting to see which way he would break behind him.

TARGETING LASER ACTIVATED flashed the message on the screen.

"That's exactly what we want," said Wright, checking his bearings and pushing his hand forward. "We're going to play tag."

Hunter continued to stare at the blinking yellow light. "Still well out of range," said the lieutenant. The general nodded, turning back to the huge screen.

"General, he's been up four hours now," said Jennifer. "We could lose him if he doesn't head back."

It was Wright's turn to run the scissors, weaving back and forth, rolling slightly in an intricate dance that kept him close, tantalizingly close, but not quite near enough to get his butt fried.

This guy was good—he hung perfectly with everything Wright did, flying almost as if he read Wright's mind. They were perfectly matched, equal candidates for the Brotherhood.

Wright suddenly had an urge to see what the Japanese pilot looked like. He could take his measure just by looking in his eyes—they could tell you everything about a pilot.

"System," Wright said, "scan target and find pilot. Can you use the infrared to show me what he looks like?"

ATTEMPTING flashed on the screen.

Wright inched the Coyote closer, slipping his weave a little wide so he was almost parallel with his opponent, trying to hold it steady enough for the radars to focus clearly. It wasn't easy; the other pilot slid around intricately, still attempting to get behind him. The onboard computer tried all sorts of different frequencies to get a good focus on the inside of the plane; all it was showing in the box it had opened was a gray shadow.

Wright moved closer, his speed inching up. He started feeling giddy as they whipped onwards, passing Mach 10, climbing as they went, soaring well over 225,000 feet.

The other pilot started to slow, preparing to turn. They were deep into Russian territory now. Wright matched his opponent's speed, perfectly parallel now, hoping he wouldn't turn off just as the System got him in focus.

"Tom, get the hell out of there," said Hunter. "Get back to base."

The cockpit window and interior jumped in and out of focus. "Hold the resolution," Wright ordered, and it was as if the System hadn't been able to decide what to do until then; everything at once became absolutely clear.

There was no one there. The plane was empty; it was being flown completely by a computer.

Wright threw the Coyote into a wild roll away, free falling back to earth and back across the world toward America, cursing.

And then the thin sky above him turned a bright orange, and he felt the shock wave of an explosion run across his wings, and he had to struggle to stabilize the plane, and his twin was gone.

10

WHO ELSE WILL THEY GET?

The general sat in the small, empty room, all by himself, staring at the vaguely peach-colored walls. Outside, feet pounded back and forth; it was always chaotic in the White House basement, but this morning frenzy had been made an art form. But at least Morse had him come here, instead of one of his clean rooms.

The general considered it a successful mission. They had shot the Japanese plane down, had gotten the Coyote Bird back to the base. And if there was any question about what sort of impact the superplane was going to have in the future, they'd answered it.

There were, of course, wrinkles. One of the navy crews had ditched in the Pacific, several miles away from its carrier; they hadn't been located yet. And the Russians had gotten a good peek at things during the operation; while it would probably take them quite a while to sort it all out, undoubtedly they had gained more data in a few hours than they would have from years of patient spying. On the positive side, they hadn't gone public with anything.

The big question, of course, was how the Japanese government would react. Hunter had the morning's *Washington Post* in his lap, and had scanned its pages carefully for some sign of diplomatic action; the only story relating to Japan in the entire paper he could find referred to a new motor scooter that would be introduced in the U.S. next month, guaranteed to outsell domestic models inside two weeks.

The Defense Department and the NSC had prepared a terse statement detailing an accident during testing, intended as a prophylactic if word leaked out. Hunter amused himself while he waited by imagining the headlines the papers would use if they somehow got hold of the full details: "Duel of the Superplanes," "Thought-Rockets in Death Struggle," "Dogfight at Mach 12."

Maybe he'd quit and find himself a job as a newspaper editor. Most likely, the Coyote project would now be folded into the normal command structure. If he stayed on, Hunter would find himself answering to a dozen senior generals, anxious to prove they were twice as important as he was.

Even if the structure remained the same, with him answering directly to Morse, Hunter thought it might be a good idea to slip out quietly. He was starting to get tired. And he hadn't seen his daughter and son-in-law in nearly a year.

The general planned to recommend that Fitzgerald take over as head of the System development team. She had a lot of potential; Hunter thought she might prove twice as smart as Elrich, and not half as arrogant.

Nor a traitor.

Morse strode into the room just as Hunter gave up trying to figure out why the scientist had gone bad.

"Come with me," said the national security director brusquely, leading Hunter out another door and down the hallway to his office. The general got up slowly, worried now that things had not gone well with the Japanese. But Morse smiled broadly once they were inside his office.

"The president got off the phone with the prime minister twenty minutes ago," said the director, easing into his chair. "The Japanese Self-Defense Forces are sending two cutters to the island today. A destroyer from the Seventh Fleet will stand by to assist them."

"We won."

"It looks like it," said Morse. "There are going to be further talks about defense arrangements. The movement to amend the constitution has been quashed by the prime minister himself."

Hunter felt his whole body suddenly deflate, and he sank easily into the chair. Morse continued speaking, talking about the possible directions the Japanese government might take in dealing with the radicals. The general grew increasingly uneasy as the lecture proceeded, however. As interested in the world situation as he might be, there were more pressing problems.

"What about the navy pilots?" said Hunter finally.

Morse, surprised that Hunter cut him off, paused a second. "What do you mean?"

"Have we gotten the guys who ditched?"

Morse shrugged. "We hadn't, as of two hours ago."

"Wright got back to the base with about ten minutes' worth of fuel," said Hunter. "He did a hell of a job flying the plane."

"I'm sure he did."

"What's going to happen to Elrich?"

"The scientist? We'll put him in jail, of course. I haven't given it much thought. There are more important details to work out, Billy. I have to advise the president on the geopolitical implications." Morse leaned across the desk, talking confidentially. "We kicked butt on this, Billy. It's going to pay off, too. I'll be in line for Dyson's job when he steps down. I'm not pushing him out, you understand. I used to think he was an enemy, but I realize I was wrong about that. No, in fact, I think he'll recommend me. The rumor is that he's thinking of leaving at the end of the year. And Jack wants me to take the post. He's come to rely on me heavily."

Hunter, exhausted with the lack of sleep, almost asked when his old friend had started using the president's first name. Instead, he told Morse softly that he was going to resign.

"Quit? Why?"

"I can't stand Washington anymore, Professor," said Hunter mildly. "I'm too old for the bullshit. And I probably have to admit I've lost a few steps. I missed what Elrich was up to; if it weren't for that FBI agent, I don't know what would have happened."

"That's not your fault," said Morse. "You don't want to quit. Who would replace you?"

"That's your problem."

"Sit down, sit down. Come on, let's have a drink. I've got a bottle of scotch right here," said the director, reaching to his bottom drawer.

"You know what?" said Hunter.

"What?"

"I'm not sure I ever really liked scotch. That was always your drink."

* * *

It was Ki, the scientist, who came to him.

"Ieyasu wants you," he said. "A boat will wait for you."

Genda nodded, and finished putting his few items into the small cloth knapsack on the bed. The master had instructed them to escape before the self-defense forces came and arrested them. It was their duty, he said, to get away, to leave Japan so that someday they might return and lead it to its rightful destiny. Though it did not recognize the true path now, that did not mean it never would.

The galling thing was that they must go on to Russia, their historical enemy. But they must keep the dream alive, somehow.

The pilot closed the sack and placed it near the door. He left his room and walked down the corridor to the room where the old parkas were kept. Suited up, he walked slowly out into the bright morning, the light so harsh that his eyes stung as he walked down the path to Ieyasu's house.

Spring had truly come. He loosened the coat, then took it off, the light breeze invigorating him. Genda paused at the doorway, then pushed the panel aside and walked into the large room.

He was surprised by how bright it was inside, the dark wood beams glowing with the light of perhaps a hundred gilt lamps. Ieyasu sat cross-legged on the platform's white mats at the far end of the otherwise bare hall. He was dressed in his ceremonial clothes. Laid out beside him on the mat was a *jimbaroi*, a war coat painted with gold, and the appropriate underclothing.

Genda approached slowly, his head bowed. "Master," he said, "I have come."

Ieyasu looked at him without emotion. "Wear these," he said, pointing to the clothes at his left.

Genda hesitated. He would have said something, perhaps protested, but Ieyasu's dark, heavy eyes stopped him. "You would not dishonor me," they said silently, and the captain, as if he'd been spoken to, nodded and went to the clothes. He took off his coat slowly, and then the heavy sweater, the boots, his socks, pants and shirt, underwear. Genda had never in his life worn vestments like this, and he marveled at their weight and craftsmanship, even as he struggled to correctly dress himself.

"You understand you are to be here," said Ieyasu when he had finished, gesturing to his left.

"Yes."

"The stand is there, against the wall."

Genda walked to it slowly. His breath filled the whole building, cold and loud, pounding his ears. The stand was heavier than it seemed, leaden, but he carried it and placed it in front of his master. Another look passed between them, and Genda shuddered, reaching down and taking the paper-wrapped *wakizashi* to offer it to Ieyasu, prostrating himself as he did so. Had Ieyasu hesitated, Genda would have lost his courage, run from the hall shouting for help. But the long knife was taken from his hand quickly and lightly, and laid on the pure white mat. He rose—Ieyasu nodded at the table, and Genda took the longer sword that sat there alone, holding it in both hands gingerly as he walked to his position on the platform.

"The spirit shall not die," said Ieyasu in a flat voice, as calm as during their happier days. "It is now in your charge." He did not give Genda a chance to say anything, his voice rising without pause, trembling slightly with the formal admission, but expressing no fear. "I, and I alone, unwarrantably gave the order to provoke the Americans, misjudging the will of heaven. I, and I alone, mistook the will of Japan. For this crime I disembowel myself, and I beg you to do me the honor of witnessing the act."

Ieyasu bowed, and now the top of his garment fell away from his chest, pushed gently by the ghosts around him. He took the *wakizashi* in his hand, leaning carefully against his knees. He smiled, and in the second that he plunged the long knife toward the slight bulge of his left abdomen, Genda gripped the handle of his sword tightly, eyeing the place on his master's neck where he must strike.

The sun had risen, but it was still fairly cold, and they held each other as much for physical warmth as emotion.

"I just feel as if there ought to be a coda," she said to him. "Some little sign that we made it."

"We haven't made it," said Wright. "Look at all the work we've got left to do."

"That's what I mean. With everything—don't you feel as if there should be some theme music or something coming, a soft fade into the sunset?"

"It's still morning," said Wright. He didn't even mean it as a joke. His attention was far away, wandering back through the clouds, high over the earth. The mission had gone well, even though they'd lost one of the navy planes. Guy hadn't known what he was doing, anyway; too slow, too dumb, too unlucky. The Brotherhood was brutal when you didn't make the grade.

Even when you did. You could go up with twenty, thirty, even eighty victories, and get it from a stray bullet. Get bumped into, or run out of luck. You crashed just the same.

Poor Millertime. Stuck back there, powerless. Never knew what he was up against. And Pelham. Dumb luck had taken him out: he'd chosen the wrong plane. Just dumb luck.

Dumb luck that it was him and not Wright.

And the Brotherhood didn't offer consolation. Those were the rules.

Were the rules the same if he never left the ground, just stayed here and thought about flying, thought about leaving the ground in a flash and streaking up toward the stars, bending into turns, diving back and forth, making and remaking himself?

Were the rules the same for computers?

If God hadn't wanted man to fly, Wright remembered one of his old instructors saying long ago, he wouldn't have given him imagination.

"Do you think they'll let the project continue?" asked Jennifer.

"Let it continue?" he said, his reverie broken. "Are you kidding? There 's no way they can stop it now. If anything they'll intensify it. You'll have thousands of people working for you."

"Working for me?"

"Of course," said Wright, looking at her face. "Who else will they get?"